THE OFFICIAL NOVELIZATION

THE OFFICIAL NOVELIZATION

J. M. BARLOG

Thank you to the *God of War* Writing Team, Matt Sophos, Rich Gaubert, Orion Walker, Adam Dolin, for making this novelization possible, and a very special thanks to Cory Barlog, Game Director, *God of War*.

TITAN BOOKS

GOD OF WAR: THE OFFICIAL NOVELIZATION
Print edition ISBN: 9781789090147
E-book edition ISBN: 9781789090154

Published by
Titan Books
A division of Titan Publishing Group Ltd
144 Southwark St
London
SE1 0UP

First edition: August 2018
10 9 8 7

A CIP catalogue record for this title is available from the British Library.

Printed and bound by CPI Group (UK) Ltd, Croydon, CR0 4YY

Did you enjoy this book? We love to hear from our readers. Please email us at readerfeedback@titanemail.com or write to us at Reader Feedback at the above address.

www.titanbooks.comwww.titanbooks.com

MIDGARD

CHAPTER 1

Atreus shut his left eye, easing the bow down until the arrow tip aligned with the sixteen-point tawny stag's shoulder. He steadied a quivering arm while narrowing his concentration on his prey.

One shot. He would get it in one shot.

Inhale, focus, exhale, release. The words drummed through his brain with a cadence that pounded like the blood vessels in his forehead. His heart raced so fast it fractured his focus, forcing him to reset and draw another breath before he might be able to release the feathered shaft.

He had to do this. He had to show his father he could do this. An avalanche of debilitating doubts stomped helter-skelter through his mind. What if he failed?

Atreus shifted his right arm slightly left. The stag continued grazing, still ignorant of their clandestine presence. They had strategically crouched upwind. *Fire only when the animal is looking down,* he recalled from his mother's training.

"Feel your heartbeat. Slow it down. Time your release between the beats," a stern, gruff voice came again, this time right beside his ear.

Despite his surging heart, Atreus focused just behind the shoulder. If his aim held true, his shot would find the beast's heart. Despite the brittle air, a trickle of sweat found its way into his eye. He was running out of opportunity. The stag's head started up.

Atreus' eyes closed without him realizing it.

"Hold," Kratos issued like a command.

Atreus released, praying the gods were watching over him. The pine shaft sailed wide, lofted left by an unaccounted-for puff of wind. It found an elm's bole nearby, sending the startled deer into flight.

"What are you doing!" Kratos exploded, steely gray eyes on fire, ashen skin as white as the clouds. Scarlet tattoos swirled across his torso as if the result of a hand's wide brushstroke. A similar tattoo, running over his hairless head and crossing his left brow, furled with anger as he ripped the bow from his son's limp hands. A three-tiered leather pauldron strapped across his chest protected his right shoulder. Other than that, his torso remained unclothed, save for the discolored bandages covering both forearms.

"Now its guard is up! Only fire—" Kratos stammered through his thick, trimmed chestnut beard. Then he forced himself to stop. He needed to check his anger. He was dealing with a child. "Only fire when I tell you to fire." He issued a low growl.

"I'm sorry..." Atreus said reflexively. His innocent blue eyes, the hue of the deep lakes dotting the land, pleaded forgiveness, though he could not fathom why his failure so angered his father. His mother always encouraged him when he missed during their hunting lessons. She was eternally forgiving compared to his father. He never felt the need to choke out an apology for his shortcomings with her. It seemed all he ever did was apologize to his father for his errors. And his mother never revealed even the slightest hint of anger toward him.

"Do not be sorry! Be better. Now find it."

Atreus reached for his bow; Kratos jerked it further away.

"You missed your mark, boy," his father muttered. He

launched himself from the cover of dense foliage to the path the deer had taken. "We are supposed to be hunting deer, not chasing them. Now we must run it down to finish the job."

The razor-sharp words clawed at Atreus' insides. He stood chest-high before his father in a rabbit-skinned sleeveless jerkin to stave off the chill in the breeze. He tried to understand why his father would act so harshly toward him. He tried to accept it. He tempered his rage. It was almost as though the man before him, his father, was a stranger. Shaking the thought away, he raced off in pursuit of the creature. He hoped it would take but a few moments to spot the fleeing animal's tracks in the sparsely covered earth.

His tenuous confidence shattered, his heart racing, and his mind reeling, Atreus accelerated his pace as fast as his skinny adolescent legs could carry him. Sweat dappled his cropped chestnut hair. Kratos loomed a dozen long strides ahead, picking his way into the forest to locate the animal's trail. Now was no time to talk, no time to think, no time to reflect on his error. Now was a time for action, as his mother had instructed him. If he wanted to eat, he had to locate the tracks and take up the chase.

"This way," he called out jubilantly.

Kratos had unknowingly drifted far left of the animal's path.

"Your mother taught you well," Kratos fired back through heaving breaths, as he pounded the forest floor beside his son to follow the now discernible trail.

Approaching a slight, pine-infested ridge, Atreus froze. He spied the stag in a thorny copse, grazing on the sparse grass jutting out every which way through mounds of dirt-speckled snow.

Atreus lowered himself onto one knee, waiting while his father eased in to return the bow.

"This time, wait for my mark. Relax. You must not think of it as an animal," Kratos instructed gruffly.

Kratos laid the bow across his son's hands, all the time eyeing their prey. "It is simply a target. Clear your mind."

The words were unwelcome and unneeded. Atreus knew what he had to do. He had learned to shoot from his mother. She was more than just an able teacher.

Atreus leveled the bow before notching in his arrow.

"Keep that elbow up."

"I can do this," Atreus whispered, more to himself than to his father.

"Draw to your chin," the God of War instructed.

Atreus eased the bowstring back.

"Concentrate on your target. See nothing else."

The stag lifted its head, sampling the air.

Having planted themselves upwind, they remained undetected as long as the prevailing breeze did not shift and betray them.

"Inhale, concentrate, exhale, release," Kratos' stern voice drummed out.

Atreus ignored the words. He paused, his own anger rising to meddle with his concentration. He cast everything aside except the target before him.

"It is merely a target," Kratos said, interrupting the boy's concentration.

Atreus felt his wavering arm drift upward. He commanded it to be still. He was off target. He began the painstakingly slow task of correcting his aim ever so gently to return the arrow tip to its mark.

"Take the shot, boy. Now!" Kratos urged, impatience riding his words.

Silently the arrow arced true to its target. It penetrated the rear of the stag's shoulder. The beast lurched skyward before pounding into the forest in a hobbling flight directly away from their location.

"I got it!" Atreus chimed. He lurched to his feet in triumph.

"Good," Kratos said, still restrained. The boy had failed to drop the beast where it stood. Now they had to chase it down again.

Atreus wanted to smile, wanted to celebrate his accomplishment before his demanding father.

But instead, he needed to focus on locating the beast before it could flee too far. All was not lost, as long as he could keep on the beast's trail and reach it before it might locate a safe refuge.

Atreus scrambled to take up the chase. The blood trail made his task obvious.

Before the deer could scamper beyond sight, they witnessed the beast's forelegs faltering. "He'll not run far, Father," Atreus called over his shoulder, his excited smile spreading across his face.

Kratos followed a dozen anxious strides in his wake.

Atreus paused, but only long enough to confirm he maintained the blood trail. "This way," he instructed his father, angling his bow in the direction to follow.

Atreus stopped suddenly at the fringe of a leafy copse. His feet remained rooted as Kratos approached a few seconds later.

The deer had fallen, blood oozing from the shaft still buried in its shoulder. Terrified, it stared up at the lad, who now stood over his accomplishment. Suddenly, it failed to feel like such an accomplishment.

"It's... it's still alive," Atreus muttered with a breathless voice.

He worked to swallow the rush of emotion flooding into his throat. He turned away rather than gaze directly at the suffering animal.

Kratos read the struggle on his son's face, his expression exactly like his mother's: caring, soulful, and compassionate.

Atreus knew what came next.

"Your knife." Kratos' voice was one of an emotionless, seasoned hunter. Atreus withdrew the blade, unconsciously offering it to his father.

Kratos planted his hands on his hips, waiting, unmoving. The God of War's thin, tight lips remained a straight line through his overgrown beard. He leveled a stare at Atreus.

"No. You must finish what you started," Kratos commanded. The lad must accept the harsh realities of his life. A forceful nod indicated the deer, still chaotically breathing in the clearing; its bleeding, however, a mere trickle while it awaited death. Until that final breath, it would suffer from the excruciating pain caused by the arrow buried in its shoulder.

Atreus reluctantly pulled his gaze back from his father to the now quivering animal.

Disbelief held him motionless. He knew what was expected of him. He understood why he had to deliver the deathblow, yet something inside held his brain in check.

Drawing in a deep calming breath, Atreus dropped to his knees before the creature. He shoved the knife forward. His hand trembled out of control.

"I can't..." he pleaded.

Kratos crouched beside him and wrapped his monstrous hand over the boy's fingers, clutching the knife, steadying the blade. Atreus flinched at the sudden, uncharacteristic contact. His father rarely made any physical connection with him. Part of Atreus wanted to bask in that moment; another part commanded he respond with the appropriate action, so as not to appear weak. In his heart he knew why he felt the way he felt. His life was to be forever changed.

Misinterpreting his father's act, Atreus relaxed, grateful in that moment that he would be released from having to deliver the fatal blow.

"Delaying what must be done only invites trouble," Kratos said.

In the next moment, with Atreus' hand still in place, Kratos shoved the blade full force into the stag's neck, ending its life with a final shrill screech and a spurt of blood splattering their faces.

For seconds—too many seconds, it seemed—they stared at the stag's lifeless form. Its sole purpose in living was to sustain them in their lives; it died so they might live on. Their lives mattered more than the lives of the creatures they killed. Atreus needed to understand that. That was the way of their world, and the boy had to accept it.

The dense undergrowth a dozen paces to their left rustled violently.

Fear swarmed across Atreus' face. Something monstrous was invading.

Remaining calm, but bracing for the worst, Kratos shot to his feet, lurching the unmoving boy up by the collar and shoving the lad behind him.

A hulking gray hand slammed over a nearby ridge, reaching for the carcass. The woodland troll, three times Kratos' height and easily four times his girth, lumbered into the clearing. Its gaping mouth, framed by two curved defensive tusks, opened in preparation for gnawing into the stag. Having caught the scent of deer blood, the creature had decided it had found something to sustain itself.

"What is that?" Atreus called out.

"Woodland troll. Stay behind me," Kratos commanded.

Kratos started to back Atreus to safety when the troll lunged for them, slamming a massive fist into the God of War's chest, while simultaneously lifting the limp deer with its other hand.

The attack sent Kratos and the boy tumbling into a hollow in the trees.

CHAPTER 2

"*Kjöt*," the troll growled.

"What did he say?" Kratos asked out the side of his mouth.

"I think he said meat." Atreus scrambled through crackling auburn leaves to retrieve his fallen bow.

"*Dauði Kaupmaðr ta*," the troll snarled.

It lofted the carcass in victory, and with the deer's limp head flopping, brought the neck toward its gaping jaws.

"No! You're not taking our kill!" Atreus fired back, understanding the last word as "take".

"No!" Kratos yelled, withdrawing the Leviathan axe strapped across his back. Issuing an unspoken command, he charged the axe with frost, aimed, then hurled it at the troll. The deer trunk came down to shield it from the strike. When the axe penetrated the stag's hide it instantly froze it, causing the startled troll to release it. The carcass shattered into a hundred pieces when it hit the ground.

"*Þú tilheyra ekki hér!*" the troll uttered. Disgust lined its voice; contempt poured out of dark, soulless orbs.

"We *do* belong here!" Atreus shouted, amazed he'd deciphered the troll's claim. His mother had anticipated that someday this exchange would come, and he should be

14

prepared to handle it. "We hunt where we please."

Raising an open palm, Kratos commanded his axe's return. The weapon, magically bound to him, responded without hesitation, whipping back into his hand.

"Father?" Atreus knew he needed to do something but didn't know what. He had never encountered such a creature when he hunted with his mother. Recovering his quiver, Atreus fumbled to extract an arrow while still on his knees. Trembling hands worked frantically to nock the shaft.

Before Kratos could mount another attack, the troll slammed its full weight into him, casting him aside like a limp ragdoll and toppling the axe to the ground a short distance beyond reach. The beast then released a garbled laugh at the human's feeble efforts.

But what the troll's simple mind failed to comprehend how the axe returned a moment later, allowing Kratos to position the blade defensively.

Now coveting the iron weapon, the troll turned to face Kratos squarely, while the axe rose over the God of War's head. The creature detected Kratos' smile. Its face turned grim and vicious.

In one smooth motion, Atreus leveled his bow on the troll, whose monstrous hand seized the axe handle to hold Kratos at bay.

"Father, move away," Atreus yelled. He struggled to line up a clear shot at the troll's vulnerable chest.

Kratos slammed his free fist into the troll's jaw, knocking it back a few feet. The troll had seriously underestimated this man's strength.

"Do not fire!" Kratos commanded.

Kratos charged, only to take a slamming fist to his chest, which drove him to the ground while the troll leaned over him with a sickening grin.

With a quivering hand, Atreus held the arrow at full draw, angling the tip skyward for fear an errant release could maim his father by mistake.

The troll hoisted the closest boulder overhead, angling toward Atreus.

"Boy!"

"I'm fine. Kill it!" Atreus yelled through clenched jaws. The true gravity of the situation took control of his brain. He saw in that instant the very distinct possibility that the troll might kill his father. Refusing to accept the possibility of losing another parent, Atreus leveled the bow, aiming the tip at the center of the troll's chest. *The easiest target is the largest*, his mind instructed him. But before he could focus his concentration and exhale, the troll lunged for Kratos. The God of War slammed the troll's neck, forcing it rearward clutching its throat to breathe.

Kratos leapt to his feet, throwing his axe up quickly enough to drive the blade into the troll's shoulder.

An agonized wail shattered the forest stillness as the troll shifted his hand over the spurting wound.

Infuriated, the troll swung his other arm to knock Kratos from his feet. Atreus now had a clear shot, but only for a moment, as the stumbling troll charged his father before he could regain his footing.

"I have a shot!" Atreus yelled, hoping his father might retreat just long enough for him to deliver a deathblow.

Atreus' heart pounded. The arrow tip wavered in his aim. His mouth turned cottony; tears blurred his sight. He had to act. He couldn't allow his father to die.

Just as the troll tightened its death grip on Kratos' throat, Kratos brought his axe up to cleave the troll's grotesque head.

Wailing and stumbling, the troll groped wildly to extract the blade, without success. With a last grasp, the troll toppled face-first into the dirt.

The clearing fell silent for a long moment. Nothing moved. Then Kratos collected himself before returning to his knees.

Atreus leapt to his feet with a grating scream. Casting his bow aside, mind clouded with rage, he dropped to his knees beside the troll, rapid-fire stabbing his hunting knife into the body. In that moment, all his bottled rage and fear and anger boiled to the surface. The thought of losing his father after just losing his mother drove him to a place where he could no longer restrain his emotions.

"This is what you get!" he screamed.

Tears stole Atreus' vision. He cast his face away to prevent his father from witnessing what was written across his face. He refused to allow his father to see him as a sniveling child. He had to be a man. He had to act like a man.

"Think I'm afraid of you!" he snarled at the troll, lowering his knife while wiping away tears.

In the next moment, Atreus released a jarring cough, forcing him to his hands and knees while struggling to breathe. Kratos responded by grabbing his son around the waist to draw him away, while Atreus sought to lash out once more at the troll.

"You are nothing to me! Nothing!" Atreus forced out between coughs.

Kratos took the boy by the shoulders, forcing him to face him. "Boy! Look at me! Look at me, boy!" he commanded, when Atreus refused to pull his stare from the beast.

"Look at me now!" Kratos snarled.

"No! No!" Atreus yelled back, yielding fully to his inner grief.

Kratos grabbed his wrists and locked on Atreus' face.

A deadpan Kratos offered no smile, no heartfelt words to console, no embrace that might indicate he shared in the grief that tore at Atreus' soul. Instead, he released his son, so Atreus could sheath his hunting knife. A cough erupted in the lad, but this time he suppressed it through force of will. He must no longer appear weak. He must no longer be the child his father saw whenever he looked at him.

"We did it," Atreus said at last, panting.

Kratos stared for a long moment. He seemed to be reading Atreus' mind. He was evaluating him in a way Atreus failed to comprehend.

"You are not ready," Kratos muttered finally.

"What?" Atreus found himself spouting. He knew he should remain silent. But he could not. "I found the deer. I shot the deer. I proved myself. How am I not ready?"

Kratos returned his axe to its sling on his back before wiping the troll's blood from his face. Then he started out from the clearing.

"What are we going to eat?"

"Badger."

"I *hate* badger," Atreus muttered with disgust on his face. Kratos kept going, ignoring the comment.

"I haven't been sick in a long time," Atreus shouted a few moments later. "I can do whatever you demand of me." Slinging his quiver and bow over his shoulder, he started after his father, now a dozen paces in the lead.

Kratos cast a glance over his shoulder at the boy.

"You are not ready," Kratos delivered with a grave finality in his voice.

"I am," Atreus whispered. As he passed the beast, he couldn't stop himself from delivering a final mighty kick to the dead troll's gut, recoiling in fear when a sudden noxious flatulence moved the carcass. Atreus pinched his nose.

"Where are we going now?" Atreus pressed, unable to prevent the pent-up frustration from showing in his words. Kratos disappeared into the thick forest.

"I *am* ready," Atreus repeated, more loudly.

"Do not speak again."

"I will show you," Atreus said, under his breath.

CHAPTER 3

Kratos emerged from the forest first; Atreus followed a few paces behind, a dead badger slung over his shoulder. They paused on the rocky outcrop overlooking the valley below.

Home.

The simple word held such a different meaning now. Home could never be the same.

Kratos scanned the surrounding fields before advancing onto the winding path leading to their house.

"Father, look," Atreus said, angling his bow at a pair of black ravens cawing aloft in an arcing formation. The boy's tone caught Kratos off guard.

"So?"

"I have never seen them before. Mother instructed me to tell her if ever I spotted ravens over our forest."

"Leave them."

Moments later a formidable gyrfalcon, half the size of Atreus with speckled black plumage and a seven-foot wingspan, soared out from the forest canopy, scattering the birds in different directions.

"Jöphie is back. I thought she had abandoned us after..."

Atreus outstretched his arm to attract the bird, which would easily consume his entire arm, to support her as a perch, but the bird of prey ignored his offering and settled onto a nearby tree stump.

"She only went to Mother. She never would come to me," Atreus said, abandoning his attempt.

Offering no more than a cursory glance at the falcon, Kratos maintained a watchful eye on the surrounding vegetation as they made their way into the clearing that opened up onto the house. They had never encountered woodland trolls so close to where they lived before. Its presence sent an unsettling rumble through Kratos' gut.

"Why do you suppose Mother insisted I inform her if I saw ravens? What could they mean? And why are we seeing them now?"

When Atreus looked skyward, the ravens were indeed gone.

"I have no answers."

Seeing his home left Atreus empty inside. The joy he had always felt in the past when returning home no longer filled his heart. Their hours of silent journey only intensified the feeling of loss.

The badger was all they had to show for their hunting trip. And that was only because badgers were plentiful, slow, and clumsy creatures that fell easily to the arrow. But at least they would eat fresh kill this evening.

Once inside their house, Kratos barely spoke, leaving the carcass to Atreus to skin and gut for their dinner. Afterward, sitting on a three-legged stool before the hearth, Atreus skewered the animal before fitting it onto the iron spigot for roasting. The flames cast his mind back to his mother's funeral pyre, where she lay enshrouded in white linens as the flames licked upward on all sides to consume her. He had shed no tears at that moment, his mind so taken by his grief that he could only stand there in shock. Then he winced from the pain he endured when he realized he had left his mother's hunting knife upon her chest after using it to cut the cloth to encase her. At the last second, he had stuck his hand through the flames to snatch the blade back, tossing it aside from the fiery pain it laid across his palm.

Tears welled as he contemplated life without her. He forced his mind to recall the warmth of her cheek pressed against his when she showed him how to use the bow she had made for him. Her gentle hands wrapped over his, to make certain he held the string properly. He would miss the way she could encourage him with just a few simple words.

"BOY!" Kratos roared in anger, surging past him to rip the burning meat from the flames.

Atreus abandoned his memories to stare blankly at the charbroiled badger coming off the skewer. The only thing worse than eating badger: eating charred badger.

"I'm sorry," he apologized weakly.

"Apologize to your empty belly, not to me," Kratos grumbled while he shifted the blackened meat to the table.

They supped in silence, and afterward sat in their chairs before the hearth to keep warm. The third empty chair beside Kratos only served to intensify the loss both were enduring.

"It is time," Kratos said, rising to retreat to his bed in the far corner. Atreus remained a moment longer, seeking to rekindle his mother's smile in his mind. It was her smile that he would miss the most. Tonight, he would force himself to dream about her. He would dig up memories of the times they were happily working side by side in her garden. She was always happiest when she tended her plants.

Atreus dragged himself out of his chair to retire to his cot, across from his parents' now half-empty bed.

He could hear his father's forced breathing rising in the night. He squeezed his eyes shut. They popped open seconds later. Sleep eluded him as he stared at the ceiling timbers. He had never felt more alone in his life than at that moment. All that he knew that made him happy was gone. Anger swelled at the thought of all that he cared about having left him. He knew he was wrong in thinking that. He had his father. He was not alone. His life was meant to go on. But why were the gods punishing him so? What had he done that angered them so much? His mother preached to him that there were gods that were good and cared about humans. So why did those same gods choose to leave his mother unprotected?

Minutes after exhaustion drew Atreus into a dreamless sleep, he was awoken by the turmoil of thrashing arms across the room. Kratos, engulfed in a tormented sleep, battled a foe existing only in his mind's eye.

Kratos held a defensive stance, his back against a rock wall, his blades out to defend himself from a trio of yowling wolves twice his height: one black with verdant eyes, one white, and the third gray. The black beast seemed to be the alpha, assuming the most forward position. A beardless God of War, clad in the clothes of his life in Greece, slashed his Blades of Chaos to keep the predators at bay. But his actions failed to discourage their assault. Kratos realized he needed to bring down at least one of the wolves if he hoped to survive their onslaught. The white wolf advanced as if on command. The movement revealed a woman behind the beasts, clad in a long cloak and cowl obscuring much of her face. Her raised arm sent all three creatures airborne to attack.

"WHO ARE YOU?" Kratos screamed with all the force he could muster, just as the black wolf ripped into his thigh to drag him away.

The dream vanished in that moment, with Kratos springing upright in his bed.

The red and orange of a rising morning sun bathed him with relief. Sweat drenched his clothes and his bed. Quiet consumed the house. His son remained asleep across the room. Kratos thought for sure he had screamed the words out loud, but his son's continued slumber indicated they had merely been part of his nightmare. For a long moment he struggled to recall the woman's face. His arms ached despite the respite of the night. For so many decades he had successfully banished the horrifying incident from his memory. Now it resurfaced to torture him, for what purpose he could not discern.

Many moments later, Atreus drew up his eyelids from his peaceful sleep. Gazing across at his father, his face conveyed a troubled mind. The disconcerting silence commanded the room.

"I did everything you asked. Why is that not good enough?" he ventured, rekindling the words his father had delivered to him while they were hunting.

Kratos buried the memory of his dream, returning to the moment.

"You surrendered control," Kratos explained, trying to constrain the harshness that so often entered his voice when he addressed his son.

"That troll was trying to kill us. It's not like you never get angry in a fight," Atreus retorted.

"Anger can be a weapon... if you control it, use it to your advantage. You clearly cannot," Kratos explained.

"I learn quickly," his son countered. "Mother told me that."

"And you risk falling ill every time your anger rules you. That is not the first time," his father said, pulling himself from his bed.

"I know, Father, but it's been so long since I was sick last. At least... The last time it was bad. I am ready."

"No, boy. You are not."

"But—" Atreus started.

Rustling tree branches stopped him midsentence. The noise began innocently enough, but quickly escalated into a resounding thud. Something big was clearing a path toward their house.

Fear choked Atreus' throat.

Kratos took up his axe, measuring the time it would take to gain a position to protect his son.

"What was that?" Atreus asked, lurching out of his bed.

"Silence."

The flapping of formidable leathery wings taking flight

stole the silence, followed by an unearthly screech that rippled through the air. Then came the sound of tree branches snapping under great strain.

Neither father nor son moved. Neither breathed. The silence filling the room choked Kratos.

Thunderous pounding battered their door.

"Come on out! No use hiding anymore. I know who you are," a callous, scratchy voice commanded.

Then came more insistent pounding. From the force shuddering the timbers, Atreus thought a thirty-foot giant beckoned them.

"More importantly, I know *what* you are!" the voice added, with such a casual delivery that it crawled under Kratos' skin.

"What's going on, Father? Do you know him?" Atreus whispered, too terrified to move.

Kratos silenced his son with a stern glare and a scolding hand before advancing to the door. Once there, he leaned his full weight against it to keep it closed.

"Quickly, below the floor. Hurry!" Kratos ordered, scanning the room for a defensive strategy.

"But... you told me—"

"Not now!"

"—never to go down there," Atreus finished.

Kratos braced the front door closed with a timber plank he stationed beside it for that very purpose, before racing over to a black bearskin rug, flipping it back to reveal a trapdoor painted with a runic symbol.

"Who is that? What is he talking about?" Atreus asked in a frightened whisper.

Atreus had never seen his father this apprehensive. Even when confronted by the huge woodland troll, his father charged rather than retreated. He had never witnessed his father showing fear in even the slightest form.

Kratos yanked open the trapdoor to reveal a five-foot-deep crawl space beneath the house. In one corner, a rectangular timber crate sat in the low light flooding the hole.

"I do not know. Get in," Kratos whispered.

Atreus obeyed, infected by the concern in his father's voice.

With his son safely ensconced in the crawl space, Kratos replaced the boards and rug before returning to the door. For a moment, he contemplated drawing his axe. That was what the old Kratos would have done. The new Kratos decided against it, hoping to defuse the imminent confrontation before it could escalate into violence.

"Just tell me what I want to know! No need for this to get bloody," the voice chimed from a distance.

Kratos removed the brace and flung the door open.

CHAPTER 4

With fists planted on his hips, Kratos marched out, his face grim and imposing. In a glance, he appraised the man presenting himself at their home. After a pause, Kratos eased the door closed behind him.

The stranger—a slight, unimposing man, appearing no older than Kratos—was bare-chested, with rune tattoos scattered about his flesh. He stood, smileless. Bead-ended braids dangled from his full brown beard. Close-cropped hair collected the snowflakes flurrying around them. Clothes tattered and threadbare, he presented himself more as a beggar than a man of means. His soulless, penetrating gaze left his face unreadable.

He stared curiously at Kratos for a time, as if to size him up. It seemed he was waiting for Kratos to speak. Kratos noticed his bony fingers curled reflexively into fists.

"Huh. Thought you'd be bigger. But you are definitely the one," the stranger said slowly, drawing out his words. His colorless lips curled into a smirk.

Kratos remained silent.

"You're a long way from home, aren't you?" the stranger said with a devious glint. If fear dwelled inside this man, he hid it completely.

Kratos raised a curious brow. He had never seen this scrawny Norseman before, yet the man seemed to know more about him than he had ever revealed to anyone other than his wife.

"What do you want?" Kratos' hands also balled into fists, his biceps and neck muscles hardening to rock. He decided on his first move should the man advance. Why would this one, so ill-equipped for such a fight, instigate a confrontation? He brandished no weapons. Surely, with an inadequate stature and impotent arms, he knew he could never defeat the God of War.

"You already know the answer to that," the stranger chided. A gloating smile crossed his face. In the next second it disappeared.

"Whatever you seek, I do not have it. You should move on."

The stranger sighed, shaking his head.

"And here I thought your kind was supposed to be enlightened. *So much better than us. So much smarter.* Yet you hide out like a frightened rabbit in these woods... you pathetic coward."

Kratos advanced a single step, removing his hands from his hips while releasing his fists to open palms by his sides.

"You do not wish this fight, whoever you are," Kratos said, his voice fraught with warning. Undaunted, the stranger advanced three steps to place himself within arm's reach of the God of War. His stare never left Kratos, who remained rock steady.

"Oh, I am pretty sure I do."

Before Kratos could react, the stranger relaxed his fists. In the next second, he backslapped Kratos hard across his face.

Kratos held his stance, reminded himself of the vow he had made when he came to this land. He forced his arms to remain at his sides, though all his muscles were ready.

Fire bloomed in Kratos' eyes. Feeling the uncontrollable rage returning, the rage he swore he would never revert to, he exhaled deeply, forcing himself to relax. He refused to allow this spineless woodsman to goad him into a fight.

"Leave my home now," Kratos spat. The stranger only smiled, revealing carious teeth and his willingness to fight. Or was it a willingness to die?

"You will have to kill me for that to happen," he responded calmly.

In a dizzying blur, the stranger attacked with a series of hard, wild punches, hurling his feeble weight into the God of War.

Kratos caught the fourth punch, crushing the man's fist within his. "I warned you," he snarled.

Unflinching, the stranger released a sigh of relief, waiting for what was to come. An elated smile formed across the man's grimy face.

Kratos could only assume the man had lost all sanity. He failed to understand the expression. Who was this man? And more importantly, *what* was this man, that he would eagerly await a fatal outcome?

Drawing back his fist, Kratos delivered a hard hook to the stranger's jaw, which sent the man awkwardly to the ground on one knee.

"Why do you not heed my warning?" Kratos said.

As the stranger remained motionless on his knee, Kratos risked a glance over his shoulder at the house, wondering at that moment what, if anything, he should tell his son. This was not the person he wanted his son to know about. The Kratos-of-the-past was not the Kratos-of-the-present.

The stranger's rising brought Kratos' face back to him.

The man's visage turned up in a strange display of pleasure at what had occurred. "No. No, no, no, no. Fine. Now my turn," the stranger said.

The stranger charged, launching a fierce uppercut, which sent Kratos flying into the air, skipping across the roof of his house, and finally coming to rest in his yard.

This was no ordinary man.

The stranger followed with an enormous leap, landing less than a dozen paces from the God of War.

Kratos rolled away, springing to his feet and planting them firmly to brace for another onslaught.

"How incredibly disappointing. Come on then," the stranger taunted.

When Kratos charged, the stranger leveraged the God of War's superior weight against him, flinging him into the side of his house. He laughed when Kratos bounced off the structure to hurl himself at him.

The stranger responded by grabbing Kratos as if he were a ragdoll, leaping high into the air with him in his clutches to slam him into the overhanging roof. Straddled over Kratos, the stranger unleashed a flurry of rapid, debilitating punches, the unseeing gaze of a madman on his face.

"This is real simple. Tell me what I want, and the pain stops," the stranger shouted.

Kratos worked his right arm free. Ramming his fist into the old man's face again and again, then throwing him off, he slammed the stranger onto the roof so hard that the thatch gave way, revealing the room's contents below through a gaping hole.

The stranger rolled Kratos onto his back, hovering his fist just above his face. But instead of slamming it into Kratos, the stranger craned his neck for a better view of the house's interior.

"Why are there two beds?"

Kratos whacked the stranger's unprotected jaw, while at the same time bucking the man off and onto the roof. The God of War dove on top of the flailing stranger, threw the man's arms aside, and unleashed his own flurry of debilitating punches.

The stranger, however, recovered quickly, deflecting Kratos' blows and using his superior strength to seize Kratos by the neck and fling him into the garden behind the house.

"Struck a nerve, did I?" the stranger asked casually, raising a brow.

The man displayed no bruising, had no bleeding, and maintained complete control of his limbs despite the pummeling Kratos had delivered.

Kratos heaved up a nearby tree trunk, one damaged from their earlier exchange, and the stranger charged in response. When he was within range, Kratos swung the trunk in a wide arc, batting him back across the yard, where he crashed into the rake of the roof.

He had to prevent the stranger from entering his house and possibly uncovering the trapdoor. Above all else, he had to protect Atreus. Was that what this was all about? Did he intend to take or harm his son?

Kratos had to shut down his brain—act purely on instinct. As he raced toward the house, the stranger slid awkwardly off the roof. Kratos rammed him full force when the stranger hit the ground.

"Who are you hiding?" the stranger questioned, while repeatedly battering Kratos' ribs. He slammed down on Kratos with both fists, sending him to the ground in a heap, then leapt to a nearby ridge where he lifted a boulder larger than himself.

"Catch!" he laughed.

Kratos commanded the frost and responded by launching his axe as hard as he could at the stranger, embedding it in the man's chest, which forced him to take a knee. But he did not freeze! Somehow this one was unaffected by his axe's most potent power. The act of Kratos recalling his axe caused the stranger to topple to the ground. In the next moment, the bleeding ceased, the wound closed up. Witnessing such supernatural power, the God of War ran at the stranger and grabbed him by the throat, dangling him off the ground.

"You are slow and old. You should never have come to Midgard," the stranger taunted.

"You talk too much," the God of War said.

Kratos pommeled the stranger's face, intent on finishing him off before he might regain his strength. As the God of War's strength began to wane, slowing his assault, the stranger leveraged Kratos' shoulder to flip him rearward and reverse their positions. He unleashed a quick, powerful flurry of punches.

"I talk too much, and you refuse to talk. Fine. Maybe whoever is stashed in that house will? Oh, but don't worry, I will be back. I am not finished with you yet." The stranger smiled.

Rage consumed Kratos. Releasing a roar that reverberated

through the forest, Kratos stormed across, grabbing the stranger by his throat and slamming him into the nearest tree. He repeatedly bashed him into the trunk until the tree teetered at an obtuse angle.

Tossing the stranger aside as if he were a bundle of rags, Kratos ripped the tree from the ground, ramming the rooted end into the man. Without so much as breaking a single stride, they crashed through the surrounding boulders and earth, ending up in a new area in the shadow of a massive carved stone monolith.

"Who are you afraid I will find?" the stranger shouted.

Kratos rammed the stranger into the monolith. He responded by jamming his fingers into the cracks of the tree trunk to tear it in half. Kratos began to realize his strength might be insufficient to defeat this one. The power this man controlled seemed far greater than any Kratos had encountered in his past life.

"Shall we find out?" the stranger said with a smirk.

Kratos leapt up to pull at the monolith with everything he could muster. It gave way, toppling on top of the stranger, crushing him beneath it.

Kratos heaved his chest to breathe, standing motionless for a moment.

It was over. Whoever this one was, he was dead now. Kratos could have spared his life, if he would have just walked away and left the God of War alone. He had no understanding of the type of person he had tangled with.

His body battered and aching, Kratos finally withdrew from the monolith, filling his lungs with deep, revitalizing breaths.

Five paces later he stopped. A low rumbling sounded. It could not be. That was impossible. No mortal could survive that.

"Leaving so soon?" The huge carving began to thunder as the stranger hoisted it above his head. He wore a relaxed smile.

"Why do you persist? You do not know who I am," Kratos said.

"Evidently, you do not know who *I* am," he responded, with

a pride that seemed out of place.

"You have engaged in an unwinnable battle against me," Kratos snarled.

"We are not done yet." The stranger's smile left his face.

The stranger elevated the monolith above his head and threw it at the God of War. Kratos caught the stone midair, and with a huge heave, launched it back. The stranger, in turn, caught it midflight, immediately charging at Kratos.

Kratos launched his full weight into the stranger, and they collided in the middle of the field. Both refused to budge. However, the thunderous fight caused the ground beneath them to give way; as the earth separated, they tumbled, still grappling, into the narrow space.

"Odin sent me for answers, but your vanity has turned this into a battle. Throw at me what you may, I *will* keep coming. That old body of yours will falter; your pain will become too great to bear. But before I end this, you must know one thing," the stranger gasped.

He leaned in close with a savage visage.

"I cannot feel any of this." He finished with a hearty laugh.

Then the stranger leapt across the gap, striking Kratos with a powerful uppercut, which launched him skyward. The stranger followed him up, and while Kratos scrabbled about on the ground, trying to regain his feet beneath him, the stranger stomped all over him before kicking him deep into the crevasse.

Kratos hit the bottom with a loud thud. He shook his head to clear his blurred vision. As he climbed the side of the crevasse, he could hear the stranger shouting.

"This fight is pointless. Your struggle is pointless. You cannot beat me."

With trembling arms, Kratos emerged to assume a fighting stance across from the stranger.

"This again. Come on then." The stranger's smile crept all the way into Kratos' soul.

Kratos charged, throwing a punch that swung the stranger

into an awkward position. Then he tackled him, sliding in from behind and locking him in a reverse choke hold. Twisting with all his might, Kratos wrenched the stranger's neck until his head turned almost completely backward.

"Come on, do it! Of everyone I have faced, I'd hoped you would have been able to make me feel something, but even you can't," the stranger taunted, straining.

Kratos grunted and heaved, finally snapping the stranger's neck. A moment later, his limp body crumpled to the ground before the God of War. Exhausted, Kratos dumped the stranger's carcass into the crevasse. He stood there for many minutes waiting, half-expecting the man to come back to life and spring up from the hole to attack once more. As his breathing slowed to a normal rhythm, Kratos accepted that he had ended the strange man's life.

Shaking his head in a mixture of anger, disgust, and sadness, Kratos sighed before turning his back on the crevasse to return to his house.

"How did he know me and my past? How did he find me after all this time?" he muttered to himself.

CHAPTER 5

Kratos surveyed the damage inside the house. The main structure remained intact, but the one corner where the roof had collapsed showed multiple cracks running the entire height of the adjoining walls. Dislodged cooking implements littered the floor throughout. Kratos kicked an iron pot into the hearth, ignoring the accompanying pain.

"Faye, what do I do?" he said in a whisper. "Our son is not ready for what you ask of us... I do not know how I can do this without you." He bent to the trapdoor.

He was grateful his son had remained safely tucked beneath the house. If the man had come for Atreus, he had died ignorant of his son's location. Yet how would he have known about Atreus anyway? They lived a secluded, sheltered life in the forest. Kratos tried to understand what had brought the stranger there in the first place. Was it a chance encounter with a man seeking to confront the fabled God of War?

Kratos had come to this land specifically to hide his identity and change the man he once was. "How did he find me?" he muttered, throwing back the bearskin to pry open the trapdoor. "Boy."

The daylight flooding in revealed Atreus curled in a darkened corner, with arms wrapped tightly around his legs and chin resting on his knees. Discerning his father through the harsh light, Atreus wiped away tears clinging to his pallid cheeks. He offered a relieved smile when he realized the chaos was over and his father was safe.

"There was so much... I thought you..." Atreus forced out, fighting back a new rush of tears, but this time tears of joy rather than anguish.

"You're all right," Atreus said, rising to his feet.

"I am uninjured. Come," Kratos said with a level, unemotional voice, as if he had expected to be fine all along.

He offered a hand, raising his son out in one smooth pull to land on his feet beside him.

"Gather your things. We leave now," Kratos commanded, leaving Atreus standing in confusion amid the disheveled room. A quick survey revealed more destruction than Atreus had even imagined. The gaping hole in the roof held his gaze. He could only imagine the force it took to batter through the roof timbers.

"What happened?"

His father busied himself near his bed, collecting everything he deemed vital for their journey.

"Why are we leaving? This is our home," Atreus said. In defiance, he remained rooted, fully expecting a response. Abandoning their house so soon after losing his mother tore his heart out. If he left, would he be surrendering all his connections to her?

"Now, boy," Kratos said from across the room, without turning to him.

Atreus scuttled about, gathering his bow and stuffing his quiver full of arrows, then adding his hunting knife and some cherished runestones that came from his mother. Seeing them in his palm brought such a debilitating sadness that he crumpled to his knees.

"What is this?" Kratos asked, clearly angered. "Are you ill?" His face softened when he realized the fragile emotion of the moment that had overcome his son.

Atreus shook his head. Inside, his heart was breaking. He was leaving the one place that still held his mother's presence. All her memories were here. Everything he needed to cling to surrounded him.

"Will we be coming back?" he mustered the courage to ask.

"Take only what is most important," Kratos responded.

Slinging his quiver and bow over his back brought Atreus back to the present, forcing those cherished memories of his mother deeper into the recesses of his mind. He needed to deal with what mattered immediately.

"Thought I wasn't ready," Atreus sniped, with a hard edge of sarcasm.

"You are not, but we no longer have a choice."

Kratos lowered the trapdoor, returning the bearskin to its place to conceal their secret. "Prove me wrong then," he said, almost to himself. Strapping his Leviathan axe across his back, he secured a leather pouch to his belt, afterward stuffing a sack full of all the dried venison, dried badger, unleavened bread and dried apricots left in the house. They could carry sufficient provisions for the first fortnight of their journey, if they consumed judiciously, replenishing along the way with whatever the land saw fit to provide them.

"Yes, sir," Atreus replied. He almost allowed a smile to cross his lips.

What must he be ready for?

Kratos stole a moment to admire his son and the strength he projected, despite the loss he had suffered. The God of War permitted himself a slight smile then quickly wiped it away, turning his gaze back to that space below the floor. His vacant stare consumed him as he considered what he must do.

"I'm ready," Atreus said at the door, jerking Kratos back to the present.

Outside, the lad surveyed the battle-scarred land and house.

"Whoa... How?" he muttered in amazement. It was impossible

even to fathom the fight that must have occurred to cause such serious destruction.

Kratos offered nothing in his defense.

"Who was he?" Atreus said.

"I do not know," Kratos snapped back, marching off resolutely toward the path that led into the surrounding forest.

Atreus scanned in a wide arc as he hurried to catch up with his father, trying to take in every nuance of what he saw. Some things seemed impossible for a man to have caused. Whoever had called at his door was no mere man. Atreus wondered for the first time in his life if a god had somehow presented himself to his father. His mother had spoken to him so much over the years about the gods, but he never dreamed he might ever get a chance to see one. Then a terrifying thought took root in his brain.

"You could have died. Never leave me alone, all right?"

"We must keep moving," his father responded.

"What could he want with us? We are nobodies," Atreus said. A silent Kratos marched deeper into the forest.

Then Atreus realized what he had failed to notice on their departure. "Hey, did you kill him?" he called out.

There was no broken, battered body cast aside, no pooled blood as would have been expected from what he heard while he hid, or by what he saw in the aftermath at the house.

"I did what I must," Kratos said simply, as if speaking the words ended the need for further discussion.

Luckily, his answer satisfied Atreus, who trotted ahead as Kratos lingered for a moment to look back one last time at the rune symbol on their door. The symbol had meant so much to his wife. All he had tried to build, all he had hoped to gain, had now been taken from him. Steeling his resolve, Kratos turned his back on the life he once had and strode off to follow his son up the trail.

"Will Mother's garden survive while we are gone? What of her falcon?" Atreus asked.

Kratos considered his response. Their garden was something special for his wife and son. It had represented their life, their future.

"It will be fine until we return. Do not worry," Kratos said, seeking to comfort.

Atreus smiled. They were coming back. They would repair all the damage and keep his mother's garden growing. She would be pleased with that.

But then Atreus thought about the softening in Kratos' otherwise hard voice. How should he interpret those words? Was his father saying that only to appease him? *Were* they ever coming back to this place?

How could he ever feel like part of a family again? He had no mother, now no home, and a father who barely tolerated him.

"Okay," he said.

As they trekked along a path leading up to a ridge on their left, Atreus stared at one of the leather pouches secured to his father's belt. His mind drifted back to his father kneeling before the funeral pyre, carefully gathering up his mother's ashes before funneling them through his calloused hand into the pouch. So intently was Atreus entangled in his memory of that terrible day that a sudden jerking hand had to yank him from the precarious edge of a steep drop along the ridge.

"Watch where you are going, boy," his father grumbled, pulling him by his collar from the rocky ledge.

"Sorry. Can I carry her?" Atreus ventured.

"No!" Kratos shot back, with a bite so sharp that Atreus knew not to argue.

"Where are we going?" Atreus asked, after meandering in silence through the trees that now lined their path.

Kratos offered no answer.

They continued to ascend the ridge, following a jagged path. As they neared the summit, a snow-dabbled mountain peak jutted against a cloudless azure sky in the far distance.

"There is where we must go." Kratos pointed.

"We are going to that mountain? How long will it take to reach it?"

"That I cannot say." Kratos assumed the lead.

"Will we see others on the road?" Atreus asked after a few more minutes of walking. He had never had the occasion to encounter other people. Friendless and isolated in their forest, Atreus had never spoken to anyone except his mother and father; and mostly to his mother, since his father was absent for long periods of time.

"Yes."

"Will they be friendly?"

"No."

"Will they try to rob us?" Atreus pressed. "Mother told me there would be men who will seek to take everything we have."

"Possibly. Yes," Kratos said, opting for honesty.

"Oh."

"On our journey, expect to face many dangers. You must be prepared for them."

Reaching the top of the hill, Atreus turned back to view their progress. Below was the Iðunn forest valley. Within the forest surrounding their house, a string of magical golden trees with glowing foliage stood side by side, forming the enormous shape of a rune amid the crown canopy. For a long moment Atreus stared at the shape the vibrant trees outlined. Their distinct pattern formed the same runic symbol of protection that was carved on their front door, and on the trapdoor in Kratos' home—except on a massive scale— forming a protective perimeter around the forest. Kratos had traveled this way hundreds of times over the years and never once noticed that the pattern formed the rune. It simply seemed unimportant to him until that moment.

"Look," Atreus said, outlining the shape with his finger in the air. He turned a perplexed face toward his father. "How can this be? Where did it come from?"

Kratos had no answers to quiet the boy's curiosity. His wife could have known of this the entire time and never revealed to him the true nature of their serene life in those woods.

"All this time… there has been a protection stave around our woods," Atreus said.

Then something troubling caught his attention. His face turned into a contemplative frown. "The stave is broken there," he pointed out.

A trio of missing magical trees formed a gap in the runic stave, severing the continuity of the stave's line.

"Those were the trees your mother wished me to use for her funeral pyre. Her handprint had marked each of them."

"Wait. She told you to cut those exact trees? Could she have known they were part of the protection rune?"

Kratos swallowed hard. Anger drenched his mind. He had no idea what he had done at the time. He had no idea of the meaning of the golden trees surrounding their life. His wife never told him… if she even knew. But she had to have known. She insisted they build their cabin in that precise location. She countered his every argument to build high on the ridge, rather than in the valley. She never spoke the words, but she knew. Who was she protecting with her knowledge of this place? Was it him? Or maybe Atreus? Or was it herself?

Sadness and grief backed up into Kratos' throat. He choked the emotions down quickly, knowing that dwelling in the past brought only suffering. Giving the forest they called home one last look, Kratos turned abruptly toward the north to continue up the path.

"Come, boy. There is no looking back," Kratos delivered with an eerie tone of finality.

But Atreus needed one more look at everything his life had been. He wondered if they would ever come back to this place, or if their destiny would send them somewhere far from what he had always known as home. Scolding himself inside for the tears that seeped out, Atreus spun around to follow his father up the path.

CHAPTER 6

The monotony of travel clawed at Atreus' brain. He viewed their surroundings as nothing more than rock and trees and meandering pathways. He wondered how long it might take to reach their destination. Asking too many questions, he knew, would only anger his father, so he remained dutifully silent. There were so many things he wanted to learn, wanted to know about his mother's life. He had always thought he would have the time to ask her about the things that mattered most. They had lived in peace for all his eleven winters. He never imagined their lives could turn so bad so quickly.

Kratos stopped suddenly, taking a knee while motioning for Atreus to follow suit.

Atreus scanned for danger. He saw nothing, felt nothing. Then he listened for anything out of the ordinary. At first, he detected nothing.

His father drew his axe, triggering a domino effect as Atreus took up his bow and quiver, quickly and clumsily notching an arrow.

Seconds passed with no discernible changes to their surroundings. Kratos returned to his feet, motioning for Atreus to follow. But when Atreus came up beside his father, Kratos forced him back a few paces.

"Remain ready behind me," Kratos whispered harshly.

Ahead, the clusters of towering birch and pine grew sparse, yielding to a wide sun-drenched clearing. As they approached, the vile stench of rotting flesh permeated the cold air, raising Kratos' alarm.

Draugr. The scourge of the realm.

"What's that awful smell?" Atreus asked, needing to suppress his gag reflex.

"Stay close. Be silent. Draugr."

"Draugr? What are—"

Kratos tugged Atreus into the midst of a densely wooded thicket capable of concealing them. They crouched battle-ready on the forest floor.

The first three draugr, carrying shields and spears, breached the clearing. Warped and distorted husks of decomposing human form, a fire burned within each of them, with an ocherous magma in what were once their veins. Faye had explained these were warriors too stubborn to die, who fought off the Valkyries that came to collect them and reanimated their bodies with their own burning rage. Now they lived only for destruction and indiscriminate vengeance on the living.

They had failed to detect Kratos and Atreus, who remained stone-still amongst the entangled dwarf willow undergrowth.

"Are they... dead?"

"Undead soldiers, very dangerous," Kratos whispered.

"They don't see us. Should I fire?" Atreus queried, his voice a terrified, restrained whisper. *How exactly do I kill something that's already dead?*

"Wait for my mark. Aim for the head."

"Do we attack?" Atreus pressed. He had never been this close to a confrontation before. His heart banged against his chest. His fingers ached from holding the bowstring taut for so long. He focused his mind on his closest target without wavering.

"Be silent. Do not question me," Kratos shot back in a stern command.

Their safe concealment evaporated when a draugr shifted

its attention in their direction. It had detected Kratos' pale skin amongst the leafy brown foliage. The draugr raised a bony, rotted arm to aim its spear.

"Fire!" Kratos commanded, leveling his axe as he charged into the clearing.

Atreus released his first arrow to whiz past his charging father. It stabbed the closest draugr in its neck. The draugr faltered, but it regained its footing to continue advancing, angling its spear at Atreus.

While Atreus fumbled for his next arrow, Kratos sliced the charging draugr with a wide swipe of his axe, severing it at waist height. Coming around in a backswing, he cleaved another draugr's head from its rotting shoulders. The move provided Atreus with the time necessary to reload.

Atreus' next arrow sailed wide of its target, quivering into the bole of a nearby linden tree. His fear kept him from concentrating on their enemies.

"Focus, boy!" Kratos scowled, while he attacked the next two who breached the clearing. Panic flooded in. Atreus fumbled to extract another arrow from his quiver.

Two more draugr, who now understood the threat the lad posed, altered their charge toward him rather than Kratos, skirting the axe-wielding God of War, who became entangled fighting off two more himself.

"Boy, guard your flank," Kratos barked, realizing his son was incapable of fighting both off at once.

Atreus tumbled away to escape the closest draugr, notching his arrow before firing it quickly, to take the first draugr down with a shot into its forehead. As the second charged Atreus, Kratos retreated from his attackers to fire his axe into the draugr's neck from behind. The corpse faltered to its knees, staring vacantly at Atreus while he loaded another arrow, just in time to launch it into a headshot that dropped the draugr poised to jab its spear into his father.

The lone standing draugr turned around to dash clumsily into the safety of the nearest undergrowth.

Silence unfurled over the clearing.

Atreus rose with an arrow still notched in his bow and joined his father, who recalled his fallen axe.

"How was that? Did I help?"

Kratos said nothing. In battle, one needed to focus on staying alive. Having to concern himself with his son's safety now meant he must worry about two people in every confrontation. Splitting his concentration could cause him to fall to one of his enemies. He needed to know that Atreus could defend himself, at least sufficiently to allow him the ability to fight and not worry about him.

Kratos was unprepared to undertake the road ahead. Could he keep either or both of them from being killed before they reached their destination? Perhaps facing his enemies head on was no longer a viable strategy. They needed to improvise ways of skirting their foes to avoid a fight.

"If you wish to help, distract them. Whoever is not my focus, should be yours. But only when it is safe to do so," Kratos offered. He searched his son for understanding. Instead, he caught glimpses of his wife's empathy in the lad. The image tore at his heart, and in that moment Kratos considered himself solely responsible for keeping Atreus safe from then on.

"I can do that," Atreus said confidently.

Kratos didn't hear his response. He had allowed his grief to infiltrate his mind. So many things flashed across his brain that it brought only confusion and anger.

"I said, I can do that," Atreus repeated, pulling an unwilling Kratos out of his vacant stare.

"Good." Kratos returned his axe to his back.

"Which way now?" Atreus said, noticing a thin crack running up the length of the sheer rock face stretching ahead.

Kratos took a moment sizing up what lay before them, after which he knelt down, gesturing Atreus onto his back.

"We go up," Kratos said.

"I can handle that myself," Atreus said.

Kratos remained kneeling.

"I can," the boy insisted.

Kratos leveled a glare at him.

"Fine." Atreus clambered onto his father's back, clinging to his shoulders while Kratos ascended the rock face. Hand over hand Kratos picked his way, choosing from many suitable handholds. The climb proved none too difficult, and Atreus was convinced he could have made the ascent himself, if his father had just given him the chance to try.

"Anything else?" Atreus said.

"Anything else what?" Kratos responded, perplexed.

"Anything else I should know if we encounter those things on the road again?"

"Time your shots. Speed costs accuracy."

"Got it."

Kratos pulled them over the summit, then swung Atreus down beside him on the ground. A part of him wanted to smile, looking at his son, but the god in him kept that part in check.

"And think. Think before you act. Know what you must do before you do it."

"How can I know what I must do before I do it, if I don't know what to do?"

Removing his sack, Kratos sat as he doled out their supper. The jagged rock formations around them would provide safe haven for the night.

"What now?" Atreus asked.

"Sleep."

A bevy of chirping larks fluttered about in the overhead branches.

"Did your mother speak to you about the gods?"

"Yes." Atreus' response seemed guarded.

"Did she ever speak of a man who felt no pain, who could not be killed?"

"That would be Baldur. Son of Odin."

"What did she tell you about Odin?"

"He's the ruler of the Aesir gods. He lives in Asgard."

A soundless night returned for many minutes.

"Anything else?" Atreus asked.

After moments of no response, Atreus fell sound asleep.

Kratos stared up at the mosaic of a nearly full moon penetrating the crown canopy. The boy's mother had taught him about the gods; he would teach him how to survive a savage world, and at the same time teach himself to be a good father. The latter thought ignited a flurry of disturbing images of his own father whipping through his head. He shook them out with a grimace before they might take root. He could allow only one thought to dominate his every waking moment: keep his son safe. Kratos allowed himself to sleep.

With the first weak rays of morning sun at their back, Kratos headed off at a determined march, taking a path that wound into a piney thicket a few hundred paces distant. Ahead, Atreus spotted an ancient rune etched on a boulder standing taller than his father. Running ahead, he mumbled the words to himself as he read.

"It says there is a Jötnar settlement ahead."

"Jötnar?" Kratos asked.

"Giants."

Atreus allowed his mind to ponder the giants while they walked. He realized he had never been this far from home before, and he had never been on such an adventure. His mother had kept him close to home when she took him hunting, and always shielded him from any dangers they encountered on their trips—if you counted a disagreeable badger confrontation as real danger. His mother seemed to display a special sense when it came to identifying danger in time to avoid it. Perhaps that was why their hunting trips always proved successful without them ever facing lethal conflict.

Atreus returned his attention just in time to spot a draugr approaching on the road. "Two more! Over there!" Atreus called, taking up his bow and bringing up an arrow.

"Hold your fire until they are close enough to hit without missing."

Anxious, Atreus waited as the draugr lifted their rusted swords into attack position. He fired to hit the closest one in the temple, while Kratos flung his axe in time to hit the other in its head. Both fell immediately.

"How was that?" Atreus asked.

"Better. But leave me enough space to fight," Kratos insisted.

Somehow, praise failed to feel like praise when it came from his father. Atreus thought he had performed well, getting his arrow notched efficiently, lining it up on the target without wasting a moment, then firing when he knew his aim was true. He decided "better" was acceptable.

"And take my time," Atreus muttered.

"Correct," Kratos said absently.

Before long, the only path ahead led to a dilapidated bridge. Frayed and weatherworn ropes secured rotted timber planks, which inspired little confidence.

Excited, Atreus ran ahead, pounding onto the planks.

"Wait!" Kratos barked, too late.

Atreus' tenth unrestrained stride shattered the plank, which sent his right leg through the splintering wood. Terror rode his scream while he clutched the ropes to keep from falling completely through.

"Father, help!"

Kratos' growl came out in a low rumble, angry and disappointed that Atreus had ignored his warning. The boy needed to learn to think before he acted; he needed to take the time to assess danger before charging headlong into it. Yet Kratos could think of no way to teach such a lesson innocuously.

"Hang on." Kratos ventured onto the fragile bridge.

Clutching rope in both fists, Kratos advanced, bypassing rotted planks in favor of the ropes.

Atreus felt his grip weakening. He knew he had to do something. He tried swinging from left to right, in the hope of throwing his arm from the left rope to bring it beside his hand on the right rope.

However, the jarring movement threw the bridge into violent

oscillations, which sent Kratos clutching the right-side rope and halting his advance.

"Do not move. I will get to you," Kratos commanded, suppressing his anger so as to deliver his words with a calm demeanor, though terror ripped at his insides.

"I'm slipping!" Atreus cried out.

The structure gave way. As the bridge unraveled, Kratos launched himself for Atreus. While his son clung to his outstretched arm, Kratos curled his son's body against his chest as they tumbled. Landing with a crushing thud, his son still atop him, Kratos endured the brunt of their twenty-foot fall.

"Anything broken?" Kratos queried, running hands along his son's arms to check.

"I'm unhurt!" Atreus said, irritated by his father's coddling.

"You must slow down. Your haste will cost us," Kratos warned, his face in a scowl, which softened when his gaze drifted away to appraise their new surroundings. He curled his fingers around his axe handle.

"Are they dead? I mean… more dead?" Atreus questioned a moment later, indicating the array of unmoving draugr planted about haphazardly like statues. Instinct drove him to nock an arrow.

Poised for the worst, they held their ground. The lingering calm, however, seduced Atreus into lowering both his guard and his arrow, while cautiously approaching the nearest draugr for closer inspection. Were they even real? How did they come to be frozen in place?

"Boy…" Kratos warned with a low growl.

As if on cue, the nearest draugr sprang to life, whirling about to levy a rusted, broken sword on the lad.

"Not dead! They're not dead!" Atreus screamed in a panic, jerking back while lifting his bow to fire.

Kratos attacked even before his son could finish his words. With fierce angled slashes, Kratos decapitated the three draugr nearest him. In an arcing backswing, he cleaved off the right arm of the next in the assault.

Atreus fired his first arrow wide of its mark, missing the draugr charging him. He ducked beneath the draugr's wild-swinging blade to come up with another arrow notched in his bow. He dropped to one knee, sending the arrow through the draugr's head before it could launch another attack.

"Remember, accuracy over speed!" Kratos instructed as he came around with his axe to repel a sword crashing down on him.

Atreus' next shot found the middle of the draugr's back attacking his father. Kratos whirled in time to bury his axe in the middle of the last draugr's chest.

Atreus joined his father in the center of the carnage scattered around them. "That was the last one. Was I better?" Atreus asked.

"Take even more time. It does not matter if you fire only once. Show me control," Kratos instructed.

"I will," Atreus said. His distracted gaze went to a slate slab scrawled with runes adjacent to the path that led away. Curiosity drew him over for a closer look.

"Father, look at this," he said excitedly, seizing upon another opportunity to demonstrate to his father what he knew.

"Read it to me."

"It says a long time ago the Jötnar would gather here to trade with the gods. This place was a marketplace. Do you think Odin himself was ever here?"

"Your mother spoke of giants?"

"She taught me the word but said little about them."

"What do you know of Odin?"

"Mother spoke to me about the god Odin on many occasions."

A loud thud erupting from behind the crumbling remnants of an ancient stone building twenty paces on their left signaled another threat.

"Something's moving over there!" Atreus said. "More draugr! We need to get back up to the ridge. But how?"

"Follow me."

CHAPTER 7

Scrambling to the wall on the far side of the ravine, Kratos swung Atreus onto his back before ascending the precipice. Even before the remaining draugr could mount a charge, the two were fifteen feet out of range. Another dozen long, hand-over-hand strides, and they crested the ravine. Atreus was hungry, though it appeared Kratos had no desire to slow or pause to eat. He wondered how long he might have to wait before they took the time to rest.

"Can we rest awhile?" he asked finally.

Kratos scanned their surroundings: open fields, sparse grass, few trees. Not a good place to try to rest. He considered the risks.

"Wait here," he commanded.

Advancing fifty paces, he turned about, signaling Atreus forward.

"I guess that's a no," the lad muttered, sensing an anger building inside.

When Atreus arrived beside his father, Kratos pointed.

Ahead, a closed iron gate blocked their path. Towering stone and mortar walls flanked either side. The barrier extended beyond their sight in either direction; the only way forward was through the gate.

"We get through that gate, then we rest. That will prevent anyone from attacking us from the rear."

A smile returned to Atreus' face.

On their approach, they discovered the rotting corpses of long-dead warriors littering the path and the adjacent fields. Kratos slowed, drawing Atreus closer by the arm.

"All these dead. You think it is safe beyond the gate?" Atreus asked.

"You think it is safer here?"

Grabbing the gate with both hands, Kratos heaved it open with a rusty squeal. Atreus led the way through, entering a vaulted stone chamber a dozen paces beyond.

"What is that smell?" Atreus asked, scanning ahead.

"NOW!" a gruff, raspy voice yelled from out of nowhere.

Atreus twisted in every direction to identify the threat.

Even before Kratos could react, the gate slammed shut behind them, trapping them inside.

A disheveled man appeared from behind a column, his look feral, and his hands tight around his broadsword.

"They Hel-walkers?" another man asked, emerging from out of the shadows.

"They are untouched." A third emerged.

Kratos placed himself between the men and his son, bringing up his axe while Atreus drew his knife, the space too confining to allow use of his bow; and besides, he had insufficient time to notch an arrow if the men attacked. A moment later, four more emerged from the darkness, while two others climbed down from scaffolding extending twenty feet high along the north wall of the chamber. In seconds they surrounded Kratos and Atreus.

"Someone start the fires, we are eating tonight," one of them said.

"Siegmund, your knives," the bandit closest to Kratos said, offering up a toothless smile. Neither Kratos nor Atreus flinched a single muscle.

"So many days without meat," another grimy man said, licking his lips.

Atreus wondered why his father chose not to address these men. Could they talk their way out of this? He risked a glance up at his father. His father's gaze never wandered from those poised before him.

"By meat, they mean us?" the horrified lad stammered.

"Behind me," was all his father said.

Atreus complied, jutting his knife out to protect himself, a feeble effort against so many.

"What if they charge?" the shortest of the band said. He stood behind one of the others.

"We keep them alive, strip the meat off a little at a time," a raspy-voiced one replied. For all intents and purposes, he appeared to be the leader of the clan.

"This fight is mine alone," Kratos said, raising his axe to display his readiness to begin.

"Oooo, now we're scared," one of them said.

Three men took that fateful first step toward the God of War. Kratos responded with a flurry, slicing into arms before the men could jab swords into him. As Atreus retreated toward the gate, Kratos whirled about to cleave the bandit who lunged for his son. Moments later, two more with severed shoulders flopped to their knees, toppling dead to the ground. Amid the moans of those dying, the leader of the bandits leveled a shaking sword at Kratos.

"It is now your turn to die," Kratos said. "Or perhaps if you linger, you can eat your comrades instead." When the man advanced, choosing death, Kratos charged, arcing his axe to disarm the clumsy bandit. Before the man could withdraw, Kratos mangled his torso, severed his right arm at the wrist. As he reached for a knife at his belt, he surrendered his left arm at the shoulder. Blood gushing in all directions, he lowered to his knees, staring vacantly at Kratos.

"Who are—" he muttered, before slumping dead to the floor.

Kratos relaxed his weapon, surveying the carnage to confirm all threats had been eliminated.

A lone bandit in tattered clothes, who had cowardly hidden in the bushy undergrowth pressed against the side wall, slid out to grab Atreus around his chest. With a haughty smile, he pressed his blade to the lad's neck.

"Father!" Atreus yelled.

Kratos turned. But even before he could raise his axe, Atreus reversed his knife, stabbing wildly and blindly into his attacker. Inky blood erupted from the man's throat, spilling onto Atreus' shoulder.

Atreus kicked the bandit's knee, simultaneously spinning about to face his assailant. In the next second, the dying man's face turned deadpan. He opened his mouth to speak, then released his arm from around the boy before slumping over him and toppling to the ground. He brought the lad down with his dead weight, never severing their eye contact. In death he flattened Atreus beneath him.

"Get him off!" Atreus screamed, thrashing in a panic. The dead body pinned him down, preventing his flailing arms from untangling himself.

Kratos yanked the body sideways, afterward extending a hand to help Atreus to his feet. A stripe of blood streaked across Atreus' cheek. Kratos kneeled to eye level with his son, placing a reassuring hand on his shoulder.

Atreus refused to meet his father's stare.

Kratos said nothing, gazing at him with compassion. Then he placed his other hand on his son's other shoulder. Still dazed from the encounter, Atreus failed to even acknowledge his father was there.

Kratos gently tilted Atreus' face to force eye contact.

Atreus stared with an expression Kratos had never witnessed before. Tears gathered. He realized what he had done. He understood what it meant to kill a man.

"Close your heart to it," was all Kratos said. It had been so long since he had experienced his first kill that he could not remember what had gone through his mind at the time.

This day, this experience, would change his son forever. From now on, he would view the world differently. This was something his mother never could have taught him. This lesson he had to learn by experience alone.

Atreus failed to process completely what had taken place. Everything had happened so quickly that he never took a single moment to contemplate his action and its consequences. He nodded to his father before sucking in a deep breath. With a swipe of his shoulder, Atreus wiped away the blood from his face, leaving a crimson smudge across his cheek.

"I am fine," he said when his father's gaze remained fixed on him, and he refused to budge.

Kratos lingered a moment longer, staring at his son, hoping for a clue as to the lad's state of mind. When none became evident, he rose to sling his axe across his back, as if nothing out of the ordinary had just taken place.

"Come then. We have a long—" Kratos said.

From the outskirts of his vision, Kratos detected movement. Fear swelled inside him. The corpses littering the ground jerked violently.

"They are coming b-back to life!" Atreus stammered.

The corpses slowly pulled themselves to their knees, seeking dislodged weapons before unsteadily drawing up to their feet.

Kratos took his axe in both hands. "Wait here. I will handle this."

Kratos slashed, hacked, and stabbed until he had decapitated the rising bandits before they could mount an assault on them.

"They will not come back again."

"I want to leave here," Atreus said, numbed by the experience.

"Then collect yourself. We must find a way out," Kratos said gently, gesturing to a beam of light flooding into the chamber from above. It seemed to be the only way to proceed.

"Okay," Atreus said, composing himself. Kratos boosted the boy onto the scaffolding.

Nearing the midpoint of their climb, Atreus suddenly stopped, lost in his thoughts. He waited.

"You are stuck in your head, boy. Let it go. He would have killed you."

Atreus turned his gaze to his father. He continued climbing. "I know. I had to do it. I do know that. It is just—"

"Then we will go home, boy."

"What?" Atreus said, alarmed.

"To give up this easily, so close to the start... is unforgivable."

His father's words rippled through him. He forced himself to bury his thoughts and focus on what needed to be done. *The only road to success is achieved by never giving up*—his mother's words.

"I am not giving up!" Atreus said. "I will do this. I just need to catch my breath," he lied, trying to buy time to fortify his courage.

Reaching the end of their climb, they skirted along a narrow rock ledge that led to a tall window at the rear of the chamber.

"Listen to me. To be effective in combat, a warrior must not feel for his enemy. The road ahead is long and unforgiving. No place for a child, only a warrior. Can you be that warrior?" Kratos said, after they leapt from the window to return to the ground.

"I understand I can be that warrior."

"Prepare yourself for what next crosses our path."

Leaving the confrontation, Kratos led the way along a dabbled winding path in the direction of their mountain destination. He did not speak, but he was worried. The boy was too young to do what had to be done. He could learn along the way, or he could be killed at the next turn. Kratos wrestled with his decision to continue on the path ahead. He was certain he could overcome anything this world threw at him. But could he protect his son from the dangers at the same time?

"Can we rest?" Atreus asked, after they had traveled three hours in silence. All he wanted was something to eat and a soft place to sleep for the night. An orange sun clung low in the sky, casting eerie shadows all around. He also wanted his father to talk to him like his mother had whenever they traveled. He never felt alone when he was with her. Yet, despite his father beside him, Atreus shook off the loneliness creeping into his soul.

"We have time before the sun sets," Kratos replied, after a pause while he checked the sun's position and scanned the path ahead. A hundred paces distant the path meandered north. He read his son's look.

"Here is where we rest," he said.

In the thick of a leafy copse, the darkness that settled upon them was startling and complete as Kratos and Atreus slept after supping on meager rations. Kratos feigned eating, returning most to the sack. He calculated seven days' worth remained if he reduced his rations by half.

CHAPTER 8

Resuming their journey at first light, Kratos walked determinedly with the flow of the path, Atreus trailing by only a few steps. After many hours, they encountered a long rickety rope bridge stretching over a deep, waterless gully.

"There is someone up ahead," Atreus whispered.

Kratos slowed, throwing an arm out to stop his son from passing him. In the middle of the bridge's span stood a formidable gray pack animal with stubby ears and a long snout, loaded down with overstuffed sacks and a collection of metalworking gear, all secured with hemp ropes. It stood on muscular rear legs, maintaining its balance with the help of a thick tail that reached the ground, since its stunted forelegs seemed all but useless to the animal.

"Move your arse, or I'll shove a boot up it," a little man scowled, no taller than Atreus, whose skin was blue in color from head to toe. He tugged on the beast's bridle to get it moving.

The beast, however, refused to budge.

As the bearded man came around to throw his full, albeit inadequate, weight into the animal's rear, Kratos concluded he presented no threat. Rather than a knife or a sword, or any weapon for that matter, the little man sported a leather tool belt loaded with hammers and files and other metallurgy instruments. Neither of them had ever seen such an odd human before. He displayed all the markings of an ordinary man, yet wore the coloring of some mythological creature.

"What is he?" Atreus asked.

At the sound of the voice, the blue man diverted his attention from the beast, and with narrowed amber eyes, studied Kratos and Atreus. His hand went defensively to the hammer on his belt.

"*Please*, get up and move your arse!" Brok said, returning to his stubborn animal, after deeming the two strangers harmless. If they weren't, they would have attacked without warning, or at the very least nailed him with an arrow from the bow the boy sported. He did, however, notice the axe slung across Kratos' back.

Still the ornery beast refused to even shuffle its cloven hooves.

"C'moooooon!" Brok moaned, pounding his fists on the animal's haunches.

"Perhaps you overloaded him," Atreus offered, without moving.

"Can't get this sloe-eyed cocklump to cross the bridge!" Brok moaned to Kratos, ignoring the boy's comment.

Kratos considered the moment. As long as the formidable creature blocked their passage, *no one* was crossing the bridge. They would have to either find another way or force the animal to move.

Kratos scanned the woods beyond the bridge, while Atreus skirted his father to lean over the side of the bridge, clinging to a fist-thick rope to maintain his balance. He followed the beast's gaze.

"She fears something in the trees over there," Atreus said.

"There's what now?" Brok said, condescension dripping into his voice. "How could you know that?"

Atreus stretched precariously over the rope handhold to point out a sprawling red-leafed elm just to the left of the trail.

"Father, throw your axe at that tree on the other side of the bridge. The one with the white-speckled trunk."

Kratos located the tree and sought to determine what, if anything, his son detected. When he failed to see anything out of the ordinary, he wondered what Atreus was thinking. His axe remained slung over his back. They were blocked from passing on the bridge. If he threw his axe, he would be weaponless until he could recall it. Though he could recall his axe across any distance, it did consume precious time to return, during which he and his son remained vulnerable. *Could this be a carefully orchestrated ambush?* If concealed bandits waited to attack, they would take advantage of the moment when Kratos had only his son's knife and bow for defense.

The God of War leveled a suspicious brow toward Brok. Could this all be an elaborate trick to disarm him?

"Can you trust me just this once. *Please?*" Atreus pleaded.

"What do you see?" Kratos asked.

"I... I just know," Atreus replied.

Kratos struggled with the boy's innocence. He would not have seen this situation the way his son did. Atreus saw nothing more than a man and his beast. Kratos, on the other hand, had to see beyond. Yet if he held back his trust, he would further cripple the bond he sought to nurture. He had to believe enough in himself, that in trusting his son he could still keep them safe from harm. He hesitated.

"And if you are wrong?"

"I am not wrong." Atreus swallowed the guilt that rose into his throat from the words. A memory of him saying those exact same words to his mother, and then having to admit he was indeed wrong, swept through his brain. Yet she forgave him and allowed his errors of judgment to fade silently away.

Throwing a leg out to kick the animal's hindquarters, the blue man missed, toppling over instead.

"I am going to grind you into fodder," he growled at the beast.

"Aim for the tree with the white-speckled trunk and red leaves. The one on the left, just after the bridge," Atreus insisted, pointing to the target.

Kratos withdrew his axe, measured the distance and direction, then fired the blade with all his might. Two black ravens erupted from the leaves to scatter skyward. Seeing the cawing birds brought a sudden unsettling feeling to Atreus, though he was confused as to why.

Making certain no threat materialized behind them, Kratos recalled the axe. "You *were* right," he said, a little too much surprise in his voice.

The pack animal chuffed, stirring nervously on the bridge.

"Look at that! You must be smart or somethin', boy. You are a boy, right? Hyaa!" Brok said, slapping the animal's backside to get the beast moving.

Puzzled, Atreus scanned the sky. Why would harmless ravens so frighten the beast?

"She have a name?" Atreus asked, squeezing around when the beast shifted, to get beside the animal when it took its first steps. Now he could look her in the eye and allow her to see him as they walked together.

"Dunno. Rude bastard ain't ever asked mine, so I ain't ever asked hers. Hyaa!" Brok said, and slapped her rear even harder. She recoiled but moved no faster.

"What's your name?" Atreus asked.

"Brok."

"Mine's Atreus."

"Oh, and you think I care? Sounds like a girl's name, anyway. You a girl in disguise?" he muttered.

Atreus ignored the comment while gently stroking the beast along its shabby mane. "*Vera logn*," Atreus said kindly.

"What does that mean?" Kratos asked.

"I told her to remain calm; the danger has passed," Atreus said.

As if the beast somehow understood what Atreus had told it, and trusted him, the animal took that first slow step toward the end of the bridge. Atreus led the way beside Brok, with Kratos following a few paces behind the animal.

Brok slowed so he could lean closer to Kratos, to sneak a better look at the axe now slung across the God of War's back.

"Huh? Say, you probably ain't gonna believe me. But that axe you got, it was me what made her; well, me and my brother. One of our best. So don't let nobody work on her but us two. You gotta handle her special, or she'll wreck beyond fixing. I can enhance her for you right now if it so pleases, you sonofabitch," Brok said.

Kratos ruminated over the little man's offer. How could he be certain the dwarf would not intentionally wreck it beyond fixing?

They cleared the bridge, following the path into the woodland where, after a short walk, they reached a disheveled campsite with a crude lean-to at its core. Brok gestured to it grandly like it was home.

"What say you?" Brok asked, raising a brow.

"You are right. I do not believe you," Kratos replied. His axe remained across his back.

"How 'bout this? There's a rune in the shape of a fork under the grip," Brok offered with a glinting smile.

Curiosity got the best of Kratos. While the God of War pulled out his axe to examine the rune located under the grip, Brok removed implements from his pack animal to assemble a makeshift work area.

"That was our brand, my brother and me, before we split. I got half of it. See here?" Brok explained to Kratos, seeing him looking at the rune. He extracted a branding iron from one of the beast's packs. He swung it up into place beside the rune on the grip. They matched perfectly, but only on one side.

"Look, you want I should upgrade her or not?"

Kratos leveled his stare, delving into the very depths of Brok's soul, deciding whether to trust him. Breaking into a slight smile, Kratos laid the axe gingerly across Brok's outstretched hands.

"Very well. But I expect an improvement," Kratos said, although some last shreds of suspicion remained in his mind.

"Where's the other half of the brand?" Atreus asked.

"My dumb dobber of a brother got it. But I got all the talent."

Pulling a looped rope hanging from a wooden box strapped to the side of his animal, Brok released a rickety workbench that unfolded like an accordion before him. It allowed him to work his magic anywhere, at any time. Strapping on a leather full-body apron, Brok drew out a blacksmith's hammer twice the size of his hand, using it to bang away at the axe blade. The determined pounding reverberated through the surrounding trees.

"Brok," Atreus said softly.

"Fuck you want?" he shot back.

"I don't suppose you have anything to eat in those packs?" The lad's empty stomach rumbled.

"Where are your manners?" Brok said, scolding himself. "Nope. Nothing to eat in those packs." He returned to the axe.

Dejected, Atreus retreated to sit near the smoldering remains of an abandoned campfire.

"Course I got somethin' to eat. Grab you some out of that pack there," Brok offered with a grin after a few moments.

Atreus smiled at the little man's infectious nature while rummaging through the pack Brok had indicated, finding small flat rolls of hard-crust unleavened bread, which he shared with his father. Next, he located apples larger than his fist and a water pouch in another pack. They drank their fill before settling into the clearing to chomp on the apples.

"Got some dried badger ifn' you're still hungry," Brok added, without looking at them.

"Really, I'm full. Can't eat another bite," Atreus lied. The only thing worse than eating charred badger was grinding down dried badger enough to swallow it. He would rather chew bark from a lichen tree.

Kratos said nothing.

"It is some gooood eatin'. You sure?"

After a series of carefully planned and executed taps, Brok laid his hammer on the workbench and raised the axe in such a way that he might examine the blade closely, after which he ran his eye down the length of the handle.

"That's gonna do it." A proud smile consumed his face.

He returned the axe to Kratos as if presenting him with the finest sword in all the realms.

"Feast them eyes," he said, like a proud father admiring a newborn baby.

Kratos accepted the axe, swinging it to test its heft. Happy with the new feel, he laid it across his hands to scrutinize the blade.

"Acceptable," Kratos grunted. His lips remained tight across his face after a protracted pause, which held the little man on tenterhooks.

"Oh, acceptable, huh?" Brok rattled back, annoyed.

"We are going," Kratos announced to his son.

No sooner had they set out than three draugr emerged from the forest trees, hurtling toward them with swords flailing.

"They're coming for us," Brok yelled, cowering behind his workshop and his beast.

"Got room for one more?" Atreus asked, scurrying behind the beast to join him.

"So long as you don't break nothin'."

Kratos advanced, whipping his axe through the air to evaluate the improvements made to his weapon. He smiled at what he felt. The dwarf had indeed enhanced his weapon. With three well-placed slashes, Kratos dispatched the undead, decapitating two with a single swipe and finishing off the third with both a forward and a backward slash, leaving them littered across the path.

"You can come out now," he said, turning back to Brok.

The little man slid from his hiding place, stopping beside Atreus. "Ya see what my touch brung!" Brok boasted with a broad smile.

"Adequate," said Kratos.

"Adequate, he says…"

"Thanks, Brok," Atreus said. "Oh, and I'll be thinking of a name for your beast," he called over his shoulder.

"How 'bout I name her Fuckin' Gratitude?" Brok screamed. "Hey! Fuckin' Gratitude, come over here!" he continued, directing his anger toward the innocent animal. "And take care of that axe. It needs regular care from an expert if you want it to keep you alive!"

The sound of Brok faded into the distance as Kratos and Atreus followed the winding trail around a bend in the woodland, until it stopped before another sheer cliff.

"Dead end," Atreus said, disappointed. "What now?"

CHAPTER 9

With no other way to proceed but up, Kratos ascended the sheer cliff with Atreus on his back.

"Back at the blue man's camp, you left me alone to fight those draugr," Kratos said after a while.

"I did," Atreus admitted, ashamed now that he hid with the dwarf.

"People are one thing. Everything else you fight, until I say stop, or we are dead. Understand? Pull your weight or we go home."

"I understand."

After cresting the summit, Kratos surveyed the surrounding terrain, and spotted the flickering flames of a meager campfire in the distance near a wharf on the river. But he spied no boat at the quay. Tracing along the river's shore, he picked out entrances to numerous caves before settling on an upper pathway of makeshift rope bridges. Further off loomed the mountain peak—their mountain peak.

They slogged their way through dense groves of dwarf juniper and bog myrtle until they reached a rusted iron portcullis set in a vaulted stone tower, meant to prevent entry to the land beyond. Overgrown downy willow wound through the portcullis openings.

Kratos inspected the gears controlling the gate. A forged

iron counterweight hung from a chain just inside the gate, routed through a series of gears. Tracing the gears, Kratos identified the lever holding the counterweight suspended. After commanding the frost, he calculated the throw he needed to make. On his fling, his frost axe slammed the gears, freezing them instantly, which cracked the attached lever. The counterweight released, but only fell a few feet due to the rust, and the portcullis rose the same distance off the ground.

Atreus slithered beneath the portcullis spikes first. Once he had safely passed under, Kratos slid on his back under the portcullis. Afterward, Kratos recalled his axe.

The portcullis protected the entrance into a wide room, and once inside they paused to assess the situation. The low ceiling struck a nervous chord in Kratos, but he spied a spiked door at the opposite end.

"Looks like the only way out," Atreus said.

Kratos studied every aspect of the door for a long moment.

"How do we get through?" his son asked.

Something still felt wrong with the room. Without advancing, Kratos launched his axe at the door. The blade contacted an iron spike, falling harmlessly to the floor. He recalled his axe to try again. The second time the axe found bare wood, splintering the door. Crossing the room, they forced the door open.

"This way," Kratos said, with a glint of a smile.

A narrow, unlit passageway led to yet another room.

"Machinery?" Atreus said, amazed and intrigued, as they wandered amongst interconnecting gears and levers. Never having seen such complicated and large machinery in his life, he paused to admire the entire breadth of the contraption. He traced along the intricate metal until it met the room's spiked ceiling, then returned his gaze to the point where the gears began. A crude crank presented a way to control the machinery.

Atreus attempted to rotate the crank. It refused to budge. Abandoning his effort, he retreated behind Kratos, who threw his axe into the crank, causing it to turn clockwise. As the crank spun, the floor rose, elevating them toward the spiked ceiling.

"Oh," was all Atreus said, realizing how the machinery worked. Then things turned bad, real bad. Gears began clanking and shuttering as they rotated under heavy strain. A series of jarring thuds from unseen large beams slamming into something resounded around them. A rock panel slid down, preventing their retreat.

"This can't be good," Atreus said.

The ceiling shuttered out of its resting place to begin a slow descent.

Atreus' blood ran cold. He needed to force himself to breathe. What had they done?

Kratos fired his axe harder this time, which made the ceiling reverse and ascend; but a moment later, it resumed its descent.

"It's sinking again!" Atreus yelled, spinning every which way in search of an exit.

Kratos lobbed the axe into the crank, halting the ceiling's descent once more. However, a moment later it resumed its slow, ominous downward creep.

The descending spikes forced Kratos to his knees and Atreus into a squat close to the floor. "It is getting a little close in here," Atreus said, trying to constrain his panic.

Kratos launched his axe once more, this time causing the spikes to retreat until both could stand upright.

"Wasn't sure we were getting out of here," Atreus said.

"Trust that I will not let us die," Kratos said.

As the ceiling continued up, Kratos used his axe to point to a tunnel that the rising ceiling revealed, high on the far wall.

"I am so happy we are leaving this place," Atreus said, climbing into the tunnel.

"It is behind us now," Kratos offered, once safely ensconced inside the tunnel. Kratos led and Atreus followed, keeping within a few paces of his father.

Three hundred paces later, Kratos and Atreus emerged into a steep-sided canyon, which led them to a sprawling overlook. They took in the sight of the distant mountain peak scraping a cloudless azure sky. The panorama took Atreus' breath away. Aside from the stories his mother had told, he had no idea such a wondrous land existed beyond his little world. For the most part, he always suspected his mother had fabricated the stories simply to entertain him on all those lonely days and nights when his father was absent. He never would have believed that what she had told him was actually true. The majesty of the mountain peak commanded the attention and stirred the soul. He wondered why that place seemed so important. What could there be on that peak worth risking their lives to reach?

Atreus struggled to bury his sorrow, when he noticed his father looking at him. The sternness in his stare forced Atreus to tuck away his grief.

"Mother told me stories of places like that. They are even more grand than she made them out to be. I wish she was here to share this with us."

Kratos drew his son closer, swallowing the grief that the very mention of her brought to his mind. He needed to drive those feelings back deep inside. He had to avoid thinking about her. He must go on; he must fulfill his promise to her, and at the same time, keep his son safe.

Kratos reached out to set a hand on the boy's shoulder, stopping himself halfway. His hand remained suspended while he wrestled with his churning conscience. He did not know how to be a father to his son; there was no one in his past to teach him. He had relied on Faye to bind their family together. They were happy in that way. Now, they were lost. But Kratos felt determined to find a path that could bring his son back to him.

At a loss as to how to convey what he was feeling, or how to ease the terrible pain now haunting his son, Kratos withdrew his hand and walked off.

"Come," the God of War said bluntly.

Atreus held his ground, to scan the breadth of the vista one last time. There was a special air to this place he had never dreamed existed. And, somehow, he felt strangely connected to it, like he belonged here, rather than in the forest where he grew up. Launching into a quick stride to catch up, he marched a few paces behind his father, stowing away those memories of his mother with the promise he would revisit them at another time.

CHAPTER 10

Before long, they encountered vibrant, leafy forest. But the sparkling ash-tree-green foliage was different to any he had ever seen before.

"I have never ventured this far from our house. And Mother never spoke of such a place. Has this always been here?" Atreus asked.

"I would assume so. Tracks," Kratos said, hoping such a detail might draw the boy out of his depression. He could think of no other way to help him.

"Boar, maybe," Atreus responded with a renewed enthusiasm, but not so much that it brought a smile to his face. This was a new opportunity to demonstrate his skills to his father and maybe earn a little more respect, as long as he did not fail.

"Find it for me."

Atreus took a knee to study the tracks in the muddy earth. The depth of the tracks indicated a hefty beast. He traced along the ground, losing the tracks in a thorny, yellow-flowered thicket a couple of dozen strides ahead. Returning to his feet, he stepped quickly in the direction the tracks led, his look roving from side to side for signs that might aid him.

Kratos lingered a few paces behind, allowing his son to lead, and relieved he could focus on something new.

They trudged up a narrow winding path that ended at the ridge of a gentle slope. At first, Atreus lost sight of the tracks, fearing he had also lost his target. As Kratos crested the ridge, he scanned the surrounding vegetation. If the beast were close, they would need to spot it before it spotted them.

Grunts from a foraging animal drifted in the breeze.

"Sounds like boar," Kratos whispered. He shot an arm out, snaring Atreus midstride before he breached the ridge. With a finger to his lips, he motioned to crouch behind a halberd-leafed willow hedge five paces ahead.

Poised at a babbling creek thirty paces downwind, the stout plum-colored boar with yellow markings tugged at the tender shoots of bird's nest spruce. The creature's golden mane undulated from side to side in the gentle wind, its ivory tusks curling from its lower jaw. It paused, ever so slowly lifting its massive head to scan the neighboring forest.

Neither Kratos nor Atreus dared even breathe while the beast remained alert. The slightest gesture could send it scurrying to the safety of the downy willow thicket a few paces across the creek. Atreus needed the beast in the open if he wanted a clear shot.

The creature returned to grazing. Kratos signaled Atreus to take up his bow.

In a calculated smooth motion, Atreus unshouldered his bow and removed an arrow from his quiver, notching it in place. He drew in a deep breath as he brought the arrow feathers to his cheek, lining up the tip with the boar's yellow marking at its upper shoulder. It was as if the creature's peculiar pattern highlighted the best point at which to aim.

His mind raced through the myriad details. *Check the wind, account for the drift. Keep the tip on target. Breathe. Bring the bow to full extension to achieve maximum kill power.*

This beast was more formidable than others Atreus had hunted in the past. For a brief second, he debated whether he was strong enough to deliver a fatal shot to the creature.

"Release when you are ready," came his father's reassuring whisper. *His father was trusting him.*

But Atreus wasn't ready. Had the creature heard his father's words? The moment seemed endless.

Yet the creature had not abandoned its grazing.

"Remember, draw to your chest. That boar's hide is thick."

Atreus could wait no longer. At any second, he expected the boar to hear their words and flee. He rushed his exhale, checked that the tip remained on the yellow target.

He fired.

The arrow whipped silently through the air.

Direct hit! The tip struck the boar's shoulder just behind the foreleg bone. The arrow, however, bounced off on impact, shattering the tip. The colored markings served as a decoy, protecting the boar from being struck in a more vulnerable spot, as long as the hunter fell for the ruse—which Atreus had.

The boar dashed into the safety of the nearest undergrowth.

Atreus sprang to his feet, angry, confused, and saddened that he had again failed his father.

"But... I hit it. Didn't I? I followed what you said, and it bounced off. Could the boar be magical?"

"What do *you* think?" the God of War asked, deciding to engage his son rather than scold, so as to raise his spirits despite his failure.

"It did not look like any of the boars Mother and I hunted in our forest. It was different to any creature I have ever seen."

"Get after it then," Kratos ordered.

Atreus scrambled down the ridge, sliding on his side when he lost his balance underestimating the steep slope. He completely abandoned his arrow that had broken, though retrieving the tip would have been a wise choice at that moment.

"I've got tracks," Atreus announced. Kratos scrambled to join him.

"What should we do once we find it? I drew the bow to my chest like you said, and the arrow still failed to pierce its hide."

"You aimed for the animal's flank. Next time go for soft belly," Kratos said.

"I understand."

As they reached the underside of the ridge, they entered a littered camp that appeared to have been abandoned for some time. Acting on instinct, Kratos grabbed Atreus to keep him beside him while he carefully assessed the place. Just because it appeared abandoned, did not necessarily mean it *was* abandoned.

"Stay alert."

"More of those people?" Atreus said, growing nervous from his father's sudden unexplained caution.

"Something else," Kratos said, trying to stay calm.

As Kratos passed a dilapidated hut, something burst from the doorway: a soldier, armed and armored, but no living man. His skin was blue and translucent, and with him came a palpable chill in the air. It lunged for Kratos with its sword. The God of War spun about, slashing his axe into the creature's head. When he did, the body burst into flames as it crumpled to the ground.

"What was that?" Atreus asked, concerned. "It's not like the other dead men. Draugr are hot—he was cold."

"I do not know." Kratos quietly recalled a word the bandits had used. *Hel-walker.*

Kratos scanned the remaining encampment for signs of others. Only after prolonged silence did he conclude that the creature was a lone warrior in the area.

Atreus lingered at the fringe of the encampment, since his father had yet to move to continue their search for the boar.

"Ready?" he asked, watching for acceptance on his father's face. "I think it went this way," Atreus said, indicating fresh tracks.

"Go then."

They followed the tracks leading them deeper into the woodland, pausing when the tracks turned north. Thirty paces ahead, the boar tugged at glistening red berries on low-hanging branches in a thorny gold-leafed thicket.

Kratos gestured.

Atreus took up his bow, dropped to a knee. His father knelt behind him just as he had before, placing his arms gently around him to help with the aim.

But Atreus shrugged him off. His father was treating him like a child. His mother would never have done that. His father needed to allow him to do it on his own.

"I got this," he risked whispering back.

Kratos retreated, allowing Atreus the space he needed. But he remained within a step of him in case anything went wrong. He feared that if his son missed again, the creature might charge, so Kratos braced to fight it off.

Atreus breathed in, aiming the tip at the boar's soft belly. The surrounding woodland sounds ceased as Atreus focused. He became so calm he could feel his own breath slipping in and out of his lungs.

"Elbow up. Relax. Accuracy over speed," he whispered to himself.

Time slowed to a crawl. He thought at any moment the boar would lift its head, see him ready to fire and dash off. He ceased his breathing.

He fired.

The boar reared up, releasing a shrieking squeal as the arrow pierced flesh. Despite the agony of its wound, the beast pounded the soft dirt to find refuge in the overgrown halberd-leafed willows to its right.

"I got it, Father!"

"Don't lose it now," Kratos said with acceptance in his voice.

Without a word, Atreus bolted into the bushes. As he vaulted over a fallen log, he brushed too close to a jagged branch that snagged his clothing and popped his hunting knife from its sheath.

Kratos followed a few steps behind, vaulting over the log just as Atreus had, in exactly the same place. He landed on something that captured his attention: his son's knife. There could be no greater error for a young huntsman than to lose what he might need to save his life. Shaking his head, Kratos retrieved the knife, tucking it into his belt. Perhaps Atreus needed to learn a lesson.

Kratos looked up. Only a few moments had passed, but Atreus was gone. Panic took over his brain like an avalanche. He had only allowed his attention to waver for a brief moment.

"Atreus!"

CHAPTER 11

"Atreus! Where are you?" Kratos yelled, stifling the anger from his voice. With each passing moment the anger turned to fear.

His heart pounding from emotions he rarely felt, he dashed down the path into a dense grove of gray alder. The overgrown, gnarled limbs reached out to snare him. He desperately sought any glimpse of movement, any tremor of disturbance that might indicate the location of his son.

Why did the boy fail to respond to his call?

"He's slowing down!"

Atreus! But he sounded far away. And the way the words echoed forced Kratos to pause and spin around, hoping to home in on the direction of the voice.

"Where are you?" he shouted. Kratos headed in the direction of the voice, but the grove was a woody maze, forcing him down many false paths. After excruciating moments of searching in the forest without a single sign of Atreus, Kratos forced himself, against his judgment, to stop. He needed to reorient himself. He was lost, and he felt no closer to locating Atreus than when he began.

"Boy!" He could no longer stifle his emotions. Withdrawing his axe, he readied himself to attack anything that might come between them.

"I found him!" Atreus called. The words, however, came from

an entirely different direction than his previous call. Kratos spun, dizzy with desperation.

"Hurry, Father!"

Kratos' mind raced in a thousand directions at once. His whole body went cold when the skeletal form of a draugr emerged from a thicket.

"Wait, boy!" Kratos shouted. It took a flurry of axe swipes before he was able to dismember the creature's arms and finally hack off its head.

"Father, please hurry!"

This time the voice seemed more distant. Was Atreus moving farther away?

"Stay in place!" Kratos seethed, repeating the words while twisting about to scatter his voice in many directions.

"Where are you?" his son called back casually.

Kratos needed deep, calming breaths before returning his focus to what he needed to do.

"What did you do?" a feminine voice snarled.

"I'm sorry!" Atreus cried, his words wavering with a panic that clawed up Kratos' spine.

Atreus was in trouble.

"Atreus!" Kratos screamed. "Where are you?" Silence seized the air; and panic seized Kratos' insides.

"Answer me!" the God of War shouted.

Snaking his way through a narrow path of spiny thistles, Kratos finally caught a fleeting glimpse of his son's clothing. Relief rushed in. Atreus knelt before the felled boar in a sun-drenched clearing.

"What did you do!" the female voice shouted.

The lad was not alone. A cloaked figure, wearing a gilded, sheathed broadsword strapped across her back, hunched over the wounded animal beside him.

Breathing hard, his pupils flared, Kratos approached, his axe ready.

"We did not know he belonged to anyone," Atreus pleaded.

"He does not *belong* to anyone. He is my friend," the shadowy figure said.

"The boy was obeying my command," Kratos said, halting a few paces short of the pair.

The cloaked woman turned a shoulder, looking with surprise at Kratos, and then continued to work her bloodstained hands on her animal.

"Then help fix this," she growled, reaching for Kratos' hand to pull him to his knees beside her.

She forced his massive palm over the boar's wound. "Hold here.

"Hildisvíni, I warned you about straying too far. I was not angry with you," she said to the panting beast.

Atreus read the terror that accompanies the fear of imminent death in the boar's human-looking pupils. It was as if he were staring at another person, not a forest creature. He could not fathom how this could even be.

With Kratos clamping the seeping wound, Atreus leaned in closer, hoping to assist, while the woman circled the beast, rolling up her sleeves and mumbling to herself as she moved. Kratos gazed up at her, seeing her face clearly for the first time. She appeared no older than his wife, with ocean-blue eyes. Her lips were thin, her jaw locked. And Kratos detected a thin battle scar running across her cheek. A sparkling blue crystal suspended around her neck caught Kratos' attention. He never expected to encounter a woman in these woods, let alone one with such a valuable gem in her possession.

However, her radiant beauty held Atreus steadfast. She reminded him of his mother, not so much by her appearance, but in the way her focus revealed her compassion.

"Hold tight, I said. He is losing blood," she said.

The boar struggled under the intense pain, releasing a terrified grunt. Its labored breathing turned erratic and shallow. The beast's great head shifted onto the boy's lap, as a helpless Atreus looked on.

"I am *not* going to let you die, you hear me, Hildisvíni?" The woman choked back waterless tears.

Atreus' discarded arrow lay beside them.

The woman extracted a handful of herbs from a pouch on her belt. She crushed them into her palm, mixing them with her spit to prepare a poultice.

"The last of his kind in all the realm, *and you shoot him*! You needed food?" she snapped, while she worked frantically to complete her preparation.

"Target practice," Atreus squeaked.

"Target practice!" she screamed, not at the boy, but at Kratos.

"I am so sorry," Atreus said. His voice crackled with guilt.

"You are sorry? *You are sorry!* Hold pressure on the wound."

The boar's stare darted from the lad to Kratos then to the witch, in such a way that Atreus was convinced it had indeed understood them.

"The blame is mine. I made Hildisvíni angry. He ran off. I warned you about wandering the woods without me. Why did you not listen to me! I should have kept a closer eye."

"Is he… going to die? Please save him!" Atreus found himself pleading.

"I will not let him die. You hear that, Hildisvíni. You are *not* going to die today," she said, with such intensity that Atreus believed she held the power to make it true.

Finishing her paste, she lathered it across both hands.

"The arrow severed a blood vessel. We must open the wound to locate both ends."

As she spoke, she motioned for Kratos to make an incision in the soft belly around the wound with his knife. Once done, the severed blood vessel became apparent.

"Now, hold the ends together tight," she ordered Kratos, who leaned in further. In a moment, amidst the pulsing blood, he managed to pinch the ends.

"Line them up. Evenly," she commanded.

Kratos complied. Once they were together, the woman laid both paste-filled hands on the boar's vessel, held by Kratos' fingers.

"*Sunnan-þoka*," she uttered slowly and distinctly. Atreus' gaze widened in amazement.

A corona of light momentarily escaped her closed palms. Hildisvíni bucked with a squeal. As the witch withdrew her hands, so did Kratos. The paste had bonded the smoking wound together.

"You're a witch," Atreus said.

"I cannot finish my healing here. My home lies just beyond the trees there. You will carry him," she said, ignoring Atreus' observation.

Atreus shot his father a pleading look.

The witch leveled a fierce, intense look at the God of War.

"He must not die," she said.

Kratos stared back at her. Reading the urgency of her words, he clutched the wounded animal in both arms before rising unsteadily to his feet. In some strange way she had convinced him to obey her command. The old Kratos would have shown no concern for a dying animal. Or was it his son who had softened his heart toward these two?

"This way."

The witch approached a formidable ten-foot-high rock wall, covered in vines. Standing before it, she took up soil from a nearby mound and released it from her hand in a sweeping gesture.

"*Greioa.*"

The vines began twisting and turning, untangling until they revealed a path through an opening in the rock wall.

Both Kratos and Atreus paid close attention to the magic at work as they followed the witch along the path. Atreus viewed it with awe, Kratos with trepidation and concern. Just how much magic did this witch possess? And could she become a threat to them? He did not like the unsettling way she had looked at him during their first encounter in the clearing. He had thought it was because they had shot her animal, now he was not so sure.

Atreus sprinted ahead, anxious about the animal. If the witch could accomplish what she said, she would remove the guilt wracking his mind. At least it might deaden the pain he suffered for what his act had caused.

Kratos found himself quickening his pace, despite supporting the boar's cumbersome weight across his arms. He slowed, however, when he came alongside the witch. He felt it prudent to keep her within view at all times.

"That bow seems rather big for you," she commented, eyeing the way Atreus clutched it as he jogged. He treated it like it was more than just a weapon.

"My mother made it for me. Said I would grow into it," he said proudly.

"Your mother is a very smart woman." The witch cast a furtive glance at Kratos.

"How much further?" Kratos said, shifting the boar in his arms.

"I have never seen either of you in these woods before. Your mother must miss you being away from home," she said.

"She... my mother is dead," Atreus said, grief churning up into his throat. He wasn't even sure why he told her that. But doing so forced him to glance at his father, with guilt across his face. If his words brought anger, his father hid it well.

Atreus pointed to the towering mountaintop visible through gaps in the trees. "We are taking her ashes to the highest peak in the realm."

"Ashes?" the witch said, an edge of alarm in her voice.

"It was her wish," Atreus added.

"Boy!" Kratos snarled.

The witch shot Kratos an unreadable stare. "I am sorry for your loss. We are here."

Atreus stopped. "Here" was not what he was expecting. They approached a strange hill shaped like a bloated clamshell, with a gnarled wych elm atop it, stretching into the gray sky.

"You live in this tree?" he asked, surprised, yet at the same time fascinated.

"Not in it. Below it." She smiled. "*Heimili!*"

At her order, the hill rose. Actually, the hill became the shell of an enormous creature resembling an aged tortoise. A cottage of tightly entwined branches and roots hung from the animal's belly, as if it had grown right into the forest.

CHAPTER 12

"It is safe. There is no threat here," the witch assured Kratos, when his face hardened toward her. Delving into the witch's stare, he realized that for now he must trust her.

Undaunted, Atreus dashed toward the gargantuan creature. "Is he friendly?"

Then he stopped. "Is it a he or a she?"

"Boy," Kratos warned.

"I promise you, he is safe here," the witch said. "It is a he."

The creature bowed its head to Atreus, who responded by reaching up to scratch its huge square chin.

"He will not hurt anyone," Atreus said.

Approaching a vine-covered door, the witch waved it open with her arm. "Quickly now."

Kratos trailed her inside, with Atreus remaining outside until his father had completely disappeared within the dwelling. Suspicion stopped Kratos a few steps in. Sunlight streamed in through four unshuttered windows, illuminating every corner. A fifth window in the farthest corner had no light beaming in, and the view through it was dreary and devoid of plant life. Kratos failed to comprehend how that window could be so different from the others. Shelves and tables, benches, and small stands were scattered throughout, all littered with the accouterments of ancient *seiðr* magic. Stacks of wooden bowls and vials lined the shelves on the outer walls.

Only after Kratos' nod did Atreus join him inside. He, too, gazed in fascination at the peculiar surroundings. The house was just as Atreus would have imagined it from the stories his mother had told him over the years about the witches in the realm. But she always described the witches as ugly, mean, and evil. Discarded bones littering the floor in an out-of-the-way location just inside the door caught his attention, as did the out-of-place fifth window.

Taking it all in, Atreus identified a distaff with flax hanging off it. On a small table across from them, he identified sprigs of hawkweed and lyme grass.

Her furnishings remained simple. There appeared to be no items of sentimental value, suggesting this was maybe a place merely for work and sleep. Surely the witch's true home, and her personal items, must be somewhere else.

Atreus drifted from his father's side to inspect the curious items scattered about the room.

"Place him there on the stave," she said, gesturing to a runic symbol painted in crimson on the timber floor. Candles marked the cardinal points on the stave, suggesting it was a sacred spot.

"And keep him still!"

Kratos lowered himself to his knees with some difficulty, struggling to maintain his balance with the large struggling animal across his arms. Once there, he gently set the beast to rest on the symbol. He knew not what the symbol meant, only that if it was important to the witch, so it must be important to save the creature.

While the witch scurried about, gathering up an armful of ingredients, the animal grunted in pain, struggling to move while Kratos held him firmly in place.

"I know! I will not do that," she retorted to the animal's grunt. "Hold him still!" she directed Kratos, who applied greater pressure onto the beast's shoulder.

Shooing the boy out of her way, the witch took up a mortar before kneeling beside the wounded creature. She remained intensely focused on her task as she placed the necessary items in the mortar then began grinding. She never looked at Kratos, the boy, or the animal. All her concentration focused on the task.

"You live alone?" Atreus risked asking.

The witch at first offered no answer, pretending his question went unheard.

"I live here with Hildisvíni," came her reply a few moments later.

"I—" Atreus started.

"It is better that way," she said.

"My father does not like people either," he added.

"Boy," Kratos snarled.

"Well, you don't. It's not true?" Atreus said. Kratos turned a frown at him.

The boar bucked wildly.

"Hold him down before he hurts himself," the witch said.

Kneeling beside the boar, she waved an open vial under its nose. Within a few moments, the animal calmed under Kratos' grip.

"Easy… rest now," she instructed the boar, rubbing her hand gently across its flank. "I need two more things: fresh red root that grows just behind the house. Can you pull a cluster?" she said to Atreus.

Up until that moment he had felt helpless. He so wanted to assist the animal, but he knew anything he did would be fruitless compared to what the witch and his father were doing.

He scurried out the open door.

"What else? You said two things," Kratos said, shifting to balance his weight on his feet. Thinking he sought to stand, the witch snared his forearm, pulling him close so as to share a secret.

"I—" she started, searching beyond Kratos' stare. Her lips stilled as if frozen.

Recognition dawned on her face. She hesitated. Before

speaking, she cast her gaze out the door, where she saw Atreus. She needed a deep breath before speaking.

"I know what you are; and that you are not of this realm. But there is no mistaking what I sensed."

Kratos sought to bury his surprise. How could she know? What powers did she possess that allowed her inside him? Failing to come up with an answer, he remained silent.

"The boy does not know, does he? About your true nature... or his own."

Kratos yanked his arm free, angry that she dared intrude into his life and that of his son. No one was meant to know the truth about them. No one in this land was ever supposed to learn the God of War's identity.

"That is none of your concern," Kratos snapped.

Snorting her disapproval, the witch rose, and, affronted by his reaction, crossed the room to return an item to her apothecary.

"You should know the gods of these realms do not take kindly to outsiders. Trust me, I know."

Leaving her bench with her bowls and cups, the witch crossed to a window overlooking her garden. Outside, Atreus crawled through the plants in search of the roots she had requested. Kratos followed to stand beside her at the window.

"When they find you—and they will—they will make things difficult. Your boy will require answers."

"That will be my problem."

"Whatever you hide, you cannot protect him forever. But you are right, this does not concern me."

Kratos read her expression, attempting to pry inside her mind. There was more he needed to know, more she knew but seemed unwilling to share. Was she an ally or an enemy? He tried to analyze her indecipherable look.

"Lamb's cress. I also need lamb's cress. Do you mind? It is a white-petalled flower in the garden. Just a handful," she said, more to herself than to Kratos, as she moved to the cottage's rear door.

"Fine. Lamb's cress," Kratos said.

"Time is critical."

Kratos joined Atreus in the garden, whose search continued for the plant the witch had requested.

Sensing there was something his son wished to confide in him about, Kratos delivered a stern look meant to coax Atreus into talking.

"I like her. I mean, she lives under a giant turtle!" he called out.

"Do not be too open with her. We do not know if we can trust her," Kratos replied in a harsh whisper.

"Has she tried to kill us? No," Atreus said with a smile.

"Yet," Kratos shot back.

Atreus finally located the red-root plant. He tugged at it, expecting it to yield to his pull. Instead, the plant held fast. Using both hands, he yanked with all his strength. The plant refused to budge.

"Can you help? I cannot quite get it."

"Use your knife," Kratos said.

Atreus reached for his knife on his belt. The sheath was empty. His knife was gone. Panicked, he scrambled in ever-widening circles, searching the nearby ground, hoping he had just lost it. His search expanded to the surrounding garden.

Kratos watched his son's desperate actions without speaking. He could see the distress spilling onto his face. But a lesson was a lesson, and Atreus needed to feel the sting of his failure to learn his lesson properly.

"I lost it," Atreus whispered.

In that excruciating moment, his mind flashed back to the funeral pyre at their house and the broadcloth linen he had used to prepare his mother. *It is your knife now*, his father had told him.

"I lost my knife," Atreus confessed. He knelt, motionless. That knife was the most important thing he had from his mother. How could he have let himself be so stupid as to lose it?

Kratos withdrew the boy's hunting knife from his belt to hold it high. "You dropped it chasing down the boar."

A mélange of relief, embarrassment, and anger poured out. Atreus accepted the knife, desperate to conceal the shame of his shortcomings.

"What is wrong with me? If I had lost this forever—" he scolded himself.

"You did lose it," his father corrected, his brow furrowed.

Atreus easily cut away some of the red roots, adding them to the flowers with the white petals that Kratos handed to him before returning to the house.

"I promise to take better care of it from now on," Atreus said, refusing to look at his father.

CHAPTER 13

Kratos remained near the door while Atreus offered the flowers and roots to the witch. "Exactly what I need," she said, revealing only the faintest glimpse of a smile.

Without delay, she added them to her mortar to grind into the other ingredients. Then she applied the salve to the boar's wound. Seconds later, the beast breathed easier, drifting off into a shallow, pain-free sleep.

"Mother told me stories about witches," Atreus said.

"She did?" the witch replied, arching a brow.

"But she said witches are old and ugly and evil."

"Am I ugly to you?"

"You are beautiful. Like my mother... was."

The witch smiled, setting a gentle hand on Atreus' shoulder.

"What is your name?" he asked.

The witch scrutinized him carefully. "For you, the Witch-in-the-woods is fine. Since that is what you deem I am." Her unexpected response brought a quizzical stare from the lad.

"He is going to live?" he asked.

"Yes, I believe so."

"Then we are leaving," Kratos interjected sternly, uncomfortable facing his son's familial interaction with the witch, the same way he had often interacted with his mother. He heard the boy's words but sensed his wife's kind heart in them. He wanted nothing more of this place, or this witch. The sooner they were gone, the better.

"Not without thanks," the witch said.

Taking up a jar, she dipped a finger in a dark liquid then reached out to touch Kratos' neck. His hand shot out to snare hers before she made contact, his face in a scowl.

"What are you doing?" he said through gritted teeth.

"You wish solitude, no? This mark will hide you from those who might make your journey… difficult."

After a pause, he released her hand, nodding approval for her to paint a *seiðr* protection rune on his neck. All the while he eyed her keenly, uncertain of what to make of this mysterious hermit witch with a boar she called her friend.

"*Leyna*," she whispered once she finished etching.

Dropping to the boy's level, and noticing blood from his first kill still smudged against his cheek, she licked her thumb to wipe it away. Atreus endured the embarrassment, yet her warm touch against his cheek made him think of his mother. However, he remained perfectly still while she painted the same rune upon his neck, finishing with the same word.

"It means 'hide'," she added, in response to Atreus' perplexed look.

The witch smiled at him the way his mother would smile whenever they were close. Atreus thought she was looking at him almost as if she forgave him for his transgression.

"A shortcut exists below the house to lead you safely out of these woods. Follow the daylight."

Kratos was already at the door.

The witch went to a wooden box in the corner, the size used to store firewood. Opening it, she withdrew dried rabbit, bread formed into small biscuits and an assortment of dried fruits.

"Take these for your journey."

Kratos remained where he stood, Atreus having to collect up the provisions in both arms and deliver them to his father to be added to their nearly emptied sack.

"We thank you for these," Atreus said.

"*Heimili*," she commanded.

Moments later the structure began shaking, sinking into the ground around them, as if descending into another world. In reality, the great creature was simply squatting to lower them to their exit. Through the windows, the view was transformed from sunlight and azure sky to root-filled, entangled earth. Except the view through the fifth window never changed.

Kratos needed to grab hold of something to steady himself. Atreus, however, seemed too excited to do anything. The cottage finally settled into place with a gentle thud. The doorway now led to a planked spiral staircase below. A strong earthy smell assaulted their noses.

The witch remained beside the door while Kratos and Atreus filed past her. "And not all witches are evil," she added, with a shade of sadness.

Her expression halted Atreus in his tracks. Why did she look at him that way? What was it about her expression that had taken over his mind?

"Will we see you again?" he felt a sudden need to ask.

Kratos snarled, continuing onto the path, turning about when he realized his son had stopped.

"As much, or as little, as you want. Now, be on your way."

She lingered only a moment longer before shutting the door, leaving them alone on the staircase.

"This underground passage should put you back on your path to the mountain. But now that the dead walk Midgard, the road ahead is fraught with peril. Watch yourselves," she felt a need to caution through the door.

Kratos checked that his axe remained secure in its sling across his back. Atreus felt the same sudden need to tighten his fingers around his bow.

"When she said the dead walk Midgard, did she mean the draugr, or that other thing we saw?"

"We will be safe," Kratos said, fuming inside that the crazy witch would raise such alarm in his son.

They followed the cave's sloping twists and turns as it gradually rose toward a distant dusty shaft of sunlight.

"She was nothing like I expected. Do you think Mother was wrong when she told me of the witches?" Atreus needed to accelerate to get within a few paces of his father's march. "What did she mean about seeing her as much as we want?"

Kratos only grunted, drawing his axe. The sooner they were above ground, the better. The tight confines of the cavern path meant it would be difficult for him to wield his axe against an attacker, and the faint light would prevent Atreus from firing his arrows true to their mark. Unease festered inside Kratos as they continued in near darkness. For a moment, Kratos fought down a concern that the witch had tricked them into following an endless tunnel that would trap them forever.

"Do you think she—" Atreus started.

"Quiet, boy," Kratos snarled. He grew more unsettled. How could he have allowed himself to be put in this situation? He considered returning to the cottage to ascend back above ground. He knew they would be safer there than wandering aimlessly in this hole in the ground.

Atreus detected his father's sigh of relief when, after turning a corner, they spied the first strong rays of sunlight peering into the cave. As the light grew brighter, Kratos returned his axe to his sling. They emerged from the cave opening to a rickety, waterlogged old jetty with rotting timbers and a two-person rowboat. They both boarded the craft, and Kratos rowed toward the sunlight.

Occupying the rear of the boat, Kratos steered with the oars, while Atreus faced him in the center.

"How often did your mother speak of the gods?" Kratos finally asked.

They drifted at a slow, comfortable pace down a meandering river. "Not often," Atreus replied, staring away after answering.

"The truth, boy."

Atreus scrambled through a number of possible responses jumbling around inside his brain.

Would the truth harm him? Could he convince his father with another lie?

"Sometimes… when you were away hunting, mostly."

"Against my wishes." Kratos' jaw clenched; his face turned hard. "That did not seem to bother her."

For a time, they remained silent.

Kratos scanned the banks on either side, cautious of what might be watching from the tall pines and overgrown shrubs lining the banks. Then they emerged into a canyon river pass. Soon, the high canyon walls gave way to jagged outcroppings and small islets. The shoreline transitioned from jagged stone to moss-covered boulders. They were entering a new territory, and Kratos opted to head for the shore. They would sup and sleep in a forest hollow for the night.

"I just thought of another thing Mother told me about Odin," Atreus said, while they lay beneath a blanket of fallen leaves at the fringe of an open meadow, a location suitable for a quick escape back to their boat should danger arise in the night.

"What is that?"

"Odin only has one eye."

"How did that come to be?" Kratos asked, though he surmised it most likely came as the result of some great battle.

"Mother said he sacrificed it."

"For what?"

"I don't know."

"We have talked enough of this Odin."

With that, silence took over the meadow.

Awakened by raucous seagulls soaring beneath the first wispy morning clouds, they launched their boat back upon the water to resume their journey.

"We flow into sea water," Kratos said, a short while later.

"How do you know?"

"Do you not smell it?"

"If that smell is the sea, the sea stinks."

Atreus had never journeyed far enough beyond their forest to experience the sea. His mother only spoke briefly of it and the vastness it entailed. He never dreamed he might actually witness it.

They rowed beneath a natural rock overhang that emerged into a vast caldera. Atreus' jaw dropped.

Then they drifted past a half-submerged monumental stone statue of a god, clutching a hammer.

"Look. That is Thor!" Atreus declared.

They approached another tall statue protruding from the water. The ornate headpiece it wore indicated it was some kind of king; it was wielding a spear and shield, and was clad in chest and vambrace armor.

"That statue, can we go look at it?" Atreus asked with growing fascination.

Kratos surveyed the tranquil water before answering. He tried to peer deep beneath it, but the water was too murky. Trusting his instinct that they would remain safe in the boat, he shifted his oar to steer toward the statue. As they got closer, Atreus pointed out the rune inscription carved into the shield.

"What does it say?" Kratos hated that he was ignorant of the symbols these people used. Now he wished he had allowed his wife to teach him. However, until now, he had had her to translate, or her axe to speak for him when confrontation crossed his path. His skills as a warrior, up until now, had been sufficient to communicate his thoughts to any who dared oppose him.

"'Sacrifice your arms to the center of the water'," Atreus read, pausing uneasily. The words sounded ominous. Atreus' gut tightened. "'Awaken again the cradle of the world.' Wait. Throw our weapons into the water?"

Puzzled, Atreus turned to his father.

Kratos grew concerned. Abandoning a weapon was always an

unwise option. Was this the work of the gods? Disobey the gods and severe punishment could result; obey the gods and become vulnerable to anything ahead. Kratos never trusted the words of a god. He knew better.

"What does it mean, throw our weapons into the water? Well, I guess that wouldn't be a problem for you," Atreus said. If he weren't so unnerved, he would have smiled. "Are you going to do it?"

Kratos only mumbled.

"Is this a command from the gods? Would the gods want us to be unarmed here?" Atreus persisted.

As Kratos scanned their surroundings, shifting the oars, the small boat drifted further from the distant shore. If he surrendered his axe to the lake, as the rune commanded, he could get it back. However, in so doing, he would reveal to any clandestine eyes the power he wielded. If he retained his axe, he might have to face an angry god.

Unsheathing his weapon, Kratos hurled it into the fogenshrouded lake. It disappeared immediately.

Seconds dragged on after the weapon vanished from sight. Kratos attempted to recall his axe. "The axe fails to return," Kratos muttered, confused and suddenly alarmed.

From all across the caldera, from the lakeshores to the high caldera walls, hundreds of white gulls exploded from their roosts. They started circling the caldera, in what began to look like a swirling snowstorm. Most soared up the caldera walls to disappear from view, but some floated in wide circles to monitor the water's surface. They were expecting something to happen; Kratos interpreted that much from the way they locked their gaze on the drifting boat.

"Father, what does it mean?" Atreus' voice quivered.

In the next moment, the water level of the entire lake began to drop, rocking the small boat angrily from side to side, causing both to cling to the edge.

"Just hold on!"

CHAPTER 14

"Remain calm!" Kratos released his tenuous hold on the craft to stand beside his son.

"I am," Atreus said in a level voice, following a scaly wall rising beside the boat.

A giant snake, so huge it consumed the entire sky before them, rose up out of the water, then lowered its head, tilting it to one side to eye Kratos and the boy suspiciously. Water dripped from its enormous snout. As if it was discarding a toothpick, the creature released the axe to drop into the boat.

Kratos made no move for his axe, knowing that to do so might demonstrate a hostile intent and lead the creature to attack. Despite his pounding heart and knotted-up gut, Kratos remained stoically still, but his mind churned.

The surrounding water grew tranquil. The flapping gulls ceased their cries, as if this monster commanded their silence. The solemn air gave Kratos the feeling they were facing some regal creature of greatness, more deity than beast.

A low rumble followed from the deepest recesses of the snake's throat. The deep harmonic voice rolled out like a combination of clicking and singing, two simultaneous layers of lower and higher pitches. Air rushing between its teeth resembled the wind swirling between rocks. The words, if that is what the creature's sounds were, all ended with a purring suffix.

"Keh-naw-nooooo. Gooooo-thooooo seh-nooooo."

"It speaks? Is it speaking a language?" Kratos said.

"I think so. But nothing I can understand."

Carefully, Kratos sank to one knee to take up the axe handle, choosing to point the blade toward the bottom of the boat.

Kratos shook his head in an exaggerated fashion to convey his confusion to the great beast.

"Father, I think he is the World Serpent that Mother spoke of."

"Gooooo-thooooo-leeeeet, air-fooooo-thooooo."

The serpent stared quizzically at him through pale yellow eyes, conveying confusion.

Neither moved as the giant creature wearily disappeared beneath the murky water. A wave taller than Kratos crashed into the boat, causing both to scramble for handholds again. But instead of disappearing completely, the serpent only half submerged, keeping its view above the surface, which placed it at eye level with the boy, as if scrutinizing him alone.

With a weak smile and an arm gesture, Atreus bid their leave from the great snake.

But before leaving, Atreus stared at the creature as if he could delve into its mind through those soulful orbs. There was not an animal behind those orbs; there was a supremely intelligent being, with great power that it chose to restrain during their exchange. It could easily have killed them on a whim, but it didn't.

"That was amazing," an exhilarated Atreus said, sitting back down in the boat.

As the serpent rose, the water level retreated. In the distance, Atreus spotted an ornate temple covered in barnacles and dripping wet, the building dominated by the statue of the ancient king that had been submerged earlier. Seven towers now appeared surrounding the lake, with a void where an eighth tower should have been. A boat dock sat just before the structure.

"That was all just under the surface of the water. There's a dock," Kratos commented. "How much do you know about this serpent?"

"He is one of the giants—so big he wraps around the whole world and bites his own tail," Atreus explained.

"An exaggeration, no doubt."

The stories his mother had shared with him years ago were, in fact, true. He never expected them to be true. And he never expected that even if they were true, he would be allowed to witness any of them. Then a dark foreboding swarmed his brain. He felt his stomach drop into an endless pit. If the stories she had told him sitting before the fire on those lonely nights were true, that meant…

Atreus snapped his brain back to the present. He could not allow himself to think those thoughts.

Reaching the dock, Kratos and Atreus left the boat, traveling the path that led to the temple's anteroom. Entering the odd-shaped chamber, they found none other than Brok pushing open a large set of temple doors.

"Well, if it isn't the bearded beefer and his sac-seed." The little blue man offered a toothy smile.

"Brok? Wait, how are you here?" Atreus asked.

"None of yer fuckin' business. And don't go makin' pig eyes at my spot. I saw it first!"

"I don't understand how… all this was just underwater," Atreus said. Brok disappeared through the open temple doors. The clanking of metal against metal drifted out.

"What do you think he wants?" Atreus said to Kratos.

"To test our patience."

"When word gets out about my new shop, they'll be clawing all over each other for my wares," Brok said, reappearing.

"Sure! Good luck," Atreus said.

"Whatever," Brok muttered, waving them off while he returned to his tools.

Finding nothing inside the temple that could be of use to them on their journey, they returned to the boat, Kratos rowing until they reached the opposing shore.

As they trekked into the foothills, Atreus cautioned himself that he needed to be ready for anything; it had seemed far too easy to reach the base of the mountain.

"Do you think that for this last leg, maybe I could carry her?" Atreus asked timidly.

"I told you no twice already," Kratos replied without looking back.

"Why?" Atreus said, growing angry at his father's stubbornness.

Kratos refused to contemplate an answer. He did not understand why he couldn't relinquish control, even for a short time. Having his wife connected to him allowed him to feel she was still a part of his life. Surrendering her to Atreus, even for a moment, might force him to allow his grief to surface. He beat down the urge to touch the leather pouch on his belt, to reaffirm she was still next to him, as she had been when they shared their marriage bed. If he closed his eyes, he could see her face, her looking into his, and the smile she displayed when they lay together.

"She meant more to me than she did to you, anyway," Atreus said.

Kratos stopped on the path.

"What did you say to me?" he growled. Fuming, his jaw locked as he came about to face Atreus squarely. The vein in his forehead pulsed.

Atreus had never seen such anger on his father's face before.

At that moment, it wasn't his son's words that seized control of Kratos' mind—it was his wife's. *He is just a boy. Above all else, you must remember that, Kratos.*

As Atreus stared, he began for the first time to understand the hurt that his tongue could inflict, even upon someone as strong and courageous as his father. He needed to correct what he had done. He somehow needed to undo what he had caused.

"I just meant... I spent more time with her. You were off hunting so much."

"Talking no more would serve you best." There was ice in Kratos' voice.

"Sir," Atreus said.

Kratos turned about to march off with a stomping, determined stride. Atreus lengthened the gap between them, finding in the distance a solitude that helped him deal with the jumble of emotions raging inside his brain. His father failed to understand how alone he felt.

He had lost his mother. He had no one now. He would never be as close to his father as he was to his mother. His father seemed incapable of understanding how to be a father to him. Did he even care enough about his son to be a proper father? Atreus sensed he would have to endure his loneliness for a long time. He panned from the path into the neighboring woods and, for a brief moment, contemplated what might happen if he just wandered away, disappearing into the woods. How long would it be before his father even noticed he was gone? Would he even care?

Atreus felt his hand sliding back to count the arrows in his quiver. He had nineteen arrows and his hunting knife. He could survive on his own. What was he doing? How could he even think about abandoning his father?

Atreus' stare turned cold, realizing his father had not even glanced back to confirm that he was still there. Perhaps he had angered him so much that his father no longer cared if he was still behind him. Perhaps he would even feel relieved if he turned around to find his son had left him.

So much anger and agony swarmed over Atreus' heart that he thought he might just drop to the ground and refuse to ever move again. Then his mother's voice intervened inside his head. Running away was not what she would have wanted from her son. Abandoning his father would only bring shame upon him in her heart.

"Hurry up, boy," Kratos called, standing in the middle of the path a dozen paces in the lead.

Atreus looked beyond his father to a stone archway, leading to a pass beneath a high peak. He banished all thoughts about himself and returned to the present. He refused to look at the leather pouch on his father's belt. He knew selflessness was what his mother would expect of him. This was what would make her proud, even if his father remained unaffected.

Against a fading shrouded sky, Kratos pushed open the doors of the archway that allowed them entry to the shadowy foothills of the pass. Ahead, they spied a small man working in an open clearing off to the right of the path, no taller than Atreus, but older and much more muscular. He wore golden chest armor while sporting forearm-length metalworking gloves. Bald and bearded, he busied himself at some kind of machine. The light flickering off the nearby campfire danced across the man's face when he turned to stare at them.

CHAPTER 15

Several crudely constructed gears and levers lay on broad cloths scattered about the floor. The man knelt beside an open gearbox, tinkering with the insides, applying a crude hammered-out wrench. From the gearbox, a long cable stretched up toward the mountain peak.

The little man rose in response to their approach.

"Excuse me," he said in a tuneful voice, "but how did you happen to come by that axe?" The weapon held his stare.

"That is my concern alone," Kratos said.

The man advanced across their path to block their passage. However, he appeared uncomfortable taking such an invasive action; as a matter of fact, his timid face practically begged forgiveness for his move.

"And while, good sir, I will not dispute that, I speak because I know that blade. It is one of ours. But we did not make it for you."

"Step aside, scrawny dwarf," Kratos ordered.

"The name is Sindri. I hate being addressed as 'dwarf'."

"But that is what you are," Atreus offered as a plain statement of fact, which received an angry glare in response.

But on Kratos' next stride, Sindri stood his ground, though his shoulders cringed while he stared up at a towering Kratos with stone-faced defiance.

"I will not step aside," Sindri uttered, with a force that proved larger than his size. "See, the special woman we made that blade for…" He fumbled. "Well, I was, I am… quite fond of her. And I would be somewhat displeased if it turned out that… you did something to her."

"So, you wish to *what*? Take this blade from me by force?" Kratos eyed the little man with an expression that bordered on ridicule.

"Rather, I would ask that you surrender it without a fight," Sindri countered plainly, swallowing his fear.

"You do not want me to have to hurt you, now, do you?"

Kratos raised the axe, causing a cowering Sindri to shield his head with his arms.

"It was my mother's," Atreus said quickly. "She left it to my father when she died."

Atreus prayed his comment might spare the little man's life.

For the first time since encountering Sindri, Kratos shot a disapproving glare at his son. He needed no diplomatic response from the lad to deal with this one.

"Faye is dead?" Sindri muttered to himself.

"How did you come to know her?" Kratos asked. "Why did you make the axe for her?"

Sindri ignored the questions.

Sadness came over the little man's face. He lowered his arms, tipping his chin down in mourning while simply shaking his head.

"I am very sorry to hear that. She was a fierce warrior, and a good woman. I will make improvements to the axe, if it pleases you."

"You knew my mother as a fierce warrior?" Atreus asked, perplexed.

Both Kratos and Atreus stared at him in confusion. Sindri knew Atreus' mother, yet she had never spoken of him, or even of how she had come by the axe. Atreus never thought of his mother as anything other than his mother, the one who cared for him with a gentle touch, who praised his every accomplishment, regardless of how insignificant, and who never raised a hand in anger to anyone. How could she be a fierce warrior?

"But no one is asking you to improve it," Atreus added.

"That is true, lad. But knowing your mother as I did, she would have insisted I repair that act of vandalism perpetrated against her axe by my brother."

"I knew it! You are Brok's brother!" Atreus exclaimed.

Atreus took the liberty of rummaging through Sindri's nearby accouterments until he located what he sought. Extracting a branding iron, he lifted it into the air.

"The other half of the brand," he said to his father.

"The blue one is your brother?" Kratos asked.

"Yes, though my talents are vastly superior. No boast, swear to Freya," Sindri said.

"How come, if you're brothers, you're not also blue?" Atreus said.

"That, lad, is a story for another time."

Kratos scrutinized him cautiously before setting the axe across his palms. "Do not undo his work, understand? Improve upon it only."

"Yeah... but can you put it down over there? That handle is..." Sindri said, his face reddening with embarrassment while he shook his head in disgust.

"No," Kratos said.

"Okay, then I will just... I will just," Sindri stammered, searching for anything with which to take hold of the weapon. Locating nothing suitable, he removed his boot, slipping it over the axe handle so he might take it without actually touching it, despite his already gloved hand. He transported the weapon to the campfire workshop, extending it away from his body as if he held a dead rat. He placed it gingerly on a plank bench.

"Yuck. Is that dried blood? It is, isn't it?" Smileless, the little man took up a file, which he began working along the blade's edge.

"Did you *really* make that axe for my mother?" Atreus asked, with more than a hint of disbelief in his words.

"We did." Sindri paused to face the boy squarely. "I see a lot of her in you, you know. She was a very special woman, who spoke the language of my people. She would say, '*Maðurinn sem gengur eigin vegum hans...*'"

"'*...gengur einn*'," Atreus finished, surprised.

"What does that mean?" Kratos interjected gruffly.

"The man that walks his own road..." Sindri started.

"...walks alone," Atreus finished.

"Ah! She taught you some of our language as well," Sindri smiled. "You and I have a kinship."

"I guess so!" Atreus said, edging closer to the little man in a spirit of brotherhood.

Sindri jerked away. "Do not touch me!" he blurted.

"What? I did not touch you."

"No, but you were becoming touch-adjacent," Sindri scolded, as if Atreus had crossed some invisible boundary Sindri had set.

The little man finished filing the axe, carefully examining his work from every angle before returning it to Kratos, again utilizing his boot as a sleeve over his gloved hand.

Kratos accepted the axe, lifting it above eye level to admire Sindri's work before whipping it back and forth to test its new heft. Satisfied Sindri had done nothing to degrade the weapon's efficacy, Kratos slung it over his back.

"It would be wise in future if you kept my brother from laying hands on it again. But if he does, insist he temper his steel longer. He is warping the bit-work," Sindri cautioned.

"What is that you were working on?" Atreus queried, fascinated by the mechanics of the gearbox.

"Sky Mover," Sindri said proudly. He replaced his tools on his bench. "Just up that mountain waits a trove of rare resources. Once I mine it, I will need a way to bring it all down."

"And you know how to fix it?"

"Not even a little. But it will tell me what is wrong, given time... probably... well, I hope." Sindri returned to working on the gondola gearbox.

"Boy!" Kratos shouted. He had already resumed their path, distancing himself by thirty paces.

"I gotta go!" Atreus said. "It sure was nice talking to you. And good luck with your fixing."

"Yeah, whatever. Best be careful. Nobody nice out there anymore," Sindri grumbled to himself, returning to his gearbox. "Stupid head sheave. Tell me what is wrong with you!"

For a time, Kratos and Atreus walked against a stiff breeze without speaking, Kratos slowing his pace intentionally so he might remain beside his son. Atreus wondered if his talking to the little man had angered his father. Recalling their exchange, he didn't believe he had said anything wrong, but felt something had caused his father to hide behind his silence.

Scaling a long, treacherous climb up a rock face, they reached a dead end at an old temple that had towering red doors with a fallen pillar blocking entry through them. There was no alternate path, so they would have to enter the temple somehow.

"Stand to the side," Kratos ordered.

With a loud grunt and a heave, Kratos lifted the pillar sufficiently to angle it aside.

Just as he did, the temple doors burst open, splintering as a result of a great force surging against them. A terrible cry issued from inside, as a Forað barreled out of the opening.

CHAPTER 16

The ogre twisted to slam Kratos into a wall, pinning him in place with a muscular forearm. With a bug-eyed face that was as cold as ice, the Foraŏ leaned into Kratos before he could reach back to take up his axe, sniffing all about his upper body.

"*þú mein líki nǫkkurr guŏ. Ganga bak nú,*" the Foraŏ said.

Atreus surged forward but stopped short, knowing there was little he could do against such an enormous creature.

"Don't you call him that!" Atreus yelled, taking bow and arrow in hand. The Foraŏ simply laughed.

"What did it say?" Kratos was able to spit out, despite the crushing pressure on his throat.

"It said you smell like a god," Atreus said, uncertain if he had understood the ogre's language. At first, he thought it had to be a mistake. What did a god even smell like? "And to turn back. Now."

Atreus leapt for the ogre's face, hoping at the same time to use his bow to tear the creature's arm from his father's throat.

"Let him go!"

Atreus plunged an arrow into the creature's tree-trunk neck.

The Foraŏ recoiled in pain, releasing Kratos, but at the same time backhanding the boy to the ground. It spun about in a rage to charge Atreus, who scrambled in terror back to his feet, where he assumed a defensive posture with his arrow ready. But Kratos intervened at the last second, jamming his bicep into the ogre's gaping mouth, just as the creature was about to seize Atreus' shoulder in its jaws.

Kratos screamed from the pain of teeth tearing his flesh. With his free arm, he swung with all his might at the ogre's head, hoping to force it to release its now clamped jaw. Despite a solid blow to the temple, the ogre maintained its bite.

Atreus scrambled about to locate a rock. Finding nothing close, he resorted to his hunting knife. Before the blade had cleared the sheath, the ogre's hand covered both his hand and his blade. Struggling to pull his other hand free, Atreus reached the dagger strapped at his father's waist.

Atreus released a desperate, angry scream. He had to help his father. He had to free his arm enough to use the weapon. In the next moment, he managed to slip his arm free of the ogre's grip. The beast angled its head to glimpse the boy's intent and before the giant creature could react, Atreus drove the dagger into its right eye.

The ogre's scream shattered the peace of the surrounding forest. The Forað recoiled, releasing its jaws from Kratos' arm, dropping the boy so it could hold its spurting eye.

Atreus breathed in relief... until he realized the ogre was drawing itself up to attack, despite being left with a single eye and a single arm for combat—it needed its other arm to keep its eye from falling out.

"*Bnǫkunr gidubð*," the creature snarled at Atreus.

"No. Now *you* will die," the lad shouted back.

Kratos attacked from the creature's blind side, cleaving the ogre's face with a mighty axe swing. The Forað toppled backward.

"Father!" Atreus called out. Kratos heard terror in his voice when there shouldn't have been.

Confused, since the ogre was no longer a threat, Kratos spun about to track where his son was looking.

Hel-walkers!

A dozen Hel-walkers were clustering at the perimeter of the

clearing, their weapons poised to take on whoever won the battle.

Kratos turned back to Atreus with grave concern across his face. These creatures would not be easy to defeat. Hel-walkers liked to swarm, and Kratos would need to find a way to fight them off while protecting his son.

"Ready yourself," Kratos ordered.

Atreus notched an arrow. If the Hel-walkers attacked en masse, he would never have enough time to fire more than a few arrows before they overwhelmed them.

Rather than take on the Hel-walkers, Kratos sought an escape route. The splintered doors could no longer be used to stop the onslaught, so entering the temple directly would be fruitless. Searching in the dim light, he spotted a path through another pair of towering doors nearby. Retreating from the approaching fighters, Kratos led Atreus through the doors, slamming them closed before the first of the charging Hel-walkers reached them.

Now safe, they continued out through another chamber, where they came upon a massive face carved into the rock.

"I can see why Mother wanted us to bring her here," Atreus said.

"Indeed," Kratos said.

They approached a cave opening in the side of the mountain. The surrounding rock was carved in the shape of a gigantic, howling face, with the cave entrance serving as the gaping, screaming mouth. An undulating black miasma spewed along the ground, smothering the pathway. "Is that smoke?" Atreus asked.

A trio of crested larks, locked in combat with each other, battled before the two on the path. When the birds noticed the approaching pair, they untangled, with two launching skyward while the third scampered on the ground until it encountered the fog. The lark began flapping wildly, now unable to take flight as if snared by the mysterious mist. It flopped out of control until, moments later, it went still, disappearing inside the miasma.

"Remain back, boy," Kratos said, stopping him with an outstretched arm.

"That's not just fog."

Kratos ransacked his memory. He'd never before encountered something that potent.

The encroaching putrid stench of rotting flesh forced Atreus to bury his nose in the crook of his arm. "Aww, what is it?" he asked.

"We find another way up," Kratos said.

"I wish the witch were here. She might be able to use her magic against it," Atreus said, realizing he missed seeing her. In her own strange way, she seemed able to comfort him during his time of grief. His father certainly seemed incapable of helping Atreus cope with all the conflicting feelings trapped inside. Maybe missing his mother so much meant that any woman could ease the hurt constricting his heart.

"What makes you think she even has the power to oppose this thing?" Kratos said, irritated that the lad even brought up the witch. He disliked that she held such a power over him that he would think of her at such a time.

"My magic is useless against the Black Breath, and as you can see, there is no way around it. Odin saw to that long ago." It was the witch's voice.

"What?" At first Atreus thought he had imagined her voice inside his head. Maybe his secret desire to see her again toyed with his mind? He spun about, hoping it was not a trick.

The witch stood a dozen paces from him, her face pale, and her lips a thin, tight line. The sight of her brought a smile to Atreus' face, a frown to Kratos'.

"What are you doing here?" Atreus asked.

"Making certain you can finish your journey," she said with an innocent smile.

"Why did you wait to warn us, witch?" Kratos said, an edge in his voice.

"I was busy saving my friend, remember?" She ignored Kratos' grunt. "The Black Breath is a corruption of magic even I cannot dispel. It consumes any who venture into it. Only the pure Light of

Alfheim is strong enough to break through it. But that road is long and perilous. What does this goal mean to you?"

"It means everything," Atreus said.

Kratos stared down at the boy, whose gaze remained on the witch. The earnestness of Atreus' response settled heavily upon Kratos' mind. How much should he risk? His son? Reaching the mountaintop to fulfill Faye's last wish was all that mattered at the moment. He would let no one or no creature prevent him from succeeding.

"Follow me, then," the witch said, leading them away.

"Why do you help us?" Kratos asked. Suspicion wrapped each word. So many thoughts churned uneasily in his mind. She knew exactly what he was. She had no reason to place herself at risk for them. Was this about his son, because he had lost his mother?

The witch stopped suddenly, spinning about to assess Kratos' expression, inhaling deeply before speaking.

"Maybe I see more of myself in you than I am willing to admit. Maybe… maybe by helping you, I will atone for a lifetime of mistakes." She paused there, reading his reaction, which was minimal. "Or maybe I just like you."

"Even though we shot your friend?" Atreus asked.

"Even though you harmed my friend, yes."

She revealed the true depth of her pain and her vulnerability in her soft gaze.

In that moment, Kratos measured the soul of this woman standing before him, and sensing no malice, he arrived at a decision.

"Where must we go?" the God of War asked.

"To a realm beyond your own."

They took the long path back down the foothill.

"We are going to another realm? Are you not coming with us?" Atreus asked the witch.

"Only for a little while," Kratos said to her.

"Only for a little while," she repeated to Atreus. There was no smile on her face, only trepidation.

CHAPTER 17

Exiting back through the shattered doors, the Hel-walkers having roamed away in search of other prey, the witch led them to the gondola machinery stairs, the same ones Sindri had been working on, where a blanket of tangled, gnarled vines prevented their access.

"We will use this. *Rotna*," she said. Her *seiðr* magic forcibly untangled the vines, despite their resistance to her urging. Then they receded.

"Wait. We cannot use this. Sindri said it was broken," Atreus said.

"Sindri?"

"An odd sort of dwarf we encountered at the foot of these hills," Kratos said.

"He was hard at work on it when we got here," Atreus said.

The witch raised a brow in concern.

"There was no one when I passed by. Perhaps he finished? Dwarves can be awfully resourceful."

"And irritating, based on the two we met," Kratos added.

"That too."

Reaching the gondola, the witch sat first, gesturing to Kratos to manipulate the cart lever. "Just give that a turn."

The gondola jerked forward, swinging as it slowly descended

the caldera from the peak. Bracing against the side walls, Kratos and Atreus sat across from the witch.

"Týr's temple is located at the center of the bay. It is from there we travel to Alfheim. Thankfully, it is no longer underwater."

"Why is that creature in the water?" Kratos asked.

"No one knows. He just appeared one day. Soon after, Thor attacked and their battle could be felt across the realms. Ultimately, their exchange ended in a stalemate, forcing an empty-handed Thor to return to Odin. The serpent remained, growing so large it now spans all of Midgard."

"See! Told you," Atreus said to his father.

"They have hated each other ever since. Destined to kill each other come Ragnarök."

"You *believe* in Ragnarök?" Atreus said, amazed.

"I dearly wish I did not, child," she replied.

The gondola reached the base of the foothills, stopping at a rock platform that facilitated their exit. Kratos paused, allowing the witch to lead the way.

"You know, we actually talked to the World Serpent," Atreus bragged.

"You did?" The witch's face showed a pleasant smile in surprise.

"An exaggeration," Kratos corrected.

"I am good with languages. Even ones I have never heard before. But when he talked, I could not understand it!" Atreus said.

"Sadly, few can. He speaks a dead tongue."

"Oh. Must be lonely," Atreus added.

The witch walked ahead, entering a rocky cave. "Watch your step. Just along here. Let me show you something."

Unslinging a bow with a glowing bowstring, she nocked an arrow and took aim at a large crystal embedded in the rock wall above the chasm.

"Are you watching?"

Once certain that she held their attention, she released the glowing arrow into the crystal, which caused it to erupt into a spray of golden radiance, illuminating a bridge of light spanning the gap. Smiling, she slung her bow over her shoulder while walking across the bridge.

"It's solid! How can that be?" Atreus muttered in amazement. He dashed across to catch up to the witch.

"Elven architecture. My bowstring was soaked in the Light of Alfheim. It can now reawaken the magic of the elves."

"Wait. It won't just disappear, will it?"

"Not as long as the light shines free. This way."

"When you moved those roots back there. What kind of magic was that?" Atreus asked.

"*Vanir*," she replied, fully expecting the boy to fail to understand.

"From Vanaheim?" Atreus asked.

"You know of it?" She raised an eyebrow.

"Just stories. Mother rarely spoke of the Vanir gods, just that they are always at war with the Aesir. I guess that compared to Odin and Thor, they are the good gods."

"There are no good gods, boy. Thought I taught you that," Kratos said.

"Yes, well, the magic seemed effective against those creatures anyway," the witch responded.

A short distance ahead, Hel-walkers made their way toward them. Kratos moved to the lead to take on the first to charge.

"I'll protect you!" Atreus said to the witch.

"How sweet," she replied, with an edge of condescension.

Kratos quickly mangled each of the Hel-walkers that came within range, preventing any of them from reaching his son or the witch. Atreus fired off his arrows to take out one of them before it could reach his father.

"Are you okay?" he asked of the witch, once all the Hel-walkers had burned up.

"I am now, my protector. You are very brave. The risen dead grow ever more numerous. I fear for the future of this realm. Once, the roads and trails would have been crowded with people. Now, all hide or flee, save for the reavers savage enough to survive such a world."

"What are those creatures?" Atreus asked. "We heard them called Hel-walkers...?"

"Restless souls denied their judgment and their peace. A plague, caused by a world out of balance. Someone or something has meddled with powerful forces."

Exiting through doors at the other end of the passage, they advanced onto another bridge, which led them to an array structure with nine separate pathways snaking out in different directions beneath an enormous glowing dome, all of which sat at the bottom of the center of the lake. Inside, the dome housed an ornate temple, almost empty, except for a lone henge in the middle.

"Týr's temple. Built with help from the giants, and great Týr used it to travel the nine realms in his efforts to keep the peace between them," she said.

"Those towers around the water—there is one missing," Atreus said.

"You are sharp-eyed, young one. The Jötunheim tower leading to the realm of the giants has been missing for one hundred and seventy winters. Nobody knows where it went or why."

She paused at the top of a staircase to wait on them, her look unreadable. What was she leading them into?

"Turn right at the bottom," she instructed, indicating they were to continue without her. Kratos refused to move, wrapping his fingers around the hilt of the knife at his belt.

"Please, take those stairs down and turn right. I will wait here," she insisted.

They descended the staircase, Kratos uneasy about what they might find at the next level. They discovered as they turned the corner that their path would take them to a broken bridge. Atreus peered at the cold lake surface below, while the witch monitored them from above.

"I think the bridge has collapsed!" Atreus called back.

"Wait there while I reawaken the light."

The witch unslung her magic bow. Taking careful aim at a large crystal below the gap, she launched her glowing arrow into it. Another glimmering bridge of light suddenly formed across the gap.

Atreus stared in amazement at the shimmering light.

Moments later, when Atreus advanced with a youthful leap of faith to take that first step onto the light, Kratos grunted, snaring his arm to jerk him back.

Was it safe?

CHAPTER 18

"I trust her," Atreus said, shaking his arm free, advancing undaunted to demonstrate the bridge's worthiness despite his father's concern. The light bridge felt as solid as if it were a rock bridge. His father still showed no faith in the witch. Reaching the other side, Atreus and Kratos stopped before an enormous wheel on a giant track, at the base of the great array of pathways.

"What are we doing exactly?" Atreus called back.

"Mending the disrepair. Start by lifting that axle," she called down.

Kratos complied.

"Good. Now push it back into place. Realign the wheel onto the track."

As Kratos pushed the wheel, the entire bridge moved from a pivot point under the array, spinning in all directions around the temple in the center.

"Excellent. Now push the bridge along the track."

"What? The whole bridge is turning! How is the whole bridge turning?" Atreus asked. "You are really strong," he added, when it seemed it would be impossible for any human to move such a massive structure without the aid of many huge beasts. His father's strength far exceeded that of the people they had encountered on their journey thus far. *What made him so different?* Atreus wondered. Appraising the disparity between their bodies, Atreus never expected to become as strong as his father. How could he, with such skinny arms?

"You must push the bridge all the way to the end for the mechanism to reset," she explained.

As the witch had instructed, when the bridge reached the end of the track, the mechanism reset with a loud clank.

"Perfect! Come back up! We are ready now!"

The witch waited at the entrance of Týr's temple.

"Through these doors," she said, with a sweeping arm gesture.

"Wait. So did the giants or the elves build Týr's temple?" Atreus asked.

"All races helped with its construction. It was the last great act of cooperation between the realms before peace vanished for good."

The witch approached another broken path. There she fired another radiant arrow into another light bridge. The glowing bowstring flickered and died.

"Your bowstring has stopped glowing," said Atreus.

"Its power is now depleted. Only a few nocks of magic remained in the bowstring and, sadly, we have used them."

Pinching the hemp bowstring caused it to unstring itself magically from her bow. "Your bow, please," she asked with a hand outstretched.

Atreus watched in wonder as she took his bow, and with a grand wave of her hand, his own bowstring unstrung itself. Then, when she held up her bowstring to the boy's bow, it magically strung itself onto his bow.

"Listen to me well," she started, her face deadly serious. "Once you claim the Light of Alfheim, you must infuse the bowstring with its power. Do not forget!"

She returned the bow to Atreus, laying it reverently across his open hands, and despite his desire to avoid it, he felt compelled to examine the new string. What power would he have now? He could only wonder how the bow might help them in the future.

Atreus and Kratos advanced more than a dozen paces across the newly formed light bridge before they realized the witch was not accompanying them.

"You talk as if you are not coming with us?" the lad said.

"I will try, but measures were taken to keep me trapped in Midgard."

"Why?" Kratos asked, his suspicion piqued. What powers did this witch possess that the gods would restrict her movements? What damage could she cause if left unchecked?

"The gods do not care much for me," she said quickly.

After a few more paces, the witch scurried up to join them, in defiance of those who sought to punish her interminably. She would show them she could fight their magic with magic of her own.

Continuing their journey, they followed the witch into a dark, ornate domed chamber. Inside, a pedestal with an elaborate table hovered at the room's center, floating above an inky hole that defied gravity.

"Is this it? It's so dark," Atreus said.

"This temple has been asleep, underwater for almost a hundred and fifty winters. It needs only the Bifröst light to reawaken it."

As Kratos and Atreus approached the hole, tree roots erupted from the edge of the floor to create a bridge over the gap.

"Those roots do not look like your magic," Atreus said.

"They are not. They are part of the great World Tree and make travel between the realms possible."

The witch positioned herself beside the table, which contained an elaborate diorama of the caldera.

"Once you commit to this journey, it might be some time before you are back in Midgard again."

Atreus leaned over in fascination. Kratos, however, maintained a safe distance from it. From where he stood he could observe all the witch had to show them, yet still maintain sufficient distance to allow him to defend them from any sudden attack.

"I can teach you how to travel between realms, but only if you are over there. Come." The witch removed a portable metallic lamp, housing a faintly glowing crystal. "You will need this Bifröst to create travel between realms."

"How does it work?" Kratos asked.

She handed it to Kratos, who examined it with guarded interest. Could this small thing actually transport them between realms? And what price did they pay for such a benefit? There was always a price to be paid, even by a god.

When Kratos nodded a willingness to continue, the witch responded by sweeping her arm across the table.

"That will capture, hold and transfer the Light of Alfheim." She indicated the place they needed to go. "Place the Bifröst there."

Kratos complied, setting the Bifröst into a power receptacle in the table. Immediately the entire room came to life, emitting a low-level humming sound.

"Every realm requires knowledge of its corresponding travel rune. Absent the proper rune, travel between realms is impossible. This rune is the one for Alfheim. Position the wheel to your destination."

As Kratos turned the wheel, inside the diorama a bridge rotated around the small model of the temple array. The bridge inside the realm travel room itself also turned in conjunction with Kratos' efforts.

"Is this moving the big bridge outside?" Atreus asked.

"Correct. Your father is lining up the bridge to the appropriate realm."

Kratos aligned to the Alfheim selection.

"Good. Now, lock in your destination."

Kratos did so.

"We are ready. Remember to take the Bifröst; you do not want to lose that," she said, inducing Kratos to extract the Bifröst from the power receptacle.

"Now the realm travel bridge will align and the path between realms will open."

The bridge inside the realm travel room automatically aligned itself to the Alfheim bridge door, and in so doing, a Bifröst bubble opened. They stared at a cosmic light shower that transcended all that existed in their realm. A kaleidoscope of colors and strange images suddenly surrounded them—bits of a reality that had fallen between the cracks, lost in this realm between realms.

"So, this is not Alfheim?" Atreus asked.

"No, we are still stepping between the two realms."

"But we are not moving?" Atreus asked.

"All nine realms occupy the same physical space, only on different planes of existence. The Yggdrasil tree cuts between those planes; its roots exist in all nine realms at once…"

Atreus could not fathom how anything could exist in more than one realm at a time. If it were here with them, how could it be in a different realm at that same time? They would travel from one realm into another, and once they arrived at their destination realm, they would no longer exist in the realm they departed. Or would they?

The witch read Atreus' confused expression.

"The magic of the realms is far beyond that which any man can understand. It is acceptable that you fail to understand what you are now experiencing. But you do not need to fear it."

In the next moment the light barrage faded, but they remained standing in the same room.

"It didn't work. We're still here," Atreus said.

Kratos summarily dismissed his son's assertion. He knew better than to trust only what he saw.

"Follow me," the witch said, with a proud smile and chin raised in defiance.

Kratos remained exactly where he stood. "The Bifröst is dark." The crystal he held had turned dead black.

"Unfortunate. This trip was its last use. There is no going back now until it is replenished with the Light of Alfheim."

"Witch, are you saying we are trapped in this realm?" Kratos snarled.

"Someone of your ability should have little trouble getting back to Midgard."

"And then we can make the Black Breath go away?"

"With the captured Light of Alfheim, yes."

Kratos didn't feel the confidence that the witch clearly felt.

However, as if to rebuild his faith in her, the witch took the first step out of the Bifröst bubble into Alfheim beyond. Feeling safe, Atreus exited next without hesitation, putting his complete faith in her. Kratos hesitated still, exiting last, his hand ready on his axe. His hawk-like stare scanned the expanse, darting quickly in all directions to catalog everything around them.

"Where are we?" Atreus asked.

ALFHEIM

CHAPTER 19

They exited the temple doors to see a long bridge stretching before them, disappearing at the horizon. The bridge stood in the exact same location as the one in the Midgard realm, but instead of spanning a lake, it now spanned a jagged chasm. Thick, gnarled and twisting trees blanketed the bridge, unlike any Kratos or Atreus had ever seen. Their towering presence proved intimidating.

"Welcome to Alfheim, gentlemen."

"Witch, that sword you carry across your back, can you fight with it?" Kratos queried, uneasy about what he saw around them.

"A spell from an angry god prevents me from wielding my blade against any living creature."

"If you cannot use it, then why do you carry it?" Atreus pressed.

The witch advanced in a determined stride, running her hand along an overhead branch that sprouted small white flowers at her touch. They became the only flowers to be seen in the landscape. The surrounding vegetation, as far as the eye could see, appeared wilted and drooping, or in various stages of decay or death. The tree branches, along with the stems of the plants beneath them, lacked the turgor normally present in all vegetation. Not a single verdant plant existed; all had deteriorated to a sickly brown color. She and Atreus marched into a spacious vista beneath a slate sky, that kept the realm in a twilight state. A cautious Kratos came last off the bridge.

"To remind me..." She paused midsentence, as if searching for the proper word. "Think you can... spot..." she choked. Her smile faded, and her tongue went still as she stared blankly into the distance.

"The light. I can barely see it. Something is wrong," she said, her tone so alarming that it struck fear into Atreus. A pasty look took over her face. She pointed to a shaft of light emitting a faint glow upward from the ground, penetrating the colorless sky.

"See that light column on the horizon? It is housed in the heart of a ringed temple. We will find what we need there," she said to Kratos.

"Why did you say something is wrong?" Kratos said.

Then he noticed her hand disintegrating. A sudden cacophony of a thousand screeching creatures pierced the air. "No, no, no, no, no! Dammit, not yet—" the witch muttered to herself. Fear, anger, and desperation swarmed her face.

"What is happening?" Atreus demanded, too frightened to reach out to help her, although he wanted to assist her.

The witch's body convulsed violently.

"No!" Atreus yelled. Fear kept him paralyzed.

Some unseen, powerful force seized her at the waist, dragging her back toward the temple.

"What is this?" Atreus said in a frantic voice.

Kratos had no idea how he might aid her. The forces that had control over her were far more powerful than any he had experienced before. If he took hold of her, would he be dragged along with her? He remained frozen in place. Yet he couldn't allow her to be spirited away.

"Father, do something!"

"The elves. Beware as you travel their realm... They can hel—"

Atreus had to take a chance. He had to help her in some way. He shot a hand out to grab hers, but her hand disintegrated before he could latch on to it. Losing his balance, Atreus toppled backward, slamming to the ground.

Kratos lunged over his son to reach the witch's arm. Immediately her skin dissolved into a thousand tiny cracks beneath his touch. But instead of the skin flaking off, the bits of her were mystically pulled back toward the temple.

"To restore the Bifröst's magic, you must step into the light. But be very careful not to get caught up in—"

"No!" Atreus screamed, his sight blurred by tears.

She vanished as every part of her disintegrated. Only a ghostly afterimage of her silhouette remained in her place, fading slowly into nothingness.

"Come back!" Atreus cried out, his voice fading.

"Not to get caught up in what?" Kratos repeated, more angry than sad that she had failed to deliver her vital knowledge.

For many silent moments, they stared into the void that was once the witch. "She's gone," Atreus said.

Was she gone forever? Would they be reunited when they returned to the other realm? Atreus refused to accept that he had lost her. Why was every woman he cared about suddenly being taken away? What had they done that made the gods so angry and vindictive toward them?

"She's not dead, is she? Is she dead?" Atreus heard himself say. He couldn't believe he was even saying the words. "Her magic will save her, right? Tell me her magic is powerful enough to save her!" Atreus searched his father's face for reassurance that he had not lost her.

"I do not know. Come, we must go on." Kratos turned.

Atreus refused to move, rooted where he stood for a long, torturous moment. How could his father not care about her? He had turned his back on her as if she no longer mattered.

His father had progressed a dozen paces before Atreus convinced himself he had to put her out of his mind. They had something important to accomplish at this moment. He broke into a jog to get alongside his father.

Kratos refused to look at him, or even acknowledge his presence.

"Look at this place," Atreus said, mesmerized by the sheer size of their new surroundings.

"Stay beside me. Touch nothing."

They traversed another long bridge toward the light, Kratos keen to observe everything in their path, seeking to uncover any signs of danger. This place was foreign to him. He knew not what to expect. But what were they to be careful of? He examined that thought from every possible angle with each determined stride. Something was lurking out there, and there was little chance they could avoid it.

"She's probably not coming back, is she?" Atreus asked, hopeful that he was wrong. Kratos said nothing, remained watchful along the length of the bridge.

"The witch said to go for the giant light shaft out there," Atreus offered.

"It is where we are going," Kratos snapped back, shooting a glare meant to silence him.

As they continued along the bridge, they glimpsed something of indistinct shape in the distance, blocking their path. Kratos slowed to assess the new potential threat; Atreus slowed in kind, to remain beside his father.

"What do you think *that* is?" Atreus said.

For the first time, Kratos gazed down at him, but he said nothing.

As they came closer, they could discern bloody snake-like tendrils the color of human flesh, curling one over another to form a crude ball-like mass. Was it something alive?

"There's something glowing inside that thing," Atreus said.

"Remain right beside me," Kratos warned, instinctively throwing a hand out to keep Atreus in check.

"I will. What do you think that is?" Atreus said, enduring an uneasy shudder rumbling through him at what they approached.

Would it attack? Could it attack?

Kratos readied his axe.

The thing reacted to the movement as if it could see it. Somehow it sensed his movement. When he chopped lightly at it, it repelled his blade.

"We leave it be, as long as it does not oppose us."

They skirted the mass, careful to keep their feet from touching it. Could that have been what the witch sought to warn them about?

Another hundred paces ahead, off to their left flank, a glowing light snared their attention. "Look, I think that is a Light Elf on that ridge!" Atreus pointed out. His father had already caught sight of it.

Further along they discovered another Light Elf, but this one stood on the bridge, illuminating the area below like a lamppost. Before they could reach it, a blurry streak shot down from the sky, colliding with the creature, knocking it from the bridge to plummet into the darkness of the caldera crater.

"Whoa, what was that about?" Atreus whispered to himself.

"Not our concern, boy. Focus," Kratos said.

They continued across the bridge, now more cautious of their surroundings.

"Did you say something?" Atreus asked, trying to take in everything around them.

"No," Kratos replied, raising a brow at the untimely inquiry.

They spied another Light Elf perched atop a rock ridge fifty paces distant, wearing a white robe. It stood no taller than Atreus, with straw-colored hair, cherub face, and armed with a glowing spear. A brilliant white aura bathed light over him. It seemed to be a sentry near the realm tower. Moments later, a Dark Elf, clad in black leather armor, with bat-like wings and piercing dark pupils, dove in from high in the sky to stab the Light Elf, retreating with it in its clutches to gain altitude before releasing the struggling body to plummet back to the ground.

"They are killing the Light Elves," Atreus said.

"It is a war, no doubt, between them—or the end of one. The robed ones lost," Kratos said, as if to dismiss what they had witnessed as none of their concern. They had no desire to become involved with any existing conflicts in the realm, only to get the light they needed and return home.

"Oh," Atreus replied, also trying to dismiss what he had seen.

A group of Dark Elves descended in a tight defensive formation to hover over Kratos as they moved.

"Be ready," Kratos cautioned.

The Dark Elves banked hard right, as if maneuvering for a full-frontal assault. The first three broke formation, with blades ready as they swooped in. Kratos deflected the attack quickly with his axe. The others remained a safe distance from the exchange, assessing their new enemy before attacking.

Atreus had sufficient time to nock an arrow and launch it at the furthest of the attacking elves. The shaft sailed wide, forcing Atreus to switch to his hunting knife to fight off the Dark Elf that dove at his chest.

"Why are they attacking us? We did nothing to provoke them!" Atreus screamed. He hit the ground to avoid the slashing blade and came back up, but he was too slow to mount an effective counterattack.

"Be ready. More will come!" Kratos barked.

The remaining Dark Elves ascended into the sky, disappearing through thick dark storm clouds.

"I suspect they sacrificed their brethren sizing us up. We must be on our guard. They will return with greater force the next time," Kratos warned. After scanning the sky in all directions, he deemed it safe to continue. After passing under the realm travel tower, Atreus spotted another dead Light Elf.

"Another one." Sadness lined his voice. "At least we are getting closer to the light."

They progressed onto a sandy beach, spotting an old boat covered with tendrils like those they had encountered on the bridge. Working together, they untangled the tendrils without harming them to release the boat, and Kratos carried it to the shore to set it into the water. The water was yet another obstacle standing between them and the light.

"Did your mother ever speak of this realm?" Kratos thought to ask, as he began rowing.

"Not much. She just said that since the elves were always fighting over the Light of Alfheim, it kept them isolated from everyone else."

The boat soon entered a tunnel under a low, overhanging rock formation.

"Huh?" Atreus said, staring up at his father. He then realized his father had not spoken. "Weird. I could have sworn you just said something."

"I said nothing."

As the boat drifted lazily into a cave, quiet returned.

In the next moment, Atreus doubled over in his seat, clutching his head at the temples, screeching from the intense pain.

CHAPTER 20

"What is wrong, boy?" Kratos asked, an unwanted edge of irritation binding his words together.

"Voices. You do not hear them?" Atreus forced out while wincing in pain.

"I hear nothing," Kratos said. Panic took over. He had no inkling of how to deal with his son's plight. He heard nothing.

Atreus struggled to steady himself in the boat. "They are fading now." He rose. "They were screaming. Many different voices. Angry voices. You really did not hear them?"

"No." Kratos remained concerned. This was never part of his illness before. He had never had to deal with anything like this in the past. He sought words that might comfort Atreus, but he realized there was nothing he could say.

"It felt... evil."

Then Atreus spotted two more Light Elves positioned strategically along a ridge, gazing down at them blankly.

"Look. Should we try to talk to them?"

"No."

The elves receded out of sight after a few moments.

"Maybe they need our help. We can help them. You have seen what those Dark Elves do."

"They do not impede us, so they do not concern us."

"But—"

"They do not concern us!"

"But what if we need their help?"

Kratos withheld his response.

Meandering around a bend, they floated out of the river canyon and onto a sprawling, calm lake with shimmering greenish-blue water.

"War has made a beautiful land ugly," Atreus said.

"War is only about survival and advantage. Battles may be won by the better soldier, but wars are won by sacrificing all for victory."

In the distance the ringed temple rose, surrounding an intense column of light projecting into the sky, while silhouettes of a few Dark Elves circled the shaft.

"Look at that temple. Is that where we need to go?"

Approaching the Temple of Light, they spied a mystical bridge composed entirely of pure white light leading to a blue temple door.

"That must be the entrance," Atreus said.

Not far from their location, a swarm of Dark Elves flooded the underside of the bridge, completely covering a light crystal located there. "What are they doing?" Atreus asked.

By the time he finished his question, the bridge had disappeared.

"The bridge is gone. They covered that crystal with that stuff. Why?"

"To prevent reinforcements," Kratos said, all the while assessing the ramifications of what they had just witnessed.

Discovering their presence, a trio of Dark Elves launched skyward to attack. Kratos readied his axe, and this time Atreus had sufficient time to nock an arrow and launch it true to take out the lead elf. As the dying creature fluttered into the water, Kratos hacked the other two down before they could become a threat.

"What is their problem with us?" Atreus asked, frustrated at being forced into a fight at every turn. He wished for some way to convey to these creatures that they posed no threat to them; they need not die needlessly.

"We are intruders upon their domain. We do not belong here. They may think we are aligned with the Light Elves," Kratos reasoned out loud.

As they continued, a dark shadow descended over them. As Kratos cast his gaze up, a horned Dark Elf swooped down, fixed on him. Kratos readied his weapon, yanking his son behind him to keep the creature from reaching him.

"Look at the horns. This one is different from the others," Atreus said.

Hovering at a safe distance, the Dark Elf issued a deafening, grating screech, while at ground level a swarm of Dark Elves flew in from all directions, brandishing knives and swords. As they attacked, Kratos worked his axe, slashing, hacking and lopping off elf heads until those that remained chose to flee. Kratos gazed up; the horned Dark Elf also disappeared.

"They are not going to give up, are they?" Atreus asked.

When Kratos advanced, the horned Dark Elf dove out of nowhere to latch onto Atreus.

"No! Father!" he yelled, swiping wildly at the creature in the hope of fighting his way free.

"Atreus!" Kratos screamed, lunging to get hold of his son's leg before the Dark Elf lifted him out of range.

With one hand outstretched and the other clutching his axe, Kratos was out of position when two Dark Elves surged to grab him. While one wrenched his neck, the other stabbed at him with a glowing spear. Kratos fended off the spear attack, but he failed to throw off the Dark Elf clutching his neck. He also lost his opportunity to grab hold of his son.

"Get off him," Atreus yelled, when he witnessed his father's struggle. "We didn't do anything. Let me go!"

In a fit of rage, Kratos flung his attackers off, positioned his axe and heaved it at the horned Dark Elf. The blade clipped the elf's wing, forcing him and the boy to spiral downward into the ground. The Dark Elf retrieved the axe before Kratos could recall it.

"Father, hurry!" Atreus cried out, fighting off a pair of Dark Elves that charged him from the shadows. "Get away from me!" he screamed in rage, slashing his hunting knife to keep them temporarily at bay. "What do you want with us?"

The Dark Elves circled, cautious of their moves, but relentless in their attack. Atreus had no idea how he was going to stay alive. The fear fueling his rage kept him from succumbing to the terror.

"Stay back!"

The horned Dark Elf dropped from above, still clutching the Leviathan axe. Kratos charged, tackling him and slamming the Dark Elf to the ground.

Reclaiming his weapon, Kratos regained his feet for a mighty swing, but the horned Dark Elf rolled away, launching into the air to flutter out of range. Atreus dashed to his father's side as Kratos prepared to fight four Dark Elves rallying to charge. Back to back, Kratos rived the lead attackers, while Atreus stabbed another, with the remaining two retreating to higher ground. Within seconds, they disappeared. Kratos and Atreus stepped carefully around the dead and dying.

Picking their way through dense, prickly foliage, they at last reached the temple, and finding the door secured and impenetrable, they moved to the side, where they discovered a gap in the crumbling walls wide enough to crawl through. They wandered the dilapidated space, traversing what had once been great vaulted golden halls that had deteriorated into a wilderness of overgrown vines and thorny broad-leafed weeds. Shattered columns littered the expanse.

"This place is great," Atreus whispered. His face wide with amazement, he drifted from his father to explore the broken-down temple.

Could this have been the scene of a great battle?

"I bet it was beautiful here, before the Dark Elves destroyed everything," Atreus mumbled. He knew his father would probably care little for the history surrounding them.

Continuing, they spied a Light Elf running across a light bridge high in the temple.

"There. Another Light Elf. What is he doing?" Atreus said.

A Dark Elf emerged from a sprawling hive above to descend upon the Light Elf. Then, two more Dark Elves spiraled down. They pounced, all stabbing him in a frenzy.

"Why are they killing him? He didn't do anything," Atreus said.

"You do not know that. We know nothing of this realm. You have no way of understanding what led to this moment."

"But he did not even defend himself."

Kratos stopped, turning a stern face to his son. "That was his choice. We make ours."

"Maybe the Light Elves were the ones speaking inside my head, asking us to help them."

"You do not know that for sure. What if the voices were from the others?"

The attackers turned to Kratos and Atreus once the Light Elf lay lifeless at their feet.

"They will find us not so foolish," Kratos muttered. He prepared for their onslaught, which came moments later. In a flurry of swinging iron, dead Dark Elves littered the ground around them.

"What now?" Atreus asked.

"The light is near. We find a way to reach it."

As he spoke, many light bridges formed around the interior of the light temple. They splayed out like a grand maze, making it near impossible to determine which would be the correct course to follow.

CHAPTER 21

Using trial and error they attempted to navigate the light bridges, progressing slowly and inefficiently from one to another, until they began to detect what was indeed a pattern that might lead them to the light. Enduring multiple missteps and retracements, they finally came to a forbidding hive that, in a puzzle-like patchwork, covered the coveted Light of Alfheim.

"I do not think we should be in here," Atreus uttered, his fear starting to choke off his breathing.

"Quiet. Here is where we must be in order to get the light for the Bifröst," Kratos scolded, barely above a whisper.

"But how?"

"We destroy the hive."

As they worked their way inward, the clamor of insects skittering rose above them.

"You hear that?" Atreus whispered, his voice shaky.

"Remain alert and at my side."

Reaching the end of a corridor, they began a torturously slow climb up the side of the hive, with Kratos studying it with every move. When they reached the midpoint of their climb, a Dark Elf emerged from hiding, striking out at them.

"No!" Atreus said.

Kratos seized the flailing Dark Elf's throat to hold it at bay.

"Boy, your knife!" he said, struggling to keep the creature restrained.

Atreus buried his blade into the elf's forehead. The creature immediately fell limp in Kratos' hand.

Shoving the carcass back into its hiding place, they continued up.

Reaching the hive summit, they squirmed down a tight, confining pathway toward the Light of Alfheim.

"Remain close."

Atreus gagged in disgust when they brushed against a tight cluster of fleshy webbing while attempting to squeeze past it.

Crawling through another small, sticky passage, they made their way toward what they hoped was an entrance to the main light chamber. Ahead, the passageway widened, but before they could get close, another Dark Elf crawled out to attack.

Atreus screamed.

Kratos seized the elf's arm, bashing its head repeatedly into the webbed floor. Although doing so killed the Dark Elf, it also caused the ground to collapse beneath them.

They tumbled out of control into the center of the hive, skidding to a stop only to discover hundreds of Dark Elves swarming the ceiling, feeding on the mystical light.

"Easy, boy... stay calm," Kratos whispered, his heart hammering in his chest.

In the midst of their frenzy, the creatures failed to notice Kratos and his son.

The Dark Elves had constructed their hive completely *around* the Light of Alfheim, to prevent anyone else from reaching it.

"This structure... See the way the tendrils holding the pieces together sag? They are the weak points," the God of War offered in a hushed voice, though Atreus appeared too frightened to even attempt to identify the weaknesses his father had discovered.

Each irregularly-shaped hive segment was secured to an adjoining piece with a sinewy black tendril. At first glance, the hive itself appeared impenetrable.

"Here," he pointed, approaching an identified tendril. He

then scanned to another near the hive's outer ring. "Destroy the tendrils, the hive falls apart."

The swarm of Dark Elves came to life. Atreus avoided them by leaping to a different hive tendril. "Father! This way!"

But Kratos joining him destabilized the tendril and forced it to wobble. Atreus leapt to the next hanging tendril. "Over here!" he said. After moving to the next tendril, Kratos hacked the one he left in two, hoping to weaken the structure and facilitate its collapse.

They climbed precariously from tendril to tendril until they reached a dead end. "Which way now?" Atreus said. They watched as the Dark Elf swarm obliterated all the surrounding light, while whipped into a raucous frenzy of noise and activity, attempting to use the tendrils Kratos hacked apart to converge upon them.

"There's so many!" Atreus said.

Kratos pushed the pack forward, trying to inch closer to the final tendril.

"A narrow path negates superior numbers. Keep shooting, boy! You will not miss."

"Okay!"

Then Kratos reached the last pivotal hive tendril holding the pieces together. "They're coming at us!" Atreus shouted.

Maintaining stable footing, Atreus struck down several Dark Elves by rapidly firing his arrows. His efforts held them at bay while his father chopped at the final tendril.

"Faster, hurry!" Atreus shouted.

Kratos battered as rapidly as he could.

"I cannot hold them all back!" Atreus shouted.

CHAPTER 22

Kratos threw out a hand for a waiting Atreus, who in turn vaulted up into his father's arms, with Kratos taking one final swipe at the tendril. The hive collapsed around them, caving in upon itself and releasing the Light of Alfheim.

Kratos and Atreus dropped for a second, before the brilliant release of light illuminated the structures and the floors that broke their fall. They crashed in a heap onto a plane of shimmering light, with Atreus landing on his stomach beside the column of light. Kratos landed on his back a short distance away.

The scaffolding that made up the body of the temple was filled in floor by floor with the Light Elves' magical light structures. Once completed, it revealed a magnificent and ornate light temple. The empyreal Light of Alfheim now stretched far beyond its earlier radius, bathing the surrounding land with revitalizing light.

Panicked, Kratos scrambled to his knees to crawl to his son. In desperation, he examined the lad's legs and arms, searching for bleeding while feeling for broken bones.

"Are you injured?" he asked.

Dust from the collapsing hive settled around them, forcing Atreus to cough. "I am fine," Atreus said, struggling to free himself from his father's arms.

Back on their feet, they realized they were finally within reach of their goal. Atreus dashed toward the intense bluish-white light, in awe of the brilliance before him. He never could have imagined witnessing such an ethereal spectacle in his life. At that moment, he thought about his mother, and how she would have felt if she could see him there.

"It is beautiful. Do you hear it? It is… singing," Atreus said. "I hear…"

He continued toward the light, mesmerized by its enchanting spell.

"I hear her!" Atreus cried. Excitement rang in his voice. He grew more excited with each passing moment. The smile consuming his face conveyed more than words could ever say.

Fearless, Atreus played his fingers across the light. The surface rippled and shimmered in response. A giddy laugh escaped his lips.

"Do you think she is in there?" he asked.

Atreus risked shoving his whole hand into the light. He had to explore this thing to its fullest. He had to know that his mother's voice was real—not just his imagination. His expression changed from playful to grim determination. He shoved his hand in further, penetrating the light up to mid-forearm.

A sharp crackle resounded, then a pop like a small explosion. Atreus yelped, his limbs vibrating as if he were being shocked.

Kratos lunged to snare Atreus' shoulder. Even before he could jerk his son free, Atreus yanked his own arm back violently in response to the pain jolting up it.

"It felt like my hand was on fire," Atreus said.

Despite the searing pain, the light called him. He obeyed; he had to obey, returning to the shaft to gingerly explore the reaches of the light's surface.

Kratos also began to examine the light, albeit cautiously, holding his darkened Bifröst crystal in one hand.

"Remain here," his father ordered.

"But I want…"

"Stay… here…" Kratos reinforced, relinquishing his axe to his son. "Use it only as a last resort."

"You are giving me your axe?" Atreus could not restrain his excitement. It felt much heavier than he had imagined, and wielding it like his father did was not something Atreus thought he could accomplish easily. He seriously doubted that he would ever attain muscles as formidable as his father's, or have the strength and stamina necessary to fight the way he did.

"I am allowing you to hold my axe. It is not a gift," Kratos corrected.

"Still…" Atreus said, his smile fading.

Kratos stabbed his fist holding the Bifröst into the wall of light. It punctured the surface easily, sinking in deep. But it felt like the fires of Hades had seized his arm. He grimaced in agony, pulling his body closer to the light.

A horrendous scream fought to escape his throat. Gritting his teeth to remain silent, he pressed forward. His pain became so great that his scream sought any way to erupt. It was as though a cacophony of voices screamed, and everything around them shuddered the moment the light enveloped him.

"Father!"

The blinding white light completely swallowed Kratos.

Then the bone-jarring pain and the screaming voices abruptly stopped. Kratos felt only peace; a calm he had never experienced in his life before. He had become wrapped in tranquility so all-consuming that he longed to remain within it for the rest of his days.

Pure white light caressed him from all sides. It appeared to Kratos that he had somehow entered the light shaft's eye.

Overcoming the inertia of fear to take that first tentative step, Kratos strode toward a single point in the distance, which appeared to open and grow closer with each stride. He detected only the sounds of a gentle breeze, his pounding heart, and his controlled breathing. The point ahead developed into a tall, wide doorway, revealing behind it an idyllic landscape of lush grasses covering hills, swaying in the wind beneath a vibrant clear sky. Nestled in the hills he spied a structure—*his home*. He recognized

Atreus standing beside a woman in front of the house; the woman's identity, however, was a mystery to Kratos. Beyond the hills stood the giant's fingers of Jötunheim, the realm of the giants.

A soft, melodic female voice sang a lonely but beautiful song that wavered in the air. Kratos knew the unmistakable voice—his dead wife's. The pouch at his belt began to rise, floating before him. As it drifted away, the pouch unraveled into a ball of pure light to illuminate the path into the darkness.

"Faye?"

Trepidation swelled as something compelled Kratos toward a spectral forest in the distance, a forest that seemed so familiar to him. What manner of magic was this? How could he be hearing her voice so clearly, so distinctly? Was it coming from outside him, or was it something that manifested itself only inside his mind? Was he going mad?

The closer he got, the further the forest stretched out before him. The surreal encounter became both peaceful and unsettling. Kratos found himself forced into the forest and toward the doorway. Any effort he expended to stop or move away was met with an unseen force more powerful than he.

With each step, the exchange between his son and his wife grew more distinct. His wife suddenly paused in her singing to calm and reassure the boy. Kratos could see his son pacing inside his house.

"He always leaves," Atreus moaned, allowing annoyance to show in his voice. Kratos would never have tolerated such behavior. He would have responded immediately and harshly if the boy ever spoke to him that way.

The hovering ball of light sped ahead, shining on the bridge of a sailing vessel floating through a mist. But there were no ocean sounds, as if the vessel were floating above the water.

"I don't know him, and he doesn't know me. Does not seem to want to." Atreus' voice came again. "I am strong, and I am smart. I am not what he thinks I am. I know better."

The ball burst into a brilliant flash, then darted along a shoreline with Kratos chasing it.

"He does not talk to me. Does not teach me. It should have been him. Do you hear me? Him, not you."

"No!" Kratos said, with a snap as sharp as a whip.

The light ball darted again, this time leaving Kratos hanging off the side of a mountain, high in the sky.

"Except… I don't mean that. You know I love him. I just wish he was better. I know he can be," Atreus said calmly.

The ball flashed once more. This time, Kratos emerged from the trapdoor of his home to see his son standing beside the shrouded body of his wife.

"So if he tries, I will try. But if he does not, please come back. I know you are out there somewhere."

Kratos stood beside the spectral ball. It stopped moving, simply floating. He reached out to touch it, thinking he might be able to touch his beloved Faye once more.

CHAPTER 23

Drops of water splashing against the stone floor marked time as Atreus stood patiently before the Light of Alfheim, his father's axe in his hand, wondering what his father was experiencing. The urge to join him permeated his very being. He wanted so badly to know what existed there, yet he knew that if he disobeyed his father, he would suffer dearly. The eerie silence beyond the regular drips soon overwhelmed him. Despite the light shaft at its core, the temple fringes remained dark. Hours passed before he realized it. He pondered what might be keeping his father so long. It should have taken mere moments to enter the light, recharge the Bifröst lantern, and return.

As time dragged on with no sign of his father's return, Atreus' attention drifted about the old structure. It had fallen into disrepair over the ages. Seeing only their footprints on the dusted-covered stone, it seemed there were no signs of anyone having entered this place other than them.

Before he knew it, four more hours passed. His stomach rumbled in need. His legs ached. Growing weary of standing, he shifted to sit atop a fallen pillar a dozen paces from where his father had left him. He dared not stray far, for fear his father might return and fail to see him.

What was he experiencing beyond the light wall? His

stomach gnawed at him, so he quelled it with a few of the biscuits the witch had provided. He wanted to eat more, yet decided he needed to save some for his father's return. He would certainly be hungry too.

The deathly still of the temple unnerved him. His bottom growing numb from sitting, with the axe weighting his shoulder, Atreus plopped to his feet to pace before the entrance where his father had disappeared.

Sudden overhead movement snared his attention. He gazed up, spotting a pair of ravens circling, floating effortlessly around the fringes of the light shaft, as if they sought to remain unnoticed. When they determined that Atreus had discovered them, they swirled higher, fluttering out of sight through a jagged crack in the ceiling the width of a tree trunk.

The birds' presence diverted Atreus' concern for his father by returning his mother's words concerning the ravens to the forefront of his mind. What made them so important? Did they possess magical powers she kept secret from him? Were the birds always in Alfheim? Or did they follow them into this place? His interest in the mystery faded into the shadows after a few minutes.

"Where are you?" he muttered to himself, for the first time allowing concern for his father to flood his brain. Surely he would only scout out what existed beyond the light and return quickly to him. Why would he risk leaving Atreus unguarded for such an extended period of time? He knew what dangers existed in this realm. Atreus looked out through the crack in the ceiling. Was night caving in upon him? He couldn't tell, since the light beyond the temple never changed. He wondered if his father was experiencing night on the other side of the light.

Then a terrifying thought wormed its way into the core of his mind. What if his father were lost, or, worse, trapped inside the light? What if he couldn't return? Atreus approached the light wall, stopping himself within an arm's length of penetrating it. He could force himself through it. He could just close his eyes, endure the pain, and throw himself through to join his father. That was if his father remained just on the other side of the light. What if his father was right now seeking a way back to him?

"Father!" he called into the eerie surroundings.

Could his voice even penetrate the light wall? Atreus grew agitated as time wore on and still he could detect no sign of his father's movements on the other side. For the first time since his father had left, Atreus began to feel the fear that accompanied being alone and vulnerable in this place.

His chest began pounding chaotically. He spun around frantically, lifting up the axe in defense, losing his grip when he thought he detected an errant noise reaching him. The only sound, however, came from the blade clanking on the stone floor.

Was there someone else in this old temple?

"Witch? Is that you?" he said, barely above a whisper.

No, it was fatigue playing upon his mind, he convinced himself. Abandoning his place before the light, he settled cross-legged on the floor nearby, tucking himself behind a fallen pillar.

He ordered himself to remain awake until his father returned. His gaze drifted from the light wall, hoping for a glimpse of movement, to the far reaches of the temple, searching for any signs of imminent danger. He felt his heart racing and his breath quickening.

Was his sickness returning? That was something he definitely could not deal with at the moment. Atreus leaned his head against the axe handle, which he had cradled in his arms.

"He is coming through that wall any time now," he said to himself as he stared, hoping that saying the words aloud could somehow force it to happen. Moments later, caving in to his exhaustion, he drifted asleep.

He bolted awake, believing he had only slept a few moments.

A slightly brighter light spread throughout the old temple, indicating morning. He had slept the entire night and still his father had yet to return. He pulled himself upright, suffering the aches of having slept in such an awkward position on the ground.

"Father, where are you!" Atreus shouted, this time in anger at the light wall, furious he had been left alone for so long.

He marched directly to the wall, ready to push his way through.

"I am here," he called, hoping if his father were lost, he could follow the sound of his son's voice to find his way back.

Then came the shuffling of feet. Atreus froze in panic for an instant, uncertain of what he should do. Terror overtook his face. Then more shuffling, followed by clanking swords.

He had to hide.

Wasting few steps and keeping low to the floor, Atreus slipped away from the light wall, ducking behind fallen pillars a dozen strides away. He disappeared from sight a mere instant before a pair of Dark Elves wandered into the open temple.

The way they meandered without purpose left Atreus confident he had gone unnoticed. His terrified heart hammered his chest. He was all alone.

Two more Dark Elves found their way in.

Atreus attempted to swallow—he couldn't. Breathing became difficult. Acrid bile backed up into his throat. His palms sweated as he gripped the axe handle with both hands.

He feebly convinced himself that, for the moment, he was safe. And as long as they failed to detect his presence, he could remain safe. He dared not try to peek around the edge of the pillar, for fear his movement might snare their attention. He wanted so badly to raise his axe in readiness to attack, but he knew better.

Atreus glanced over to the light wall. What if his father came through at this moment? He would be unarmed against four of them. His father would have at least a few strides before they encountered him.

"Please do not come through now," Atreus found himself praying. He clamped a hand over his mouth. Had he actually said the words out loud?

Tightening his grip on the axe, he attempted to shift his weight into a battle-ready crouch, so he might be better able to reach his bow if time allowed. Sooner or later, he was going to have to peer around to locate the Dark Elves.

But the temple remained deathly silent. Nothing beyond the pillar moved. Perhaps the Dark Elves had left, convinced there was no one there?

Should he risk a confirming look? Instinct argued against it. His pounding brain urged him to find out if the danger had passed. He would not be able to lower his guard until he had determined it was safe again.

Atreus' thoughts turned to his mother. *When fear seizes you, Atreus, that is the moment you must become fearless.* What would she expect of him? Would she want him to rise and fight, or remain hidden until the danger passed?

Slowly, Atreus inched his trembling body forward until he reached the edge of the pillar. Silence was baiting him into a quick peek. First, he used several deep breaths to fire up his courage. Moments later, his courage wilted. He had to know if he was safe. He needed to assess the situation in case his father chose that moment to return. He had to be ready to fight and return the axe to his father's hands before any of them could reach them. Sizing the distance from his position to the light wall, Atreus determined the number of strides necessary to reach his father, if it came to that.

Atreus eased forward just enough to gain a glimpse of the open temple. Nothing presented out of the ordinary. He allowed a small smile.

They were gone.

Atreus slid his head back, allowing a moment for his anxiety to calm. He was safe. Cradling the axe, he waited. His father had to return. His father had to come back to him. He couldn't face his life without a mother and a father.

Then, a change in the light reflecting off the wall stole his attention. His father was returning. It had to be.

Without thinking, Atreus burst from his hiding place behind the pillar. He was going to be safe. But before he could take that first step toward the light wall, Dark Elves emerged from a shadowy corner of the temple. They saw him. Atreus squared his shoulders, braced for their attack.

They formed up to charge, first two, then two more. Atreus had no time to think.

"Father!" he screamed with all his strength, releasing the axe handle to take up his bow and the first arrow from his quiver.

CHAPTER 24

The ball of light remained elusively beyond Kratos' reach. "Faye, do not go!" he uttered in a breathless voice.

Seeing this vision of his wife crumpled his heart. He had exiled her from his mind to focus on what needed to be done and to care for his son. He buried his grief so deep inside that it could find no path to worm its way into his head. Now it gushed into his brain like an arterial bleed, taking over every corner of his being.

"I miss you so," he muttered, wishing that wherever she was, she could hear him. He extended his arm further, hoping to touch her, to make any kind of contact with her. He had never realized how much she meant to him, despite the fact that he was a god, and, as such, immune to the frailties of the human condition.

Did she exist in this new realm he was in? Was there a chance he could speak to her, if only for a moment? She never once turned her head in his direction. She never once acknowledged him standing so near to her.

Kratos yelled when a hand broke the plane of the light to snatch him from behind. In a jarring blur, he left the light against his will.

* * *

Landing on his back, Kratos stared up at the dilapidated ceiling of the old temple. He was back. He pushed up quickly from the ground, blinking away the blinding brightness.

"No! No, what have you done? Why did you do that?" Kratos spat, angry and disoriented. Why had he been forced to endure that moment from a past he needed to let go? Why did he have to face the darkness of what was, rather than the light of what should have been?

Atreus stood a few steps away, rising from where Kratos had tumbled to the ground. He scrambled to find his axe. Still struggling to shake off the pain he had just endured, the God of War prepared to fire back with anger of his own.

"I saved you! You were trapped in there. I waited and waited, but you never came out. So I pulled you out," Atreus barked.

He removed an arrow from a fallen Dark Elf for emphasis. Then he began coughing.

His coughing escalated quickly into choking, choking on his own rage. He dropped to a knee in an attempt to recover.

Kratos knelt beside him. Had the boy's sickness returned? "Son, I was only gone a few moments."

"No, you were not. You have been gone a long, long time," Atreus wheezed.

Once Kratos adjusted to the dim temple light, he surveyed the space. What he observed forced him to accept that he *had* been gone longer than the few moments he experienced in the light.

Slaughtered Dark Elves littered the surrounding floor, some from Atreus' arrows, others decapitated by his axe. A pile of coarsely dismembered body parts strewed the floor a few paces from where Kratos had come through the light. It appeared that a bloody heap marked where Atreus had been forced to stand his ground and fight for his very life.

Atreus stared at Kratos, hurt but mostly disgusted. His blood-splattered jerkin and breeks were ripped in places. He wiped the blood from around his mouth, coughing and gasping for air.

"Where is my axe?"

"Your axe?" An edge of disappointment seeped into Atreus' voice. Of all the things he expected from his father at that moment, concern for his axe was the least of them. Dead elves scattered the temple. Was he proud of his son? Atreus brimmed with pride over what he had done. He had proved himself, surviving an onslaught by himself. He had fought with the same ferocity as his father. In his mind, he was no longer a child. He was a man; no, he was a warrior, like his father. Was his father concerned that his son might have taken a life-threatening injury that could end his life? Or that Kratos might have lost his son, along with his wife? No, he sought the comfort of his weapon first.

Silently, Atreus indicated the doorway through which they had entered. On the far wall, his axe was stuck deep into a Dark Elf's chest.

Determined not to yield to his sickness, Atreus returned to his feet, swayed until he caught his balance, then trudged about the room to retrieve his arrows from the corpses.

"I did not know what I was supposed to do. You left me here. Again. Why do you not care?" the lad said, fighting back tears. He had to bury his emotion. *A warrior never cries, ever.*

"I... That is impossible," Kratos muttered, shaking his head.

Atreus' cough subsided, though anger still smoldered beneath the surface.

"What is impossible?" Atreus shot back.

"I was only away from you for a short time."

"We need to go before more come," he said impatiently. "I hope you got what we needed." Bitterness remained in his words.

Kratos stared at the now glowing Bifröst crystal.

"Yes," he said, with a regret-laden voice and heart. He realized at that moment that something was indeed watching over them. His son had survived.

Kratos yanked the axe from the Dark Elf, allowing it to slump to the floor.

"You could have told me the axe only returns for you!" Atreus said.

He stomped over to an inactive light bridge crystal, pointing to it.

"Look! There's our exit, but there's no light to make a bridge. We're trapped. And the witch's bowstring is useless."

Kratos considered his son's words before removing the glowing Bifröst from his belt.

"Your bow," he commanded.

Seeing the brilliant light emanating from the Bifröst, Atreus quickly unslung his bow. "Hold it out toward me."

As Atreus extended the bow across his hands, Kratos slowly ran the Bifröst over the string. As he did, Bifröst light saturated the bowstring, giving it a glow of its own.

Kratos returned the Bifröst to his belt while Atreus examined the glowing string.

Standing beside the bridge crystal, Atreus readied a now glowing Bifröst arrow.

"On my mark, fire your arrow into the stone," Kratos commanded.

The Bifröst arrow struck the bridge crystal, illuminating it to create a light bridge. "It worked!" Atreus shouted.

"Now we can make our way back."

Walking up the right-hand path, they discovered a fallen column blocking their way.

"That way's blocked," Atreus griped. They diverted to an ornate doorway leading out of the temple. When Kratos pushed open the enormous oak doors, a parade of Light Elves waiting outside pushed past them, reclaiming their temple. Atreus turned about to stare in silent awe while they floated majestically by. But as he tracked them, his look landed on his father. His wonder turned to a scowl.

They began their walk across the main light bridge without speaking. As they reached the middle of the bridge to return to the travel room, the horned Dark Elf raced past them, stopping to hover.

"And the one with the horns is back. What does he want

now?" Atreus said. After what he had endured, his fear for the creature had diminished. If a fight was what this creature wanted, then a fight to the death it would get.

As if in response to the boy's question, the Dark Elf released a guttural screech before disappearing into an open trench beside the bridge.

"I hate that thing," Atreus said.

"It will be back."

They braced for the worst.

Seeing the horned Dark Elf king coming back at them, Kratos charged without flinching, slashing back and forth to drive the Dark Elf rearward. The elf fought back using its spear. When Kratos realized the elf could defend itself against him, he changed tactics, using his axe as a diversion while he reached across to snare the spear, which he plunged into its chest.

Struggling to breathe at Kratos' feet, the Dark Elf gazed at Atreus when he joined his father. The creature stared up with sadness and disappointment. Blood spurted from its mouth when it attempted to speak.

"You... grave... mistake. Oppressors... will... enslave... all."

The Dark Elf ceased breathing.

It took a long moment for the words to sink in.

"No. That cannot be!" Atreus said. "What did we do?"

Kratos dismissed the Dark Elf's words. What happened in this realm had nothing to do with them or their quest.

All around them, Alfheim had undergone a dramatic transformation while they were inside the temple. The Light of Alfheim now shed glorious light upon the realm, restoring the vegetation to their verdant lives.

"So..." Atreus started.

The simple syllable sucked Kratos out of his thoughts to face his son.

"Was she in the light?" he said.

"Was who in the light? The witch?" Kratos said, attempting to divert him, though he knew exactly what Atreus wanted to know.

"You know who!" Atreus said, sparks of anger in his voice.

The moment demanded a decision. Lie to his son? Or face the difficulties sure to arise from the truth?

"No. She was not there," Kratos offered at last, in a voice that trailed off. A part of him felt angry and disappointed for dodging the truth. Another part consoled himself for it. A pang contracted through his insides, constricting his heart like a giant snake.

Atreus' stare never wavered from his father's.

"Mind your tongue, boy. Until our journey is over, one of us must remain focused. Do not mistake my silence for a lack of grief. Mourn how you wish; leave me to mourn on my own."

Returning to the dome array and the travel room with the now fully-powered Bifröst, Kratos placed it in the power receptacle while Atreus drew the rune for Midgard, which allowed them to align the realm travel bridge to Midgard and leave Alfheim behind.

MIDGARD

CHAPTER 25

The moment they exited the travel room they encountered Brok, hammering behind a shopfront.

"Brok! We just came back from another realm, and we met your brother. Wait... not in that order," Atreus said, racing ahead to join the little blue man.

Brok ceased hammering, then he wiped his brow with his sleeve, while at the same time leveling a suspicious look at them.

"You did not let that seed-sop put hand to your blade, did you? You do know he lost his talent, right? Just up and left him one day, tried taking me down with him. Did he botch up our girl?"

Kratos handed over his Leviathan axe. "Quite the opposite," Kratos said.

With a squint, Brok appraised Sindri's handiwork with a quick, disapproving once-over before taking up his hammer.

"Hmm, well, even a blind pig farts up a truffle every now and again. But you know what really counts?" He smashed the hammer down once on the cheek of the blade. "Consistency. And I got that comin' outta alla my parts."

Once he had finished working on it, Brok returned the axe, with Kratos carefully inspecting the little blue man's work. "What did you do?"

"It is better now, trust me."

Kratos only grunted at the dwarf.

"See how that treats you. And don't be letting that spit-fister of a brother of mine lay hands on it again."

"I promise nothing."

"Do you remember the way back to the Black Breath?" Kratos asked to test his son's memory, while they walked along a trodden path away from Brok and the realm travel temple.

"Of course. We need to cross the bridge to the Vanaheim tower."

They jogged the length of the bridge, with Atreus pointing out the statue of Thor in the distance.

"Look. We rowed past that statue of Thor earlier, when we left the witch's cave," he said.

"And what direction is that?"

"It is midmorning, the sun is over there, soooo..." Atreus said, thinking. "That is south... southwest?"

"Excellent."

They came off the bridge to make their way back through the foothills. "Well, at least the curse is gone," Atreus said.

Getting through the hills without encountering any draugr, they climbed back into the gondola for the ride up to the Black Breath.

"Do you... do you think I could carry her now?" Atreus asked.

"No," Kratos replied too sharply, too quickly. He made it seem as though he never even considered his son's request. A fear dwelled deep inside of him that his son would lose what remained of his wife.

"But—"

"I said no," Kratos said calmly.

The lad grew sullen; inside he was angry and disappointed. He hoped holding her might rekindle her image in his mind. He found it troubling that he was slowly forgetting what she looked like.

Atreus wallowed in his thoughts as they rode the gondola, reaching the path shrouded with the black fog.

"There's the Black Breath again. What do we do now?" Atreus said.

"See if that witch was right."

As they approached the Black Breath, Kratos activated the Bifröst. Nothing happened. They drew closer; still nothing.

"She was wrong," Atreus muttered. All the danger they had been through turned out to be for nothing.

A snarl grew on Kratos' face. Was their journey to Alfheim nothing more than a ruse by the witch to get them to do her bidding? Either of them could have been killed by those Dark Elves, and for what? Kratos scolded himself for listening to the witch in the first place. If that hag's quest was to serve them up to the Dark Elves, then she had failed miserably in her quest. However, there could be no dwelling on their latest failure. They would just have to find another way to get through the Black Breath.

Then the fog reacted. Reluctantly, it retreated as if angered, curling back as they moved through it, revealing a path littered with the skeletal remains of those who had foolishly underestimated the evil of the magic. Then the Black Breath succumbed, dissipating entirely.

"She was right!" Atreus said.

Smileless, Kratos looped the Bifröst onto his belt. "Come. We finish this."

Continuing up the path, Atreus noticed stone steps leading to the mouth of a cave blocked by fallen boulders.

"What do we do now?" Atreus said.

"We climb."

After surveying their latest challenge for a few moments, Kratos leapt to a long crack in the rock, with Atreus following a few feet behind.

"You know, Mother said the giants used to visit the Midgard mountains before they disappeared."

"Disappeared?"

"I guess they just up and left one day. No one knows why."

"Perhaps they returned to their home."

"To Jötunheim? Maybe... I wonder if the face in the mountain was a tribute to an important giant?"

Finally reaching the face carved in the side of the mountain, they approached the entrance.

"The mouth—we made it!"

Inside, more Black Breath oozed toward them. But they dispelled it handily using the light, which enabled them to proceed to a large plank door deep within the cave, that had a diamond-shaped plaque in the center depicting a mountain in the shape of a hand.

"That emblem matches the one on the door to Jötunheim in Týr's temple. The giants did come here," Atreus said.

Beyond the door, they moved through a mountain tunnel, a small amount of glimmering light guiding them ahead. As they neared the tunnel's end, a silhouette bloomed into view.

"Is that... a deer?" Atreus asked.

The tunnel opened into a vaulted room bisected by a jagged chasm falling into a pit. Across the void, a tall statue of a stag with a man's body, seated on a throne and clutching a scepter, stared back at them. On its side a lever jutted out into the middle of a semicircular dais, with a sand bowl at the center. It was bookended by two pedestals, one empty, the other holding a fist-sized light crystal.

"Look at him. I don't remember any stories about a giant with a deer head. I wonder who he is?" Atreus said.

Atreus ventured near the chasm's ledge, causing loose gravel to sprinkle into the black hole.

"No way across, but there is a sand bowl. Want me to read this one?" Atreus said.

"Read it."

"'No yoked beast, nor fearful thrall, nor rooted tree doth know my call.'"

Kratos pulled the lever, to no response from anything in the chamber. "The floor, boy," he said, indicating that maybe the seemingly random markings on the floor would provide a clue to unlocking the lever's use.

"Those marks don't mean anything to me. Maybe something is missing," Atreus replied. Atreus thought for a moment, scanning the expanse for any sign of a solution. "Maybe it requires a second light crystal."

"Seek it out," his father commanded.

Atreus searched quickly about the space, delving into every crack where a light crystal might fit.

"I've looked all over," he said, after searching for a long time in silence. "No crystals anywhere."

Then Atreus turned his gaze upward. "How do you think that got up there?" he asked.

Using his axe, Kratos broke the second hanging crystal loose from the ceiling of the chamber.

"This place must have been important to the giants. It's as if they test us," Atreus said while Kratos retrieved the fallen crystal, placing it on the empty pedestal. "That looks right."

Kratos pulled the lever again while the crystals remained lit, revealing runic words on the now-illuminated floor.

"That's it!" Atreus ran to the sand bowl. "It means 'freedom'."

When Atreus carefully scribed the rune in the sand with his knife, mysterious lights drifted skyward.

"*Frelsa*." Atreus recited the runic incantation.

The statue responded, tapping its scepter three times, after which it emitted a light beam. "What is it doing?" he asked.

Kratos shifted the weight of his axe in his hands.

The light beam revealed a hidden door on the opposite wall.

"Oh! Thought maybe there would be a bridge," Atreus said.

"The giants mean to test us further."

The God of War shoved the door open, allowing them to drop into the passage below. "Guess we must go down to go up?" Atreus said.

Approaching a tight section of tunnel, so confining that swinging an axe might be near impossible, Kratos drew closer to Atreus to protect him.

"These passages seem too small for giants," Kratos commented, which brought a giggle from his son.

"You laugh, why?"

Atreus stifled his laughter. "Oh, you are serious."

"I am always serious."

"I forget. Mother said you never took an interest in our history. The giants are just a race, like elves and Huldra folk. It doesn't mean they're actually big. They come in all shapes and sizes," Atreus explained. His sadness grew as he recalled how his mother had explained it to him when he, at first hearing about them, also thought they were towering, fearful creatures. Her smiling face flashed across his mind, sinking his heart a little deeper inside his chest. If only he could reach out to brush her cheek one more time. Maybe even hug her...

"Then what of the World Serpent?" Kratos asked.

The question forced Atreus only reluctantly to abandon his vision of his mother.

"In that case, giant also means big. But there is only one of him. Giants are... complicated."

Kratos decided to allow the conversation to die there. He needed to focus on what lay ahead, and not on useless information only a mother would convey to her child.

They reached an extremely cramped passageway, with Kratos' shoulders scraping the sides.

Dead bodies littered everywhere, all the victims of an assortment of different traps. "There are a lot of bodies. They look like men, though, not giants," Atreus said.

"Thieves seeking treasure. See the traps."

"Lucky for us they set them all off."

"Be grateful these stay dead."

After pushing through a barricade at the end of a hall, whose floor was shin-deep in skeletons, they emerged to the rear of the stag statue, realizing that along the way, they had somehow crossed the chasm.

"We made it across!" Atreus said.

Their entrance suddenly collapsed. "Won't be going back that way," Atreus said.

As they turned to leave the statue behind, several Wulvers—blacked-furred, wolf-like creatures with glowing yellow eyes that stood erect—charged with jaws gaping and fangs dripping. The two had but a few moments to brace for the onslaught.

CHAPTER 26

While the Wulvers' attack proved fierce, Atreus' barrage of arrows distracted the beasts sufficiently to allow his father's axe to dispense with them before they might become a threat to his son. Amid the carnage, Atreus picked his way over headless carcasses to examine a writing of sorts that he identified on the rear of the stag's throne.

"This is Duraþrór, one of the four stags of the World Tree. He is supposed to safeguard the entrance to Jötunheim while the giants slumber. Do you think it's possible he is still there? Could we be close to Jötunheim?"

"I do not know," Kratos admitted, cleaning his axe of blood before slinging it over his back.

As they pushed open the doors leading from the statue room, they found themselves facing a crossroads. Surveying their choices and determining none seemed to reveal imminent danger, Kratos chose the path to their right.

As they approached a broken-down pulley contraption, several more draugr emerged from hiding places to attack. But by the time Atreus could get off his second arrow, his father had killed the remaining three. Witnessing his father's vicious and relentless assault, Atreus could only wonder if he might ever become as proficient, and as fearless, a warrior as his father.

"Where to now?" Atreus asked, scanning the dead and dying.

"The peak is still our goal. We need to find a way up."

"We are seeing more and more of those things. Is the situation getting worse here?" Atreus asked, as they picked their way along. His father had no answer.

Was this to be their future? Atreus wondered. *Would they have to fight every day for the rest of their lives?*

As they neared the apex of the rock face, Kratos pointed out to Atreus some runes etched into the rock.

"What do those...?"

"It's a name, I think. Hraezlr. It means 'terror'."

After completing their ascent, Kratos and Atreus stood before a long path lined with flickering torches, with a steep drop-off on their left. Light from an exit to the path ahead beckoned them.

Atreus stopped suddenly.

A ripple of uneasiness rumbled through Kratos' gut, stopping him a moment later. He turned back to his son. Each read the other's face.

"Hey, who do you think lit these torches? The dead need no light."

Kratos initially dismissed his son's words. Whoever lit the torches would face the God of War's wrath if they opposed them.

"Stay alert," Kratos replied.

They emerged from a passage leading up to a large open space cluttered with primitive mining machinery, most prominent of which was a huge two-pronged metal claw dangling at Kratos' eye level.

"Whoa. What is all this? Where are we?" Atreus asked, scouring every inch of the machinery. Having never seen such work before, he had no idea these things even existed. His life in the forest had sheltered him from ever being exposed to such marvels.

"We're in some kind of mine. And if those gears and levers will draw this claw up to the summit, our goal is near."

"All right. So how can we use it?"

Kratos shifted from gear to lever until he came to a rope-wheel contraption. Yanking the rope wheel activated the contraption and caused the claw to sway. Atreus studied the movements, identifying how each of the fifteen gears meshed with its mate and connected through a pair of levers to the chains.

"I think I see how this works. The claw is on one side, and if we can get this lever here unstuck…" Atreus said, tugging at the gears that kept them from turning freely.

"Wow!" Atreus screamed when, as a result of his action, the chain with the claw shot up into the darkness, pulling him with it.

"Boy!" Kratos growled.

As Kratos pulled the boy to safety, a nearby chain with a large tree trunk counterweight attached fell—and with it rained debris and a huge boulder, which pinned the chain beneath it on an unreachable platform to their left.

"Great. Now the chain is stuck," Atreus said.

"That was careless."

"Yes, sir. Sorry, sir," Atreus apologized, angry with himself for not first considering the consequences of his actions. He needed to take the time to visualize the outcome before he acted.

Kratos pulled at the chain, testing the mechanism, while the counterweight remained pinned.

Atreus wandered away, his interest snared by something he saw in a corner. He lofted the strange lantern candleholder—which had its candle set within a parchment bag inverted over it—to eye level, to examine it more closely. "Huh, no wick."

"That is of no use to us. The Bifröst lights our way."

"I know. But it is interesting, anyway."

Hastily casting the lantern aside, Atreus rushed to catch up with his already-moving father.

They made their way through a side tunnel that rose toward the platform with the boulder pinning the chain.

"I think we can get to that rock now," Atreus said.

Sizing the distance and the surroundings, Kratos leapt onto the right platform to reach the rock pinning the chain. Once on the platform, but before reaching the rock, Atreus discovered another broken lantern cast aside on the floor. As he took up the lantern, it moldered in his hands.

"Broken. Go," Kratos ordered.

"What could they be for? There is something special about them. I can feel it," Atreus persisted.

Kratos dismissed his son's comment, moving on with Atreus trailing reluctantly behind. They reached the huge boulder pinning the claw counterweight chain.

"That looks really heavy," Atreus said.

Kratos tipped the huge boulder out of the way.

"How? No way," Atreus muttered in disbelief.

The boulder tumbled off the platform, freeing the chain.

"You did it! But how? I bet we can make the chain-wheel work now. Might be our way to the top!"

But then he considered more deeply what he had just seen. No man he had ever seen in the forest could have moved that boulder. No man alone could have done that. How could his father be so strong, when no other men were? What explanation could there be for what he had just witnessed?

CHAPTER 27

Atreus had little time to wonder. Returning to the ground floor, a dozen Tatzelwurms emerged from holes in the floor to attack. Reptilian-skinned creatures, with cat-like bodies and huge upper fangs, they lurched, exposed razor-sharp claws and jagged teeth.

Kratos took the lead, smashing into them and cleaving one after another. Atreus launched his first arrow to take out one charging him, just seconds before it could reach him. His second arrow pierced the neck of the next charging Tatzelwurm attempting to join the fray against his father. Kratos flashed a smile toward his son, then he hacked into the next wurm within range. Four more lost their heads just behind their shoulders.

Calm returned.

"Back to the wheel," Kratos said.

Operating the chain-wheel mechanism, the freed chain now allowed the counterweight to rise. "We got it working!" Atreus piped up, all the time watchful of their surroundings.

The chain holding the claw returned to the ground. "We got the claw back!"

Kratos held the chain taut, used the frost axe to jam the gears in place.

"If we could just ride up with the claw somehow, we could get to the top in no time," Atreus said.

Kratos positioned himself beneath the chain. Using the chain-wheel, he brought the claw down, where it locked into place.

"That is perfect," Atreus said. "That should hold it."

When Kratos recalled his axe, the claw began to rise. As they ascended, they watched the draugr clustering below, seeking ways to climb up.

"Do you think this goes all the way to the top?" Atreus asked.

"We will see soon enough."

A shudder of concern rippled through the boy. "Something feels strange up there. We are heading into danger."

"Do not concern yourself with what might be. Focus on what is, and always remain vigilant," Kratos counseled.

"Yes, sir."

When the claw stopped short of the summit, Kratos and Atreus abandoned it to land on an adjacent platform. Atreus dashed to a nearby lantern, hidden behind some rubble.

"Wait! This one is not broken!" he said, holding it overhead, looking beneath it to reach the candle. Pulling it out, he paused, finding a note attached to the end with a hemp string.

"Look at this," he said.

He passed the parchment to his father, who angled the Bifröst light so Atreus could read it.

"A giant's prayer. They are asking their ancestors to watch over them and guide them home," Atreus said. He studied the candle and the lantern. Then he gazed up the elevator shaft. A broad smile flashed across his face.

Setting the lantern down, he rolled the candle's burnt wick between his fingers. Then, using the soot on his fingers, he scrawled something on the back of the parchment.

"Boy," his father grumbled impatiently.

"Wait, wait! I think I know how it works!" Atreus responded. Excitement overflowed in his voice. Quickly pulling two runestones from his pouch, he struck them together over the candle's wick.

The spark ignited a weak blue flame. Carefully, he eased the candle back into the lantern. Afterward, he brought it to his father, eager to demonstrate what he had deduced.

"Watch."

He released the lantern. It wobbled at first, then it began rising slowly skyward up the shaft, ascending the mountain interior. The lantern's light illuminated the path upward, revealing the massive structure and the carved walls in the darkness. They watched in silent awe.

"Wow," Atreus whispered.

"What did you write?" Kratos queried.

"I asked them to watch over Mother." He craned his neck, looking up, which caused him to lean into his father. Kratos recoiled slightly, gazing down at his son. Seeing the expression of joy and wonderment on Atreus' face tempered his apprehension. He leaned in to allow Atreus to rest fully against him.

"Do you think they will watch over us on our way to the peak?"

"Come. It is a long way up."

Locating an iron counterweight discarded on the platform, he attached it to the chain then motioned Atreus back into the claw, after which he pushed the weight off, which pulled the claw upward.

"We are almost there. Nothing is going to stop us now," Atreus said. He released a silent sigh of relief.

Only he was wrong.

Before they could breach the summit, an ebony-scaled, yellow-eyed, three-clawed dragon lurched out from an unseen alcove in the wall to attack with a beam of pure electricity. Latching onto the lift with razor-sharp talons, it drew closer while simultaneously spreading gaping jaws.

Atreus panicked, screaming in abject terror.

"Calm yourself, boy," Kratos demanded. Panicking at such a crucial moment could get both of them killed. "Just remain behind me."

Despite the tight confines of the claw and the surrounding

shaft, Kratos worked his axe free from his back to maneuver it in such a way that it allowed him to hack at the talons holding them.

"It's not letting go!" Atreus yelled.

The dragon ripped the claw from its bindings to drag it down a side tunnel, where Kratos and Atreus were able to escape. The dragon, meanwhile, dashed away before Kratos could fire his axe at it. For a long moment both just stared into the darkness.

"How do we defeat that?" Atreus asked.

Kratos offered no answer.

Taking the new passage up an incline, they worked their way past gnarled red roots overrunning their path.

"That looks like a root of the Yggdrasil tree," Atreus said.

They continued through the tunnel, facing daylight when they followed a bend in the passage.

"I can't believe we fought a dragon. I was aiming for his eyes, but I kept losing my footing. Do you think this is its home? Did they move in after the giants left? Or are they why the giants left?"

"The air grows thin up here. No more questions. Breathe," Kratos said, emerging into the bright sun near the mountain's peak. He scanned for a path that might take them higher.

They had progressed no more than a few dozen strides on a winding path when distant screaming stopped them in their tracks.

"Go away! Help! Help me somebody!"

It was Sindri yelling as he crouched behind a jagged rock formation, hiding from the dragon.

"Sindri's in trouble. Can you kill something that big?" Atreus asked.

"If we can force it off balance."

"I can distract him." Atreus withdrew his bow and an arrow.

Kratos knew the arrow would have little impact on the dragon, whose scaly hide kept meager projectiles like arrows from penetrating.

When Atreus started for Sindri, Kratos drew him back. "What are you doing?" he growled.

Sindri screamed. The dragon ripped away a chunk of the little man's hiding place, causing him to curl into a tighter ball as the beast sniffed ever closer. He shut his eyes as if to pray, or maybe to keep from witnessing what was about to become his gruesome fate.

Atreus sought his father's response with a look of desperation. "We *have* to help him!"

Assessing the situation as quickly as he could, Kratos released his son. "Go to the right, find an angle, then wait for my mark," Kratos instructed.

Atreus nodded. "Thank you."

The lad hopped across a series of rock pillars spanning the chasm between them and the dragon, firing arrows along the way. As he had hoped, the arrows distracted the creature, shifting its attention toward him rather than Sindri or his father, who at that moment was skulking along the underbrush to a place where he could take the dragon by surprise.

Kratos attacked with a flying axe, which failed to penetrate the beast's shoulder. The dragon whirled about, as if only mildly irritated. Kratos went in again for the dragon's long neck, this time gashing deep enough to draw blood.

Atreus used that opportunity to race to Sindri's side behind the rock formation. "You okay?"

"For now," Sindri replied in a shaky voice. His hands trembled out of control, and he quickly shifted to place the boy and his nocked arrow between himself and the monster.

The dragon returned to Kratos, swiping its tail wide to knock him from his feet. As Kratos scrambled back upright, the dragon lurched. Kratos threw his axe up just in time to force it into the dragon's gaping mouth, preventing the beast from taking off his arm in one bite. The God of War retreated, needing to gain sufficient space in which to launch his next assault.

A panicked Atreus shifted his arrow this way and that, trying to maintain his focus on the target. He figured he would get one shot at best. He had to make it count.

"Now!" Kratos yelled, while the dragon turned away.

Atreus sucked in a breath, exhaled, and fired without a second's hesitation.

The deadly shaft whipped silently through the air, true to its mark. The tip punctured the dragon's right eye, sending it reeling in agony and slashing its head from side to side in a vain attempt to knock the arrow out. When that failed, the dragon lowered its head, using its right front claws to rip the shaft free. In that moment of the dragon's vulnerability, Kratos charged, hacking at the beast's head now hovering at his height above the ground.

The great beast collapsed, unmoving.

After a few moments of inertia, Sindri mustered the courage to creep out from behind the protection of the rocks. Seconds later, Atreus jumped down to join his father. They stood over the dead dragon, while Sindri dashed over clutching a bag.

"Wow. We actually did it! Sindri!" Atreus said. He went to hug Sindri, but the little man would have none of that, jerking away, preventing any contact with the boy.

"But, but, but, no one has killed a dragon for hundreds of years. Not since the grand culling of the Wyrms!" an astonished Sindri uttered. "And unless I am mistaken, you did all that for me!"

"You are mistaken, small one. The dragon was simply blocking our path... nothing more," Kratos said.

"Ha! Deny it if you wish, but you have saved me. And that," Sindri said, reaching deep into his small bag— his entire arm disappearing while he rummaged about, "deserves compensation."

Noticing Atreus' quiver was nearly empty, Sindri removed a bundle of arrows that could never have fit into such a small space, presenting them to the boy.

"How did you... These are not just arrows, are they?" the lad asked, sizing them up.

"Braided mistletoe arrows. Straighter than Heimdall and perfectly weighted," Sindri said proudly.

"Oh. Thanks?" Atreus said, disappointed.

"Oh, okay... Hold on... uh," Sindri added. Returning to his

magical bag, this time he withdrew a Dark Elf's spear. "Ew, not that. Umm."

He continued, withdrawing an ornate horn, then a pickaxe, followed by a large stirring spoon, all of which he spread around him. After looking them over and rejecting them, he piled them back into the bag.

"Have you seen my brother again?" he asked, changing the subject.

"Yeah! He said you lost your talent."

Kratos snorted.

"Oh, and that I am selfish, I am sure. That I also value a weapon's look over its purpose. That I am pretentious and uptight. Fussy. I know what he thinks. But he cannot hurt me any..." Sindri continued, rejecting the unwanted items he had extracted.

Next, he pulled a dead fish from the magical bag. "Ah! This could be your next dinner," he said. Then he dropped it.

"I do not have time for this," Kratos said, marching off impatiently.

"No! No, no, no, wait, wait, wait, wait... I have a better idea," Sindri said.

Kratos turned back, albeit reluctantly. "What?"

"I just need one tooth. I promise you are going to like this."

Kratos took hold of the dead dragon's snout.

"Watch where you grab— oh, never mind. So unclean. So, so unclean," Sindri said.

Kratos twisted the head sideways to pry open the mouth, yanking out the first incisor presenting itself.

"Perfect. That should do."

"Why do you need the tooth?" Atreus asked. Sindri only smiled.

CHAPTER 28

K ratos offered the tooth to Sindri, who, of course, recoiled with palms downs, preventing the God of War from setting it in his hands.

"I'm not touching that. Just break it open," Sindri grumbled. He scurried about, assembling a makeshift workbench that he extracted in parts from his packs.

Annoyed that the little man refused to handle the tooth, Kratos only grunted a response. Slapping the tooth onto the plank to crack it open sent a fluorescent, bluish powder spilling out.

"Is that magic?" Atreus asked.

Sindri offered a wry smile.

Extracting a red powder from a container in his bag, the little man blew the powder across the exposed tooth root, resulting in blue arcs and white sparks.

"What's it doing?" Atreus watched with fascination.

"You ask a lot of questions."

"My mother said that was how I would learn."

"So, it is her I should blame," Sindri retorted with a dour expression.

Kratos shot Sindri a scornful glare, which Sindri shrugged off with a smirk.

"What? My brother could never do this," he responded

finally. "It is part of why we split up, truth be told. He wanted to stick with what we knew best: weapons. Change or die, I say. Learned this in Vanaheim. It is the least I can do to repay you." He gestured to Atreus, "Now, run the tooth along the string of your son's bow."

Sindri leaned in while Kratos complied with his request. "Two passes should do it. Let's see that blue bastard do *that*," the little man boasted, with a smile and a wink for the boy.

The Bifröst on Kratos' arm extinguished its glow.

"So, now how do I explain this? The powder added a new vibrating pattern to the crystal's lattice. Aiming it at crystals will vibrate their patterns to their fracture point," he explained, more like a wizard trying to impress than a teacher working to instruct.

"What does *that* mean?" Atreus said.

Sindri stared down his nose, as if the lad were stupid.

"Makes crystals go BOOM! Trust me, you will love it."

"We leave now," Kratos called back.

"Before you go: I'm thinking there may be something Odin has taken a special interest in, up there on that peak. Just a warning."

Atreus shook his head in disbelief as Kratos started his climb. After a boost, Atreus dashed ahead of his father, his quiver flapping loosely around. Regardless of how he repositioned it, it kept sliding off his shoulder.

"What is wrong with this thing?" he stammered.

"What is happening with your quiver?"

"Strap broke fighting the dragon. Lucky that's all that broke. It is all right, I can hold it," Atreus said.

"Stop," Kratos ordered. Exasperation peppered his voice.

He lowered to a knee to get on eye level with his son and inspect the damage.

"Your weapons are what keep you alive. Even something

as simple as a broken quiver slows your draw. Pain we endure, faulty weaponry we cannot."

The strap had split at the center, with the remaining attached overstretched fibers creating the loose fit. Kratos gathered the split ends tightly to hold them with one hand, while pulling out a mistletoe arrow with the other. He jammed the tip through the leather strap and the quiver body to stitch it together, breaking off the unneeded feathered end of the shaft.

"This will do for now. Good?" Kratos said.

Atreus tugged the strap, at the same time rotating his shoulders forward. "Good."

"Go," Kratos said.

They resumed their climb toward the apex of the mountain, surrounded by the sound of a swirling wind. Then a more distinct pattern of sounds emerged in the air. As they neared the summit, the sounds became a flurry of grumbling words.

"You hear those voices too, right?" Atreus asked.

"Yes. Be silent."

"You know why we're here. Did my last visit manage to loosen your tongue?" a voice said.

The stranger. Kratos immediately recognized the voice.

"That sounds like the man from our house. You said you killed him," Atreus whispered in a breathless voice a moment later.

Kratos shushed Atreus to silence.

As they inched nearer the summit, they caught sight of three men milling about, questioning someone beyond their view.

"I see you brought your companions this time. Must be important if the sons of Thor deign to grace me with their presence. Tell me, you two still tripping over yourselves to impress your da?" the unseen voice delivered, without so much as a tinge of fear.

"The tattooed man. Tracks show he travels with a child. Where would they go next?" the stranger pressed with an intimidating snarl.

Kratos froze, clinging to a rocky cliff, forcing Atreus to remain out of sight.

"Why in Odin's name would I even know that?" the voice offered innocently in response.

"You *are* the smartest man alive, aren't you?" another voice shot in.

"Smarter than all the dead ones, too."

A tense pause clung to the chilled air.

"Look. You help me; I help you. Tell me where they are, and I speak on your behalf to Odin," the stranger said.

A breathless laugh came in response.

"Your father will never let me go, Baldur, and he will never let you kill me. So we are at an impasse. You have nothing to offer me. So take your questions, take your threats, take your two worthless wankers, and piss off."

"When no one's looking... we will be back for that other eye," the third man said.

"Do not forget, we are everywhere," the second voice chimed in.

"We really are."

"Shut up, you idiots. Let's go," Baldur said.

Kratos and Atreus breached the summit, turning the corner in time to watch Baldur and his two companions retreat down a path on the opposite side of the apex.

Nearby, the older man, still with his back to them, faced a stone henge. Encased up to his neck in crystalline gnarled roots, only his head and one arm remained exposed. The man was chuckling to himself when Kratos entered his view.

Surprise flashed on his face when he saw Kratos, rather than Odin, coming before him. "Ah, the very topic of our conversation. A pale, red-tattooed man traveling with child."

"Boy, check their path; make certain we are alone."

"But we just saw them leave."

"Do as I say," Kratos fired back.

The man—with goat-like horns protruding from a hairless head and entwined with hemp—watched with curiosity as a confused Atreus wandered off to the other side of the ridge. His long gray beard displayed a collection of food scraps. Once the lad had moved out of range, Kratos spoke.

"Oh, I see. He does not know what you are, does he?"

"And I expect you to keep it that way. Who are you?"

"Me? Why, I am Mimir, the greatest ambassador to the gods, the giants, and all the creatures of the nine realms. I know every corner of these lands, every language spoken, every war waged, every deal struck. They call me the smartest man alive, and I have the answer to your every question."

"Good. Then why does the son of Odin hunt us?"

Mimir looked him over with a blank face and a single white eye, his other eye socket vacant. He blinked after a few moments, clearly stumped.

"Fine. So there are a few gaps in my knowledge. But Odin's had me imprisoned here for a hundred and nine winters. However, I am a clever lad. I can piece it together, I promise. Just give me time."

"Nobody there, just like I said," Atreus complained on his return.

"The boy's mother is dead. She wished that we—" Kratos began.

"She requested her ashes be spread from the highest peak in all the realms," Atreus interrupted.

"Well then, you've come to the wrong place, little brother. The highest peak in *all* the realms is not in Midgard. It is in Jötunheim, in the realm of the giants."

Kratos and Atreus gazed around the open vista with a growing sense of defeat. "No," Atreus said.

"That could not be what she meant," Kratos said.

"Take a look," Mimir said, trying to move his arm to indicate where they should turn.

Mimir's eye suddenly glowed with a golden light. The light striking the nearby henge projected what appeared to be a tall, unframed window that revealed another realm. In the distance, a craggy three-fingered peak rose majestically.

"That is the last known bridge to Jötunheim in all the realms. See that mountain that looks like a giant's fingers scraping the sky? That is the highest peak in all the realms. Not here."

"Then can we just take that bridge? We have a Bifröst," Atreus said.

"When the giants destroyed all the other bridges to their realm, they locked this one up with a secret rune. If it still exists, only a giant would know it."

"And all of them left Midgard a long time ago," Atreus added.

"True. But today the Winds of Fate have kicked up a strange vortex of coincidence. Fact is, there is only one person alive who can get you where you need to go... and lucky for you, my schedule is wide open."

Thinking, Kratos stared at the pouch of ashes on his belt, then at the henge, then at his son, who looked on uneasily, fearing his father might be considering spreading her ashes right there.

"We *are* going to Jötunheim, right?" Atreus said.

"Tell us what we have to do," Kratos said.

"Yes!" Atreus chimed in.

"First, you need to cut off my head," Mimir said.

CHAPTER 29

"Wait? What?" Atreus said.

"Odin made certain no weapon, not even Thor's hammer, could free my body from these bonds. But fortunately for you, you do not need my body. The trick is, we need to find someone who can reanimate my head, using the old magic," Mimir explained, as casually as if he were talking about the weather.

"Old magic... We met a witch in the woods, she is knowing of the old ways," Kratos said.

"And she will help? Yes, she just might do. It is worth a try!" Mimir said.

Atreus felt the need to interject. "Wait. If she fails, you will be dead."

"Your concern is admirable, young one. But misplaced. I am willing to chance it."

"There is no guarantee you can live," Kratos said.

"He tortures me, you know, every day, brother. Odin himself sees to it personally, and believe me, there is no end to his creativity. Every—single—day. This... this is not living."

"Very well," Kratos said. Without any hesitation, he drew his axe.

"Wait!" said Atreus, reaching out his arms. "We do not even know if the witch is still alive. What if she did not survive what happened to her back there?"

"What happened to her?" Mimir asked. Both ignored his question.

"We must take that chance," Kratos argued.

"Fine. I cannot watch this," Atreus said, walking away until he was out of sight. Kratos raised the axe overhead.

"Are you certain of this?"

"Just be sure to locate a witch capable of performing the old magic."

"I will."

In a tense moment, neither of them spoke.

"Brother, in case you fail to resurrect me, there is something you must know. The boy…"

Kratos lowered the axe.

"The longer you delay telling him his true nature, the more damage you do. He will resent you, and you may lose him forever. Are you willing to risk that?"

"There is much about me I would rather he never know."

"Aye… so you value your privacy more than your flesh and blood?"

"It is more than privacy. I am going to cut off your head now, so you will be silent."

"Fair enough."

Kratos lifted his axe. From afar, Atreus watched, unable to look away from the sight. However, he turned away at the very last moment and only heard the guttural chopping sound of the head leaving the body in a single clean swipe of the axe.

Atreus rejoined his father while Kratos placed the fallen head into a sack on his hip. Then they began the long return to the witch's house.

"Jötunheim. We are going to Jötunheim, the long-lost realm of the giants. That's…" Atreus said, with exhilaration pumping in his chest. The thought of seeing the witch once more made him feel good. Each time they were together, he felt like he became more capable of dealing with the loss of his mother. The witch could never replace her, he accepted that, but being around her gave him a sense of family, of being wanted by someone.

"Inconvenient?" Kratos finished.

"That's what I was going to say…"

"Do you remember the way back to the witch's house?"

"Of course. The woods with the blood-red leaves, south of the bay. I know just where to go," Atreus replied.

Silence swelled between them as Kratos thought about what he must do, and Atreus thought about a decapitated head slung on his father's hip.

"Hope she made it back from Alfheim, and can bring him back. He seemed nice… before you cut off his head. What if no witch can bring him back from the dead?" Atreus asked.

"Worry more about what is… not about what might be."

"Makes sense. Maybe Odin will not even notice that his head is gone."

They continued for several hours in silence. As night fell, they left the traveled way to favor a hollow in a sprawling thicket in which to sleep for the night. They consumed the last of their dried badger and the remaining dried apricots, along with what the witch had provided them.

"How long will it take to reach the witch?" Atreus asked, from his place on the ground.

"Maybe a day or longer," Kratos said.

"We are out of food."

"I know. We will hunt for something on the morrow if we do not reach the witch."

Then Atreus blurted out, "I still cannot believe the god Baldur came to our house. And you fought him and won!"

"Yes," Kratos said.

"Odin's son. Thor's brother. And now he hunts us with his nephews. Why is this happening?"

"If the witch can bring the head back, we will ask him."

Silence grew between them, Atreus looking over at the sack with the head every few minutes, still in disbelief. His mother never talked about anything powerful enough to bring a head back to life.

"I had secretly hoped we might find a giant somewhere back on this mountain. I guess they really did leave Midgard... except for the World Serpent. He may be the last of his kind..."

Saying the words kindled a thought in Atreus' mind: "Are you the last of your kind? Is that why you do not like to talk about it?"

"My kind?"

"I mean, your family. Before Mother and I? Where you came from..."

"Now is not the time for such a discussion," Kratos snapped.

Within a few more hours of traveling, they reached the boat at the caldera dock. "You remember the way back to the witch from here?" Kratos tested.

"That way, toward the big statue of Thor. And row under him." Atreus pointed in the direction they needed to go.

"Correct," Kratos acknowledged, rowing toward the witch's abode with Atreus keeping a lookout.

"I know she is really powerful, but do you really think the witch can actually bring a head back to life?"

"She seems capable in her craft. And we have nothing to lose."

"If she can't bring it back to life, can we keep the head anyway?"

"No. But you may feed it to the fish."

Kratos drew the boat to the water's edge, steering to the dock. From there, they trekked through the dense forest until they came to the hag's cottage. As they entered, not bothering to knock or call out, the place appeared unoccupied.

"She is dead," Atreus said breathlessly, his words so crestfallen that they leeched under Kratos' skin.

CHAPTER 30

"Who is dead?"

The voice came from a ladder in a dark corner, where the witch busied herself hanging herbs from her garden to dry. Her face brightened with a welcoming smile at the sight of Atreus.

"It is so good to see you again! I knew you weren't dead," Atreus said.

He ran to hug her, which caught the witch unguarded. She had no idea how to react. "Hello to you, too!" she laughed. Her gaze drifted to Kratos to welcome him.

"Oh, can you bring a head back to life?" Atreus asked.

She stared down at him still embracing her, stunned and more than a little confused. "I am… not sure I understand what…" She shoved Atreus away, forcing the lad to arm's length. "Where did you get those?" Her tone turned sharp, more than just accusatory. The sight had clearly angered her; when she examined the mistletoe arrows in his quiver, her face turned ashen.

"They are just arrows. Why do you look at me that way?" Atreus said.

Kratos advanced to place himself between his son and the witch.

"Those arrows. Give them to me. Now!" she demanded, her glare never straying from the shafts.

"Why? They were a gift."

"Do as she demands, boy," Kratos commanded. He read a grim determination on her face that convinced him to trust her, though he had no idea why at that moment.

After Atreus reluctantly handed over the bundle of mistletoe arrows, the witch immediately crossed to the fireplace, where she tossed them into the flames, making certain not a single shaft escaped.

"Those arrows are dangerous, wicked. Should you find any more, destroy them. Promise me you will do that?" she said with a stern jaw.

Confused, and with his mouth wide open, Atreus just stared at her.

"Do you understand? Say it!" she shouted at him, with a streak of meanness neither had seen before.

"I understand! If I see them, I promise to destroy them!" Atreus shouted back rudely.

Relief washed across the witch's face. She scrutinized his expression before her expression softened.

"It is all I ask. Forgive me." There was a long pause. "Please, take my arrows in their place. I have no need for them anymore."

Atreus crossed cautiously to the witch's quiver, hanging nearby. He glanced back at her, making absolutely certain he could take them. She offered a nod of reassurance.

"Now, what's this about a head?"

Kratos removed Mimir's head from his bag, elevating it so the witch might see it clearly. Aghast, the witch stepped back in shock at the sight. A few drops of blood dripped from the severed sinew and dangling blood vessels.

"Do you have any idea who this is? Did you kill him?"

"At his request. He claimed you could revive his head," Kratos said.

"Me? Are you certain you heard him right?"

"Please," Atreus begged, with an innocent look she could not ignore.

The witch just sighed, studying the head, as if still deciding whether she should fulfill their wish. "Take him to the table," she said finally.

Filling her arms with jars of ingredients from her shelves, she moved them to the table beside the head.

"It has been a long time since I practiced the old magic. Hold him there so I can have a look."

This time she examined the head more closely. If no maggots or drill worms had invaded, she might just be able to pull it off.

"How long dead?"

"Three days," the God of War responded.

"Cut looks clean, no infestation of any kind, and very little decay," she said.

The witch set about mashing her ingredients into a thick paste. Filling one hand with it, she slathered the neck wound with her concoction. She had no idea if her efforts might work, or if returning the head to life was such a good idea. Leaving the dead to remain dead was most often the wiser course to follow.

"Cutting off *his* head, of all people. I sure hope you know what you are doing," the witch muttered, while she worked her magic at the base of the skull. Next, she dumped grubs from a jar into Mimir's open mouth, afterward jamming it closed. Without speaking, she gestured for the cauldron of water sitting near the fireplace.

"Now hold his head submerged, and don't let go. I mean it."

Kratos plunged the head into the cauldron. The water immediately began to bubble and froth. A pattern of bright light wavered over the water. Moments later, the water calmed.

The cottage fell silent for a seemingly unending moment.

"I have done what I could. You expect far too much from me. The old magic has not been used for a hundred years. What can you possibly…" her rambling sputtered out.

"May we take some food for our journey?" Atreus asked, while they waited.

The witch nodded, indicating the wooden box across the room.

Atreus opened the box to fill a sack with biscuits and fruit, along with what dried venison existed there.

After a few more moments, she nodded for Kratos to remove the head from the water. He held it up until the dead eye was level with his own. The clouded orb remained unseeing with the face utterly motionless.

"Anything?" she asked, hopeful.

Atreus stared at the head, mumbling under his breath, as if trying to pray for the magic to work.

"I failed. The old magic is too complicated…"

Then Mimir's eye blinked. The clouded iris turned clear. The head gurgled up a mouthful of grubs, spewing them down the front of Kratos' chest.

"It worked!" Atreus whispered in amazement.

"Let me see him. Mimir, you there?" she asked, shifting around to stand beside Kratos so she could look at Mimir's face. A smile played across his face.

"Yes," Mimir said simply and without fanfare.

Kratos angled the head to allow the witch to see him.

"Good," was all she said, though relief was evident in her voice. Then she spit in his face.

"Oh, hello Freya. Been a long time! You do look well."

Freya's look revealed disdain; her lips drew a thin, tight line across her hardened face. "What I did, I did for them. As far as I am concerned, death suits you better."

"You know I would bow if I could, your majesty. Forgive me, had I known the witch in the woods was Freya herself, I never would have suggested this," Mimir said.

"Freya? The goddess Freya?" Atreus uttered in awe.

"You did not know either?" Mimir asked Atreus. "Forgive me," he then said to the goddess.

"Do you not understand? When word gets out that Mimir is free, the wrath of Odin will not be far behind," she said.

Kratos looped Mimir's head onto his belt by his hair.

"You are a god," Kratos said, feeling betrayed by her deception.

"Leader of the Vanir once, yes, but no longer."

"You did not think it important enough to tell me?" Kratos said, with anger seething through his teeth.

"Are *you* really going to lecture me about that?"

Kratos examined her for a long moment.

"We are leaving, boy."

"But..." Atreus said.

"Now!"

Atreus' glance bounced from Freya to his father, before he shuffled out of the door. Kratos shot Freya a grim, disappointed face as he trailed his son out.

"You're welcome!" she shouted, slamming the door behind them.

CHAPTER 31

"Why did you do that?" Atreus questioned, having progressed no more than a dozen strides from Freya's cottage. He stopped in his tracks.

"We cannot trust her." His father stopped also.

"Because she is a god?"

"Have I taught you nothing, boy?"

"But she has helped us. A lot."

"She lied."

"I do not understand. Why do you hate the gods so much?" Atreus persisted.

"Some people value their privacy, brother. Best not to judge," Mimir said.

"When I require your counsel, I will ask."

"Fair enough. Get me to Týr's temple, in the Lake of the Nine, and I'll get you to Jötunheim as promised."

"We know the temple. What's there?" Atreus said.

"Only the last living giant in Midgard. Who better to tell us the way?"

"The World Serpent? Wait—do you know how to talk to him?"

"Indeed. He speaks an obscure tongue, more ancient even than these mountains. None are left in Midgard who can speak it. Except for me, of course."

Kratos marched toward the dock. After a few moments, Atreus resumed his progress, but lagging behind intentionally. His father remained silent while they climbed into the boat and he took up the oars.

"Let us just hope the snake remembers me."

"The same way Freya remembered you?" Atreus asked.

Kratos continued to row, growing more confident with the head on his belt. If anyone could reach the serpent, it was Mimir.

"Head, why does this Baldur hunt us?" Kratos asked.

"I have been trying to puzzle that one out. Odin must want you badly for him to send his best tracker after you. And there's few things Odin wants as badly as a way to Jötunheim."

Atreus blinked at this. "But... how could he have known we were going to Jötunheim? We've only just found out that's where we need to go!"

"Yes, well..." Mimir paused for a time, appearing confused, or perhaps lost in his thoughts. "Odin's a tricky one. Give my brain a little time to wake up and I'm sure I can explain it properly. Dying is a disorienting business."

Kratos murmured something indecipherable to both Mimir and Atreus, who shifted from the bow to settle beside Mimir, wanting to scrutinize the head more closely. Pressing the nose rotated the head sideways.

"Could you release my nose?"

"This is nasty. I can see the hole where food goes down," Atreus said.

"Perhaps you would like to feed me something, to see what happens?" Mimir offered with a laugh.

"Do not waste our food, boy," Kratos said.

"Sir," Atreus replied, disappointed.

"Spoilsport," Mimir said to Kratos.

An hour passed, Kratos rowing in silence into a glaring midday sun, shining down on verdant hills lining both shores. Atreus decided to return to the bow of the boat. "I cannot believe I actually met a god," he said.

Mimir smirked at the child's naivety. In time, he would come to learn the truth about "the gods". Then he would think differently of them.

"Hey, why did she spit in your face?" Atreus asked.

Mimir took a few moments to compose his response.

"Well, Freya blames me for many, many things. Some justified. Some not."

"She was leader of the Vanir. Why is she now a hermit in the woods?" Atreus asked. "That is quite a tale in itself, actually..."

"Mind yourself, boy," Kratos interjected. "Her past is her own."

"No, he is right. Best not to gossip," Mimir admitted.

"Mimir, what is that weird window I noticed in Freya's house?" Atreus said suddenly.

"Yes! I noticed that as well! It appears to be a window created from Bifröst crystal, aligned to the realm of Vanaheim. Odin's punitive magic prevents her from leaving Midgard and returning home. That window may be the next best thing, tormenting her with unattainable visions of what she has lost."

"Why did Odin do that?" Atreus said.

"Plain and simple: he's a sonofabitch, that's why. And Freya was leader of the Vanir, the Aesir's mortal enemies."

"She must miss her home," Atreus said.

"Could be worse. She could have ended up a head dangling from someone's belt," Mimir chided.

Reaching the caldera array, Kratos eased the boat to the dock, where they disembarked. A hundred paces from the dock they encountered small, blue Brok, sitting beside a campfire with a large spit of meat hanging over the flames. The little man gnawed away at the fleshy leg bone of some creature.

"Brok! Brok!" Atreus said. He was famished.

The little man remained focused on the fire, displaying no response.

"Brok!"

"What?" he screeched. "I'm on a fuckin' break. You don't hear me screechin' at you whenever you're twiddling your short and curlies, do ya?"

"Come, boy," Kratos scowled.

Kratos pivoted to walk on, though his stomach rumbled. He figured his son was also hungry. A dejected Atreus followed.

"Oh, fer… You already spoiled my solitude. Ya may as well join me." Brok's voice seemed anything but accommodating.

"We are not hungry," Kratos lied. As a god, he never allowed himself that human failing of becoming obligated to anyone for anything.

"Good. That is not what I was offerin'," Brok fired right back.

Setting the meat on the anvil to wipe his hands along his legs, Brok released a rare glimpse of a smile as they walked over.

"Eat. That's some good meat."

Atreus wasted no time pulling at another meaty bone, tearing it into two, one for him and the other for his father. Ripping off a chunk, the lad chewed it down quickly, so he might clear his mouth to speak. He smiled. The meat wasn't that bad. It wasn't deer or boar, and, for sure, it wasn't badger. The little man had cooked it a bit too long over the flame, but it was still quite tasty.

"None for me, thanks," Mimir said.

"Saw your brother again!" Atreus said.

"Well, con-grat-u-la-tions. They giving out some kind of medal for that? I'm sure you let him go and roger my axe good and plenty again, didn't ya? Let me check the damage."

Kratos tossed him the Leviathan axe, which Brok flipped over so he could examine the double-edged head, mumbling to himself something that neither of them could understand.

"Little canker-throat wouldn't know proper weight and balance if it were dangling off his chut," Brok said louder and more clearly, wanting to make sure Kratos heard. "You know what a chut is, boy? Oh, never mind."

Brok carried the axe with reverence to his makeshift

workbench a few paces away. "He eatin' well enough?" Brok asked Kratos.

"The boy?" Kratos responded.

"No, why would I ask about your little spit weasel?"

"I guess," Atreus said.

"Good," Brok replied under his breath.

The blue man hammered at the axe.

"You doing what I think you are about to do, means you'd better have the best axe I can make." Brok motioned to the sack hanging at Kratos' belt.

Atreus tore more meat from the roasting carcass to offer his father, keeping a large charred chunk for himself.

"Times he gets so wrapped up in his work, Sindri hasn't the sense to sip or sup. And if he does remember, good luck getting him to cook his own meat. Guess I got all the stomach in the family, along with all the smarts," Brok said, offering a rotten smile.

"Whatever happened between you two could not be all that bad. Can't you two just patch things up? You are family," Atreus said.

"I don't need no lecturin' about family from a half-size speckle-frosted yapper. I ain't the one what forgot what our name stood for. What we made—the weapons we made—were legendary across nine realms. You just don't throw that away on account of one bad—"

Brok abruptly stopped talking, as if remembering something painful. Just as quickly, he shook it off and returned to the work at hand.

"There. All better now," Brok said, returning the weapon to its true master.

"Hey! Where's Fuckin' Gratitude?" Atreus asked suddenly.

Brok indicated the meat on the spit.

Atreus dropped his chunk, spitting out what remained in his mouth. His face soured. "What is wrong with you? It's ruined now," Brok sniped.

"*Me?* What is wrong with *me*? What is wrong with *you*?"

"What? Her milk ran dry."

Kratos discarded what remained of his meat, marching off.

"She was your friend," Atreus muttered back, as he caught up to his father.

"Then she'll be happy I'm so well fed. Don't go getting all sentimental..." were the last words they heard from the dwarf.

"Head, how do we speak to the serpent?"

Silence. Kratos turned the head to face him on his belt. He shot Mimir a look that demanded a response.

"All right. There's a horn on a platform at the middle point of the bridge. Take me to it."

After wending their way up to the bridge, they approached a giant brass clarion horn resting on an ornately carved oaken frame.

The World Serpent's head followed them from the water's surface below.

CHAPTER 32

"Good. Now place my lips to the horn," Mimir ordered.

Once there, Mimir blew into the reed mouthpiece to create a low, mystical note that echoed across the vast caldera. Atreus watched in excited anticipation as the giant serpent rose from beneath the dark water. The snake advanced, but it seemed distracted by the large Thor statue on the caldera's outer ring. Before uttering a word, the serpent reared back, releasing a loud hiss, and bit down on the statue, shearing Thor in half at the waist.

"Why did it do that?" Atreus whispered.

"Odin ordered that statue made in Thor's honor. Seeing as how the World Serpent absolutely abhors the fat dobber, it was probably sick of looking at it," Mimir whispered back.

The serpent angled its head back to swallow the statue.

"But doesn't that hurt?" Atreus asked.

"The serpent and Thor have a bit of an unpleasant history between them, or will, anyway. Guess waking up to it was worse than the thought of solid stone passing through its gullet. Want me to ask it?"

"No! Our only concern is Jötunheim," Kratos interjected.

The serpent shifted its attention to Mimir. Once again, its deep, harmonic voice emerged. "Ennnnndooooooooo. Thoooooo blooooooo tooooooox," the serpent said.

"You again. Have you come to sacrifice the axe?" Mimir translated.

Kratos yanked Mimir's head from his belt, offering it up to the giant snake.

"Wish me luck!" Mimir shouted.

Clearing his throat before contorting his lips into an unnatural shape, Mimir released an equally deep harmonic chant, a low rumble with concurrent tongue clicks.

"Yoooooor-moooooooo hin meeee-meeeeeeeeer," Mimir said.

"What did you say to it?" Atreus asked.

"Jörmungandr, it is me, Mimir."

The serpent leaned in for a closer look.

"Yaaaaw-ehhhhhhh-thaaaaa foooooh-raaaaah," it offered in response.

"Yes, but there used to be more of you," Mimir again translated, with a slight laugh. "Shift me closer," he ordered Kratos.

Kratos complied, though he could see no reason for the head to be any closer to the giant creature.

"I've still got it, lads. He remembers me! Lyoooooooooo... Oh! That's not it!" Mimir muttered when he realized he had erred. "Maaaaaw-lon-gooooo vih-nooooor kooooon tooooon," he then tried. Kratos and Atreus waited anxiously.

"My friends here are searching for entry into Jötunheim," he translated for them.

The great serpent recoiled suddenly, baring monstrous fangs.

"Oh, dear," Mimir muttered.

"Ehhhhhh-kooooo... nooooooh oh-thooooo voo-nooooor," the serpent spat in response.

"No, no! They are no friends of Odin, quite the opposite. They seek only to pay final respects to the boy's mother. I mean, Ehhhhhhh-yooooounaaa tooooob sooolaooooo megaaawoooo."

The serpent twisted its neck to further scrutinize Atreus and Kratos.

"Mooooon-veeeee-taaaaah. Thaaaaaw-toooool Teeeeer," the serpent uttered.

"Ahh. First, we need a sliver from the tip of the sacred chisel. We must also learn the Black Rune, secreted away in the Temple of Týr," Mimir said.

"Yooooo soout aaaaaaaz keeee soooo luuuu paaaaut," the serpent doled out next.

"What else is it saying?" Kratos grumbled.

"He understands the pain of your loss," Mimir said.

"Baaaaaw-thooooor-thaaaaah. Gooouul-dooooo," came next from the serpent.

"Efni. Ooooo-foooooon-goooor," Mimir offered in response. "Curious, though," he muttered.

"What is?" Kratos asked.

"Nothing to be concerned about," Mimir said.

The serpent suddenly pressed its massive head against the caldera bridge. Exerting its colossal strength, it pushed the structure—with Kratos and Atreus still on it—in a different direction.

"W-what's he doing?" Atreus stuttered.

"Making certain we head in the right direction. To etch the rune to Jötunheim, no ordinary mortal instrument will suffice. Hence, sliver from the tip of a very special chisel. Luckily, that is not too far away," Mimir said.

The bridge completed its rotation then locked into place.

"Thanks!" Atreus called up with a wave.

Kratos and Atreus proceeded to the lower level of the bridge, noticing that the serpent's shift further reduced the water level, which now exposed a new ornate door. Reaching the boat dock, they climbed into a boat to take them through the canyons.

"It looked like the World Serpent was gonna eat us!" Atreus said.

"My fault. A misplaced click or two created some confusion. He thought I said you were friends of Odin. You will have to forgive me. Truth is, I have never spoken the ancient tongue while sober."

"It did not sound like you were saying a lot... but you were saying a lot!" Atreus said.

"Well, the ancient tongue makes use of multiple streams of communication at once. Tricky, but efficient."

"You think maybe I could learn it?" Atreus asked.

"You? I gather you might be uniquely suited for it. Just watch you don't destroy your voice."

For monotonous hours they rowed in silence through the canyons, with stacks of snow-covered pines towering on both sides. Mimir seemed at peace with his new condition.

"Before, you said I should not be concerned with what the snake said. I am concerned," Kratos said.

"It is really nothing. He just said that the boy seemed already familiar to him when he encountered him that first time you two met."

"Me?" Atreus interjected.

"How can that be? This is the first time the boy has ever left our forest. The snake does not know him," Kratos insisted, though the notion churned inside his mind.

"Well, that may not exactly be true. You see, the World Serpent is fated to kill Thor during Ragnarök, and the God of Thunder is fated to kill him. As they fight, the Tree of Life shakes so violently, it splinters—and the World Serpent is cast backward through time. Now he is trapped in a time before he has even been born. It is all much clearer in the ancient tongue."

"Um... What?" Atreus said.

"Your future is actually his past. This was the first time you met him, but it may not be the first time he met you," Mimir said with a sigh.

"Fate is but another lie told by the gods. Nothing is written that cannot be unwritten," Kratos said.

"Whatever you say," Atreus said. "So, Mimir, why is the World Serpent the only giant left? Where did they all go?"

"That, my boy, is one of the greatest mysteries of the nine realms. Nobody knows. Not even me. The leading theory is that they called it a day and went home... smashing all the realm bridges to Jötunheim along the way, so no one could follow. Others think it was somehow Odin's doing."

"What do *you* think?" Atreus asked.

"Me? I think after centuries of suffering at the hands of Thor and that damn hammer, they chose to lick their wounds in private, and plan their next steps in peace. It is too bad. I was fond of every giant I ever met."

"So, Mimir... why is Odin so desperate to find a way into Jötunheim, anyway?" Atreus asked.

"He is convinced the giants hold the key to changing his fate when Ragnarök comes. They are the Aesir's oldest enemies. It's their army that is supposed to do him in, in the end. But more than that, he covets their gifts of prophecy."

"Wait. Isn't Ragnarök what is fated to happen? You can't change that."

"Try telling Odin that. He is one of the few who does not believe it is a foregone conclusion. Things do not end well for him and the Aesir, or even the world, for that matter. He chooses not to believe in the event. It all turns out to be tommyrot."

"Mimir, Freya's magic is pretty strong, right? I saw her heal her boar when it was badly wounded, and she even brought life back to you. Do you think she could do that with... you know, other people?"

Mimir's pause suggested he was weighing his words.

"Boy, what she has done to me should not be visited upon someone you love. Look at me. I will never be completely what I was."

Sadness washed over Atreus as he came to understand Mimir's meaning. His life would also never be the same. He could never go back to the past, when he had his mother. He could never go back and change the relationship he had with his father. But maybe it was not about going back. *Maybe it's about changing the future by altering what is done in the moment.*

"I see."

"Fact is, I am not entirely certain this is not all just some horrible, horrible dream," Mimir said. "Not... that... you and your father are not just lovely people... uh," he added moments later.

A long silence ensued.

"It's getting colder," Atreus said, vigorously rubbing his arms. "Do you feel it getting colder?" he directed to Mimir.

"Yes, I do believe it is," Mimir said.

"Tell me about this chisel we seek," Kratos said.

"Gladly. A giant named Thamur—a very giant giant—was without question the greatest stonemason in this world. He set out to build a great wall around Jötunheim to protect his people from the Aesir. Proud Thamur hoped to one day pass his vast knowledge on to his son, but young Hrimthur had the heart of a warrior. A quarrel of theirs spiraled out of control, and the overworked stonemason struck his son in anger. Hrimthur ran off. Thamur chased after him, but soon found himself wandering Midgard, lost and alone. Sadly, he caught the eye of the one person he didn't want to meet alone at night, so far from home... Thor."

"What happened next?"

"You will soon see."

The river soon funneled them into a cave with a low opening, forcing Kratos to almost double over to make the entry. Once inside, the cave ceiling arched many feet into the air, allowing Kratos to return upright.

"It is freezing now. This doesn't seem right," Atreus commented to nobody.

CHAPTER 33

They emerged from the cave, only to be forced to a stop by a frozen lake. A dock came into view across the ice. Beyond, a huge, petrified hand of a giant stonemason's corpse jutted out from the lake. The stonemason's giant hammer towered a short distance from it.

"That thing is huge beyond imagination, and Thor killed him," Atreus said, awestruck.

"Turn my head so I can see it," Mimir asked.

Kratos attempted to row, ignoring Mimir's request, hoping the ice might be thin enough that it would crack and split open as they rowed through it. A dozen rowing strokes in, they abandoned the craft to trek the rest of the way on foot. As they neared the mostly-submerged corpse, Atreus picked out various rectangular-shaped silhouettes under the ice jutting out beneath the giant's palm.

"Oh no, it looks like he fell on a village," the lad said.

"Aye. When Thamur fell, he crushed a charming place famed for worshipping the Vanir god, Njörd. Thor always took credit for planning that one, but the truth is, the sweaty bawbag just got lucky."

"We seek its chisel?" Kratos said.

"We do. The tip of it, more precisely. A very, very large chisel."

They approached a hut still standing close to the palm on the frozen beach. Kratos attempted to force the hut door open, but failed.

"Magically sealed, I'm afraid," Mimir said.

Finding a long, curled rope beside the hut, they located a partially collapsed building under the giant's palm, using the rope to descend into it. Their first objective was to locate the chisel, presumably under the ice. "What happened to the survivors?" Atreus asked, while surveying the surroundings.

"Thamur was a frost giant. When he died, his final breath froze everything. Everything."

Using another nearby rope, they ascended back to the edge of the frozen lake. They could make out the outline of the stonemason's giant head under the ice. The chisel they sought was buried in the head. It had cleaved his skull and was now set deep in the ice beneath him.

"There it is," Atreus whispered.

"Locate the tip of that chisel. That's the magic we need," Mimir said.

As they worked their way closer, the chisel's magical tip became visible, separated from them by many feet of solid ice. Kratos and Atreus knelt on the lake for many long moments to appraise the situation more closely.

"How are we getting down there?" Atreus pondered aloud.

Kratos scanned their surroundings.

"I have a plan," Kratos announced.

"You do?" Mimir and Atreus chorused.

"Why do you act so surprised?" Kratos grumbled, a frown furling his brow.

"No offense, brother, but I do not even think Thor with Mjölnir in hand could get through this much ice."

"Then Thor is a fool," Kratos said.

"Oh. This should be entertaining."

Suddenly, the yowling of Wulvers rang out.

"Boy," Kratos said, a single word; all that was needed.

"Ready," Atreus replied, nocking a feathered shaft into his bow.

A tight pack of five Wulvers attacked. Atreus' first shot took out the lead. As they came in range, Kratos cleaved two in rapid succession. Atreus' next arrow took down the Wulver nearest his father. A flurry of well-timed and expertly aimed slashes slaughtered the remaining beast.

Atreus' gaze left the bodies to track along a snowy rock ledge to a rise fifty paces distant. Sindri waved from atop it.

"Is that Sindri? Is he following us? We should ask him to help," Atreus asked.

"We have no time now," Kratos said, shaking his head. The last thing he wanted was further delay caused by a dwarf. Kratos steered Atreus in the direction of a vaulted circular building, with the hammer sticking out the top of it.

"Sindri, what are you doing here?" Atreus called out.

"Looking for skap slag."

"What?"

"What are you doing here?" Sindri called.

"The chisel," Atreus called.

Sindri indicated he had failed to hear him.

"Never mind. We keep moving," Kratos said.

"Mimir, you knew this place? Before?" Atreus asked.

"Came here on a diplomatic mission once, trying to broker peace between Asgard and Vanaheim. That war... So many lives lost. What I didn't know was Thor had already gone on a killing spree of giants."

"What did the giants have to do with the war between the gods?"

"Nothing at all, lad; that is the tragedy of it. They took no side in that madness... But Odin's paranoia and his viciousness are surpassed only by Thor's lust for blood."

They entered the building, where they began ascending the shaft of Thamur's hammer coming out of the ice.

"Why are we going up, when what we need is all the way down there?" Atreus asked.

"Think," Kratos responded simply.

"Well, the chisel tip is under thick layers of ice, so melting it won't work."

"Correct."

"That just leaves smashing through the ice. But we would need something heavy to… Oh, now I get it."

"Good," his father said with a glimmer of a smile.

Nearing the top of the hammer, Atreus realized his father intended to use the falling hammer to smash the ice, if they could only control the fall to make it hit directly over the chisel.

"But how do we turn the hammer so it lands where we want it to?" Atreus asked.

"Not possible. We cut it free, ride it down, and figure out what comes after."

"So your plan involves a whole bunch of luck then," Atreus said.

"You are welcome to suggest a different one."

Reaching the hammer's head, they examined the lashings of leather straps securing the head to the shaft.

"Hold tight," Kratos said. Slashing the straps caused the hammer to come loose and shift. It toppled but failed to fall all the way to the ice, instead lodging against a nearby snowbound ridge alongside the building.

"Uh. This plan seems ill-advised," Mimir said.

"Quiet, head," Kratos grumbled.

Slashing another strap allowed the hammer to shift and fall further—just not far enough. Now it crashed halfway through the building's vaulted roof, with Kratos and Atreus jumping off to land beside it.

"That didn't work. It only fell a little way," Atreus said.

Kratos pushed the giant hammer. A moment later, Atreus joined him. It broke free and began sliding in through the hole.

"How are we getting back down?" Atreus asked.

"Jump." Kratos grabbed the boy before leaping onto the hammer. Lying flat against the metal, they rode it down.

"Do not panic!" Kratos instructed his son.

"Why should I panic?" Atreus called back.

Then he spied their landing site. Fear tightened around Atreus' heart so much that his grip on the hammer faltered. Kratos shot an arm out to catch him before the lad fell away from the stone. Landing in a booming explosion of ice and stone, they came to rest in a narrow-angled pocket beneath a dome of ice debris. Kratos shifted his body to shield his son as ice chunks rained from the ceiling.

"You truly are cracked, you know that?" Mimir said. "You are well?" he directed to the boy.

"Wow, can we do that again?" Atreus responded, after realizing he had safely made the drop.

"We need to keep moving."

Leaving the collapsed space, they discovered a split had opened up in the lake, revealing a crevasse zigzagging to the giant's skull and their end goal—the chisel.

"The chisel tip," Kratos said, pointing and gloating over his handiwork.

"I give you due credit. You do have a talent for destroying things," Mimir replied.

"Remember that, head."

"Never leaves my mind, actually." Mimir allowed a sneer to cross his face. Luckily, his face was out of Kratos' line of sight.

"Look out!" Atreus shouted.

To avoid ice chunks that were caving into the crevasse, Kratos and Atreus jumped across the opening to a rock handhold, where they began climbing around old frozen city structures. A deafening thunderclap forced a monstrous chunk of ice to separate from the side, altering the path through the chasm.

"Where are they?" a voice wavered to them in the cold air.

"Magni," Mimir whispered. That single word choked off his breathing.

CHAPTER 34

"I fucking hate Midgard," another voice said. "How do we even know they're here?"

"You think that hammer fell on its own?" Magni, the taller and more muscular of the brothers, said. Both Odin sycophants wore full rubiginous beards and wielded broadswords.

"We find them, the kid is mine, right?" Modi queried a moment later, his face lighting up at the very thought of the potential carnage.

"What is the matter with you?" Magni said. Inhaling deeply, he filled his lungs to capacity with the biting air. "I smell a dwarf. You smell a dwarf? Let's go hack up the little shit."

Their voices trailed off as they seemingly progressed away from Kratos and the boy, who remained perfectly still. The last thing they wanted was another fight. *Just get the chisel tip and get clear of those two*, Kratos reminded himself.

"Stay quiet," he said.

Resuming their climb out of the crevasse once they felt certain the danger had passed, they leapt onto a small ledge. Returning to their feet, Magni and Modi stood less than fifty paces upwind. Kratos had mistakenly concluded the two men had wandered away, but they hadn't, they had just gone silent.

Drawing swords, a swaggering Magni and jittery Modi charged Kratos, while Atreus drew his bow and nocked an arrow. His first shot zipped high and wide of Magni, which only brought out a wolfish grin. Kratos parried wildly to keep the brothers from launching any semblance of a coordinated attack. The brothers, realizing the unstable ground beneath them might fail to support their fight, retreated quickly to regroup on the other side of an icy ridge.

"They're running!" Atreus called. "Do we go after them?"

Kratos climbed to higher ground, heading directly away from where the brothers had disappeared.

"That would be a no," the lad concluded. He then asked Mimir, "Those were the men threatening you on the mountain?"

"Aye. Magni and Modi, sons of Thor. Be wary of those two, desperate to impress their da. They are far more powerful and more dangerous than they appear."

"Mother always said the Aesir were the worst gods, and Thor was the worst of the Aesir. Guess he's a terrible father as well," Atreus said.

"They are no longer children. They have no excuse," Kratos said.

Just as Atreus and Kratos crested the ridge, the path behind them completely collapsed, toppling them through the roof of a spacious vaulted room with a large dining table, which Mimir immediately recognized.

"Ah, the great dining hall. Envy of all Midgard. Funny, I remember there being a massive candelabrum adorning the table. Really livened up the place."

Kratos scanned the space.

"If memory serves, the Jarl's throne was just on the other side of that wall of ice," Mimir said.

Kratos hacked into the wall until he created a hole large enough to peer through.

"I see a throne. I think we can get through there," Atreus said.

A few more powerful hacks and the wall split open enough for them to climb through. Atreus immediately went to the runes scrawled on the wall behind the throne.

"I think this is Njörd's own mark. The god they worshipped came to dinner?" he said.

"Sounds like Njörd to me. Affable fellow, formidable drinker. The Vanir always were a more personable sort of god than the Aesir."

As they made their way out of the chamber, voices echoed off the crevasse walls, making it impossible to discern the exact direction from which they came.

"We should've stayed and fought them right there," Modi harped.

"We fight on our terms. We needed better footing," Magni shot back, trying to act as the voice of reason.

"Is that what you tell yourself, you spineless weasel?"

"Shh! You hear something?"

Kratos and Atreus skulked around a corner into the ruins of an ornately carved domed rotunda. Across the expanse, the vital chisel tip glowed in a chunk of ice larger than Kratos.

"Enough. Uncle said to bring them back alive. We can't just attack without figuring out how we—" Magni said.

"Uncle said? Uncle said. Then why isn't he here? It is because he *wants* us to fa—" Modi stopped.

"*They're here*," Magni declared.

"Hurry, brother, we need to get a piece of that chisel and be gone before they spot us," urged Mimir.

Kratos and Atreus had advanced no more than a half-dozen strides when a hulking ogre dropped down from the rotunda dome to block their path. Magni, covered in speckled ogre blood, rode its back with a wide grin across his face.

"Too late," Mimir said, catching only a glimpse of the desperate scene from his position on Kratos' belt. His eye swiveled frantically from side to side.

With a sickening crack, Magni wrenched the ogre's neck to kill him dead where he landed.

Jumping off, he planted his feet in a fighting stance, fixed on Kratos. His smile faded. Hatred took over his stare.

"You're next," he said bluntly.

From a ledge on the other side of the chamber, Modi dropped into the rotunda to join his brother.

Hoisting the ogre's limp body overhead, Magni heaved it out of the way.

"Surrender!" Modi demanded.

"The Allfather demands it," Magni added, his vicious stare all-consuming.

"Never," Kratos shouted, with raging fire in his voice. He tightened his grip on his axe, widened his stance, and braced to take on both demigods himself. He had witnessed the one brother's strength, but had yet to determine just how powerful the other might be.

"This fight is mine alone, boy. Go," Kratos ordered.

Atreus attempted to flee, but before he could advance three strides, Modi shifted his charge, cutting the boy off. There would be no escape.

"Where you think you're goin', you little cretin worm?" Modi sneered, with a vicious gap-toothed smile. "Look, brother, the little shit's got a bow. What are we gonna do?"

Kratos juggled his fight between the two demigods, alternating blows back and forth to keep both men at bay. Magni focused his assault on Kratos, while Modi seemed intent on hounding the boy, who was raining hastily-aimed errant arrows his way.

"Come 'ere, half-breed. You're done holding your father's hand," Modi goaded.

Kratos worked to fight Modi off, but the demigod, with sword clutched in both hands, delivered a flurry of well-placed vicious parries, effective against the God of War's assault. Following up with repeated fierce jabs kept Kratos at bay. Each time Kratos focused his attention on Magni, Modi renewed his charge at the boy.

"Look at you, all weak and half-formed. How did you manage to crawl out of your crib?" Modi chided.

"Shut up!" Atreus yelled.

"Ha! Those skinny little arms can barely draw back your flimsy bow."

"I said shut up!"

"Calm yourself, boy," Kratos warned.

Modi only laughed, inching closer to the lad, waving his blade menacingly.

"Why do you hunt us?" Kratos gasped between cuts of his axe, returning his fight to Magni.

"Don't know. Don't care," Magni replied.

"Hey, boy, your mother must be some whore to lie with the likes of him," Modi jabbed.

Fear, anger, and despair all collided in an explosion of emotion in Atreus' brain. Discarding his bow, he charged Modi with his hunting knife, snarling like a crazed animal.

"I *will* kill you!" he yelled.

"Control, boy!" Kratos shouted.

Atreus' unexpectedly foolish charge captured Magni's attention, but only for a moment. And in that unguarded moment, Kratos caught the demigod with a hew of his axe. The blade sliced effortlessly through Magni's neck, the screech of his death wail ripping into his brother's ears. His body quaked uncontrollably for a few seconds, before collapsing lifeless to the floor.

Modi half turned, frozen in place. A demigod killed by a mortal?

"Magni! No!" he uttered in a panic, retreating. "How did you? You have no idea what—" he screamed at Kratos, while flailing his sword wildly to fend off the God of War. "Who are you, you sonofabitch?"

"You're next," Kratos said calmly, devoid of emotion. His stare turned vacant, soulless.

Unleashing his weapon on a now frightened Modi, Kratos

advanced. Modi's courage, however, evaporated, so he fled. Atreus rapidly fired off a volley of high and wide arrows at the demigod, before Kratos took up the chase.

"Come back, you damn coward! I will rip your head off!" Atreus shouted, his heart pounding out of control, his chest heaving.

Without warning, the lad doubled over, forced to his knees, gasping to breathe. A moment later, he erupted into a coughing fit so brutal that he felt his guts being pulled into his throat. His suffering forced Kratos to abandon any chase and, instead, spin about in time to see his son buckle to the floor. Visibly frustrated, all he could do was watch Modi escape before rushing to his son's side. Atreus continued to cough violently into his hand.

"The sickness… your fever has returned," Kratos said, taking a knee beside the boy.

"No… it… hasn't," Atreus forced out weakly.

Kratos turned Atreus' hand over, to see splattered blood covering the lad's palm.

CHAPTER 35

"I... will be... all... right," Atreus spat between coughs.

"Son," Kratos said. His voice rumbled with frustration, but mostly fear for his child.

Atreus read the dire concern across his father's face. There was more anxiety than he expected to see.

"The coughing, the blood. Your boy is sick. He needs help," Mimir said.

Shaking his head, Atreus brought his coughing under control; he staggered to regain his footing, wobbling like a newborn fawn struggling to its feet for the first time.

"Steady," Kratos said, doubt clouding his response.

Atreus fell, unable to keep his rubbery legs beneath him. Angry, and refusing his father's assistance, he pulled himself erect by sheer force of will. He ventured a few uncertain strides toward the stonemason's chisel, growing steadier with each footfall.

"There you go, lad," Mimir encouraged.

Kratos extended a steadying hand; Atreus shoved it away.

"I am fine. See," he declared. "Let's get what we came for and go."

Unconvinced of his son's state, Kratos unsheathed his Leviathan axe, and turning to face the chisel, he hacked at it with maddening force. The ice cracked and broke away, surrendering the chisel tip, which Kratos tucked away into the sack at his belt.

"What now?" Atreus asked.

"Back to the boat," Kratos said.

"Yes. We must not linger. Magni might have been a minor Aesir, but his father is not. There will be repercussions you do not wish to face."

Kratos, however, remained skeptical. If he had to fight their gods, he knew he could defeat them.

Atreus released a throaty cough, which escalated quickly into moaning.

"I do not think the wee one is doing too well. His face is now the color of your skin," Mimir said.

"I am fine! Nothing to worry about," Atreus growled, still attempting to stifle his cough.

"If you are, then keep up," Kratos said.

"Yes, sir!"

Kratos spotted a way for Atreus to jump onto a ledge to assist them out of the crevasse. "There," he said, pointing.

"I can get it," Atreus said. But he couldn't.

Kratos had to hoist Atreus up. The boy climbed, rolling weakly over the ledge. He slipped, but regained his footing in the next moment before managing to pull himself over completely.

They wound their way around the giant's corpse and over the frozen lake to reach the boat. Atreus appeared exhausted and weak. He collapsed when he attempted to climb in, rocking the boat. Slowly, he crawled to his position in the center, where he slumped, head lowered, with his elbows resting on his knees.

"Is it colder than it should be?" the lad said, his voice growing frail.

He began shivering uncontrollably.

"Hurry, we need to get him back to the warmer air," Mimir said.

Kratos had already determined that on his own.

"What now? Maybe Freya ought to have a look at the boy," Mimir suggested.

"There must be another way," Kratos said.

"Anyone else I know who is capable of helping will refuse. In fact, they will try to kill us. No, he needs Freya. And look at him, brother, we are running out of time. You will lose him if we do not hurry!"

"Freya. Very well then," Kratos conceded. He rowed as fast as he could, consuming every ounce of strength to keep the boat moving at optimum speed.

"I'm sleepy..." Atreus said, unable to lift his head to even look at his father.

"Boy, wake up! You must not sleep," Kratos ordered. He had been in the company of men who fell into their final sleep when ill. "Talk to me to keep me awake."

"Oh. What would you like me to talk about?" Mimir offered.

"Odin. Tell me about Odin. He wants to prevent Ragnarök, right?" Atreus said.

"Odin, the Allfather, and the Lord of the Hanged."

"Why is he called the Lord of the Hanged?" Atreus asked.

"The god is so obsessed with gathering knowledge that he actually hanged himself, so he might enter the realm of the dead to plunder the World Tree for its secrets. I think, and quite rightly, that the realm got so fed up with him that it sent him back to the land of the living. Did I mention he was barking mad?"

"But I don't understand how Odin can prevent Ragnarök, if the World Serpent has already experienced it. Doesn't that mean he has already failed?"

"Fate's a tricky thing. And Odin is just arrogant enough to think he can get the best of it."

"Fate is but another lie told by the gods," Kratos butted in.

"Nothing is written that can't be unwritten. Yeah, I got that already," Mimir finished for him.

Disregarding Kratos' comment, Mimir let slip a smile. Keep the boy engaged, maybe he could keep him awake and alive, at least for the time being.

"Odin seeks to control his future and thereby control his

fate. The god would control all nine realms if he could. Even if Odin cannot prevent Ragnarök, he hopes to acquire enough details to tip its outcome in his favor. Remind me later to tell you about the wolves."

Atreus' eyelids dropped against his will. His breathing slowed to a trickle, indicating that the lad had lost consciousness.

"The boy asked for you to keep him awake," Kratos interrupted.

"Odin's eye is on you, brother. Especially now that you have taken to killing his kin. Freya's forest is a blind spot for him, making it our smartest move. And if anyone can heal him, it is her."

Kratos shifted from rowing to steering the boat toward the shore. In the distance, Freya's cottage appeared out of the trees.

"He's unconscious," Mimir announced. "Boy, wake up!"

Atreus tugged his eyelids up halfway.

"Why did Freya spit in your face?" he asked.

"Oh, that. In an attempt to end the bloodshed between the Aesir and the Vanir, I brokered a peace between the gods. It took some convincing, but ultimately Odin was persuaded to marry his deadliest enemy—Freya. She only agreed as a sacrifice to save her people..." Mimir's voice trailed off.

Atreus flinched, but his head remained slumped, his eyelids closed.

"What happened after that?" he asked.

"Simply put, he won Freya's trust, used her to steal the Vanir magic—then robbed her of her warrior spirit and banished her forever to Midgard. No living thing may she harm, by blade or spell. Should I go on?"

Mimir waited for some indication that Atreus was still with them. None came.

"You will lose him if you do not hurry," Mimir said.

Kratos withdrew the oars from the water just as the boat slammed into the shoreline, lodging itself in the weedy mud.

"I take it this isn't the first time this has happened?" Mimir asked.

Without responding, Kratos leapt from the boat, shifting the craft sideways so he could more easily remove his son.

"Sickness plagued his childhood. We thought it was behind us," he grumbled, while taking Atreus into his arms to press him against his body. The boy's skin felt cold, lifeless.

"And you really have no idea what causes it?"

"No," Kratos snapped, struggling to steady his footing in the marshy ground. The cottage was fifty long strides distant.

"It is possible that a conflict of the mind is expressing itself as an ailment of the body. That would be rare in his case... Hey, you forgettin' something?" Mimir shouted, when he realized Kratos was leaving him behind.

Kratos stopped midstride. He stared back at Mimir's head. If he left it behind, it might be gone when he returned. The God of War scanned the sky for predators, then the surrounding woods. He noticed nothing more than a pair of ravens perched near the canopy of a towering tree. He had no choice but to return the twenty paces back to the boat to collect the head.

Setting Atreus down, Kratos dashed to the boat and secured Mimir to his belt, then, in a graceful swoop, returned Atreus to his arms.

A distant horn warbled through the trees, then a slight rumble followed. Behind them water sloshed, thumping the boat against the shore.

Kratos kicked into a slow run with his son in his arms.

"Somebody just called the serpent," Mimir muttered with an ominous tone.

"Now his fever burns. He is quaking," Kratos said.

"It is serious. I tried to tell you nothing good would come of keeping the boy from his true nature. You will have to tell him. And I do not want to be around when he finds out you have been lying to him his whole life... keeping the most important part of his life secret, ashamed of what he is," Mimir blurted out all at once, to prevent Kratos from interrupting. Then he paused, realizing this moment was possibly the worst time to criticize a god. "I should stop talking now."

"Yes," Kratos agreed.

The God of War halted at the door, cradling his limp child in his arms.

"We'd better hope old Freya is home," Mimir said.

CHAPTER 36

"Witch! Open the door! We need your help!" Kratos yelled. He refused to set Atreus down in order to break down the door.

"Perhaps addressing her by her name, rather than 'witch', might achieve better results?"

Kratos detected shuffling inside the house, despite no response to his call.

"Woman, do you hear me? It is urgent!" he growled.

"I am still a god! Go away and leave me alone," she shouted.

"Freya, it is the boy. He is ill!" Kratos said breathlessly. "I need your help."

The door flew open, banging the side wall. Freya rushed out, immediately laying the back of her hand on the boy's forehead. Then she slid it down to his chest to evaluate his breathing.

"He is ill," Kratos repeated, with a helpless father's desperation. Freya read the sadness on Kratos' face.

"Hurry inside. We have little time if we are to save your son."

Kratos followed her in, setting Atreus onto a braided thatch cot. Freya wasted no time or movement going to work on him.

"We cannot let him die," she muttered, before turning her gaze to the God of War. "This is no ordinary illness. The boy's true nature, your true nature, fights within him."

"I did this to him…" Kratos paused as the truth sank in. "Will you help me?"

"Of course. But I need to think. This illness is more virulent than I would have thought. What is the nature of this thing?"

Freya observed the state of Atreus' eyes, moved next to examine his neck with agile fingers, after which she listened closely to his heart beating in his chest. Her face turned grim, almost angry. What had Kratos done?

She left the lad for a time to pace. Movement stimulated thought, thought led to focused analysis.

Kratos' worried gaze never left the woman, tracking her every move, anxious for her to speak or do something that would help his son.

"Say something!" Kratos snarled.

She had to help him. She had to…

"There is a rare ingredient found only in Helheim. Máttugr Helson."

"What is Máttugr Helson?" Kratos asked.

"Not what. Who. Máttugr Helson is known as Helheim's son. He is the keeper that protects the Bridge of Death… I need his heart if I am to save the boy."

"Are you certain?"

"As certain as I can be at this moment. Do exactly as I command, if you desire your boy to live." Her face soured, as if she were somehow laying blame for Atreus' condition on him.

"Helheim?" Kratos said.

"Yes, the Realm of the Dead. Do you know it?"

"Not this one," Kratos had to confess. Fear wormed its way into his soul.

"It is a land of unyielding cold. Fire will not burn there, magic or otherwise. As for the dead… your frost axe will be useless. You will need something more powerful to achieve what I ask of you."

"Then I fear what I must do," Kratos said, contemplating what was to come. He wished there might be another course of action, but searching Freya's face, fraught with concern, he knew there was to be only one way to save what mattered most in his life right now.

"I know what I must now do."

Freya snared his arm before Kratos could make a move toward the door.

"Who you were does not matter. That boy is not your past. You are his father, and your son needs you now."

Kratos nodded his understanding while Freya took his palm and drew with her fingertip on it. The rune persisted, as if it had been written in blood.

"This rune opens the bridge to Helheim. When you are there, do not under any circumstances cross the Bridge of Death. There is no road back. Understand?"

Kratos nodded. Stirring on his cot, Atreus released a soft moan. Freya crossed to her Norse battle bell to ring it. As she spoke, the mythological creature outside stood up, which caused the house to shudder and rise around them.

"*Heimili!* You must hurry. Through my garden, there's a path leading to my boat. Take it. Do whatever you must. Just bring back Máttugr Helson's heart, and your son may survive."

With a wave of her hand, Freya threw open the rear door, and then began preparing a poultice.

Reaching the door, Kratos lingered, turning back to her.

"When last we spoke… I was…" Kratos started, struggling with words he was unaccustomed to using. Apologies were never part of his vocabulary. Freya remained with her back to him as she busied herself with her preparations, refusing to allow him to finish.

"No. You are wise to distrust the word of a god. No need to explain. Not to me. Not for that," she said. Only then did she face him. "I will keep him safe. I will do everything in my power to keep your son alive. That is a mother's promise."

Kratos needed one last look at his son, wishing he could say something that would make everything right again.

Atreus' skin had become ashen, the color of the dying, his face slack, his eyelids barely open. Voiceless, Kratos left the cottage, determined to return with the crucial heart.

Freya's boat awaited him at the riverbank behind her garden, just as she had said. A primitive but adequate creation, it looked more like a mud slurry in the shape of a boat that had hardened into glass.

"Helheim, of all places," Mimir muttered. "You all right, brother?" he responded to the silence.

"I will do what I must. Leave me be."

"As you wish."

Kratos climbed in and pushed off, steering the small craft into the fast-moving current that would carry the God of War along a shortcut back to his home. He could arrive there in a matter of hours if the current remained strong. Rowing with a grim determination, he cast his gaze to the horizon, where crimson clouds were forming. Their sweeping formation indicated difficulty had positioned itself across his path. A red storm was gathering strength to oppose him. The gods of this land sought to do whatever they could to keep him from saving his son.

Biting rain began to pelt him as the river carried him along. Angry winds whipped the small craft left and right, forcing Kratos to struggle with the oars to keep the boat near the river's center and clear of the dangerous rocky shores.

Kratos refused to allow the elements to sabotage his mission. When he turned back to check his way ahead, the goddess Athena stood behind him in the boat. She appeared more statue than flesh and blood creature, with her sandstone skin emitting a netherworld glow. Her face showed gloating confidence.

The two gods stared at each other in silence. Did she come at this moment to boast? To tell him he would fail? He would not fail!

The fierce wind forced Kratos to turn around to steady his

meager vessel through sloshing waves. After the next wave passed, he turned back. Athena was gone. Kratos shook the rain from his face, believing the goddess was nothing more than a phantom of his tortured mind.

Within another hour, Kratos reached the riverbank near his house, just as the red storm intensified. He leapt from the craft to the shore. The glass boat melted, dissipating into the water as soon as he stepped on land. As if refusing to accept defeat against the God of War, the winds and rain battered him with driving force and angry thunderclaps, while inside him, anger and guilt battered his mind.

"You will not succeed!" the God of War snarled, shaking an angry fist at the gods guilty of this treachery.

He pounded through the mud to reach the door to his home. Throwing it open, he escaped the barrage outside. Quiet and calm enveloped him. Wasting no steps, he dropped to his knees before the bearskin rug. Burying his axe tip into the floor with a quick flick of his wrist, he threw the rug back, tore open the rune-painted trapdoor, and reached in to extract an unblemished oaken box the length of his arms.

CHAPTER 37

*T*he Blades of Chaos.

Kratos stared at them, a whirlwind of terrible memories flooding into his mind.

Locked deep inside of you, Kratos, is hope, a soft feminine voice whispered inside his head, from a life he had buried away so long ago. *Hope is what makes us strong. It is why we are here.*

Jarring memories of his tortured past flashed across his mind: splayed on a stone floor, motionless and bleeding from a self-inflicted wound, Kratos came to realize the gods would never allow him death by his own hand. So, to spite them, he collected up his blades, determined to find a way to free himself of their terrible curse. He watched a veritable menagerie of creatures fall to his indestructible weapons. His existence of relentless killing accumulated a mountain of men who perished needlessly at his hands. Their screams clawed at his imprisoned soul. At first, the God of War tossed the blades from the highest cliff. But a vicious wind swirled the steel upward to deposit them at his feet. The gods, it seemed, had delivered their edict, yet Kratos refused to succumb. Another image played across his mind: he cast the blades into a calm sea. His action induced such rage from the gods that a shipwreck ensued, washing him up upon a black sand beach amid the flotsam. He lifted his head to find his blades leaning against craggy rocks, awaiting his arrival. Despite countless more failed attempts that drove him to the very brink of madness, the gods unfalteringly rejected every desire to be free.

In his final desperate act, Kratos had concealed the blades beneath the floor of his house five decades ago, vowing never to take them up again. They represented the evil that was once the god, an evil that still haunted him to that day. Determined never to return to that life, he had promised himself he would live not for the evil the gods do, but for the good a god could do.

Now the same blades fueled his hope that he might save his son.

He brushed his fingers along the gleaming surface, pausing at the skull face on the hilt. The blades hummed with a power that would never die, never be silenced. They could never be broken or dulled. Thunder reverberated and jagged lightning veins spread across an angry sky as the red storm raged full tilt. It seemed even the gods became aware of what was to come. He gazed at his bandaged forearms—now soaked with blood, never-healing wounds from the chains used to fuse his flesh to his blades. That part of him he had grown to hate now wormed its way back into his tortured soul.

He lifted the blades out, slowly wrapping the chain links over his forearms, wincing from the jolting pain accompanying each coil. A firestorm of conflicting emotions raged inside his brain, more intense than the tumult raging beyond his door. Part of Kratos felt complete; a darker part felt terrified that this return to his old life was not to be a brief detour.

A reflection in a blade seized his heart. He turned. Athena, the one goddess that so tormented his mind, filled the doorway. A fierce lightning flash illuminated her silhouette as she watched him silently with a smug, satisfied smile on her otherwise stone face.

"There is nowhere you can hide, Spartan," she said.

Kratos chose to ignore her, returning to the task of wrapping the chains.

"Place as much distance between you and the truth as you wish. It changes nothing. Pretend to be everything you are not... teacher... husband... father."

The word *father* triggered a fierce snarl from the God of War.

"But the one unavoidable truth you can never escape is that you cannot change. You will always be a monster."

Kratos completed chaining the blades to his arms. His stare held Athena's.

"I know, Athena," he admitted. The shrill screams of those he had killed flooded every corner of his mind. His voice carried no strength, no defiance, only acceptance. Without breaking his stare at the goddess, he fastened the blades securely on his back.

"But I am your monster no longer."

Retrieving the axe from the floor, the God of War holstered it now on his belt, on the side opposite Mimir, before marching for the door, walking through the apparition to dispel the goddess into a cloud of rainy mist.

"I knew it! You're Greek. Suspected it all along."

Kratos glared.

"What? I am familiar with the goddess Athena."

The violent red storm lashed at Kratos as he exited. Surging rain pelted him. Thunderclaps resounded from within angry, churning clouds, accentuated by powerful jagged lightning streaks aimed at the trees near Kratos as he journeyed back to the caldera.

As the storm shook the world around him, all manner of forest creatures prowled for things to kill. Employing his powerful blades with the same efficacy as in his past, Kratos easily dispatched each that chose to attack him.

"Release the worst of your monsters! You will never defeat me," he roared into the storm, his rage pitched by the thought of losing his son.

As if to surrender, the storm diminished by the time Kratos reached the temple, marching past Brok at his workshop. The dwarf glanced up casually at first, but then he did a double-take, salivating when he saw the Blades of Chaos.

"Sweet Nanna's nethers, what are those?" he asked, held transfixed by the sight.

When Kratos slowed, Brok stepped before him, forcing him to stop. The little man circled the God of War, indulging in a more discerning examination of the gleaming steel. The glinting light held him spellbound as he admired the craftsmanship with wonder.

"I have never seen the like... not from any of these realms... That has gotta be a family heirloom," he said, awestruck, his words laced with a metalworker's reverence few others could ever understand.

A cacophony of screams from the dying who had met their fate by those blades ripped through Kratos' mind.

"No. Nor will it ever be," Kratos said, to silence the torment raging within.

"Son, my brother and me created Mjölnir for the big idiot... I know quality. And them... them are special," the little man replied. He scanned beyond Kratos. "Say, where's the little turd?"

"Fallen ill." Kratos' voice cracked.

"No. What happened? Aesir?"

"The fault is mine... and the responsibility to make it right."

Kratos' words struck an uneasy chord. Lost in thought for a moment, Brok nodded, releasing a deep sigh.

"We all gotta take responsibility some time, huh? Say, what can I do to help him? I can do things, you know. You want I should tag along?"

"No."

"Where are you going with them, if I might inquire?"

Prying into the comings and goings of a god was not necessarily the smartest move a dwarf might make.

"Helheim."

"Shiiiit!" Brok returned his interest to the blades.

Kratos remained motionless while Brok accepted the blades to hone their edges with his hammer and file while still chained. When he finished, he returned them.

"You have done well," Kratos said, as a way to thank him.

"A privilege. Say hi to the pimple-flap for me when he's better."

The roads leading back to the caldera proved even more

dangerous than before, with warriors of the Aesir flocking to the area after hearing reports of Baldur and Thor's sons in the area. The foreign magic of the blades, however, did not go unnoticed by them.

Kratos left the Midgard forest, taking the boat back to the caldera. In the dome array at the caldera's center, he discovered the bridge already lined up with Helheim. Referencing the Helheim rune Freya had drawn on his palm, he copied it into the sand bowl, using the Bifröst crystal to light the way across the bridge.

Kratos swallowed any trepidation worming its way into his heart. He tightened his grip on his blades. Only one thing mattered now: his son.

A frigid foreboding miasma awaited him.

"What you are about to do is absolutely insane. Not even Odin can survive this cold, so I hope those blades work."

HELHEIM

CHAPTER 38

As Freya had warned, Helheim proved blisteringly cold, with icy fog permeating the air. The realm existed absent a day or night sky, bound in perpetual darkness, which made observation of their surroundings extremely difficult. Kratos sucked in a frostbitten breath before speaking to Mimir at his belt.

"Freya spoke of a bridge."

"There is not a more inhospitable place than here."

"What do you know of this bridge?"

"The Bridge of the Damned? The dead use it to cross into their permanent home, the *city* of Helheim. The bridge keeper who minds admission, he is the one we want. Just follow this path to the bridge. By the way, there is no avoiding it, or the bridge keeper."

"What exists beyond the bridge? What dangers should I be apprised of?"

"I couldn't tell you," Mimir said.

Kratos busied himself with cataloging every detail of anything observable in their vicinity. He had no inkling of what to expect in this realm.

"You know, I had really hoped I would never see this place again," Mimir added, after a discerning pause.

Kratos shifted the head on his belt before beginning a climb up a rocky slope which, at its crest, revealed a dark, forbidding vista before him. The Bridge of the Damned stretched over a yawning, murky chasm that disappeared into the mist beyond. Dead men marched across, oblivious to Kratos' presence. Some seemed confused, uncertain if they were walking in the right direction.

"These dead... what awaits them in this Hel?" Kratos asked.

"If they pass muster with the bridge keeper, they can cross the Bridge of the Damned into Helheim proper. There, the dead are appraised, sorted, processed, and otherwise put to rest. But judging by the number of dead walking in the wrong direction, the gates of Hel may indeed be closed. We will find out soon enough."

They continued across the bridge against the steady current of dead.

"Oh, this is all wrong. Only the newly dead should be here. There's too many. The gate must be closed... and if the gate is closed, then it's true—Hel is full up. Odin, you old fool, what did you do?"

"This is Odin's doing?"

"It's the only explanation. He always coveted the power of the Valkyries; hoped to control them somehow. I don't know what magicks he tampered with, but if they're out of commission, I'm certain it's down to him. And without the Valkyries to sort and cull the dead, Hel is overwhelmed... and soon Midgard may be as well."

Kratos remained silent while he monitored each of the dead as they passed. He cautiously retarded his pace when he spotted the bridge keeper, a towering horned creature, whose flesh was permanently blue from the terrible cold, standing watch over the parade of dead awaiting their turn to enter. He wrapped three-clawed fingers around a magic totem resting against massive arms.

"The Bridge of the Damned. And there's the keeper, making sure the dead are really dead," Mimir explained in a whisper.

Kratos sized up his prey, who rose taller and stouter than the mountain trolls he had faced in the past. He must take the monster down in short order, as the frigid air would drain him of strength more quickly during a fight. The bridge keeper, being native to this place, would be comfortable with his environment.

They watched the dead soldier at the front of the line advance before the bridge keeper. The entire line shuffled forward behind him. The bridge keeper watched dispassionately as the dead man moved under a spectral lamp. When the lamp changed color, the dead's exterior burned away, leaving behind a persistent glow. The lamp's spectral light then returned to its original color, and the glowing soul proceeded across the bridge. Behind it, the train of dead took a few steps forward, and the process began anew.

"Are you capable of defeating that thing?"

Kratos grunted a response.

"Then just get his heart so we can leave."

"How?"

Mimir pondered for a few moments.

"Start some trouble. You can do that, right?" Mimir smiled.

They advanced, not entirely certain if their meager plan would succeed. Passing under the lanterns spaced at regular intervals along the bridge, Kratos' color appeared different to the dead. Spotting the anomaly, the bridge keeper sprang to life, spinning around to square off against him.

"Here we go!" Mimir said with a hollow voice.

Unleashing the Blades of Chaos, Kratos attacked. The bridge keeper leveled his totem in both hands to fend off the assault, believing the small man would prove nothing more than an easy and pleasant distraction to the monotony of his job. Lunging at the God of War, the beast slashed his totem from side to side, deflecting each strike from the glistening blades.

"Mind your left!" Mimir trembled, referring to the side he was hanging on.

When the bridge keeper raised the totem to smash it down onto Kratos, the God of War slid the blades underneath to rend the bridge keeper's chest, raising the shocked creature off his feet. When Kratos dropped the bridge keeper, the monster's totem sheared in half, hurtling off the bridge. The bridge keeper stared lifelessly at the God of War.

"Good show," Mimir said. "Never doubted you for a moment."

Kratos grunted. In the next second, he mounted the corpse, carving deep into the cavity to pry it open with a sickening crunch. In the distance, across the Bridge of the Damned, the sky behind Kratos turned to fire.

Sheathing his blades, he plunged into the wound with both hands. While Kratos fished amongst the squishing entrails, a swirl of clouds on the horizon formed into an apparition of the Temple of Olympus engulfed in flames.

With a fierce yank, Kratos extricated the steaming heart in a spray of inky blood, which quickly froze in the subzero air, causing the splashes on Kratos' arms to dangle in red icicles. Kratos jumped away from the body, turning back to stare at his gory creation; a flash of remorse crossed his face, and he shook it out of his head. He did what he had to do to save his son.

"Will killing the bridge keeper help the dead leave Midgard?" Kratos asked.

"I don't expect it will. Though I don't suppose it will make things any worse, either. It'll be one less obstacle for the living to reach the inner sanctum of Helheim... but who'd be mad enough to go there?"

"What backlash will come as a result of this?" he said to Mimir.

"You need to see this," Mimir said, instead of answering his question. After packing the heart into a pouch, he held up Mimir's head.

"I have the heart. I need nothing more?"

"You are set. But best not to linger here, yeah?" A silence followed. "Uh, you need to..." Mimir persisted.

An angry lightning bolt sizzled through the frigid air above the bridge, forcing Kratos' attention for the first time to the burning mountaintop temple across the bridge. Above the temple, the fog and clouds swirled to create an eighty-foot bearded face with glowing white eyes of flickering lightning.

"Kratos," the voice bellowed.

"W-who are you?" Mimir stammered.

"Zeus?" Kratos responded, his voice tempered with confusion.

"Zeus?" Mimir repeated, exuding a mixture of shock and surprise.

Kratos gazed in disbelief at the apparition. "My father," he confessed. "How is he here? This is not possible."

"An illusion. Hel tortures its inhabitants with the darkness of their past. We need to focus on getting back to your son."

"The boy must never know what you have seen here."

"No. The boy must know. He can never be whole without the truth."

"You will tell him nothing!"

"Very well."

"What is that place?" Kratos asked, to divert the conversation toward a temple situated on the far side of the bridge.

"Never go there, understand?"

MIDGARD

CHAPTER 39

Entering Freya's cottage, an eerie sensation of déjà vu overwhelmed the God of War. Atreus slept nestled on the thatchwork cot. Freya knelt beside him, applying a moist rag to his forehead as a hearth fire flickered nearby. But in the scene playing across Kratos' grieving mind, his wife Faye knelt in place of Freya. A welcoming warmth spread throughout the room, seeping into Kratos' soul.

"Faye," he muttered on impulse.

"You have it?" Freya asked, hope and excitement filling her voice as she sprang to her feet.

Sadness swarmed Kratos' heart. He held up the leather pouch, bringing his mind back to what was most important at that moment: his son. Freya took it, only to dump the heart into a bubbling cauldron near them. Shimmering blue light emerged in a burst of steam.

Kratos reached out with hesitation, touching his son's forehead with the palm of his hand. "Back of your hand," she corrected.

Kratos corrected his touch, holding it there. "He is still sick?"

Freya poured a steaming ladle full of the concoction into a wooden bowl. "I can break the fever, but to heal…"

"He must know the truth of what he is," Kratos admitted.

"Yes, he must."

"That is not so simple," Kratos countered.

Freya motioned for Kratos' help in sitting the boy up as she readied her remedy. She sat beside Atreus, holding the steaming magic under his face.

"Did I tell you I also have a son? It has been forever since I last saw him. At his birth, the runes foretold a needless death. The babe in my arms was so small, so helpless. I knew right then I would do anything to protect him. No matter the sacrifice..." Her voice trailed off as her own loss flooded her head. "Of course, everything I did was really for me. I put my needs, my fears, ahead of what he needed... and I didn't see his resentment until it was too late. Do not make the same mistake. Have faith in him. I know the truth is not simple, but nothing is, when it involves your child."

Rising, Kratos turned away. "It is a curse. The boy has been cursed," he said plainly.

They waited for any sign that Freya's remedy might be working.

Atreus stirred suddenly.

"Do not leave without me," he muttered, his legs thrashing as if trying to walk from his prone position.

Kratos' tone softened instantly. "I will not."

"Are you angry?" Atreus asked.

"No," Kratos replied.

Atreus stumbled as he rose from the bed.

"I am better now."

"I see that," Kratos said. "Is he well enough to travel?" he said to Freya.

"For now."

"It will not happen again," Atreus said.

"See that it does not," Kratos offered with a weak smile, the stern words tempered by the tone of a caring father.

Hollow-eyed, Atreus nodded solemnly before going to Freya. "Thank you," he said, hugging her waist. He wished in that moment he could remain with her for eternity.

She brought her hands to his temples, caressing him as if he were her own. The beginnings of an endearing smile flashed across her face. Tears crept in.

Atreus lingered in her embrace, feeling not Freya in his arms, but rather the touch of his mother. If only he could reach out to hold her once more. An unfathomable emptiness consumed his aching soul.

"It was your father who did the heavy lifting. You should stay, though. Recover more fully," she said.

"You have done enough," Kratos was quick to interject. "I will not forget this."

Freya wiped tears from her cheeks, directing her stare at the God of War.

"He will be safe here until he has fully regained his strength," she responded, though her statement lacked insistence. She would never convince Kratos to leave his son behind.

"What is beyond that window?" Atreus asked, indicating the strange view that did not match what existed on the other side of the wall.

"Vanaheim. My home."

"That's Vanaheim?"

"Yes. All I have is that view through a Bifröst crystal."

"We must go," Kratos reiterated.

"What happened to you in Alfheim—that prevents you from traveling to other realms?"

"Yes. My punishment from a cruel husband."

"Time goes short," Kratos said, forcing an end to the exchange. The last thing he wanted at the moment was to spend more time in this place. The sooner they were gone, the better for them.

"My door will always be open to you." Something in her face changed after the words left her lips, her shoulders slumping in regret.

With only unfathomable stares in response, Kratos and Atreus departed the cottage with Freya crowding the doorway. She watched them trek through the forest until they were beyond her view.

241

* * *

"Head, what next?" Kratos asked after they had been walking a while.

"As luck would have it, we are only a stone's throw from our goal: the home of the ancient god Týr. That is where we will find the Black Rune, the lost password that allows us to create a Bifröst bridge into Jötunheim."

"Why did the World Serpent not just tell us the rune?" Kratos asked.

"Because there is no spoken equivalent. We must see the rune if your boy is to learn how to scribe it. Nothing comes easy, does it now?"

"Those blades... where do they come from?" Atreus asked.

"They are from a time before your birth."

"And you do not wish to talk about it."

"No," Kratos said.

Reaching the underground cave beyond Freya's cottage, Kratos pulled the old boat through knee-high mud with Atreus in it.

"You are quiet," Kratos commented. Atreus offered no response.

"Are you not better?"

"I guess," he said.

Kratos continued to drag the boat in silence for a dozen strides.

"I know you overheard my talk with Freya. You think you understand. But you do not."

Silence.

"Why do you say nothing?" Kratos said.

"You said I was cursed. You think I am weak, because I am not like you. I know I was never what you wanted. But after all this, I thought... maybe things were different." He allowed long-buried bitterness to creep into his words. After he had spoken, he regretted the biting inflection in his tone.

"You do not know everything, boy." The harshness in his father's response cut into Atreus.

"No. But at least I know the truth now."

"The truth. You think you know the truth," Kratos snapped, his anger and impatience mounting. An expression of pain flashed across the God of War's face. He knew what he had to do... but he refused to force himself to do it. So much would change if his son knew the truth; so much would have to be dealt with. Their lives could never remain the same.

"The truth," Atreus said.

Kratos needed a deep breath, using the moments it took for the air to slip in and out to reconsider his fragile decision. He studied every nuance of Atreus' face, read into his soul in that instant. Could his son accept and deal with the truth?

"I am a god, boy, from another land, far from here. When I came to these shores, I chose to live as a man. But the truth is... I was born a god. And so were you."

Relief swarmed Kratos' head. He had revealed his deepest secret to his son. He had taken a step which he had thought until now he could avoid. But what came next?

Silence came next.

Atreus stared off into the distance, as if he wished to hide what was running rampant through his mind. All the stories his mother had told him about the gods. They were good, benevolent gods, not monsters. Did she know about his father? If she did, why had she kept it secret from him?

Kratos reached the dock, where he pushed the boat into the water. He watched Atreus, who sat speechless, staring.

"Son?"

Kratos climbed into the boat to sit squarely across from him. "Have you nothing to say?"

"Can I... turn into an animal?" Atreus asked.

Relief flooded the God of War. Kratos was uncertain whether his son actually understood the full gravity of what he had told him. His perception of gods was rooted in his mother's biased teachings, rather than reality. Perhaps he could avoid confronting the ugliness that so cluttered his past life.

"Can you turn into an animal? No... no, I do not think so," Kratos responded.

"I am a *god*," Atreus muttered to himself. "Mother knew? She was a god, too?"

"No, your mother was not, but she knew of my true nature."

"I am a god. Why did you wait so long to tell me?"

"I hoped to spare you. Being a god... can be a lifetime of anguish and tragedy. That is the curse."

Atreus nodded, understanding now why his father felt he had been cursed. "What sorts of things can I do? Can I fly? Turn invisible? I don't feel like a god."

"I do not know the reach of your godhood, but over time, we will learn."

Breathing easy, Kratos settled back, took up his oar, and used it to push off from the dock.

"You're sure I cannot turn into a wolf?"

"You are welcome to surprise me..."

Kratos rowed, the creaking oars the only sounds, as he watched Atreus come to grips with his new identity. His young face bounced between elation and consternation. Kratos could only wonder what thoughts ricocheted about his mind.

"Is that why I hear voices inside my head?"

"Every god is unique. As you grow, your capabilities will become clear," Mimir said.

"Wait. If I am a god, how come I get sick? Gods do not ever get sick, do they?" he asked.

Kratos had no answer.

CHAPTER 40

Leaving the boat, they crossed the bridge toward Týr's temple. They reached a platform beside the dome temple, which began a slow descent the moment they stepped onto it, stopping at a position that allowed temple access.

"Look, do not be mad, but I have seen those blades before. I saw them when I was hiding under the house. Where did they come from?"

"They are my burden. From a life left behind me."

"They are in my life too, now, and I would like to hear that story."

"Those days are dead. To relive them is… needless."

"How can it be needless if it is the truth?"

"Er, laddie, up on the wall there," Mimir interjected, in an attempt to change the conversation.

Two panels from a triptych of panels hung on the wall, illustrating a god being attended to by a small group of peasant people.

"It is Týr! But… the middle panel is missing. Wait, I thought Týr was a god, not a giant," Atreus said.

"Aye, you are right. But Týr was loved by everyone, including the giants. Other than me, he was the only one they gifted with their special sight."

"I wonder if the giants left a triptych about me somewhere

too?" Mimir added, after pausing to reflect.

Then he returned his attention to the triptych before them.

"Aye. A god of war... but one who fought for peace. He had a reputation for being heroic and lawful, using his power and knowledge to stop wars, rather than start them."

"So then there *are* good gods."

"All gods choose to either serve themselves or serve others. Týr chose the latter," Mimir said. The platform lowered to a second runic panel, which Atreus ran to.

"This one mentions places I have never even heard of. Seems Týr really liked to travel," Atreus said.

"Týr believed the mind, not might, was the key to preventing war and chaos. And he also knew visiting other cultures would give him a perspective that staying in one place could not. While Odin always hoarded knowledge, guarding it jealously, Týr openly shared his learning and wisdom. For this, mortals adored Týr, showing their love by bringing him gifts from the world over."

The platform reached a third runic panel showing Odin and Thor at the center of a dais, presiding over Týr, who stood before them with his head hung. Atreus scanned it for a second, then turned back to Mimir still hanging at his father's belt.

"So whatever happened to Týr?"

"Odin came to power, regarding Týr as a threat to his rule. He suspected Týr of collaborating with the giants instead of helping to steal their secrets. Something he accused me of, though in Týr's case, I believe he was right."

"So you think Týr was helping the giants?"

"I do. He felt responsible for the suffering visited upon them by Odin. I suspect he had something to do with helping them cover their tracks."

"The missing Jötunheim tower!"

"Correct. Whatever happened to it, I believe it could only have been done with Týr and the giants working together."

"But why did Týr feel responsible?"

"Odin deceived him into believing he wanted peace, so

Týr brought Odin to Jötunheim to negotiate. The giants saw through it, and banned Odin from their realm. That's when Thor began using Mjölnir to wipe them out, and they retreated from Midgard. No man nor god has set foot in Jötunheim since."

The platform stopped, allowing Kratos to move toward a set of doors. "Where is this Black Rune, head?"

"Don't know. I've never been in here."

As the doors swung open, they spied down the hallway before them a black stone dangling from the ceiling in the center of a majestic room.

"The stone! That has to be it!" Atreus said.

As they approached the stone, a spherical barrier formed around it, encasing it within three swirling, ornate metal rings, as the entire array rose into the air.

"Naturally," Atreus said, exasperated.

Then a hand appeared out of the hole in the floor that the rings rose out of. It planted itself on the stone, waiting for the other hand to appear. A draugr head followed. As the creature slithered out of the hole, another followed immediately behind, moving with more urgency. Three more draugr followed.

Kratos attacked without a moment's hesitation. A dozen mighty slashes of his axe left mangled corpses littering the floor.

"Did not think it would be that easy?" Mimir said.

"No," Atreus agreed. "Was kind of hoping, though," he muttered under his breath. "So what now?" he asked his father.

Kratos strayed to an alcove containing a statue of a mountain troll.

"The Stonebeard King," Mimir said.

"A king?" Atreus asked.

"Only because he proclaimed himself king and no other troll could defeat him."

A narrow passage forced Kratos to sidestep along its length, with Atreus leading the way through. He held his hunting knife out before him just in case they encountered anything, knowing his father was incapable of defending them in such constricted confines. A treasure room filled with an array of artifacts from across the known world greeted them on their exit from the passage.

"Wow," Atreus muttered, taking in the gold, silver, and precious gems. He had never seen such a display of opulence. His life had been simple and unadorned. He had no idea such treasures even existed. Even his mother had never spoken of such things.

On a nearby table, littered with plumed helmets and shining armor plates, something stole his attention.

"Look at that!"

While he raced over to examine it more closely, Kratos crossed to another table, scanning for anything useful. He examined a rotund bottle briefly, discarding it over his shoulder to shatter on the floor. A tall, slender vase next to it suffered the same fate. Spying a clay flask with distinctively familiar markings, he snatched it up, removing the cork to smell it. A slight smile crossed his face. He jammed the cork back in before stashing it in his pouch.

Then his smile faded.

Two Greek vases sat on twin pedestals, illustrated in the silhouetted black-figure style of Greek antiquity. The first depicted a Greece in ruins being rebuilt. The second illustrated a Spartan warrior, standing atop a tall mound of mangled bodies.

Moving closer, Kratos picked out the pale skin against the telltale scarlet slashes of his tattoos. He was the Champion of Athena depicted on the vase, screaming in rage at the heavens. Kratos stared at the vessel with a haunted face. At that time he had been feared and hated in his land, and he had accomplished feats that were the envy of all the gods, yet they portrayed him to the world as a monster.

Unaware of exactly what was consuming his father's intense concentration, Atreus approached from behind, an ornate pharaoh's crown wobbling on his head with each step.

"What did you find?"

With a sweeping hand, Kratos slammed the vases into a thousand pieces on the floor before his son could see them. He wanted no questions about that world he'd left behind. How could he possibly explain the scene they depicted on the pottery? What could he possibly say that might nullify the savagery meant to endure in clay forever?

"What was that?" Atreus said, reading the emptiness haunting his father's expression.

CHAPTER 41

Leaving the treasure room, they progressed to another large, circular room. On the opposite wall, a massive mural of two wolves perched on a rock outcropping amidst a dense forest snared their attention.

"It's the wolf giants, Sköll and Hati," Atreus pointed out.

Kratos stared at the beasts with a shiver of recognition. The image of him dressed in his Greek attire, being dragged by a verdant-eyed black wolf while the others flanked either side, flashed like lightning across his mind. Were those the creatures that had brought him to this land? He could not recall them being that large. The beasts that attacked him had determined his fate against his will. But for what purpose? Why was *he* meant to be in this land?

"That is correct, lad, the bringers of day and night. It is prophesied Ragnarök begins when they catch the sun and the moon. And Odin controls them. He believes by controlling the wolves, he can control the timetable for the ultimate battle, a battle he hopes to win."

They continued through the room.

"Don't you enjoy it at all? Being a god? Out on an adventure in some amazing place? Maybe Mother wanted us to have a little fun. Everything we've seen and done. Maybe it was her gift?" Atreus said, with embarrassment tingeing his cheeks.

At last, Kratos and Atreus breached the inner chamber deep within Týr's temple. Once inside, however, the door slammed shut, sealing them in.

"This can't be good," Mimir muttered.

Kratos made his way across the room to a wheel crank he suspected was necessary to force the doors back open.

"Wait. Look, the runestone is coming down," Atreus said.

When the rings spinning about the runestone reached the floor, a wrist trap clamped shut on Kratos' hands, locking him in place on the wheel crank.

"What's going on?" Atreus called to his father.

"A trap," Kratos said, yanking on the clamps to try to break free.

The floor beneath him began to sink, while bursts of water sprayed him from pipes in the floor.

"Father!" Atreus screamed.

Frothing water churned in, pooling at Kratos' feet, with him still trapped on the crank. "Boy, get out of here."

"I am fine. How do we get you out?" Atreus shouted.

"Pull chains, there on that wall."

"But... there are three of them. What do I do?"

"Atreus, focus. You can do this."

"Please hurry, lad, I don't know yet if I can drown. And I'd rather not find out," Mimir said.

"Okay... think. Hati's the silver one. He hunts the moon. Sköll is gold and chases the sun. For Ragnarök to happen, they have to eat them. But these are out of order."

"Good, boy," Kratos said in encouragement, while the water level crept up his legs.

"So the moon goes on the left, sun on the right, with Midgard in the middle. But which chain do I pull?"

Atreus could consume no more precious time analyzing. He pulled the chains in left to right order. Nothing. Then he tried right to left, to no avail. On this third try, he progressed from the center chain to the left chain, followed by the right chain. Success! The water began to drain as the platform rose, but Kratos remained locked to the wheel.

"We did it!" Atreus cried.

"Almost," Mimir said.

The lad's excitement turned to horror when the platform beneath his father continued to rise toward spikes, which simultaneously began descending from the ceiling.

"Father, above you!"

Frantically, Atreus searched for some way to save his father. Seeing nothing he could use, he unsheathed his mother's knife, dashing over to the rotating mechanism to jam the blade into it. A moment later, the blade snapped and the mechanism continued to turn. There was a gut-wrenching moment when Atreus was out of options, before a shard of the knife wedged in the gears, forcing the mechanism to stop.

"Her knife?" Kratos said.

"There was no other way." Sadness crushed Atreus' heart. It was all he had left from his mother.

"That was cunning, boy," Mimir said.

"Except I ruined it."

"Saving my life," Kratos added. He gazed at his son.

Atreus nodded, coming to terms with what he had done. His expression, however, changed to alarm when he suddenly noticed Kratos' neck.

"The rune Freya drew on you is gone."

"Is it?" Kratos said, unconcerned.

"What do we do?" Atreus asked.

"We keep going."

After working Kratos' hands free of the crank, they moved on to an iron gate. With three mighty axe swings, Kratos destroyed the grating, which allowed them to escape the room. Reaching the main balcony, they witnessed the rings receding to reveal the Black Rune.

"The rune is free," Atreus said.

Kratos spun his son around, kneeling before him. "Take this." Holding out his open palm, he offered Atreus another hunting knife, this one with Greek engravings on the hilt.

Atreus hesitated, but then wrapped his trembling fingers cautiously around the handle. Kratos closed his hand over his son's—gripping it tightly—then he curled his other hand around both. Pulling their hands up between them, he drew Atreus close.

"The day of your birth, I made two knives, mixing metals from my home and this land. One was for me, and, when you were ready, the other for you," he said. He released his fingers, leaving Atreus holding the knife. The lad turned it over, admiring the exquisite craftsmanship.

"Today is that day."

"So I am a man now, like you?"

"No. We are not men. We are far more, which makes our responsibility far greater," his father corrected. Could the boy even comprehend what that meant? "And you must be better than me. Understand?"

Atreus stared at the knife, then at his father. He nodded absently. "Say it," Kratos demanded.

"I will be better."

Kratos, unconvinced his message had sunk in, placed a reassuring hand on the boy's shoulder. "The power of this weapon, of any weapon, comes from here." Kratos indicated the boy's heart. "But only when tempered by this," he added, indicating Atreus' head. "By the discipline and the self-control of the one who wields it. That is where the true strength of a warrior lies. You must never forget that."

Atreus nodded.

"Good. Come."

They continued on their way, plunging deeper into the temple until they reached a sealed vault, where Kratos discovered the Black Rune inside a glass orb. The sacred rune was etched on an obsidian tablet in the orb suspended from the ceiling. Behind it loomed the stone statue of an ancient mountain troll, whose curled horns on the sides of its head angled away from its cheeks. Massive stone hands supported stone pillars.

Using his axe, Kratos brought the glass orb crashing to the floor.

CHAPTER 42

With a growl, Kratos smashed the Black Rune orb open. The glass shield protecting the tablet shattered into a thousand fine shards. Carefully reaching between the shards, Kratos extracted the tablet. Finding nothing on it, he handed it to Atreus.

"Blank," Kratos muttered, his mind mired in confusion. How were they to get the Black Rune they needed so badly?

"Wait," Atreus said.

The tablet began emitting a flickering glow. The light intensified into a magical crescendo under the boy's touch. Then a brilliant flash filled the room, followed by a concussive air burst, as glowing light radiated.

An ancient symbol flickered across the tablet, then faded. But as it did, the light seemed to penetrate Atreus' skin—spider-webbing up his arms into his chest.

In the next moment, the stone troll burst into life. "Boy!" Kratos cried out.

A huge fist swooped toward Atreus, who stood staring trance-like at the blank tablet.

Kratos surged forward to intercept the powerful punch. Shielding his son and the tablet, the God of War took the full brunt of the troll's attack, which drove him to one knee. He barked angry commands, while preventing the troll's fist from crushing them both.

"Did you see it?" Kratos asked.

"Yes!" Atreus shouted.

"Are you certain?"

"Positive. It is in here!" Atreus pointed to his head.

"Good. Then aim for the face!" Kratos replied over his shoulder.

Atreus removed his bow and notched an arrow, while his father fought to keep from being crushed. The lad realized there was only one way to stop the troll in time to save his father. He took steady aim, watched that the tip of his shaft held true, and fired. The arrow pierced the troll's left eye, forcing it to reel back. The retreat allowed Kratos to pull his blades and attack while the troll struggled to maintain its balance. Slashing left to right, Kratos gashed the troll's neck just below the head. The monstrous creature dropped to its knees, staring not at Kratos but at the boy as it toppled face-first onto the stone floor.

The stone troll defeated, Kratos and Atreus left the vault chamber, following the only path ahead. Soon they reached what appeared to be a dead end—a circular room hanging from an ancient chain-pulley system. A pool of sunlight illuminated the center of the floor. There, the torso of a twenty-foot broken statue of Týr lay on its back, the legs and the foundation positioned nearby, severed at the knees.

Atreus stepped into the sunlight to peer up a tall chimney-like shaft that stretched all the way to the surface. Suspension chains attached to a counterweight ran the length of the shaft.

"Sunlight," Atreus said.

"Our way out," Kratos said.

Using his axe, Kratos broke through the support holding the counterweight in place, which caused the entire room to slowly rise in the shaft like an enormous elevator.

"We are so close to the end," Atreus said.

"Sit," Kratos commanded.

They were safe, and had nothing to do but wait for the elevator to deliver them back to the sunlight.

"Why?" Atreus asked, then reading his father's expression, he complied. Kratos lowered to sit across from him. Reaching into his bag, he withdrew the horn flask he had pilfered from the treasure room.

"Lemnian wine. From the island of Lemnos, near my place of birth," he said.

Atreus drew closer. His father rarely spoke about his life. There was so much Atreus wished to know. But he held his questions in check, fearing they might only induce his father's silence.

"Lemnos," Atreus said, relishing the sound of a Greek word rolling off his Norse tongue.

Using his teeth, Kratos pulled the pine-resin stopper from the flask before handing it to the boy. "To our journey's end."

Atreus brought the flask to his lips, hesitating after sniffing the foul odor wafting from the opening.

"Smells like rotten egg. You sure this is still good?"

"Possibly."

Breathing only through his mouth, he risked a small drop on his tongue. His face immediately contorted while he choked it down. But he had to swallow; a true man would knock back a generous drink. Keeping the liquid down, he returned the horn flask.

Kratos drained what remained in the flask without breaking eye contact. Then, with a face as hard as stone, he tossed the flask over his shoulder. Only then did he crack a smile for his son.

Atreus smiled in kind, still uncertain if he was going to be able to keep the liquid from coming back up.

They sat, staring at dusty rays of sunlight streaming in. There was so much Atreus wanted to say. He had never felt this awkward around his mother. She always knew how to talk to him.

"I don't want to forget anything about her," Atreus muttered, with a sadness that consumed his face and his heart. Inside he was angry for feeling the way he did, angry for saying what he said. How was he supposed to act as a god? Should he even feel things for people? He wondered if that was why his father seemed angry all the time. Maybe a god feeling anything for mortals was forbidden, or at the very least, frowned upon.

Atreus looked to his father, hoping for some acknowledgement for his feelings. Kratos merely nodded before casting his gaze back toward the sunlight.

"Why did you leave your home to come to this land? Does it have to do with the other gods there?"

Kratos gave no answer. It was the best he could offer under the circumstances. He had faced so much death, and so much pain, that he no longer even knew how to deal with it.

"Týr proves there are good gods. You are a good god, right? You only kill those who are deserving."

A sudden avalanche of violent images roiled across Kratos' mind: scores of men fell without mercy to his blades. His face, however, remained stoic, unreadable.

"Ah, but who shall be deemed worthy enough to judge?" Mimir interjected.

"Quiet, head. We are," Atreus fired back.

"Now you sound like your da," came Mimir's rebuttal.

A moment later, they cleared the top of the shaft to find themselves looking down the caldera bridge. In the distance, Peak's Pass beckoned them.

"Ready?" Kratos asked.

"Ready," Atreus said with a confident nod. Time to act like a god.

CHAPTER 43

"Okay, we have the chisel, we have the rune. Can we go see the giants now?" Atreus asked, pulling up Mimir's head.

"Aye. Head back to the peak where you found me, and we will open the bridge."

"We go where we want, we do what we want, and now we're gonna go see the giants! Nobody is getting in our way this time," Atreus said.

They continued, Kratos becoming more vigilant with each passing stride. Something felt wrong around them. He could sense it, yet could not identify exactly what was niggling at him.

"Do you realize we will be the first gods to set foot in the land of the giants since Odin and Týr? That makes us important! But... what if we get to Jötunheim and there are no giants there either?" Atreus asked.

"Makes little difference to us. Fulfilling your mother's wish is what is important."

Silence returned for a time. Kratos was still uneasy about their surroundings as they progressed steadily upward toward the Midgard peak.

"Why don't you let me carry her from here?"

Kratos continued without even acknowledging the request.

"No," he announced finally, delivering his response

with such a sharp bite that it was meant to shut down any further requests.

"Why not? We are almost there. And after all we've been through, you must believe I can handle it."

A silent Kratos refused to even look at him.

"Fine. Carry her yourself," said Atreus.

The words cut deep into Kratos' heart. Ruminating, Atreus continued in silence.

Kratos accelerated to gain a few strides over his son, remaining silent.

At a turn in the worn path through overarching branches of elm and willow, they abruptly stopped. Modi wobbled near a deep chasm that flanked their right, except he was barely recognizable beneath bruises and blood.

Hunched over and limping with the aid of his sword, Modi approached. Through battered, swollen lips and labored breath, he did his best to force out his words.

"Thor... Thor blamed me... me, for what you did to Magni. My own father called me a coward."

"Appears he did more than that. Move away, or we take up where he left off," Kratos commanded, with no sympathy for the demigod.

"I will kill you!" Modi said.

Kratos only laughed when Modi attempted a hobbling step toward the boy. His beaten legs collapsed beneath him before he came within striking range. Helpless, he groaned, a useless heap of beaten flesh upon the cavern floor.

Atreus stepped up to the struggling demigod and, standing with his head held high and legs in a defensive stance, he stared at the pitiful sight. Modi cowered, turning his gaze upwards, his face a display of sadness, desperation, and defeat.

Without so much as a single word, Atreus unsheathed his knife, glanced over his shoulder to his father for permission, then raised the blade.

Kratos seized his son's hand as it reached the apex of its arc.

"No. He is beaten... not worth killing."

"He must pay for what he said about my mother," Atreus seethed.

"I said no!" Kratos barked, with sufficient force to keep his son in check.

He released the boy's arm only when he sensed no downward force applied. Atreus accepted his father's command, for the time being...

"But we are gods. We do whatever we want. We administer the justice for the realm."

The words set Modi chuckling. "That is what I said... to your mother... before I gave it to her."

Kratos reached for his son's arm. He was too late.

"Now you die!" Atreus shouted.

The lad expertly delivered his blade to Modi's throat, watching with delight as dark blood spurted everywhere.

"Boy!"

Kratos yanked him off Modi while Modi gurgled something unintelligible. Drawing in his last breath and ounce of strength, he crawled desperately toward the chasm's edge.

Atreus allowed the swell of his anger to take full control. Without a sound, he tore free from his father, lurching forward to kick Modi clean over the edge and into the darkness below.

"What are you doing?" Kratos said, grabbing his son's shoulders.

With an unnerving calmness, Atreus wiped the blade clean on the leg of his pants before gazing up at his father. There was something unfathomable there. Atreus was no longer the innocent child Kratos had sired.

"Odin's wrath will not be far behind..." Mimir started.

"Enough about Odin and his whole stupid family. Is this not what we are meant to do as gods?" Atreus paused for a contemplative moment. "This is a much better knife than Mother's," Atreus added plainly.

Kratos' gut tightened. What was happening? How could his son have changed so dramatically?

There was no way for him to undo what he had done.

"You killed against my wishes, boy. You lost control."

Atreus stared at him, empty, soulless. The very same expression Kratos had had so many years ago. "I must seek your *permission* to kill? Have you not been teaching me all along to kill as a god? You're a fine teacher for the act of killing."

Kratos dropped to a knee, squeezing his son's shoulders so tightly that it forced Atreus to maintain their eye contact.

"I have been teaching you to survive. We are gods, boy, and that makes us targets. From now until the end of your days, you are marked. So I teach you to kill, yes... but in defense of yourself. Never as an indulgence."

"What about for justice?"

An eerie silence hung between them.

"Nobody cared about him anyways. What is the difference?"

Kratos' heart sank. "There are consequences for killing a god."

"Why should there be? How do you know?" When Kratos didn't reply, he asked again in desperation, "How do you know?"

"Watch your tone, boy. I will not warn you again."

Kratos released his son's shoulders, Atreus rubbing the points where the pressure had been applied. He nodded and then jogged away, leaving his father behind.

Kratos stared as his son ran off, no longer seeing the innocence of a young boy—instead seeing only the worst of himself. The sight crushed his soul. Faye would hate him for eternity for what he had allowed their son to become.

The surrounding trees thinned to wide expanses of thatchy grass when they reached the peak. Kratos' sense for imminent danger flooded his brain. Something was close.

"Caution, boy. If the nephew found us, the uncle cannot be far behind," Kratos said.

"Good! I have a few words for him, too."

"No, you do not, boy. You leave him to me. Do you understand?"

"I can't learn if you won't teach me."

"You do not heed my lessons."

"I have done everything you have asked. And all I wanted was the truth."

No response. The boy was prying into something Kratos refused to accept. Was he afraid that he would revert to that monster Athena had accused him of being? Did he choose evil, or was he forced into it? He thought about his own father. A moment later, he banished the thought. He stared unblinking at his son. What was he really seeing?

"Where did you get those blades?"

Horrible images of the severed limbs, the decapitated heads and the torsos oozing bloody entrails from Kratos' past carnage flashed across his mind.

"Why did you hide them?"

His father refused to acknowledge him.

"Fine," he muttered after a time, then he diverted his attention to Mimir's head. "Mimir, guess what. I know everything I need to know now. I have nothing else to learn."

"Uh? Congratulations?" Mimir said.

CHAPTER 44

Navigating about the summit, a half-dozen draugr emerged from a thicket before them. Atreus' anger intensified; he dispatched his arrows in furious flurries, screaming in a rage, spending less time aiming and more firing, becoming more like the *old* Kratos in the way he dispatched his enemies. Kratos recognized the signs that his son was sliding further down the path he had never intended for him. Was this his destiny? A future unalterable by anything he might try to do?

"Boy, the rune," Kratos said, once the threat had been neutralized.

Atreus jabbed his fingertip with his hunting knife without the slightest flinch. Then, using his own blood, he sketched the Black Rune from memory on the Bifröst henge.

"Carve along that." Atreus indicated where he needed Kratos to carve using the chisel tip. Kratos traced the rune to activate the stone.

Vibrant prismatic light burst in all directions as the Bifröst bridge opened. The brilliant light erupting from the open henge made everything pulse and radiate in an ethereal way.

"This is it. Let's go!" Atreus exclaimed.

They approached the bridge, penetrating the intense energy emanating from its gate, and then backed up, shielding their faces as the gate began to open.

"Wow! Jötunheim. We made it!" Atreus cheered.

"Beautiful, isn't it? Why, I remember once—" Mimir started.

Before he might complete this thought, all color drained from his face. "Brother! Look ou—"

Wham!

Baldur crashed into Kratos from behind, ramming him face-first into the gate's pillar with such force that it cracked the stone. The attack's explosive force threw Atreus off his feet.

Ripping the Leviathan axe from Kratos, Baldur hacked it into the God of War's shoulder. When Kratos reached back for it, Baldur snared his wrist to wrench his arm beneath the axe handle, pinning it in place. Then he grabbed the back of Kratos' head to slam it into the pillar again.

"Miss me?" Baldur asked. A wicked smile contorted his face.

"Run, boy! Cross the bridge!" Kratos yelled.

A hastily aimed arrow pierced Baldur's left cheek, the tip exiting through his right, leaving the shaft dangling in his mouth.

"No! I'm a god, too! I can do this!"

Atreus rapid-fired several more arrows as he advanced toward the fight, striking Baldur in the back and shoulder. Despite the direct hits, none caused any devastating effect.

"Really?" Baldur garbled out of a mouth encumbered by the shaft.

Atreus stopped a dozen paces from his target, leveling an arrow directly at Baldur's temple. "Get off of him!" Atreus ordered.

In a vicious sweeping motion, Baldur backhanded the boy, slamming him to the ground. Then he ripped the arrow from his face with disgust.

"Ouch. He landed kind of awkwardly there," Baldur mocked.

"I will kill you!" Kratos screamed.

"Ah, if only you could."

Kratos grabbed Baldur by the throat, unleashing a flurry of punches. Feeling none of them, Baldur shoved Kratos backward.

An unstable boulder tumbled from above, landing beside Baldur. When another dropped, Baldur grabbed it, smashing it into Kratos' face, stunning him. With Kratos motionless, Baldur seized the opportunity to grab the first boulder, which was sharp at one end, and impale Kratos to the gate pillar. Cracks spider-webbed across the rock.

"Baldur, let 'em go. Take me instead. I will do whatever you—" Mimir pleaded, before getting Baldur's knee in his face.

"Shut up," Baldur ordered the head. "I am an idiot. All this time, I thought I needed you," he said to Kratos, "but the little one's the brains. You're just meat. My father's going to get what he needs from the boy, no matter what it takes."

Baldur drove wild punches into Kratos' head and face. Then he drove the shard deeper into the God of War's bleeding gut.

Twenty paces away, Atreus pulled himself back to his feet.

Kratos issued a vile scream, filled with rage. He broke off the end of the protruding shard to allow him to push himself free. When Kratos doubled over in agony, Baldur stomped on his back. Kratos attempted to get his feet under him, but Baldur slammed him back to the ground and began beating his head from behind.

Through the power of rage alone, Kratos surged to his feet and hammered Baldur with multiple punches to his face and gut. As Baldur retreated, Kratos charged, driving him with his shoulder into the gate pillar. The stone exploded on impact as the pillar finally gave way.

"No!" Baldur and Atreus screamed simultaneously.

The gate crumbled, crashing down in an explosion of light. Debris buried Kratos and Baldur as a billowing dust cloud rolled over them. Atreus clawed through the rubble, seeking his father. But Baldur was first to regain his feet. Standing unsteadily, he used a chunk of gate to keep himself upright. Without waiting to determine the fate of his father, Atreus drew his knife and advanced on Baldur.

"You broke the gate. That was our only way to Jötunheim!" Atreus yelled.

"Oh, you stupid sonofabitch!" Baldur said.

It was at that moment Kratos pulled himself out of the rubble, got to his feet, then shoved the large boulder away that had toppled onto him.

"Get out of here, boy!" His stare never left Baldur.

"By all means, little boy, flee, like a frightened rabbit. Let your da do all the heavy lifting for you."

Atreus snarled, surrendering to his emotions as he charged recklessly at the Aesir god.

Kratos intercepted his son a few paces before he reached their nemesis.

"Let me go!" Atreus shouted.

"Calm down, boy! You are not ready for this."

"I am ready!" Atreus screamed. He shoved his father with everything he had. Kratos, who instinctively responded to violence with more violence, shoved him back. In that second, Kratos realized he had allowed his inner rage to usurp control. He had taken his anger out on his son, something he had told himself a thousand times in the past he would never, ever do.

Baldur burst into raucous laughter at their ridiculous father–son moment.

"Boy, I—" Kratos started.

Atreus adroitly drew his bow, nocking an arrow without giving it due thought. "Þruma!" he shouted.

He released the arrow at his father. The impact of the projectile propelled Kratos backwards, smashing him into what was left of the gate and forcing him to his knees.

"And I thought I had a fucked-up family." Baldur offered a theatrical clap.

Abandoning all control, Atreus charged Baldur, brandishing his knife. Vaulting off a nearby rock, Baldur snared the lad by the throat, suspending him at arm's length. Atreus futilely stabbed at Baldur's forearm, but the Asgardian face indicated he felt absolutely nothing.

"You should feel so lucky that I can't kill you right now."

"No," Kratos said weakly.

Baldur simply stared at the knife embedded in his forearm. "Your da is right, boy. You are far from ready." He smirked. "Now, would you be so kind as to hold this for me."

Withdrawing the knife from his forearm as if it were nothing more than a thorn, he chopped it ruthlessly into the boy's shoulder. Atreus screamed from an electrifying pain tearing up his neck into his brain. Panic overtook his face, and for a long moment, his breathing ceased. He felt about to retch his empty stomach.

Baldur turned a demonic gaze to Kratos on his right, offering a haughty smile before giving a wave. Then, grabbing the boy with his free hand, he tucked him under one arm, carrying him like a rolled-up sleeping blanket. He turned and gave Kratos a furtive glance before dashing for the edge of the mountain— leaping off into the blue before Kratos could regain his feet.

"Atreus!" Kratos screamed.

He forced himself onto shaking legs. Wasting not an instant for contemplation, he raced to the edge to leap off.

CHAPTER 45

" Atreus!" Kratos wailed, spreading his arms wing-like to catch as much of the updraft as possible. The fierce wind caught his torso, stabilizing him after the initial drop from the edge.

Below, Baldur, still carrying the boy, landed on the back of a monstrous green dragon that swooped upward, away from the mountain.

Kratos angled right, dampening his wind resistance to increase his speed. He needed to reach them before the dragon gained altitude. Seconds later, he slammed into the dragon's broad, scaly tail. Instinctively, he drew the Blades of Chaos, flinging them at the dragon's neck, where they successfully pierced thorny flesh to take hold. The great beast would now keep Kratos airborne. Yanking hand over hand on the chains, the God of War propelled himself forward toward Baldur.

"Did you think I would ever allow you to take my son?" he growled with an unexpected calmness to his words, seizing Baldur's neck.

In order to defend himself, Baldur had no choice but to release Atreus, who slid helplessly along the dragon's back.

"Father!"

Kratos was forced to release Baldur, to swing his weight rearward on the dragon in order to save his son. He shot an arm out just in time to snare Atreus' wrist.

"Grab onto a thorn," Kratos yelled above the wind roaring over the dragon's back.

Atreus twisted to press his chest against the beast. When he did, his hand slipped free of his father's grasp.

Before Kratos could regain his hold, Atreus slid away.

"No!" Kratos groaned in agony, watching his flailing son flutter away.

Baldur released his grip on the dragon's back to slip closer to the God of War.

Nearing the dragon's tail, Atreus threw his arm out in a last-ditch effort to keep from being thrown from the beast. Latching onto a spine at the tail's base, he threw his other arm over it to cling to the creature's back.

Before Baldur could reach Kratos, the God of War shook one of the blades free from the dragon's flesh, swinging it wildly in an attempt to keep Baldur at bay. But Baldur desired the boy more than the God of War. As he worked his way past Kratos, he twisted in a way that allowed him to slide on his back toward the tail.

Kratos whipped his blade, burying it into the dragon's neck at the base of the skull. The majestic wings fluttered chaotically in response. The beast's head slumped as the dragon degraded into a death spiral toward the caldera temple below.

Baldur decided in that moment that he had a better chance of reaching the God of War than the son, so he pulled himself back toward the dragon's head, surging in the last second to latch onto Kratos' ankle.

"Let's see how long you can stay in the air," Baldur said.

Tugging and pulling, Baldur attempted to force Kratos to surrender his grip on the dragon. But Kratos knew that as long as he kept one blade buried in dragon flesh, he could remain safe on the creature.

Baldur swung himself over Kratos' back and, using the

chain against him, forced the blade free of the beast. As Kratos turned for another swing of his blade, Baldur kicked Kratos' chest, breaking him away from the plummeting beast.

Kratos plunged toward the caldera. The edges of his vision blurred with panic as he tumbled toward the caldera bridge, and he flung his body so the momentum would turn him back to face up at the dragon. Atreus still clung to the tail as the massive body descended. Slamming into the soft earth, Kratos pulled himself back to his knees in time to watch the careening dragon pass over the temple. A second later, two figures abandoned the beast on the opposing side of the temple.

Kratos drew his feet beneath him, immediately launching into a slow trot for the temple. He needed time for his head to clear before he attacked again.

"Baldur!" he screamed. An uncontrollable rage drove his voice. He ran like a demon thirsting for blood toward the realm travel room, where Baldur and Atreus had fallen. As he neared the chamber, the bridge shifted position on him.

Baldur was aligning the Bifröst travel table to somewhere new.

Kratos burst into the temple, heading for the realm travel room, where Brok had set up his workshop. Before Brok could even register he was there, Kratos was already halfway across the space.

"Who is activating the bridge? Hey! I asked you a ques—" Brok said.

Kratos timed his leap perfectly to fly through the shifting realm travel room door.

Tumbling and then rolling back to his feet, he saw Baldur hunched over the realm travel table. Having completed the sequence of locking in the bridge destination, Baldur extracted his Bifröst from the table when he realized the god was bearing down on him.

Without breaking stride, Kratos slammed full force into him, pinning Baldur to the table. The God of War cast his gaze at the bridge doors just as the inner and outer rings of the room made their slow, continuous rotation toward Asgard. Then he spied his son lying motionless on the other side of the table.

A glowing, spectral nebula of dust swirled around the realm travel table like a growing tornado.

Baldur recovered enough to push back on Kratos.

"Too late, it's locked in. When the bridge opens, the full weight of Asgard is gonna crash down on you," Baldur taunted with a smug cackle.

The room began rumbling; an electric hum sizzled through the air. Baldur grabbed Kratos' head, slamming it into the table.

"It is over."

The room's inner and outer rings rotated past the Alfheim bridge door. Baldur tried for another slam, but Kratos resisted.

"Is it?" Kratos said calmly.

This time Kratos slammed Baldur's head into the realm travel table. He did it with so much force that the table shuddered, leaving Baldur dazed. Then the God of War threw Baldur aside, and, in an act of desperation, pulled out his own Bifröst to jam it into the table's power receptacle—but it failed to slide in.

Atreus stirred, issuing a weak moan.

Baldur regained his feet, leaping onto Kratos' back to choke him from behind. Jamming both feet on the realm travel table allowed Baldur to push with all his strength, arching his back while attempting to separate Kratos from the table.

The God of War held fast.

The inner and outer rings rotated past the missing Jötunheim bridge door.

Atreus regained sufficient consciousness to yank the hunting knife from his shoulder, returning clumsily to his feet to advance on them.

"Now you will die!" he shouted.

"No! You need to listen to me!" Kratos yelled.

"Let me help!" His voice was gaining strength.

Kratos had to check his anger long enough to reason with his son; Atreus did not understand the creature they were opposing. Until the boy fully fathomed Baldur's true nature, any attempt he might make to help would be futile.

Baldur looped his other arm under Kratos' arm, trying to rip it away from the Bifröst as he tightened his choke hold.

"Release it, or I kill him. You know I will." Baldur savored the words as he whispered them slowly into Kratos' ear.

Through gritted teeth, Kratos released a vicious roar, the way a mother lion snarls when protecting her cub. He pressed down harder on his Bifröst.

The receptacle yielded; the Bifröst locked in. The brilliant light dimmed. The electric hum dwindled to static. The temple itself rumbled and groaned. Kratos suspected jamming his Bifröst into the table was not something that was allowed.

The inner and outer rings continued toward the Helheim bridge door.

"What did you do?" a horrified Baldur said. His face turned ashen.

Roots from the spectral World Tree lifted the travel crystal out of the center of the realm travel table and into place, while other roots lifted the Helheim bridge crystal into position.

A beam of multicolored light shot through the two crystals.

The malfunctioning Bifröst bridge to Helheim burst open in a terrifyingly brilliant display of light and sparks. Then came a vortex of swirling air. The entire room felt like it was in the eye of a tornado. Debris swirled everywhere. The open bridge sucked everything in like a vacuum.

The vortex lifting him airborne, Atreus grabbed the roots stretching toward the bridge. On the opposing side of the realm travel table, Kratos was pulled hard into it, lurching forward as the winds swirled around him. Violent air currents caused Baldur, still clinging to Kratos' back, to flip over the God of War and sail through the spectral tree toward the open bridge.

As he flew by, Baldur shot an arm out at the very last second to snare the boy. His face turned a smile as they disappeared into the swirling Bifröst bridge.

"Atreus!" Kratos cried out in anguish.

He had no choice but to release the table and spiral off toward the open bridge.

HELHEIM

CHAPTER 46

The violent wind swept them miles skyward.

Kratos twirled through the air in a wide arc, all the time locked on his nemesis and his son. Ahead of him, Baldur maintained his grip on the boy as they broke through a stream of clouds.

Kratos lowered his chin, tucked in his arms to streamline his aerodynamics. A second later, he was buffeted to within arm's length of them.

Seeing his father, Atreus reached back, stretching his fingers out, hoping.

Fighting the wind, Kratos rolled his right arm out of its tuck to grab for his son. He felt his hand brush across his son's fingers, but the wind lofted him to keep him from latching on. Kratos twisted his body left to decrease the drag, allowing him to slip in closer. This time his swipe latched onto Atreus' outstretched hand.

A thrill exhilarated him.

Baldur responded by twisting onto his back, enabling him to seize Kratos by the throat. "You actually think you can save the little shit," Baldur scoffed with a forced smile.

Kratos hammered Baldur's face with a fist that delivered little force, since it had to fight the rushing wind.

Baldur swung wildly, accomplishing only a glancing blow to the side of Kratos' head.

When Kratos buried a fist into Baldur's gut, he felt the other's grip on his son weaken. Kratos had to act immediately if he wished to take advantage of the moment.

Tugging Atreus free, Kratos simultaneously kicked Baldur in the ribs to separate him from them.

But his action made him lose his grip on his son. Atreus, now free of both of them, was buffeted through the air just beyond Kratos' reach. Tumbling through a cloud layer, all three hurtled toward the edges of Helheim proper and what appeared to be a harbor populated with warships.

As they flew past the end of the bridge, Baldur slammed into the architecture, before landing out of sight.

Kratos nearly met a similar fate, but in the last second, he whipped his chain blades out to snare a bridge stanchion, which altered his trajectory. But he was still hurtling too fast for a safe landing. The God of War smacked into the Helheim docks.

Regaining his feet while reeling from excruciating pain, Kratos clutched his shoulder in the piercing cold. He hastily scanned the landscape. His son was nowhere in sight.

"Atreus!" he shouted.

"I am here." The voice came from somewhere in the dark abyss of Helheim.

"Remain where you are." Kratos climbed the stone structure in the direction of the sound. "Where are you?"

"Here."

Kratos dashed quickly but carefully through the misty boatyard, filled with ships in varying states of war readiness.

"It's so cold... Where are we?" Atreus called out.

The voice sounded closer than when Kratos had heard his son's first call. He was moving in the right direction, he was certain of that. Yet he still had no idea how much further he needed to go to find Atreus. The mist could be altering the sound, making him think he was close, when in fact he still needed to travel a long way.

"Helheim… Describe what you see around you."

"This is Helheim? The mist's thick around me. There's rubble on me," Atreus said.

"I am close."

"I can't move my arms or legs," Atreus responded, discernible fear rising with his words, which gave Kratos a sick tremor in his gut. He needed to reach his son before Baldur did.

Kratos homed in on the direction of his son's last call, dropping to his knees when he came upon a heap of rubble. Digging furiously at the chest-high pile, he uncovered his son's arm, which then came flailing out.

"I am here," Atreus called in relief.

Kratos cast off enough rubble to bring his son out. But instead of wrapping his arms around him, grateful he was still alive, Kratos allowed his anger and his past to swarm in. He knelt over Atreus with an angry finger pointed at a still-terrified face. When Atreus tried to regain his footing in the rubble, Kratos forced him back into his position on the ground. There was no mistaking the fury on his father's face, or the throbbing vein on his forehead.

Yet Atreus stared at him in disbelief. How could he be angry? What had he done wrong this time to warrant his father's wrath?

"You will listen to me, and not speak a word. I am your father—and you, boy, are not yourself. You are too quick to temper. You are rash, insubordinate, and out of control. This will not stand. You will honor your mother and abandon this path you have chosen. It is not too late."

Atreus wanted to speak, needed to refute everything his father had just accused him of. He was acting just like his father, so how could Kratos be angry with him? Was this not the way a god was supposed to act? How could he act differently from the man he looked up to most?

Footsteps.

The military precision and cadence of a marching patrol grew louder. Hel-walkers were coming.

Kratos peeled back from his son to peer out over a large stone: a band of twelve approached.

Lowering himself out of sight, he turned to his son. "This discussion is far from over," he growled. Atreus nodded acceptance, still confused and somewhat shaken by the outburst.

"We are here because of you, boy. Do not forget that."

Kratos had to turn his attention back to the oncoming enemies.

"Now you die!" Atreus said with an ethereal echoing voice, clearly not his own.

"Boy?"

Kratos led them to the boatyard to plan a defense against the Hel-walkers. They sought refuge in a wooden structure close by.

"For a thousand mortal lifetimes, the bridge keeper kept the living out of this place. But now that you've ripped his heart out, here we are. Funny how it all comes around."

A bright flash of intense light momentarily blinded them.

"He should pay for what he said about Mother," a phantom voice carried in the wind: Atreus' voice.

"Boy?" Kratos muttered, confused and now concerned.

"That wasn't me," Atreus said from behind him.

Not far inside the structure, they stopped in their tracks. An ethereal image of Atreus occupied the center of the room.

"But we're gods. We do whatever we want," the phantom Atreus continued.

Kratos spun to find Atreus standing behind him, despite having witnessed him ten paces before him a moment before.

"I saw myself," Atreus said astonished, his face ashen, his breathing coming in terrified gasps.

"I saw it also."

"What was that?"

Once the image vanished, Kratos and Atreus progressed into a new room. Another bright flash briefly stole their vision. Now an image of Atreus appeared. But Modi was there as well, appearing exactly as he had when they saw him in Peak's Pass—collapsed on the ground, bloody, beaten, and pitiful.

Modi began chuckling from the floor.

"That's what I said… to your mother… before I gave it to her," Modi said in an ethereal echoing voice.

The ethereal Atreus unsheathed his hunting knife to expertly stab Modi. Dark blood gushed from Modi's throat. Atreus knelt before the man, grabbed his hair and yanked his head off the floor. He leaned into Modi's face, who watched horror-stricken.

"My mother still a whore? Huh? She still a whore?" the phantom Atreus spat. Modi gurgled unintelligible words, then Atreus released him.

He turned from Modi, wiping his hands across his thighs, staining them with Modi's blood as if he wished to wear the stain as a badge of honor. Behind him, Modi crawled desperately away, toward the edge of the bridge.

The phantom Atreus, turning back to see Modi crawling away, wordlessly kicked him over the edge.

A muddled Atreus stared blankly at the spot where his actions had replayed before him. "I couldn't have done that."

CHAPTER 47

"Why must I relive the things I have done? Is that part of being a god? Will these things haunt me all my days?"

Kratos offered no explanation, despite knowing the answers to his questions.

"I, I don't even recognize myself anymore," Atreus said.

"This place corrupts the mind. Do not dwell on those thoughts. Not here. Not now."

"I understand."

"We must move. Quickly."

Navigating through various boatyard structures, Kratos and Atreus came upon a vista overlooking a deep chasm and a spectral bridge.

"There. We need to be on the other side of the bridge," Kratos said, pointing out their destination.

"Is it safe to cross?"

"Only the dead can cross."

"Then... how?"

"We must find another way," Kratos said.

Before they could leave the boatyard, a squad of six Hel-walkers assigned to patrol the boats surged toward them. Only the fire from Kratos' chain blades was able to defeat their onslaught. Kratos spun about to locate Atreus once he had dropped the last of the undead.

"We must hurry to reach the bridge," he said.

As they neared a tower adjacent to the bridge, a surreal voice echoed through the stone corridors.

"I would never have wanted this!"

Baldur.

"He is near," Kratos cautioned Atreus, swallowing with great difficulty.

Atreus' hand tightened on his bow, though he knew the weapon was all but useless against their nemesis.

They eased closer to the structure, Kratos realizing another confrontation with Baldur was now inevitable. *But the man could not be killed!* He would keep coming until he succeeded in destroying one or both of them. Kratos ransacked his memory, desperate to unearth some skill, some trick, some nuance of being a god that might allow him to defeat this monster in human form.

They had not progressed far when another bright flash of light brought an illusion of the phantom Atreus across their path. They stopped, at a loss as to how to approach it. To their flank, separated by a translucent energy barrier, stood Baldur in the flesh. He was entranced, witnessing his own illusion of himself in which he held a knife threatening someone unseen.

"You had no right," the phantom Baldur spat.

"I had every right. I am your mother," a gruff feminine voice fired back with a venomous tone.

"No right, witch!" the phantom Baldur screamed, his neck veins bulging.

Nearing the scene, Kratos and Atreus discovered the object of Baldur's tirade: Freya.

Undaunted, she stood facing him, despite the knife poised to eviscerate her.

"Can't taste. Can't smell. Can't even feel the temperature of this room. Feasting, drinking... women. It's all gone!" the phantom Baldur sobbed in insurmountable misery.

"But you will never have to feel pain. Death has no power over you. You would rather die?"

"Than never feel again? Yes! Take it away, Mother. Now!"

"I cannot."

"Did you not consider all that would transpire as a result of your decision?"

The phantom Baldur curled a hand around the back of Freya's head, pulling her close to set the tip of the blade to her delicate flesh.

"Take it away! Now!"

"It does not work like that. In time you will thank me."

"No... I will *never* thank you."

He pressed the knife more forcefully. A trickle of ruby-red blood leaked out. Freya's otherwise stoic demeanor revealed the first signs of fracture. Fear and concern took over her face.

The real Baldur ventured closer, but only by a single step.

"You ruined my life," the phantom muttered.

"My child, my lovely child, we can—" she started.

"No!" he screamed. "If you can't fix it—"

The phantom Baldur slid effortlessly behind Freya, driving her to her knees, never releasing the knife from her flesh. His muscles tensed as if about to slice her throat.

"Do it," the real Baldur spoke out loud, hoping the force of his words alone could tip the exchange in his favor. "Come on," he whispered anxiously, but only to himself.

"Son." Freya's helpless whisper came faint and breathless.

"Come on, do it."

The phantom Baldur released Freya with a shove. Disgusted, he staggered from her.

"Coward!" Baldur screamed at his phantom self, as if he were addressing a different person.

Freya stared up at him, unmoving, drowning in tears, her lower lip quivering out of control.

"I never want to see you again!" the phantom Baldur blurted, his anger exploding, his free hand clenched in a fist.

The knife remained in the striking position, as if his inner battle still raged.

In the next second, the phantom Baldur vanished, leaving a seething real Baldur dumbfounded at the illusion of his stunned mother.

Kratos signaled silence with a finger to his lips. They had to hope they could slip by Baldur unnoticed. His son acknowledged the signal with a slight nod.

Baldur advanced several steps toward Freya.

"What you did to me," he said calmly, like a man in complete control of his every emotion. Snatching up a discarded plank nearby, he raised it high enough to smash Freya's head. "What you did to me!" he half-shouted, half-growled, surrendering some of his control.

But, like his phantom, he hesitated.

The board hovered ominously overhead. Like his phantom, he lost his nerve. Dropping the board, he began to sob, unable to kill even an illusion of his mother. He slumped to his knees. The battle inside his head had ended and the victor had emerged.

"Coward. Worthless coward," he cried.

Kratos had never expected to witness Baldur's human, vulnerable side. The man's relentless pursuit and vicious attacks on him and his son seemed like they had been initiated by a person very different from the one now kneeling twenty paces away, still ignorant of their presence.

Kratos and Atreus crawled beneath broken sections of the stone structure, keeping directly behind a sobbing Baldur. As long as Baldur stayed stone still, they remained safely beyond his field of vision.

Once out of his sight, but still within range of his sobbing, they slithered beneath a broken gate, leaving Baldur to wallow in his sorrow.

CHAPTER 48

Only after they were far enough from Baldur did Atreus release a sigh of relief.

"Freya is his mother. How did that escape your memory, head?" Kratos said, astonished.

"I'm at a loss. I assure you I have no reason to keep such a thing a secret. I said my memory was slowly coming back."

"Why did she keep that from us? Does she not know he hunts us? We never told her."

"For what it is worth, I do not believe she colludes with her son. Those two have not spoken in years," Mimir said.

"Time will tell. There is the bridge," Kratos said, to change the subject. As they advanced toward it, another voice rode the wind. A bright flash came from behind them.

"I will put an end to this chaos," an old man's voice said.

"Who was that?" Atreus asked.

"No," Kratos muttered to himself. Fear pervaded his face, and Atreus noticed. That voice was familiar to his father, a voice powerful enough to force his father to falter. A knot tightened around Atreus' stomach; his hand sought the reassurance and comfort of his blade.

Then they stopped.

Poised before them, a phantom Kratos wore the garb from

his life in Greece. Appearing much younger, beardless, and more muscular, he was speaking to someone unseen.

The ground transformed into a bloody stone floor.

"Such chaos. I will have much to do after I kill you," the old man said.

"Face me, Father. It is time we end this," the phantom Kratos responded.

"Yes, my son. It is time. Only one of us will be left to live."

With the sound of crackling ice, the illusion vanished.

Atreus struggled to fathom what he had just witnessed. His father looked so different from the man he grew up with.

"Mind nothing you see here, boy."

Atreus knew he could never just dismiss what he had seen, and what he might see, as they progressed toward the spectral bridge. He ruminated over the visions he had witnessed earlier about himself. They were stark; they were brutal; *but they were true.*

"Come on. We have to go," Atreus pressed.

"Yes."

They found the only way ahead was onto the deck of a single-mast, two-tier warship with an enormous sail, moored at the end of the dock beside the bridge.

"What now?" Atreus asked, scanning around them.

"Yes... what now? Only the dead can cross that bridge, and, last I checked, I'm the only dead one in our party," Mimir said.

"I could roll you across, if you would like," Kratos offered, annoyed.

A siren shrieked like a chorus of a thousand dead voices wailing in unison.

"What is that?" Atreus said.

"That would be the city being alerted to our presence," Mimir informed them.

Areas of the dock were now illuminated with harsh light, as if the place were being jarred awake. Soldiers of the dead charged down the pier at them.

Screaming, Kratos charged the incoming horde, cleaving

the clamoring Hel-walkers in two with his chain blades. Legs toppled in one direction while torsos spun in another. The corpses became a littering of small fires dotting the ground. Only after the last one had fallen did Atreus advance to huddle on his knees beside them, to gather their warmth.

"We should not stay," Kratos said.

"Wait... but these bodies are burning," Atreus said.

"So?"

"Yes. And if we wait around here long enough, we can have ourselves a bonfire," Mimir added sardonically.

Kratos ascended the warship's mast, hacking it in half. Then, using the chain blades and his weight to pull down the top of the sail, he formed a makeshift balloon. From his vantage point at the top of the severed pole, he spied hundreds of undead mustering for an organized assault. His hastily concocted plan had better work.

CHAPTER 49

Scanning the deck, Kratos studied the thick black tar that covered a large area of the ship's rigging. "Not entirely sure this thing is seaworthy," Mimir said, unable to keep his own fears out of his words.

"She will do," Kratos grumbled. They had no other options at that moment.

He had to free the rigging, and free it quickly. Using his chain blades and a stone, he set the tar ablaze, which disappeared from the water-soaked rigging timbers as it was spent. Racing over to the sail crank and working it with both hands, the now-freed sail began to fill with hot air. His idea had to work.

With a lurch that jolted both father and son, the vessel surged forward and upward into the air. "We're moving upward! Just like the lantern!" Atreus called out. He could see a smile on his father's face.

They could get out of this wretched place.

"Great. Just bear in mind—this boat can only take us part of the way. Týr's temple is near the top of a tremendous waterfall, which, sadly, we are downstream from. That means even if we get there intact, we'd still need to sail up a waterfall somehow," Mimir informed them, much to their dismay.

"The Vanir built the greatest ship that ever was, and it can fly," Atreus said.

"*Skíðblaðnir?* Because it was *designed* to fly. This was not," Mimir corrected.

"Nevertheless, this is the boat we have. We make do," Kratos said.

They had not floated far when the ship collided with a giant jagged iceberg, drifting lazily through the frigid air.

"We're stuck," Atreus called back.

"On perhaps the biggest iceberg I've ever seen. We are now officially sunk," Mimir said.

"At least the fire's still making heat," Atreus said. "What now?"

Kratos did the only thing he could think of at that moment. He withdrew his Leviathan axe and began chopping feverishly at the catch that impeded the sail's full release.

"You're chopping it?" Atreus said. It seemed an impossible feat.

"Give your father room," Mimir butted in.

After a dozen forceful hacks, the catch broke apart, releasing the mainstay and fully untethering the sail.

"Great. So now the sail is loose…" Atreus commented, still unable to visualize his father's plan.

Kratos jumped onto the balustrade to fasten the sail in such a way as to create more makeshift balloon pockets above the deck. Once he had finished, the pockets caught the warm air to glide the ship over the iceberg.

"It's actually working," Atreus said, amazed such a feat could actually be accomplished. He dashed to the side of the deck for a better view of what lay ahead.

Before he could react, the ship jolted sideways, throwing both him and his father to the deck. The half-mast struck the towering bridge architecture.

"And we're stuck again," Atreus announced, pulling his feet beneath him and moving to the site of the contact.

"Not for long. Stay with the boat," Kratos said.

"I can't believe it. You just turned this ship into a huge sky lantern," Atreus said, impressed with his father's sudden ingenuity.

Kratos crossed over to the tower that snagged the ship.

He pulled on the tower crank, and the lodged bridge section fractured just enough to free the ship.

"That did it. We're loose!" Atreus said as the ship began to rise anew.

"Wait for me there!" Kratos ordered.

"We need to talk, brother," Mimir said. "You do realize it's over, don't you? Even if we make it back to Midgard, you and Baldur destroyed the only gate to Jötunheim. We are out of options. And that boy there... he's in nine kinds of pain. His head's turned so far around, he..."

"Atreus is not your concern," Kratos said.

"Well, he might become everyone's concern if you don't do *something*. You don't have to be the smartest man in the world to see that."

A few seconds later, Atreus informed him, "Look! Now we're stuck on *this* bridge!"

Kratos repositioned himself where the edge of their ship was lodged under a tower bridge. He looked back over his shoulder to his son watching nearby.

"Atreus." He gestured at the tower. Atreus rushed over to join him.

"I can help." Atreus moved next to his father.

"Together now."

With all their strength, they pushed the tower structure. Atreus felt the vessel move, though just a little. He couldn't believe the strength he had surging in his arms. A moment later, the ship became dislodged from the tower.

"We did it. We're free," the lad called out.

The ship surged forward across the cold Helheim sky. "We *are* going to get out of here," Atreus said.

Another bright flash spread over their heads.

"Face me, Father. It is time to end this," a phantom voice wavered through the air. It was Kratos' voice from another time and another place.

"Yes, my son. It is time," responded the old man's voice.

"No…" Kratos whispered to himself. His worst nightmare presented itself for his son to witness.

"It's that voice again. Do you know who that is?" Atreus said.

"Head, how long before we reach the temple?" Kratos asked loudly, hoping to divert the conversation.

"Yeah, it's freezing," Atreus agreed.

"As long as we maintain this speed and those fires don't go out, we should be there in no time, lad," Mimir reassured.

"How'd you even think to do this, Father?"

"I… do not know."

"Are you all right?" Atreus said, upon seeing the distracted look on his father's face.

"Yes. Now stay close to the fire and rest," Kratos said.

As the ship continued to float across Helheim, Hel-walkers launched themselves off the roofs of the passing architecture. Kratos attacked them as they landed, hacking and slicing them before they could launch a fight. After a few moments, some of the Hel-walkers broke away from the fight.

"They are trying to put out the fire! Right-hand side! I mean—starboard!" Atreus yelled to his father.

The Hel-walkers sought to extinguish the fires keeping the ship aloft. The harder Kratos fought, the more other Hel-walkers reached the flames to dampen them.

"Hurry! We're going to flip over!" Atreus said, feeling the ship listing to the port side. "We're sinking."

As the boat soared close to another iceberg, knife-like shards scraped its sides. "Iceberg! Port side!"

"Hold on!" Kratos called out.

Even before they could react to the latest threat, a huge harpoon flew out of nowhere to snare the ship. Its impact jarred them on the deck.

"Something is stopping us! Port side!" Atreus called.

Kratos hacked the last of the Hel-walkers in time to reach the balustrade and gaze down at the harpoon.

"Harpoon! I will free us!"

Using his chain blades to secure him, Kratos went over the side of the ship to hack the harpoon free of the hull.

The ship surged toward the next obstacle in their path. "We're going to hit that bridge!" Atreus shouted.

Kratos swung himself back onto the deck, but before he could react, the ship ricocheted off the bridge with an explosion of dust and rubble. Luckily, the craft remained stable in the sky as it cleared the chasm and sailed over the foothills of Helheim. Watching the ground racing by below, they passed the carcass of the bridge keeper at the bridge entrance.

"We're almost back! Look! Straight ahead. I see it!" Atreus said. He smiled at the thought of leaving such a formidable realm.

Slam! Slam!

Another set of harpoons slashed into the hull.

"We've stopped again!"

"More harpoons," Kratos reported.

"We're pitching!" Atreus called.

The harpoons' weight drew the ship's foredeck downward.

Using his chain blades, Kratos had to sacrifice the ship's bow to break them free of the harpoons.

"Guess we didn't need that part of the boat!" Atreus said.

Kratos looked up to see the realm travel temple in the distance. They were almost there.

"The temple! We made it!" Atreus said. "Wait. We're going too fast. We're going to fly past it!"

Before they could reach the temple, a dense fog cascaded in from their starboard side, completely enveloping the ship. A flash spread through the air.

"It is time, my son," the phantom voice of the old man said.

In a panic Kratos spun about, following the mist as it drifted over the deck, where it solidified into an old man with a white beard and glowing white eyes.

Zeus was collapsed on the ground, bloody, beaten, and pitiful. A moment later, the younger, beardless phantom Kratos appeared in Greek attire. He threw down one chain blade, then the other, then he rushed at Zeus.

The phantom Kratos grabbed Zeus by the throat, lifted him into the air, then slammed him to the floor. He punched the old man several times, following up with a knee to the face. Then came more punches, finishing with a head slam against stone. Blood splattered with every punch. Viciously, the God of War battered him, repeatedly and unrelenting.

Across the deck, Atreus stood in disbelief, witnessing every brutal punch. Then something caused his face to change from horror to panic. He rushed to his father, shaking him and pulling him away from the vision as it disappeared.

"Come on. We gotta go," he said to his father.

"You saw…"

"There's no time, look!"

The floating ship struck another tower on the bridge, crashing through it. Caroming off the structure, the ship's trajectory shifted, putting it on a collision course with the realm travel temple.

"I have a plan!" Atreus said, seizing his father's arm. "Jump!"

They leapt from the boat, falling into the realm travel temple below, landing in an antechamber.

Moments later, gazing back at the sky, they watched the ship crash into the temple.

"*That* was your plan? You're both cracked!" Mimir said, elated that they had survived the fall.

"We are leaving this realm. Now," Kratos said.

"As long as we didn't wreck our way back…" Atreus added.

Debris sealed off the entrance to the domed room, forcing them to find another way inside. They navigated through a series of hidden rooms under the dome.

"What is this place?" Atreus asked, scanning what might be a library.

"This is Odin's. I'd recognize his atrocious taste anywhere," Mimir commented. "Look at all this… The amount of arcane knowledge hidden between these walls."

"I would rather not be here when Odin returns. Come," Kratos said.

"Look at that! It's the missing panel, about..." Atreus said, indicating a panel on the other side of the room depicting Týr moving through the air over the watching commoners.

"Odin must have stolen it. But why?" the lad asked.

"He always has his reasons. Might I have a look?" Mimir asked. Kratos lifted the head so he could examine the triptych panel. "Well... this is most unexpected."

"Why? What does it mean?" Atreus asked.

"Haven't the foggiest. Isn't that unexpected?" Mimir laughed.

"Head..." Kratos snapped.

"Look, clearly that's Týr... traveling, somehow, perhaps magically. But what's that to do with the giants, that they should devote a shrine to it? I'm afraid that's none too clear."

"What are those runes in the corners?"

"Not runes. Symbols... from different lands. They mean..."

"War," Kratos said.

"Aye."

"How do you...?" Atreus asked.

"This one I know too well," Kratos said, pointing to an Omega symbol in the upper right corner.

Kratos broke the ensuing awkward silence. "His eyes. They are jewels. Like yours," he said.

"No doubt signifying the gift of sight the giants granted us... Give me a closer look," Mimir said. Kratos elevated and angled Mimir's head to the metal depiction of Týr.

"Interesting..." Mimir commented, squinting his one good eye as he inspected the triptych.

As he stared, a golden light erupted from his eye, striking the jewel in Týr's eye. The metal symbol above Týr's head began to shudder, the whirring sound of clockwork gears behind a wooden facade becoming audible.

"Now, this is most interesting," Mimir said.

Then an image formed at the panel's base. As it came into

sharper focus, it appeared to show a diagram of an ornate key, beside the door that it fit into, which Atreus imprinted on his memory. It also displayed a talisman in Týr's hand.

"So that's what it is," Mimir said, trying to make it sound like he knew what it was all along.

"What *is* that?" Atreus queried, examining the panel more closely.

"I'll tell you what it looks like. I think it is some sort of secret plan, concealed by Týr so no one could access it but him... and those few others the giants trusted. And right under Odin's nose—ha! I did promise I'd get you to Jötunheim..." Mimir boasted.

"What do you mean, head? You said we were out of options," Kratos snapped.

"Don't you see, brother? Odin never gave up hope, and neither should we. He knew there was a clue in here, but we're the ones who found it. These plans are for a key to some chamber Týr's kept hidden. I don't know where it's leading us, or what we'll find... but it's a path."

Kratos cast a glance at Atreus, who immediately looked away.

"How do we make this key?" Kratos asked.

"We ask one who specializes in this sort of thing. A dwarf."

"That symbol on the temple door... it's a bunch of runes together. Peace. Unity. Hope. Other things too," Atreus commented, as they made their way out of the room.

"Týr's own design. He made this door himself," Mimir said.

Kratos' mind churned as they ascended to the realm travel room. He vacillated between remaining silent and speaking. He understood that the longer he delayed facing what they had witnessed, the more difficult it would get.

"Before... what you saw..." Kratos started slowly.

"I didn't see anything," Atreus responded quickly and adamantly.

"You did not see me with someone? An old man?"

"What old man?" Atreus replied.

Kratos analyzed his son's look—he was lying.

"Can we go? I hate this place." He rubbed his arms vigorously for effect. He could only hope it worked. He just wished his father would let the conversation die there. He wanted no more confrontation. As a matter of fact, if they never spoke of it for the remainder of the journey, he would be happy. And he suspected his father would be happy also.

"Yes... very well."

The lad escaped onto the glowing Bifröst bridge the moment it lined up. Why would his father beat a helpless old man? Is that something a god would do? Atreus thought not.

"So, let's get back to Midgard and see about making that key," Mimir said, when he felt a tension rising between father and son.

Silence resumed until they returned to the caldera temple complex, where they activated the realm travel mechanism to allow their return to Midgard.

MIDGARD

CHAPTER 50

Leaving the dome array in Midgard, they immediately took up the trail they hoped would lead them back to where they had last encountered Brok. If the blue man had changed the location of his workshop, they might lose days roaming about the woods in search of him.

As luck would have it, Brok had remained in the same place. On their approach, he lifted his head from his workbench, which was set up beside a crackling campfire.

"Can you make it?" Kratos asked, about the detailed drawing of the key from Atreus' memory he sketched in the dirt.

Brok stared at it quizzically.

"Is it a weapon? Armor? Or likewise an instrument of war, of which I am a master at shapin'? No? Then forget it. Even if I wanted to make such an insignificant gewgaw, I'm liable to chink my tools making something so delicate and ladylike."

"Then shingle it," a voice came from behind them.

They all turned to see Sindri standing ten paces away, clutching his workbag.

"Pattern weld the thing with skap slag. Keep the layers thin, alternate the overlay."

A sneer formed on Brok's face as he stared dumbfounded at his brother.

"Okay, smart guy. And where d'ya propose we find a lump of quality skap slag? Last time I saw one, I could still get rigid down south," Brok said. "You probably gonna have to ask your da what that means, boy."

Sindri withdrew a fist-sized hunk of shiny slag from his pocket, lifting it like a trophy. "Duh, right here!"

Brok gasped as if experiencing a true wonder of the world.

"You shut your mouth. Is that...? But where did you...?" Brok's voice rattled, his lower jaw hanging open.

"Had to get my hands dirty," Sindri responded casually. "If you know what I mean." He offered a wink, indicating a meaning only the two dwarves would understand.

Brok stared at him for a long moment, then started to laugh. "Well, don't just stand there—let's do this!"

"You... you are suddenly fine working on something that is not a weapon?" Sindri teased.

"Ah, hell, why not? They're good people."

Sindri and Atreus stared at Brok like he was some sort of alien.

"What? I can grow, too."

The brothers crowded Brok's portable smelting furnace, both feverishly hammering away. "Watch the spine! Keep your wrist loose," Sindri growled.

"Help yourself to whatever I got to eat in my sack," Brok offered.

Kratos and Atreus pulled out apples and bread, dried venison and dried apricots. After consuming it they settled beneath a sprawling oak to fall fast asleep, despite the raucous banging. Hours later, they awoke to loud talking.

"You keep *your* wrist loose. Get more heat here!" Brok ordered, gesturing with his hammer.

"Coming up. You going to temper that steel longer?" Sindri said.

"Don't need to. I triple-quenched it in draugr oil. See?" Brok smiled in a boastful way.

"You clever little beaver. How inventive. And sanitary! Never too late to learn a new trick, is it?" Sindri said, matching his brother's smile.

Atreus watched with obvious glee, happy the two brothers were finally working together. He looked over to his father, who watched stone-faced, which caused Atreus' smile to fade.

"Here it is!" Sindri declared finally.

He held up a broad-angled key with pride. It matched exactly the drawing still visible in the dirt. Brok returned to his smelting furnace, to extract a branding iron with a glowing tip.

"Don't forget this!" he said.

Together, the dwarf brothers branded the item with a hiss.

"A creation Dvalin would be truly proud of." Brok grinned.

"Is Dvalin your father?" Atreus asked.

"Your mother never taught you about Dvalin? Sure, of course not, he's not a god. You people only care about the gods. He's the ruler of all the mountain dwarves. We don't answer to *your* gods," Sindri said.

"I have work to do," Kratos said sternly, grabbing the key.

Atreus shrugged, while Kratos stomped away.

CHAPTER 51

"Now we just need to figure out what door this key opens. It has to be somewhere around the temple…" Atreus said.

"And beyond that, hopefully some trace of a secret path to Jötunheim!" Mimir added.

Returning to Týr's temple, Kratos located the door that matched the one they had seen beside the diagram of the key. Unlocking the door with the key, he threw it open to reveal a small antechamber at the foot of a narrow staircase.

"Great. We're inside! But… what *is* this place?" Atreus asked.

"Your guess is as good as mine, little brother," Mimir answered.

Suddenly, the large Jötunheim door swung open by itself, along with a simpler, smaller door they could reach, which led across a Bifröst bridge to another door with an ornate carving on it.

"Does that mean something?" Kratos asked of the carving.

Atreus shook his head.

"Lift me up to see it," Mimir said.

Kratos placed Mimir's eye squarely before it.

"The talisman! I suspect we'll be needing that," Mimir said.

Using his knife, Kratos pried the talisman in the form of a carved wolf's head from its socket on the door. He swung open the door to reveal a mystic gateway to a strange environment, like a tree branch stretching out to infinity.

"There it is! We've got it!" Atreus said.

"The panel in Odin's library showed him holding this," Kratos said.

"Yes... yes! That's it. I understand now. It showed Týr walking the realm between realms. Normally to stray from the path is certain death. Well, Týr always followed his *own* path, if you catch my meaning."

"The realm between realms..." Kratos said.

"So you're saying Týr's shrine was showing him stepping off the branch of the World Tree. And you're thinking, to reach the secret path to Jötunheim, that's what *we* need to do?" Atreus asked.

"I am," Kratos replied.

"Oh, dear. That *is* what you're thinking, isn't it?" Mimir said.

They stepped into the nebulous mist of the realm between realms, where light swirled around them as if scrutinizing the invaders.

"If you're thinking about hurling us all into the void, I hope you're quite sure," Mimir cautioned.

"Wasn't it your idea? Find our own path, right?" Atreus said.

"Bollocks," Mimir said.

Without hesitation, Atreus sprinted along the branch to the edge of a precipice resembling that in the triptych panel.

Kratos peered into black void. "This is where Týr stepped beyond. Ready?" Kratos said. He looked at his son.

Atreus climbed onto his father's back.

"Well... if this is it, lads, it's been an honor," Mimir said, with a shaky voice.

"Have faith, head," Kratos said.

He stepped off, gliding into a controlled descent.

"This is incredible!" Atreus shouted.

"I... thought... there'd... be... a... bridge!" Mimir said, against a fierce wind contorting his face. He floated away from Kratos' body as if weightless, only to return to the God of War's side as they neared the ground.

Kratos landed cat-footed, braced for anything. Atreus slid off his father's back the moment they were on solid ground, anxious for what lay ahead. A twisting path before them led to the lost tower of Jötunheim. The tower had been constructed of ornately carved sandstone, with tall, narrow windows on all sides.

"The tower! I *knew* there was something down here," Atreus said.

"Amazing. How do you hide something that exists in all realms? Cast it out of any realm to the space between realms. Clever old Týr," Mimir said.

"Is Jötunheim on the other side?" Atreus asked.

"Can't be that. It is not like you go through Vanaheim to reach the Midgard peak," Mimir said.

"But how do we use the tower?" Kratos asked.

"I suggest we look inside. But stay alert; Týr's little challenges are never as simple as they appear," Mimir said.

Entering the tower, they found it empty, with the exception of a simple pedestal.

Seeing nothing that could be used with the pedestal, Kratos decided to place the talisman on it, thinking it might act as a key to unlock something within the tower. However, the talisman disappeared a moment after making contact.

"Don't know if that was such a good idea," Atreus said. "It's gone, and nothing happened."

Kratos gazed around, hoping to notice something changing.

"What if we needed—" Mimir started.

The tower room began shaking, silencing the head midsentence.

"I don't know about this," Atreus said.

The tower began to rise.

"The tower is absorbing the talisman's energy!" Mimir said. "It knows what to do. The artifact served its purpose. We're fulfilling Týr's spell!"

"What happens now?" Kratos said.

"No idea, brother. But after that fall, I'm guessing we're past the worst of it."

"We've stopped... I think it's over," Atreus said.

"Aye... but where are we now?"

As Kratos threw open the door to the Jötunheim tower, they watched the realm travel bridge outside rotating past the other realm pathways.

Without warning, as the realm travel bridge passed Alfheim, two Dark Elves lurched through the opening to attack. They came with such speed and voracity that they left no time for either Kratos or Atreus to prepare their blades or the bow. Kratos shoved Atreus from the opening, latching onto the neck of the first Dark Elf to enter. That slight bit of time allowed Atreus to withdraw his knife and brace for the attack of the second elf. The lad's scream was lost in the screeching of the elves slashing with their knives.

Kratos snarled the next Dark Elf through, to slam it with all his might into the adjacent tower wall. Dark blood spurted from the elf's mouth as Kratos ripped the wings off with one hand.

Atreus slid on his knees beneath the slashes of the charging elf. Before it could bank around in the air, Atreus attacked it from its vulnerable back, stabbing viciously between the wings. An agonizing wail sundered the air. Blood spurted across his face. He relented, unsure if the creature was yet dead.

Kratos ripped the head off the elf he held, discarding the limp carcass at his feet. He spun around, hoping to help his son, witnessing instead Atreus plunging the knife into the elf's temple in a deathblow, while maintaining control on top until it lay lifeless.

"It's dead," he reported to his father.

But they had no time to lower their guard. The bridge approached the Vanaheim opening; they had no idea what to expect.

The yowling of Wulvers answered their concern.

As the realm travel table passed Vanaheim, three Wulvers leapt for the doorway. Atreus' first arrow took out the lead. Kratos chopped down the other two the moment they breached the tower.

Kratos turned to observe the realm travel table. The Midgard tower came next.

They kicked the dead aside when the travel bridge locked into place with the Midgard tower.

"We're back in Midgard! There's the bridge! We did it—the tower's back where it belongs!" Atreus said.

"Just when I thought I'd seen it all."

"Now Týr's travel room can take us to Jötunheim," Kratos said.

"What are we waiting for?"

"Odin suspected the giants secretly possessed some remnant of primordial Jötnar creative essence—the stuff all realms were made of. The talisman must have been fashioned from that. They must have been desperate, even to trust Týr with it," Mimir said.

Kratos moved to the realm travel table.

"I must tell you, I don't know what we'll find when we get to Jötunheim, but it is imperative that we cover our tracks. Huginn and Muninn will tell him of the tower's restoration, and we mustn't let our efforts be to his benefit."

"Huginn and Muninn?" Atreus said.

"A pair of ravens: Odin's spies. The war-god dispatches them throughout the realms to observe from on high and report everything to the Allfather."

"The ravens..." Atreus muttered to himself. Now he understood why they saw them on their journey, and why his mother needed to be informed if he saw ravens in their forest. They were the ones informing Odin of their whereabouts. That could have been how Baldur kept finding them.

"Activate the table for Jötunheim," Mimir said.

"Yes, let's go," Atreus chimed in.

"Wait. This isn't going to work. There's no travel crystal," Mimir said. "Týr must have used his own eyes to refract the energy. It was his final failsafe."

"But *you've* got eyes like him, Mimir," Atreus said.

"I've got an eye. One! Odin plucked out my other eye precisely to keep me from traveling."

A Bifröst beam shot out from the realm travel table, striking the receptacle with the missing travel crystal.

"Sorry, lads. Hoped that might work."

"What did Odin do with your other eye?"

"He'd have kept it in any of a hundred places, I'm afraid."

"We've come so far. There has to be a way," Atreus said.

"Look, bit of a long shot, but for years I would see Sindri, and sometimes Brok, lurking around on that mountain when Odin came for his visits. Maybe they know something."

"Brok! Sindri! I'm so glad we found you," Atreus exclaimed when he came upon Brok's shop. Both dwarves stopped to face the lad.

"Where's your da?" Sindri asked.

A moment later, Kratos entered the clearing.

"You got another job for us?" Brok asked, in a way that made it sound like he was preparing to refuse it.

"We are always glad to help," Sindri butted in.

"Not a job. A question. Do either of you know where we might find Mimir's other eye?"

"His other eye? What for? He's got the other one. Nobody needs more than one good eye anyway," Brok said.

"How can you say that?" Sindri bickered. "If you had only one good eye, you'd end up pounding your thumbs until they were flat slivers."

"I can out-pound you on metal with one eye any day!" Brok fired back.

Kratos growled at being forced to endure their senseless banter. "Guys, the eye?"

"Yeah, yeah, yeah. Oh. No, no, no. That's... I'm sorry. As a matter of fact, Odin asked me to... he wanted me to build a... he *showed* it to me, you see, and I... declined," Sindri stammered out nauseatedly, before excusing himself.

"Well, that was useless," Mimir commented.

"You *know*... it was about the same time that Odin came around lookin' for me to build a statue with some sort of hidden compartment. Now, that not being a weapon and the Aesir being a bunch of pock-speckled cockers, I saw fit to decline. But I know he got it built just the same," Brok said.

"A statue of what?" Atreus said.

"It's that one of Thor, out there flashin' his sac to the bay."

"The statue the serpent ate," Kratos said.

"He ate it? He actually ate the statue?" Brok said.

Atreus voiced the question they were all thinking: "How are we supposed to look *inside* the snake?"

CHAPTER 52

They wound their way through the forests of Midgard, back to the giant horn. Approaching it, Kratos lifted Mimir's head, holding his lips to the horn of Jörmungandr. Atreus covered his ears while Mimir blew a sustained, deep mystical note that echoed across the vast caldera.

Within a few minutes, the World Serpent rose out of the water, leaning forward to observe his audience. The resulting wave shook the bridge beneath them.

"Thooooor stuh-tooooo… eeeee-kneeeee smooooo-thooooo thooooor-fah," Mimir uttered in the snake's language.

"Skeeeeel-yaaaaah. Pvooooo-meeeee-thooooor," came the reply. The great snake leaned back into its resting position.

"Is the statue lost to us? What did the snake say?" Kratos said, his anxiety rushing to the surface.

"Well, he thinks it might still be in his stomach. He is open to allowing you to row into his mouth for a look inside."

"Eww. Really?" Atreus said.

"By his expression, he is not wild about the idea either," Mimir said.

Kratos grunted while pondering the snake's offer. Could it be a trick to get him inside, where the snake might consume him? Dare he risk both of them entering the snake's belly?

He started toward the boat dock.

Once they were seated in the boat, Kratos navigated toward the snake's gaping mouth.

"Wait! We are actually going to do it? We are going to let that thing swallow us?" Atreus said, his concern written across his brow.

"Do we have another choice? If so, then tell me," Kratos said. Atreus was silent.

"You do not have to come," Kratos said, though the tone of his voice betrayed the fact that this was a challenge rather than a genuine offer. There was no way he was returning to the dock to allow his son off the boat.

But he got the answer he had hoped for.

"What? And miss this?" said Atreus.

The massive beast leaned down as they neared, settling its head on the surface while fully opening its huge gullet. Massive fangs framed the mouth, its constricted throat visible in the distance.

"Hurry, row faster!" Mimir blurted out.

"Why?" Atreus asked.

"There, in the sky! Huginn and Muninn. We must get us inside before they spot us."

Kratos ripped the oars through the water with all the strength he could deliver, while Atreus scanned the horizon.

"I see 'em," the lad called out.

"Pray we make it before—" Mimir said, just as the shadow of the serpent's mouth swallowed them up. Darkness consumed them.

"You are certain about this?" Atreus asked, gazing about. He stared up at the curled fangs.

"No," Kratos responded.

Flowing deeper into the serpent's body, Atreus peered into the total darkness looming beyond the throat. He had no idea what to expect, how they would navigate once inside, and how they intended to get safely out. Yet he still never thought about dying. Somehow, he knew his father would come up with solutions for whatever challenged them along the way.

Perhaps that was what being a god was all about: being able to overcome any obstacle they encountered, human or otherwise. The very thought inspired him. Could he possibly become as invincible as his father appeared to be?

Kratos rowed undaunted into the abyss, progressing into the roar of rushing water, followed by a splash that shuddered the small craft. Then all fell silent. But only for a moment, as the fugue of the snake's digestion took over.

Activating his Bifröst crystal and extending it to arm's length, Kratos illuminated the snake's cavernous stomach. They could see the gullet surrounding them, half-filled with bubbling, steaming gastrointestinal juices. Objects defying digestion bobbed along like so much flotsam: half-eaten boats, wine barrels, and boat chains.

"You see the statue anywhere?" Atreus asked.

Kratos only grunted a negative response.

"What?" Atreus asked, when he saw his father's look.

Kratos steered the craft around wine barrels and sinewy strings of kelp that stretched on into the distance, clinging to a graveyard of boats.

"I think I see something," Atreus called.

Kratos slapped his oar hard right to steer starboard.

"There!" Atreus said.

Rounding a bend, they spied Thor's statue listing half-submerged, the face concealed. Kratos rowed to the nearest side, toward the helmet.

"Mimir… any idea where Odin might have hidden your eye?" the lad said.

"No. It is not like I can still see through it," Mimir shot back.

"The hammer," Kratos said.

Kratos leapt from the boat, grabbing onto the side of the statue. Stabilizing himself, he climbed to reach the hammer, where he noticed a glow inside of it. He banged it with his axe handle.

"There is something inside," Kratos called back.

When he removed an outer plate, by hacking it repeatedly with his axe, a chest slid out.

Fishing around inside it, Kratos located, then extracted, Mimir's eye, holding it up in triumph.

"Gently now, gently..." Mimir said. If he still had his heart, it would have been racing at that moment.

Kratos carefully lifted Mimir off his hip, bringing him eye-to-eye. "Maybe it's best you should stick that into my head for safekeeping," Mimir said.

When Kratos pushed the eye into Mimir's empty socket, it immediately began looking around. "Thank you, brother. You don't miss *depth* until it's gone."

Kratos lowered himself back to the boat.

"So, now how do we get out?" Atreus asked.

"We signal the snake," Kratos said.

"Okay. How?"

"Row back to its mouth and we force the boat into the narrow opening. When the World Serpent senses we are there, he will open up for us," Mimir said.

"Perfect," Atreus said.

"We now have all we need," Kratos said.

"How's it feel, Mimir?" Atreus asked.

"Well, I wouldn't say I'm feeling whole again, but it's a right improvement."

"The Bifröst is intact?" Kratos asked.

"It'll serve."

"Finally, we're going to Jötunheim. There's no stopping us now," Atreus said.

"Laddie, have you ever heard the term 'tempting fate'?"

"Fate is another lie told by the gods," Atreus responded.

"Told by the gods, yes, of course. You really are your father's son, you know."

A low rumble erupted as the caustic stomach acid churned and bubbled.

"Hold on tight!" Kratos shouted, just before the slimy green liquid began sloshing into the boat.

The gurgling rose into a deafening roar. A wave of acidic

liquid crashed down on the small craft, dousing Kratos and Mimir's head first, then plastering Atreus, before plunging them into darkness. Despite their burning skin, they clung to the sides to remain inside the boat, while they traversed the snake's insides to reach the throat in utter darkness.

"What is happening?" Atreus cried out in terror. "Are you there?"

"Yes! Hold on, son!"

The roaring water escalated to a fever pitch. Then it receded into the calm of rippling water as they drifted, still engulfed by the darkness.

"Are you still there?" the lad asked.

"I am."

"I am too, if anyone is wondering," Mimir added.

"My fingers are numb from holding the rope so tight," Atreus said.

BOOM!

The sudden thunderous sound reverberated around them, echoing through the snake's entire body.

CHAPTER 53

"Uh, what was—?" Atreus began.

Fumbling about the boat's deck, Atreus located Mimir's head to lift it. Mimir used his eyes to illuminate the passing fleshy walls as they continued their slow drift within the snake's throat.

BOOM!

Another shock wave rippled across the snake's flesh, as if something had struck the animal from outside.

"What is that? Is he getting hit?" Atreus asked.

They floated into a larger chamber: the snake's closed mouth. Peering toward a narrow slice of white light, they spied the fangs awaiting them at the exit.

BOOM! BOOM!

"Something bad is happening out there!" Mimir shouted.

"How do we avoid it?" Atreus asked.

They listened. A bombardment was taking place outside the snake. The shuddering impact rocked the boat, causing Atreus to drop Mimir's head, plunging them back into darkness.

Then a blinding light erupted. The snake was opening its mouth to speak. "Maaaaaaaaaah-dooooooooooh-tooooooooooooh."

The expelled air buffeted the vessel, slamming it into the snake's cheek. "What's he saying?" Atreus shouted to Mimir over the rush.

"Impossible!" Mimir said.

"What is impossible?" Kratos said.

"No, he's saying 'impossible'," Mimir said.

"Why?"

"How could I possibly know?"

Peering out the gaping mouth, they stared at the ground below from a dizzying height. The snake arched its head back suddenly, skewing their world topsy-turvy, after which it emitted a sick retch, ejecting them from its mouth. As they fell, debris from the boat tumbled beside them as frozen terrain rushed up. Kratos realized just how far away they were being deposited.

They crashed hard into the ice. Kratos shook off the dizziness before scanning to get his bearings. He drew his feet under him just in time to see the World Serpent's massive head drop toward a large bluff.

"Atreus?" Kratos called out in panic.

The lad emerged from a pile of debris, ejecting a mouthful of water. "Pffah! I'm good. I'm getting kind of used to this," he retorted.

He peered up at the towering serpent, which appeared to be losing consciousness. "What happened to him? Something we did?"

"No. Something else," Kratos said, scanning for any signs of a threat. Atreus spun about. They were perched near the stonemason's corpse. "The dead giant... Why did the World Serpent leave us here?" he asked.

A shadow forced Kratos' look skyward. Overhead, a lone peregrine falcon swirled, almost as large as Kratos himself, with burning red eyes. Kratos jerked his son's arm to rotate him, in time to witness the bird settling on the ground and transforming into Freya.

"Freya? Keep your distance," Kratos commanded.

"Why?" Atreus asked.

Before Kratos could answer, Freya advanced on them, gesturing toward the unconscious snake.

"The World Serpent has fallen. What has happened here?" she asked.

"It was not us," Atreus replied.

"You are far from home," Kratos said.

"I seek my son. The two of you..." Frey paused. "Seeing you together... helped me to see things more clearly."

"You do not know where he is, then?" Kratos said.

"No. But the woods and fields speak his name. I know he walks in Midgard." Freya directed her attention to the snake. "We should tend to the serpent."

"When did you last see your son?" Kratos said, unable to quiet the suspicion permeating his every thought.

Sensing his distrust, Freya stopped dead in her tracks.

"Long ago. Before your boy was even born. Why do you maintain your distance?" she questioned. Kratos turned suddenly. Atreus drew his bow, targeting what had diverted their attention from Freya.

Baldur clawed his way out from beneath the World Serpent, straightened out his rumpled clothes, then strode casually toward them as if nothing unusual had happened.

"Oh, you are going to pay. You have no idea what you cost me—what you cost the Allfather. No more games," Baldur sneered, staring menacingly at Kratos. As he accelerated his stride toward them, Freya emerged from behind Kratos. She advanced a few paces toward her son. Her expression changed instantly, she became overrun with tears.

"My son," Freya said, weeping with joy.

Baldur paused in his tracks to gaze at her, but absent was the loving face and joyous heart, rather his body language projected confusion and contempt.

"Mother?" he said, his voice riddled with disdain. There was accusation in his cold stare.

"I am here. Please, do not run away," she pleaded, as if addressing a child younger than Atreus.

"I am going nowhere, Mother," Baldur spat back.

Atreus advanced a stride toward Baldur, his concern for Freya written across his face. But Kratos signaled him back.

Recognizing the drama about to unfold, the God of War edged himself into a defensive position between them and his son. Atreus was too callow, too naïve to fathom what might result from this reunion.

"I know you are angry. I know your feelings toward me have not changed, but—" she whimpered.

"How I feel? You *know* how I feel?" Baldur said, as if trying to spit on her with his words. His face fell into an expression of insane rage. Helheim had destroyed all reasoning left in his mind.

"How I feel?" Baldur's voice suddenly turned casual, almost disinterested. It was as if another being had taken control of his body. "I have spent the last hundred years dreaming of this moment. I have rehearsed everything I would say to you, every word, to make you understand exactly what you stole from me. But now I realize I do not need you to understand. I do not need you at all."

Baldur advanced three bloodthirsty steps toward Freya.

Kratos lurched forward, inserting himself between them, though he failed to understand at that instant exactly why. He cared little for either of them. His focus needed to remain on fulfilling his wife's last request. He knew what might come of his action, and yet he chose it instead of his real purpose. He did it not for himself—he would rather allow these two to kill each other, for all he cared. He did what he did for Atreus, whose concern for the goddess had become apparent, and infectious.

Freya pressed a hand to the God of War's shoulder, as if to persuade him to stand aside. "Back off, Kratos. This has nothing to do with you," she said. Her stare clearly remained on her son.

Ignoring her words, Kratos advanced on Baldur until the two men stood nose-to-nose. The God of War never backed down from a fight, though at that moment, he had no idea how he might defeat someone who could not be killed. This vile creature of hate had to have a weakness. He just needed to uncover it.

"This path you walk... vengeance. It will bring you no peace. That I know," Kratos said.

CHAPTER 54

"I will deal with you in my own good time. But family first. I mean, you understand… You being such a model parent and all," Baldur chided. His stare never wavered from Kratos. He shoved with both hands, attempting to cast the God of War aside. But Kratos remained steadfast, shoving Baldur back with a force far greater than the man had exerted upon him.

"You do not understand. If you did, you would stand aside," said Baldur.

"And you would yield to the woman who gave birth to you."

"Ha! Are you one to speak of the honor afforded those who spawn us?"

"Then make me understand."

Atreus drifted from his father closer to Freya's side. His hands were balled into fists, ready to respond if Baldur launched an attack on his mother.

"Look, I have tried killing myself a hundred and twenty-nine times. I have tried hard. It cannot be done. So… exactly how do you see this ending?"

Baldur launched a battering attack upon the God of War, punching his face as hard and as rapidly as he could. Kratos endured the barrage while retreating to fortify his footing, which enabled him to launch an effective counterattack. Baldur, however, proved relentless, flailing wildly while still trying to reach his mother.

"My misery can never end as long as she breathes. Do you not understand that?" Baldur screamed.

Kratos delivered punch after punch, holding Baldur at bay but unable to force him to abandon his fight.

Atreus jammed his body in front of Freya, hoping to provide that last line of defense should Baldur find a way past his father. He quickly fired arrow after arrow, hoping one might find a way to slow the crazed man down.

"You will not harm her," Kratos shouted.

"Why do you care? Get out of my way!"

Freya restrained herself no longer. When Atreus twisted to improve his shot, she slid past him to wedge her body between the two fighting men, forcing both to yield or strike her in error.

"This is not your fight! I can reach him!" Freya spat at Kratos, who lunged to jam his body between her and her son.

"There is nothing to reach! He will kill you, woman! Do you not understand that?" Kratos urged. "Then he kills me! Stay out of it!"

"No!" Atreus screamed, which caused Freya to lower her guard when she glanced back. She read agony and suffering pouring out from his innocent face.

Throwing all his weight into Kratos, Baldur pitched him aside, lunging over his shoulder to seize his mother's cape, and in turn, forcing Atreus to abandon his arrows, fearing an errant shot might strike Freya by mistake.

"I did everything for you! If you were a parent, you would see that," she cried.

"But I will never be, will I? You saw to that," he fired back with venomous words.

"That was never my intent."

"That's right. Nothing is ever your fault!" Baldur shrieked, his rage now unfettered.

Without any forewarning, magical roots erupted through the

icy ground, seeking to ensnare the two warring gods. Kratos became the first prisoner, wrapped chest-high; but this time Baldur had anticipated his mother's magic. He dove, successfully evading the roots, while snatching up a small ice rock to hurl at her. The projectile ricocheted off her head with a sickening thud. She dropped unconscious to the ground.

"Nooo!" Atreus screamed. In that moment, indecision flooded his brain. He had to decide in a single second which one he must go to.

Atreus rushed to his father's side with knife drawn. Shredding wildly at the roots, he tore away sufficient strands to enable his father to breathe. The roots, however, continued to wrap the God of War and constrict his chest.

Baldur rushed at the trapped Kratos.

"You might want to turn away, son. This will not be pretty," Baldur said.

Atreus ceased chopping, turning his blade on their nemesis. "I will never allow you to hurt him," Atreus spat defiantly.

"No, boy," Kratos ordered. But Atreus refused to move.

"Show me what you got, you little shit."

Atreus lunged, vaulting into the air like he had seen his father do a hundred times, slashing savagely side to side.

"No!" Kratos yelled. "Leave the boy be!"

In desperation, Kratos worked a hand free and began ripping with all his strength to break his bonds. Freeing his other hand, Kratos shredded roots until he could return to his feet. Throwing his arms out, he broke free of the roots with a final pull.

"Stop!" he yelled.

Baldur bobbed and weaved to dodge the lad's attack, launching his own counterattack with a fist slamming squarely into the boy's chest.

Atreus left the ground, tumbling backward into Kratos' arms.

"Stop!" Kratos snarled. His face contorted in anger.

Wheezing and incapable of speech, his son fought for each breath. Kratos used a few precious seconds to check his son's chest. He drew back a bloody hand. The front of Atreus' shirt and his quiver strap were blood-soaked.

"Atreus, breathe… please…" Kratos pleaded. His heart was breaking. He couldn't let his son die.

He couldn't fail his wife.

Atreus shook his head. Between labored inhalations he murmured, "Not mine."

He extracted the broken piece of the mistletoe arrow shaft from his quiver strap. Unable to eject any more words, he pointed to Baldur.

Baldur stood unmoving, staring at his hand.

Blood.

"What is this? Pain," he muttered to himself.

The arrowhead and wood splinters stuck out of his fist at obtuse angles. His incessant laugh echoed off the nearby ridges.

"I can feel it," he announced. He reluctantly lifted his stare from his hand to the boy.

A thin, and until that moment unseen, layer of magical protection that rendered him invincible became visible as it cracked, with the shards toppling off Baldur like sheets of ice. Freya's enchantment evaporated from Baldur's body while he flipped from hideous laughter to sobs of realization.

"The spell is broken!" Mimir said.

"The mistletoe arrow was his weakness?" Atreus said.

"He can be killed?" Kratos asked.

"You've seen it yourself, he's vulnerable now."

Kratos and Atreus drew their weapons, simultaneously advancing on Baldur.

"No!" Freya screamed, having regained consciousness. Now horrified, she stared from a distance. The arrowhead used to repair the lad's broken quiver strap had been mistletoe, one Freya missed when she burned the lad's mistletoe arrows back at her cottage.

Kratos attacked, slamming a fist into Baldur's jaw.

"Yes. Yes!" Baldur cheered, as if experiencing some ecstatic pleasure from the attack.

Kratos pummeled him to the ground.

"Oh, the pain. It is wonderful!"

Atreus hastily launched an arrow at Baldur on the ground while his father retreated a step to recover his fighting stance. The tip winged Baldur's shoulder.

Baldur let out a wretched scream, staring quizzically at the blood. "I can feel it. More. Give me more!" Baldur taunted.

Kratos obliged.

Baldur rolled away from the God of War's battering attack to bounce back to his feet, counterattacking with flying fists that landed about Kratos' face.

"Feeling! Glorious feeling!"

Kratos blocked Baldur's fists to force him to retreat.

"I never knew how much fun this could be!"

"I will kill you!" Kratos yelled.

"Ha! Killing you is going to feel so rewarding now!"

Baldur grabbed both Kratos' arms to prevent him from reaching his blades.

"I will not allow you to kill my son!" Freya snarled, slamming a fist into the ground, which caused the earth to tremor with violent rumblings.

Behind Freya, an enormous silhouette emerged in the distance.

CHAPTER 55

The stonemason's corpse, which Freya reanimated with her ancient *seiðr* magic, gazed at them through the twilight mist. In the next second, the stonemason charged, and in response to Freya's sweeping arm movement, the creature's monstrous hand slammed in front of Kratos and his son, knocking them from their feet, at the same time cutting them off from Baldur and herself.

"You will stop this now!" she demanded.

Realizing Freya now controlled the stonemason's every action, Kratos needed to find a way to reach her to prevent her from using it against them.

"Do not do this, Freya!" he growled. His words would land on deaf ears. The goddess intended to do anything necessary to protect her son, even at the cost of her own life.

Releasing the Blades of Chaos, Kratos attacked the giant corpse. But the blades were all but useless against it, and nothing he could do could break the magic Freya had employed.

"Father, we need to get around it," Atreus barked, when he realized Freya's intent was not to harm them, but simply to block them from reaching her son.

Kratos consumed a precious moment calculating a leap timed perfectly against a chaotic wind, in order for his action to carry him atop the giant hand. Atreus followed a second later. Jumping down the other side, they charged Baldur, forcing him to retreat from his mother. When Freya raised her hand to bring the giant hand up, it crashed into the rock cliff, sending snow and ice shards raining down upon them.

"Ah! I feel it. I feel the cold and the ice. Glorious!" Baldur shouted, spreading his arms to take in the new sensations. But his respite lasted only seconds. He launched a furious attack on Kratos, simultaneously kicking Atreus to the ground on his way to colliding with the God of War.

Baldur now had to become deft on his feet in order to sidestep Kratos' swipes with the Blades of Chaos. Since he could be harmed, and even killed, he had to change the tactics in this fight. He had to bob and weave to escape Kratos' assault. Taking up a large chunk of fallen ice, he swung it wildly, forcing Kratos into a temporary retreat.

A hastily launched arrow sailed wide of its mark. "I will get to you shortly, little boy," Baldur taunted.

"You will stop!" Freya yelled from her place a safe distance from the confrontation. She slammed the hand down again, hoping to knock both men off their feet. But it didn't work. Baldur scrambled to his feet, to charge Kratos before he could position his blades to defend himself.

But instead of meeting Baldur's attack, Kratos dodged his assault and jumped up onto the stonemason's hand, when he remembered a ring on one of the fingers. Lifting the ring exposed a crystal beneath it. That had to be the source of the magic Freya was using to control the creature.

"Atreus, the crystal!" he called back, remembering what Sindri had done to the bow with the dragon's-tooth magic. He had no time to act. Baldur jumped him from behind and threw him from the hand, back down to the ground. Kratos squirmed beneath him to reach his blades. But Baldur knew how to keep the God of War from harming him—keep him from using his blades.

Atreus nocked an arrow and swung around to level it at the crystal.

"Noooo!" Freya cried out.

The arrow hit its target, producing a blinding explosion, just as Sindri had said it would. When he landed, Kratos spun about, chaotically searching for his son. He had no idea what had happened to Baldur, and at the moment he couldn't care.

"Atreus? Atreus!" he called in a panic.

"I'm up here! I'm okay!" the lad called down from a twenty-foot-high snowy ridge, where the explosion had deposited him.

A thud turned Kratos' attention away from his son, who disappeared over the ridge, dashing away in the direction opposite to the fight.

"And I am doing won-der-ful, thanks for asking. Why, I've never felt so alive!" Baldur said, with a voice loaded with excitement.

Baldur relaunched his assault on Kratos, grabbing him by the neck and throwing him into a choke hold. Behind them the stonemason's corpse struggled to regain its footing and return to life. Shattering the crystal had only slowed the corpse; it had failed to destroy the magic controlling it.

"Before you die, I want to thank both of you. You've done what even the Allfather himself could not. I've never felt more alive!"

"*Frjósa!*" Freya called out, summoning an Ice Breath spell.

The stonemason responded by blowing a fierce frost blast that separated Kratos from Baldur.

Beyond the ridge, Atreus stopped fifty paces before the serpent's head, which appeared dead. His mind raced through the earlier exchanges Mimir had had with the serpent. He just needed to piece together a few words to communicate with the snake.

"Mooooog-taaaaaaay-oooooom!" he shouted. He couldn't be certain, because he had loosely stitched the shards of sounds together, but he hoped his clumsy plea could gain the World Serpent's help.

He then raced back to help his father in the fight. Three errant arrows whizzed past Baldur harmlessly. He scolded himself for firing without thinking. He stopped, nocked a fourth arrow, and cleared his mind to take aim on Baldur's back. A deep hiss and the rising shadow stole his attention.

"Father, look!"

All turned from Freya and Baldur.

The World Serpent towered over the ridge, with jaws gaping open to engulf the entire stonemason's head. It dragged it away while lifting it skyward to swallow the creature whole.

"Damn you. No!" Freya screamed, her magic severed.

Finally free of the stonemason's attack, Kratos dashed at Baldur, clamping both hands around his throat, tightening slowly to choke the life out of him. Freya, still weak and exhausted, watched from the ground nearby, unable to muster the energy to defend her son.

"Come on, do it!" Baldur taunted, the corners of his mouth inching into a grimace.

"Stop… please!" Freya cried, surrendering to the agony of her breaking heart.

"This must end," Kratos snarled.

"But he is beaten, Father. No longer a threat."

Something in Atreus' voice stopped Kratos in his tracks. He stared first at Baldur, then at his son, then back at Baldur. It was Freya's influence that tugged at his son's heart. Was Atreus allowing emotion to cloud his thinking? Was it the way he cared for Freya that made him wish compassion on this fiend? The old Kratos lived only to kill, and would have snapped this one's neck then pummeled him until every bone in his body splintered. That Kratos could find no reason to let this monster live. But he was no longer that man.

Hearing Freya's whimpers behind him, he yielded to the god he desired to be, rather than the god that was.

He released Baldur's throat.

"You will never come for us again. You will never touch her in anger," Kratos commanded, his face hard as stone.

"I need no protection from you," Freya said, her voice growing stronger from the realization that her son would live.

Kratos cast his gaze to Freya as if to dismiss her words. She stared back at him, disappointed, hurt, and broken.

The God of War turned his back to her. Then he walked away. Atreus looked at her sadly, wishing he could change the way these things had come to be. He so wanted to be close to her. He needed to feel even a surrogate mother's love. But instead, wordlessly, he trailed after his father.

Speaking in hushed tones, so neither of them might hear, Baldur addressed his mother where she lay spent on the ground.

"You just cannot help yourself, can you, Mother? No matter what I say or do. You won't stop interfering in my life," he muttered, while he himself still lay battered in the snow.

"I was always trying to protect you. I was—" She stopped, knowing she was just regurgitating the same old excuses. "Wrong. I held on too tight. Out of fear... but also out of love. It is not too late for us to build something new," Freya continued.

"New? No. We cannot. I will never forgive you. You still have to pay for the lifetime you stole from me."

"Do you not understand? I pay every day that you hate me. But if my death is the only way to balance this wrong—if that alone will make you whole—I will not oppose you."

Freya looked up. The sadness and acceptance consuming her face were more than any human soul could bear. But they meant nothing to a fiend like her son. Baldur loomed over her, his hands clutching a huge, jagged ice rock, poised to smash her head.

"I know," he said.

"I love you," she said in a whimper, now at peace with her destiny and her decision.

Baldur drew back. His face lit up with a perverted gaze of sick satisfaction.

In that moment, Kratos delivered a killing blow to the rear of Baldur's head. Blood gurgling from his lips, Baldur turned in disbelief. He released a strangled croak. The God of War leaned into Baldur's ear. "You chose this end," he whispered.

A fluttering snowflake landed on Baldur's face. He winced at the cold and smiled faintly, being reintroduced to a feeling he had been forced to live without for over a century.

"Snow," Baldur uttered, before all life drained from his face. He crumpled dead to the ground, landing curled in the fetal position beside his mother. Screaming, Freya crawled atop her son's body as plump snowflakes swirled around them. First a few, then the air filled with them.

"No, no, no! My child… my dear, sweet boy," Freya sobbed, wailing as she surrendered fully to her heartbreak.

Kratos stared at her, unfeeling. Atreus joined him with the same empty face, battle-scarred and grown-up.

"I will rain every agony, every violation imaginable upon you. I will parade your cold lifeless body through every corner of every realm, and feed your despicable soul to the vilest filth in Hel. That is my promise," she screamed at him.

"He saved your life!" Atreus said.

"He robbed me of everything that mattered to me!" Then she turned to face Kratos directly. "You are a monster… passing on your cruelty and rage to the product of your vile loins. You will never change."

"Then you do not know me."

"I know enough." Freya's face glowered.

"Do you?" he asked, so plainly that it forced Freya to pause. He addressed his son over his shoulder. "Boy, listen close. I am from the land called Sparta. I made a deal with a god that cost me my soul. I killed many who deserved death… and many who did not. I killed my father."

The weight of his father's words fell heavy into the core of Atreus' very being.

"That was *your father* in Helheim?" Atreus said, shaking his head. He cast a glance at Freya, then at Baldur. He tried to make sense of it all. "Is this what it is to be a god? Is this how it always ends? Sons killing their mothers… their fathers?"

Kratos finally turned to face his son. Were those words the universal truth of the gods? An inescapable truth beyond anyone's control, mortal or otherwise?

"No. We will be the gods we choose to be, not the gods who

have been. Who I was is not who you will be. We must be better."

Atreus nodded, convinced and at the same time relieved.

Freya pushed her way back to her feet and composed herself before picking up her son's lifeless body. With her head high, and her dignity on full display, she turned her back on Kratos and Atreus, walking away.

"I don't understand… I know saving her was the right thing, but she seemed all evil at the end," Atreus said.

"Not evil. You killed her son, lad. Her son. The death of a child is not something a parent overcomes easily," Mimir said.

"But he was gonna kill her!"

"She would have died to see him live. Only a parent can understand," Kratos said.

"So you'd let me kill you?"

"If it meant you would live… yes."

"Look, there was no easy choice, for anybody, brother. But I think we can all agree you did the right thing. The world is a better place with Freya in it. Just… give her time, she'll come around."

Responding to a sudden impulse, he hugged his father, with Kratos sliding a hand to his son's head, too tired to oppose the turmoil raging inside.

"We must finish our journey while I still have strength," his father said.

"You have achieved the impossible, Kratos. That insufferable sonofabitch is finally dead," Mimir spoke up after a long silence. For the first time, Kratos detected a subtle ring of respect in his voice.

"I'm not sorry we saved her. We had to," Atreus said.

"Even if she curses us?" Kratos replied.

"Even if she curses us," Atreus agreed.

"She's *always* hated *me*… I'm finally remembering how much! But it's true—the world's a better place with her in it," Mimir said.

"Why *did* mistletoe break the spell?" Atreus asked.

"Vanir magic is powerful, but its rules are slippery and elusive.

I'm sure it makes sense if you're a witch. Oh, but it's all so bloody tragic… Baldur was the greatest gift Odin granted Freya, the one thing she treasured from their marriage. She only hoped to spare him pain, and spare herself loss—but such impulses can lead good parents to make terribly stupid decisions," Mimir said.

Kratos and Atreus wasted no time returning to the realm travel tower on the caldera. Once inside the realm travel room, Kratos inserted the Bifröst into the receptacle to activate the device. Once was it activated, he positioned the table to the new Jötunheim tower.

Atreus removed Mimir from his father's belt, placing him in the location where the Jötunheim crystal should be.

"Hope you don't explode," he said.

"Wait! Should we talk about this?" Mimir cried.

Kratos locked the destination into the table and started the sequence. A blinding light beam shot across the room into Mimir's eyes.

"Oh, most unpleasant!"

Atreus pivoted while holding Mimir's head out front, shielding his own as best as he could. The exploding energy from Mimir's eyes struck the center of the Jötunheim bridge door. The doors shuddered, then opened.

JÖTUNHEIM

CHAPTER 56

A golden staircase awaited them. For the first time on their journey, they advanced without trepidation.

"A staircase? I was expecting another bridge," Atreus commented. The glinting gold dazzled him.

"A word please, before we continue," Mimir asked from Kratos' belt.

Kratos paused, snaring Atreus' arm to halt his advance while he lifted Mimir's head to bring them face-to-face.

"Listen, the last thing you two need up there is a decomposing head ruining your moment. Why don't I wait here for you? This should be between you and the boy."

"That is true. But if someone were to find you…" Kratos replied.

"By Lady Sif's soft, perfect sloshers," a voice erupted from nearby. All heads turned. Brok smiled, with Sindri beside him.

"You done did it!" the blue man continued, amazement lacing his words.

"Sorry for the intrusion. But we had to see this," Sindri added sheepishly.

Kratos stared blankly at the brothers, then back at Mimir's head. His face turned up a smile.

"Oh no, no, no! Fine, damn it, fine," Mimir caved, anticipating what was to follow. He knew whatever Kratos intended would not prove beneficial to him.

"Watch the head until we return," Kratos commanded the brothers.

"I knew it!" Mimir blurted just before Kratos released him from his belt, tossing him to Sindri. "Whoa, you do realize throwing me like that makes me dizzy."

"Oh no. I cannot do this. No, no. I can't," Sindri cringed, crossing his legs impulsively. He immediately shoved Mimir onto Brok, who just stared at the head.

"Okay, but why?" Brok said, extending the head to arm's length. He breathed only through his mouth, hoping to minimize the stench wafting to his nose.

"Ready?" Kratos turned to Atreus.

Atreus smiled, scaling the staircase leading into the sky.

In hours they reached the summit, still covered in blood and mud, where they stood near the crest of the mountain. A light snow spattered their faces. To their north were two more finger-like mountains nearby.

"Look, we're on the giant's fingers. I see the highest peak ahead, right over there. We *did* it!" Atreus said.

"We did do it, *together*," Kratos replied. Relief swept through him. They had survived to fulfill his wife's dying wishes. They had battled more than anyone would have expected to reach this place.

Kratos unwound the bandages protecting his forearms, exposing his grotesque never-healing wounds to the snow.

"What are you doing?" his son asked.

"I hide nothing." Kratos discarded the bandages into the swirling mountain winds, which accepted them skyward with a flutter.

"Can we go? We are so close now!"

Atreus took off impulsively up the mountain path.

"Boy," Kratos growled.

His demanding tone stopped Atreus in his tracks. He turned back.

Kratos removed the leather pouch from his belt, staring at it for a long moment. Visions of life with Faye played across his mind: her smile, the love in her eyes when she looked at him. He so wished he could reach out to stroke her rose-petal cheek. Finally, Kratos held the pouch out, knowing what he had to do.

Their moment seemed frozen in time, as Atreus stared at the pouch, his hands in check. It was something he had wanted since their journey began. Now, faced with the moment that he had wished for, he wrestled with uncertainty. Should he?

"Carry her," his father said.

Atreus stared at him. Overcoming an inertia that he could not explain, he advanced to his father, where he gingerly accepted the pouch—his mother. His heart ached at the touch of her in his hands. He felt so close to her now. After adjusting the leather tie, he looped the pouch carefully on his belt. With tears undetectable in the snow, he offered his father a nod of gratitude. Maybe his father no longer saw him as a boy. Maybe his father had accepted him for what he truly was—a fellow god.

The snow turned to flurries, becoming nothing more than a cleansing mist when the flakes melted against their skin, stripping away the blood and the mud as they began their final ascent to the mountain peak.

Within a few more hours, they reached the Jötunheim summit, a massive crest with jagged and multi-pronged rock formations like the very fingers of a giant. A maze of sharp angles, chipped, knife-edged corners, and steep granite faces stood between them and the final location. Carefully picking their footing, Kratos and Atreus weaved their way up the precarious, narrow path that twisted at times on a forty-five-degree incline, snaking in and out of the mountain.

With the sun drifting lower in the western sky, they arrived at a half-collapsed Jötunn temple, which had been constructed within the mountain. The shrine stood as a final way station between them and the highest peak. Kratos entered first, through a large crack along the northern wall, with Atreus following a few steps behind. As he passed through the fissure, his hand brushed the wall unconsciously. His contact ignited a bright latticework of light spider-webbing along the surface.

Atreus stopped to watch the magical effect spread from where his hand made contact. With the light came a series of carved images, covering the entire wall.

"Father, wait. Something is happening."

Kratos came about, saw the light, and returned to join his son at a wall carving. At first neither understood the meaning of the drawings. A rotund woman ripe with child stood defiantly before a seated council of giants. Her face clearly angry, she was yelling at them, *and she held Kratos' axe*. One of the giants pointed, as if to cast her away.

"That axe is just like yours, Father. Is it not?" Atreus asked, moving closer to the wall to examine each line of the etching more carefully. "Is that... Mother?" The exquisite detail of the drawing clearly indicated it was. "The word says *Laufey*. Is that her?" The resemblance was undeniable.

Before Kratos could form a plausible answer, Atreus raced to the next image, on the opposite side of a jagged crevasse. This one totally consumed his attention. It looked exactly like him, on a bed, the same way he was when he was ill. Around him was the interior of Kratos' house.

"How can this be? What manner of magic has conjured this? When were these etchings made?" Atreus rattled off in rapid fire. He turned to his father for answers.

Kratos had none.

Neither could understand how these things could come to be. Did they foretell the future, rather than record the past? And why would they record him and his mother?

The woman from the previous image sat beside the boy, tending him with cloths. But this image was of his wife and son, with him in the background.

Consumed with questions and disbelief, Atreus sought words to convey what his mind churned about uneasily. "That is her, isn't it? And that... that is me?"

Kratos could conjure no response. Instead, he stared blankly at the carvings, then at his son. He needed no more convincing.

Atreus had never witnessed his father in such a state of helplessness. He didn't know how to understand the things that someone had presented before him. Was he even meant see what they depicted? Was he meant to ever know the truth that these gods sought to convey? Who he was plagued his young mind. And just as importantly, who was his mother, that she would be on these walls?

Kratos commanded himself to find words that would ease the burden caving in upon his son. Before he could formulate a response, Atreus darted to the next carving, anxious to learn more about what his life was meant to be.

The next carving showed Atreus locked in a fight with Baldur, stripping away his invulnerability.

"Father, look, this one *is* me... and Baldur. But how can this be? This has just happened. What... what does this all mean?"

Joining his son, Kratos studied the latest carving with a new sense of comprehension. There was so much now that he understood. There had been so much left unsaid between him and his wife. She was not who he had thought she was.

"I was not the only parent with secrets," Kratos muttered, more to himself than to his son.

"You did not know?" Atreus asked, with unmasked surprise.

Kratos stared blankly at his son. Was he saying that he knew? His own son knew more about his mother than Kratos knew about his wife. Would she have confided in the lad before revealing the deepest of her secrets to the man she loved?

Did she even love him?

"She was a giant," the lad said, realizing that Kratos would now understand what that meant.

"You knew?" Kratos asked, with a breathless voice.

"I did not. She never told me who she was," Atreus said. Minutes passed. Neither spoke. Then Atreus returned to the carvings. "I am a giant," he added in revelation.

Kratos stared at him, then at the carving. What was her

true nature? How could she have kept such an important truth from him?

"Why did she not tell us?" Atreus asked. "Did she think we would not understand?"

"Maybe she could not reveal her true self to us. She sent us here, hoping we might find this and learn the truth on our own," Kratos said.

"But why conceal the truth from those she loved most dearly?"

"You ask questions even I cannot answer."

"But why not just tell us the truth?"

"Because maybe the truth would prove too dangerous, even for a giant."

The words churned inside Kratos' brain. There was something in these etchings he had failed to understand. There was something in their lives he could not fathom at the time. But now…

"We must trust that your mother would have had good reason to—" Kratos stopped himself. He needed to understand his past. He needed a moment to reassemble the puzzle pieces of his life.

"Baldur was never sent to find me," he muttered. "It was her he was tracking all along… unaware at the time that she had become only ashes."

Kratos laid a hand upon his son's shoulder.

"She was here. She saw every step we took before we took it. Like she was always with us… watching over us… leading us home," Atreus said.

The lad retreated toward the shrine's exit.

"Come on! Look, we're on the giant's fingers. I see the highest peak ahead—right over there. We *did* it! We are so close to the end now."

Kratos' gaze lingered on the final image of the mural—a fragment only partially intact. It showed an enigmatic image of the boy holding a dead body, gazing up at the sky, weeping, and cursing. The rest of the fragment had been destroyed, making the identity of the corpse an eternal mystery.

"Yes… yes, we are," he said in a distracted voice.

Leaving the shrine, Kratos and Atreus continued their tentative ascent, eventually reaching the tip of the highest finger. Billowing gray clouds crowded the sky for as far as they could see. The swirling air wrapped them with a sense of peace and calm.

Awestruck by the sight, Atreus dashed ahead, stopping at the very edge. In that moment, he thought not about himself, but about his mother. He wished he could have shared such magnificence with her.

Kratos approached, forcing Atreus out of his sadness and back into the world he must face every waking minute.

"Father?"

He offered his father the ashes. It would be the last time he would touch his mother. It felt like this was to be their final goodbye.

"No. We do this together," Kratos said. "She would have wanted it this way."

In this life, Kratos had experienced more death than any one man could ever fathom. Yet this loss tore at the very core of his being. Gods were never to feel the way he felt at this moment. Gods were never to surrender to their human feelings.

Kratos released the strap securing the pouch. Spilling the ashes between their hands, together as father and son they released her. The last of Atreus' mother and Kratos' wife spiraled away, caught up in a now snowflake-laden breeze.

Neither spoke as they paid tribute to her in their minds. There could be no words that could convey what this moment meant to each of them. Kratos' life was never supposed to come to this point. Unconsciously, he put his arm round Atreus' shoulder to bring him closer. Atreus turned away, hiding tears. He wanted to speak, had things he needed to say, but refrained, fearing a tremulous voice might make him appear weak. He had to keep his frail emotions in check, just as his father was doing. He was a god, and he must always act like one, though there was still so much he needed to learn and understand about who and what he was.

Atreus stared out at a vast graveyard of giants sprawled before the horizon.

"They really are all gone. There is nothing for us here," he said, allowing sadness to stitch his words together.

"Come. We must go. We have accomplished what we came here for. We must leave this behind," Kratos said.

Atreus pulled away reluctantly. He wanted to remain with her, remain part of her for as long as he could. Leaving meant turning his back on her, yet he knew staying served no earthly purpose. They had to turn around, begin their long journey back.

For the next few hours, they carefully and swiftly picked their way through the rocks. Each had so much to think about.

"So... I understand that Mother was a giant. Which makes me part giant and part god," Atreus said finally.

"And part mortal," Kratos added.

He shot his father a puzzled look. How was he to interpret what he was? How was he expected to live? And what was his destiny that his mother spoke of?

"I am. Still I do not understand. My name on the wall... Mother called me Loki." The words forced Atreus to stop, and Kratos paused beside him.

"The giants called me Loki? Is that supposed to be my name?"

The word triggered thoughts buried deep in Kratos' memory. "Your mother bestowed that name upon you at your birth. She may have called you that to her people."

"But why? How then did I come to be called Atreus instead?"

"By my choice. Atreus was the bravest of all the warriors in Sparta. I sought to honor his death by bestowing his name upon my only son. Now I understand why your mother eagerly agreed when I asked that of her. You were meant to remain hidden from your own kind. She intentionally instructed me to destroy the protection rune in the forest, to force us on this journey of discovery."

"Why would she do that?"

"A question for another day. It is time we go home, son."

MIDGARD

EPILOGUE

In the fading light at the end of another day, Kratos and Atreus left the Bifröst bridge from Jötunheim, crossing the surrounding caldera lake thick with ice, the aftermath of their battle with the stonemason now covered in deep banks of snow.

As Mimir explained it, Baldur's death had seemingly unleashed Fimbulwinter upon Midgard, even though it was not prophesied to fall for another hundred winters at least. Now, by virtue of their run-in with the local gods, fated events were already underway. Three winters with no summers between would plague the land. It would become a time when all creatures sought refuge from the bitter elements, burrowing in extended hibernation until warm winds arrived to thaw the frozen tundra.

But those same winds were to usher in something else.

Kratos and Atreus continued through the biting cold, traveling mostly at night under the light of the moon, while sleeping hidden during the day to avoid confrontation with any who might be seeking them. In time, they reached the snow-shrouded forest overlooking their valley. In the distance, their house sat quietly tucked within the folds of drifting snow mounds.

Atreus searched the sky.

Huginn and Muninn lazily circled the crown canopy.

Ensconced safely within the shadowy depths of an entwined

thicket, father and son patiently held their position.

Atreus slowly nocked an arrow to his bowstring. He raised it skyward; his father lowered it back down with a calm, firm hand.

"I can hit them. I know I can," the boy said.

"Hit one, and the other knows we're here, lad," Mimir said, hanging at Kratos' belt.

Upon their return to Midgard, Kratos had intended to abandon the head with the dwarves, but Mimir surprised him by requesting to join them on their journey home. As he consumed no provisions and could prove an asset in dealing with the uncertainties of their future in this land, Kratos acquiesced.

"So what do we do? I'm so cold and hungry," said Atreus.

Kratos thought. They could attempt to slip into their house under the cover of night, though neither wished to remain in the elements for such an extended period of time. As Kratos pondered the problem, as if Laufey herself was watching over them, a solution came. Jöphie swooped in from high above to attack the ravens, forcing the Allfather's feathered minions to abandon their surveillance and flee noisily away to the north.

"They're gone," Atreus said.

Creeping slowly out from their hiding place, Atreus snagged the badger carcass slung over his shoulder on some thorny branches. He tugged viciously to set it free, uncertain of why such a trivial matter should so ignite his anger.

"You were right. Mother's falcon knew we would return," Kratos said.

"I knew she'd never desert us. From now she'll protect us from Odin's little spies."

They were home.

But for Atreus, home could never be the way it once was. The moment he saw his house again turned bittersweet. He was returning to a place without a mother, and he was no longer the same person who had departed what seemed so long ago. He could never be that person after what he had experienced with his father. He would follow a path much different than the one he and his mother had talked about before her death.

Would he instead follow a path similar to his father's? Would he become what his father was?

But above all else, would he choose good over evil? Could it be that simple? He would grow into a god and a warrior, but to what end? What would his mother expect of him?

Atreus lay on his cot and thought back to his last conversation with Brok and Sindri, after returning from Jötunheim. Having learned of his mother's true nature, he found the brothers more forthcoming of their experiences with her. She had come to them, as the last Guardian of the Jötnar left in Midgard, seeking a boon to protect her people. In that, they saw an opportunity to restore the balance of power, and crafted for her the Leviathan axe to be Mjölnir's equal.

For after all, it was Mjölnir, and the wholesale slaughter of Jötnar that Thor had put it to, which had so torn at them that the guilt would ultimately come between them, in a long and finally-concluded cycle of recrimination. Atreus smiled at the thought of their reconciliation. It brought him some comfort to see the bonds of family prevail over so much division.

But what had mother used the axe for?

"They called your mother Laufey the Just," Mimir said, as if sensing where the boy's mind must be. He had settled in on the mantel by the stove, overlooking the room.

"You knew her?" Atreus asked.

"I never had the pleasure. Laufey was a rumor in the halls of Asgard—a giantess warrior who thwarted many an Aesir god's plans. Freeing those who they would enslave, feeding those who they would starve, and generally making a nuisance of herself in the most noble of ways. Thor was terribly frustrated he could never find her to fight. Once my imprisonment began, I could only wonder what became of her, and who she would turn out to be. Yours is quite a singular lineage, lad."

"Then she fought to protect the innocent from the evil gods."

"Aye, she did."

Atreus turned pensive for long moments. Kratos welcomed the silence.

"Then that is what I must do to honor her."

"As well you may, little brother. But remember—in the end, she didn't choose the fight. She chose you. Both of you. I suppose she thought it was the best chance for the giants to live on. But your path is your own."

Finally, with that thought lingering in his mind, Atreus closed his eyes and succumbed to his exhaustion.

Kratos had listened quietly, sharing his son's interest in this new perspective on the woman he loved, and appreciating Mimir's wise words of caution. But somewhere within, he already knew what path the boy would choose. It was in his nature to help people. And if Mimir was right about what befell the Valkyries, then this realm was sure to need more of their help, and soon.

Kratos put the thought out of mind, and closed his eyes.

Kratos sprang awake, lurching up in his bed, every muscle alert. Something had taken him from his slumber.

Or was he truly awake? Kratos struggled to recall how much time had passed, or what he last remembered. He felt at peace only a moment ago. Now something terrible sundered him from his dream of the woman he so loved.

Warm winds whistled through the cracks in the windows and the door.

Moments later, thunder rumbled every wall of their house.

Atreus tumbled awake, stumbling to plant his feet beneath him. Instinct drove him for his hunting knife.

"W-what is that?" he stammered, searching the darkness for his father, who was no longer in his bed.

Kratos planted his feet in a fighting stance. His blades were out of reach to help them. He rummaged for his Leviathan axe. Across the room, he shared a knowing glance with his son. There would be no hiding in the cellar this time.

"Your bow, quickly," Kratos commanded.

Atreus crawled around the unlit room. His hands trembled as he located his quiver and bow. Owing to his father's tutelage, he had become a superior archer. And now he believed his training was about to pay off.

Kratos balanced his axe in his hand.

Both knew the thunder had not come from nature. It came from something else.

A lightning bolt sizzled just outside the house, causing a blinding flash to flood in through the windows and cracks in the walls. For an instant, the interior became as bright as day.

Then the pounding of heavy footsteps slogged through the mud outside.

Glancing back to confirm that Atreus stood ready, Kratos advanced to the door, throwing it open.

A towering stout figure in a black cloak and cowl stood in the darkness, the driving rain obscuring his identity. The sounds of bloated drops pelting the roof and the trees was all that was heard.

Notching an arrow to his bow, Atreus planted himself beside his father at the doorway. The figure flipped back its cloak, an iron hammer hung from its belt.

It was Mjölnir; the hulking man was Thor.

In the heavens above, Sköll and Hati hurled to pounce on the sun and the moon. Ragnarök was about to begin.

ABOUT THE AUTHOR

Chicago native and Vietnam veteran, J. M. Barlog's novel *Windows to the Soul* won Best Thriller at the "Love is Murder" Mystery Conference. Barlog was story consultant for *God of War 2*. *God of War* is his twelfth novel.

www.jmbarlog.com

To receive advance information, news, competitions
and exclusive offers online, please sign up for the
Titan newsletter on our website.

For more fantastic fiction, author events,
competitions, limited editions and more...

VISIT OUR WEBSITE
titanbooks.com

LIKE US ON FACEBOOK
facebook.com/titanbooks

FOLLOW US ON TWITTER
@TitanBooks

EMAIL US
readerfeedback@titanemail.com